WARKON

Sam Beckett

Publisher: Inspiring Publishers,
P.O. Box 159, Calwell, ACT Australia 2905
Email: publishaspg@gmail.com
http://www.inspiringpublishers.com

A catalogue record for this book is available from the National Library of Australia

National Library of Australia The Prepublication Data Service

Author: Sam Beckett
Title: Warkon
Genre: Fiction
ISBN: 978-1-922792-56-3

Author's note

This book is an invention. It is not an autobiography. The town of Warkon does not exist. Neither does the escarpment. Or magic. With one exception, the characters are completely fictitious. Hoots, I'll always miss you.

Sam Beckett

sdbeckett@gmail.com

ACKNOWLEDGEMENTS

I would like to thank the many people who have helped me to get this book down on paper. Wayne and Philippa Rowlands, at the start – I wouldn't have kept going without your kind support. Lesley Livingston, your encouragement has kept me pushing forward. Tania Morton, Troy Cairns and Amanda Nott saw interim drafts and didn't laugh too loud. Alison Thompson saw a more recent draft and told me to keep going. Robyn Martin has been patient throughout. JB Lazarte provided an editorial critique that left the book infinitely more readable. And a huge and special thanks to Christie Cooper for the beautiful artwork.

Cover photo is of Simpson's Gap in the West MacDonnell Ranges and is reproduced with permission from Bill Robinson (https://pbase.com/billrobinson).

PROLOGUE

The eagle looked down at her two half-grown chicks. They were sleeping at last, after fighting over the remains of a kangaroo's leg retrieved from beside the dusty highway.

Satisfied that the chicks would be resting now for most of the day, she rose up on her long legs and looked out over the rim of her nest. Until recently, she had shared this nest with her smaller mate, but he had not returned one evening and now she was alone. When it came time to breed again, she would seek out another.

The nest was set into the crown of a long-dead bloodwood that had grown from a seed blown deep into a fissure in the escarpment. It leaned precariously out over the cliff face, anchored by a network of strong roots knotted among the sandstone boulders. Alive, the tree had weathered countless storms, but since its death the once-flexible timber had hardened and become vulnerable and one day it would fall to the plain below. The eagle could sense this and would not stay on in the nest once her chicks had flown.

Carefully, she climbed up on to the lip of the nest. She looked down, and instead of launching outward with beats of her strong wings, fell forward as though shot and allowed her body to plummet towards the rocks below. As the wind rushed around her, she savoured a feeling of abandonment, yearning to be free.

Completely free. But hunger woke her and she opened her wings. Gradually, at first, to permit a controlled stoop, and then to their full span.

Her fall broken, she floated forward in a gentle arc, resting on a thermal, and felt the warm air buffeting her and playing through the fingers of her wings as she flitted her wedge-shaped tail for balance. From this height she could see everything. Every tiny detail of the escarpment. Every rock and blade of bush and every dead and living thing. The broken men were barely specks on that sparse landscape, but she knew that they were there. She had watched them die and had later taken their eyes to prevent them staring up in death at the ancient beauty of her world.

The eagle now turned from the scene and urged the thermal to bear her upward, circling away only as she felt herself to be leaving the earth. One day, she would let the warm breath of the escarpment carry her all the way to the sun. She knew that it could. It was pure magic.

CHAPTER 1

Sydney 1986

I first met Dania in the Jungle Bar, near Wynyard station, where I worked one or two nights a week. She had come in with a group of people from her office on George Street for a combined birthday party—a sleepy looking bloke with thin brown hair and a loud chick with too much lippy and hysterical hands. Both were taking turns sculling spirits and were already half squirreled. Dania was sitting slightly apart from the others, with one leg over the other. She wore a thin gold chain with a pearl pendant over a sheer black turtle-necked jumper, her long hair pulled back in a colourful silk scrunchy. Small-boned, delicate hands took the margarita. She smiled at me, blinking away the sudden taste of salt and lime.

The others were clamouring for their drinks and I turned to hand out the rest of the glasses. The place was still pretty quiet. One other office group had come in, as well as some sweaty, rumpled businessmen looking for an hour or two of relief before the train home to the suburbs. Soon the construction and demolition workers would arrive. Sydney was exploding, with cranes and skip bins everywhere. Cement barricades. Jackhammers. Suits interspersed with hard hats and blue cotton singlets. The Jungle Bar catered for everyone. Always dark and over-cooled, and infused with cigarette smoke and the residual smell of carpet laced with beer and cheap spirits.

Dania was still smiling at me. Easy-listening bullshit music came quietly from speakers in each corner of the room as the disco ball turned listlessly in the heavy, vented air. I wanted to say something clever but have never been any good at that. I nodded self-consciously then picked up the empties and gave the table a wipe down, and went back to the bar.

Jilly was putting racks of steaming glasses back in the cooling shelves. She nodded at Dania's table. 'That mob getting pissed yet?'

'Some are. Two of them having a birthday. Office mates.'

'Used to hate those office things. Nothing in common except the photocopier. And then there's the food chain. You know, is the boss still the boss when you're talking shit over beers?'

Jilly bent to take another tray of hot glasses from the dishwasher. Her long spare limbs stretched and folded. All cantilevers. Not graceful. A thin hard girl and very tall, with sandy red hair and freckles sprayed all over like mud splatters. Amazing green eyes.

I nodded. 'A lot of the uni things are the same way. Someone puts a keg on in the cafeteria every now and then. Private school kids get pissed. The rest stand around. I've stopped going to them.'

I was doing second year veterinary science at the University of Sydney. I had spent the first year living in one of the colleges on campus. It was a good way to meet some people and get to know Sydney a bit. I was older than most, as I'd taken a year off after school. I had worked for part of it on a little run-down logging place in the mountains near Nundle in northern New South Wales, helping a poor old bloke with terminal emphysema. He was an alcoholic and basically fucked, but it was beautiful country. Cold forests with deep snow in winter. I lived up there in my own little cabin and spent a lot of time exploring and shooting pigs with an old rifle that had been left over from the first war. Every now and then I would take the boss's broken car down the hill to Tamworth for supplies. Food and grog. Brown Muscat in flagons. It was awful stuff, but seemed to keep him alive.

I left the hills one evening on the spur of the moment. A nurse had been to visit the old bloke and gave me a lift. It had been snowing and she was nervous about driving through the silent forests alone. I had also come to realise that I would never be paid. From Tamworth, I hitched west for a week or more until it seemed that I had come to the edge of the desert, then turned north to the big cattle stations in Queensland. One place near Charters Towers was amazing. Over a million acres of hard, open country. Tough blokes, but not in a Marlborough Man way. Two gay bikers, deeply in love. Then there was Big John, with a huge body, a little head and no speech; and Lanky Aaron, who could ride anything. Half a dozen others. We each took a handful of horses out for the three weeks it took to get the cattle together and back to the homestead. Some of the horses had been ridden after stock but most were freshly broken. I remember eating breakfast in a stock camp one morning and watching Aaron work a new black filly. She was a big horse and every muscle in her body was trembling—poised to explode in a flimsy little pen made from ropes tied around bush saplings. Aaron was on her back, calmly rolling a smoke with both his hands and wearing the horse down through the weight of sheer nonchalance. I doubt I'll see riding like that again.

I came back from Queensland towards the end of the year to our little farm near Tamworth. My parents had split up and the place was being rented to a mate. It was a bit of a strange time, really. I had no money and ate a lot of cabbage. I felt a bit stressed by the uncertainty about what I should do with my life. The travel and station life had been brilliant but I had the hollow feeling you get when skipping school. I played a lot of guitar, grew a thin blonde beard and wore a Mexican poncho made out of an old army blanket. I didn't really have any direction but with good school marks and both parents doctors, felt pushed towards uni and some sort of a profession. I ended up choosing vet science because of the horses. I wasn't a particularly good or talented rider, but loved working with them and thought I might try to be a horse vet.

I knew pretty much straight away that I was a fish out of water. I struggled through first year with bugger-all study, and somehow passed everything on smarts, but could feel it slipping. It was second year now, and still slipping.

Jilly was pointing over my shoulder. 'You've got a customer.'

I turned. Dania was standing at the bar. 'I'm sorry, what would you like?'

She looked at me. Another small smile. Fine wrinkles appeared around her eyes and nose. A face that smiled a lot. 'Can we have exactly the same order again? I can't remember it all.'

I found a sticky note on the till and read the order out to her. She paid with lots of small notes and coins. I watched her hands and felt each finger as she counted the money out into my palm. Stared at the top of her head. Thick dark hair. A few strands escaping from the scrunchy.

'Is that right?' She was looking at the complicated pile of notes and coins in my hand.

'I've got no idea.'

She laughed. A short burst, as her hand flew up to her mouth.

I smiled. 'I'm Devlin. Devlin Mack.'

'I'm Dania. Do you work here a lot?'

I told her it was usually just Fridays, although I sometimes stood in for the others. I felt myself suddenly nervous and blurting. I said that I was at uni and didn't have time for too much bar work. She asked me what I was studying.

'Vet. I'm in second year. Three more to go.'

Her face lit up. 'Really? I've never known a vet. I love animals. I've got a cat and I'm learning to ride horses. I have lessons at Centennial Park.'

I dropped some of the coins and had to chase them around under the dishwasher. When I stood up again I was a bit flushed, but still smiling. 'I ride horses, too. I've been riding since I was a kid. Horses were why I decided to try and be a vet.'

She looked at me for a second. I felt foolish and wished I had been a bit more guarded, but she didn't seem to mind. 'Sunday's lesson will be a ride around the outside of the park. We do that every three weeks. If you wanted, you could probably come with us. They seem to have lots of horses.'

I told her that I'd love that and asked for the riding school's number so I could call them and line it up. She ferreted around in her purse and produced a business card. I wrote down the details on a beer mat.

'Can I call you tomorrow to let you know what they say?' This was bold for me.

'That would be nice. I live with my mum, so she might answer.' She gave me her number and I added it to the beer mat. I was still smiling and probably looking very stupid. She pointed at the post-it note. 'Those drinks, Devlin?'

I snapped out of it. 'Onto it, Dania.'

'Devvo, my little mate.' A slap across the back that felt like an oar.

'Chatting up all the beautiful girls again, mate?' A friendly punch on the arm that knocked me into the till.

Dania smiled again and went back to her friends, as I turned to see our bouncers Ray and Sharky calmly helping themselves to drinks and packets of chips. Ray was short for 'ray of light', the Tongan meaning of his true name, Huelo. Sharky's real name was Anga, which in Tongan means shark. Ray and Sharky were cousins, although at that time the term seemed to encompass most of Campbelltown. Both had come to Australia on rugby league scholarships. Neither had performed well, but they liked the place and stayed. They liked the food, too. Ate almost constantly, fuelling exponentially expanding guts. But they carried it well. Both were several inches over six feet and built like fridges. Huge smiles. Slow to anger. And they loved to sing. They would sing to each other, like lovers, with eyes closing as they found complex little harmonies. Neither seemed to have the upper hand. It was as though they were two parts of one huge being.

'Ray, mate. You'll kill me if you keep hitting me like that. Seriously. Have to go easy on us little whiteys.'

'Devvo. Need to eat more food. Get bigger. Pretty girls like big fat boys.'

Chuckling, they took some more handfuls of chip packets and waddled over towards the door. A female cover of The Doors' 'Light my Fire' started up and the two of them were off. Ray took one line, crooning as Sharky hummed a falsetto harmony. Then they swapped. No explanation needed. Face to face. Holding hands. No hesitating. No wallowing in the mire.

There was a spattering of applause from the office party. Raised eyebrows exchanged between two businessmen. A chance to glance across the room to Dania, but she turned and caught me. I smiled and looked away.

Ray and Sharky took up their places, still humming quietly. One would station himself outside to keep out the drunks while the other remained inside to break up fights. The construction workers knocked off at five and started to drift in around half-past. Same for the demolition teams. A lot of the demo workers seemed to be Maoris. It was hard work and they're tough people. They'd come in happy, but almost always started a fight once the jugs of beer took hold. It was usually just among themselves—a disagreement about something that had happened on the site, or maybe a family thing—and quickly extinguished by their mates. But every now and then the fights would get out of hand and Ray and Sharky would have to earn the chain-eaten packets of chips and use their enormous weight to smother the flailing arms.

But as the evening wore on, there was no sign of that and Dania's group were quietly winding down. The birthday boy and girl had transitioned to a sad, weary resignation and the talk had dried up. The others were looking around self-consciously, then one made a move and they all stood up and gathered coats and bags, chatting again now that escape was imminent.

Dania made her way back to the bar. 'Are you sure you'd like to come on Sunday? You won't be bored?'

'I'm dead sure. Really, I'd love to. I haven't ridden a horse for over a year now.'

'The horses might not be what you're used to. They're very quiet old things.'

I told her that I didn't care what sort of horse they gave me—it would just be great to sit in a saddle again. We were both smiling. Inspired, I added, 'I'll give you my number in case you change your plans.'

I found a dry beer mat and wrote out the phone number of my flat in Balmain.

A tired, smudged face appeared behind her, the voice a whine. 'Dania, we're heading off now.'

Dania nodded and smiled again at me. 'Bye, then. See you Sunday.'

I watched her walk off with her friends. She stopped at the door and turned to wave. The others were milling around her like sticks in a flooded stream, then someone took her arm and she was gone.

The last part of the evening was uneventful. Jilly had been trying to tell me about her flatmate who had developed schizophrenia from smoking too much dope. He was paranoid and angry with it and convinced that the TV was watching him. Followed him around the room. I was immediately interested in the idea of belief in something so completely and provably fictitious. So completely imagined. It occurred to me that if a person's brain could do this, perhaps it could also excise the memory of something completely real? Just remove it from the record, or at least lock it in a safe. Would you also have to be crazy for that to work?

I was thinking this through and only half listening to Jilly's stories, our conversation relayed between shouted requests for drinks. Then a girl at the bar smiled in a way that reminded me of Dania. I could picture the little turtleneck jumper and the way it clung to her body. And the black skirt as she walked to the door. She was just gorgeous. She seemed subtly different to other girls I knew. Somehow more grown up. More like a woman. I thought about the weekend ride. The horses would probably be rubbish—fat hairy ponies and ancient racehorses. But it wouldn't matter. We could ride side by side and I could find out about her world. Maybe I could fit in it somewhere. Maybe she'd like Balmain. We could have breakfast at Ernie's cafe. I might even be able to scrape up enough money for dinner somewhere.

The night dragged on, but eventually it was closing time and we locked the doors. Ray and Sharky helped us to tidy up the bar and stack chairs on tables. Cleaners would come in later in the night. I fetched my bike and backpack from the staffroom and walked Jilly to the bus stop. I knew she liked that, as she felt a bit nervous about being alone at night—even on George Street— and the big fellas had another gig to go to in the Cross.

With Jilly on her way, I set off for home. The Jungle Bar was close to Circular Quay and only a ten-minute ferry ride to Balmain, but the ferries stopped after eleven and the bike was always a lot quicker than buses.

The house I shared was a little renovated weatherboard terrace on Colgate Avenue, not far from the Darling Street wharf. Balmain had been built as a working class suburb with narrow two-story terraces cheek-by-jowl from the ferry terminal right up to the shops at the top of the hill. But by the mid-eighties the demographic had changed, as moneyed arty and professional people cottoned on to the charm of the old buildings and the way they made the area feel a bit like a little fishing village. Many of the houses had now been stripped back and repainted and the beautiful Sydney sandstone that appeared here and there had been cleaned and re-grouted. Doors and windows were new, and those houses with any sort of a front garden displayed strange succulents and manicured shrubs in expensive earthen pots.

Our street ran down to the old Colgate building, right on the water. The factory was still churning out toothpaste and shampoos, and was a busy little hub on working days, so most of the locals parked in a small service lane that ran behind the houses. Our house had its own covered parking area, just off the lane, and a small paved backyard. I chained my bike to a post at the side of the walkway and took my backpack through to the kitchen. A note on the fridge told me to remember to turn off the outside light. I smiled and turned off the light. Another note told me there was a homemade pie in the fridge and that the oven was still warm. I found the pie and put it in the warm oven. A third note attached to the oven door told me to turn it up to about 200°C. So I did that, and didn't need to look to know that a final note would be attached to the door of my room, telling me to check that I had turned off the oven.

I sat down at the table and took the beer mat out of my pack. The kitchen had already started to fill with the smell of warming pie. I propped the mat up against the pepper grinder and stared at it. Small spidery writing. A Randwick address. There was also a phone number. I looked around the kitchen, then back at the beer mat. Thought about Dania. Late at night like this I wanted so badly to find someone who could get close to me and unlock some of the secret bullshit that I knew was in there but couldn't visualise or understand. Get rid of it, then help me to get on with life. With her. Always with her. I was dead scared of myself, really. Just a ticking bomb.

I realised I was stinking up the kitchen a bit in my smoky bar clothes, so had a quick shower and put them in a bag outside the door. I had to be quiet as Aud, my flatmate and landlady, and the author of the helpful little notes, would be asleep. Aud was nice. She was dumpy and hesitant and not very smart, but really nice. Aud was the same age as me. She worked in a trendy bookshop in Glebe. This was the house she grew up in. Her mum and dad had moved up the coast to Queensland when her dad retired, and had left her to look after the place.

Aud's dad had been a senior copper and was a bit of a scary dude. After I moved in, a couple of his mates came around for a quiet word. 'We hear little Aud's upset, goes hard for you. Aud's happy, you got some mates in the police.' They had looked at my hair, and my jeans, and then at each other. One had added, 'Never know when that might be a good thing.'

I did my best to keep Aud happy, and that included leaving my reeking bar clothes and shoes in a bag outside the door. Helping with housework. Cooking. Shopping. Maintaining the little yard. It worked really well. I loved the place and knew I might otherwise have ended up living like most other students, in a filthy room with greasy clothes and shit food, yelling at each other.

Aud's mum and dad had come home for a weekend, early in the piece, and I was taken outside to the barbie for a beer. Called 'son'. I didn't mind it. Her dad wanted to know how Audrey was coping. His soft little dumpy daughter. Very much loved. All alone. No dangerous blokes hanging around? Black jeans seemed to be his chief criterion. And there had in fact been a dorky bloke who wore black jeans and seemed a bit keen. Morris, his name was. He was very tall and painfully thin, with acne scars, lank black hair and obscenely long white fingers. I wondered once whether Morris had stayed the night, but didn't share this with the Chief Superintendent. Morris was okay. He had actually seemed to be a bit scared of me, which said enough. But I hadn't seen Morris lately.

I could hear Aud mumbling in her sleep as I tiptoed back down the steps from my room in the loft. Aud's parents had converted the terrace's attic and ceiling space into a self-contained flat, which her mum had wanted to run as an upmarket inner-city B&B. The idea had never really taken hold and when her dad retired and they moved to Queensland it seemed natural for Aud to have a house mate. The flat was enormous by student standards. The spine of the ceiling ran lengthways, with eaves coming down on either side to about head height. Two big dormer windows faced towards the harbour, one with a view to a snippet of water and McMahon's Point on the other side. The far end of the room had a glass sliding door that opened to a tiny balcony above Colgate Avenue. The near end had the main entrance, as well as a small *en suite* with a shower and loo. There was also a slatted deck outside the entrance and, again, this looked down the hill and out to the harbour. The flooring was polished wooden slats, and with wood panelling on the ceiling as well, the flat had a warm and quasi-Scandinavian feel. Aud's parents had left a queen-sized bed and an antique wardrobe and writing desk. I had strict instructions about where I could and could not put coffee mugs. My only contributions were an old Persian carpet that my mother had given me and a ridiculous lime-green beanbag shaped like a frog that I could take out onto the deck on weekends.

Balmain's two ferry terminals were only a few minutes' walk, and in the mornings, you could hear the big girls ploughing around the harbour and a signal blast as one or other approached a wharf. The house was also very close to Ernie's cafe on Darling Street. Ernie was a fat little Turkish bloke and a well-known purveyor of delicious coffee and the lethal sweet pastries that his wife churned out from their home in Darlinghurst. I had an arrangement with Ernie, such that he would give me a free breakfast for each three hours' work I put in at the cafe. We kept a tab. It was usually just kitchen stuff, but sometimes I'd mow the lawn out the back or take care of little repairs. Aud's dad had suggested the job to Ernie, who had said yes on the grounds that everyone said yes to Aud's dad. The original idea was a little wage that might then help me with the rent, but once Aud's dad had gone back to Queensland, Ernie had quietly explained that he couldn't afford casual staff—but could pay me in food instead. I was happy with that. Ernie made amazing breakfasts that soaked up cup after tiny cup of his thick Turkish coffee and were a luxury I would never have had otherwise.

I had bugger-all money. But no-one I knew had much, except Aud. Aud had a bottomless allowance as well as her salary from the bookshop. She'd always try to pay more than her share of the food and stuff, but I never let her. I couldn't see that going down well with her dad. And it was not inconceivable that her bank account was watched.

The Jungle Bar gave me a small income and I had a little coming in from Mum. I also had a scholarship given out to some of the country kids studying vet science. It was bequeathed by an old small-town vet who must have done it tough in his time. The scholarship paid for books and other uni expenses, like surgery gear and gowns. Transport around Sydney would also have been expensive, but I rode the bike pretty much everywhere. It was great exercise and I enjoyed it. That said, I did actually have a car. It was an old XB Ford Falcon utility, ute, originally Dad's. Mum paid for the rego and reimbursed my fuel. I didn't abuse the privilege, and outside the long trips home I only used it to drive to band practice sessions and gigs.

The band was huge. It even made me a bit of extra cash. We called ourselves The Stain, which was a bit lame but tended to get remembered. We had a regular slot at the Shakespeare Hotel, in Surrey Hills, and also played at university formals. I'd met Rick, Scotty and Dom at college the year before. Rick played guitar and was a year ahead of me in vet science. Scotty sang. He was doing law. Scotty was a bit of a prick, really, but he had a great voice and the chicks loved his clean, arrogant rich-boy look.

Dombo played drums. He was a physics student and probably the only true genius I've ever known. Dom came from a little town down in the Riverina somewhere. His old man was a welder and sheetmetal worker. But Dom had come second in the state in four-unit maths. Without a teacher. No-one at his little school was qualified to teach four-unit maths. He was short and a bit tubby, with a full black beard. His hair fell in ringlets and was generally pretty filthy. Dom was a brilliant drummer, but played a bit of guitar as well and he and I usually did an acoustic set within each gig where we both played and sang. Harmonised. Tin whistles. Harmonica. I played a bit of mandolin sometimes. My voice was okay, but quiet. Dom sounded harsh but he had a good range and could belt it out. We took our acoustic act out busking every now and then. It was a lot of fun at the Quay and Martin Place, and on suburban late-night trains, and we usually made enough to pay for a good meal and some drinks.

I took the warmed pie from the oven and wrote Aud a little thank-you note. Added a smiley. Aud liked smileys. I switched off the lights and oven and carried the pie up to my room, then propped the beer mat up on a little table by my bed and adjusted the bedside light so that I could see it properly.

Outside the dormer windows, the city was grinding on as it did day and night. I had become used to it now, but at one time I cried for the muffled quiet of the country. For the small, unplanned noises. Nights without light. Sometimes when anxiety started crowding me I would think myself away—think up a story, then put on headphones to shut out the city and live the story in tiny detail. It was always the same story and with the exaggerated simplicity of a comic book. I had started to write it down. Self-conscious and a bit afraid, I stopped. It was set out west in the oven-dried and beautiful arid bush. A small place, with no expectations. Dusty. Very hot. An open and endless sky. Huge birds drifting slowly on thermals. And there was always a girl just like Dania.

The Warkon story

It was a Thursday . . .

Ben never saw the roo, or emu, or pig, or whatever it was. He recalled a shape to his left, which had seemed to materialise out of the glinting splintered dust and flow with the bike like a bow wave before veering into and over it . . .

It was a Thursday . . .

Ben never saw the roo, or emu, or pig, or whatever it was. He recalled a shape to his left, which had seemed to materialise out of the glinting splintered dust and flow with the bike like a bow wave before veering into and over it. Dusk, and Ben was travelling pretty much due west. The dwindling sun had been in his eyes for an hour or more and though now below the horizon, its memory was held in the tiny shards of burnt sand and rock that lined his screen and goggles.

It was always like this in the late afternoon and evening in western New South Wales. The sun dominated everything, pouring itself into each tiny grain of life and matter. Beyond the glare and heat you could feel the way it shaped the landscape, giving it fickle and fleeting beautiful colours. Stands of rock could be pale in the morning, then a deep red in the heat of the day before fading to purple. Stark trees would appear browned and strangled at one glance, then suddenly be bathed in a lime-green eucalyptus aura.

The next few seconds were furious and catastrophic. The front wheel lost traction in the deep red dust as the animal's weight pushed the bike sideways. Ben felt the left side go down and the bike turn over itself as the bars dug in and he was flung forward, directly down the road and out of its path. There was a braking abrasion of dust and rock as he seemed to bounce along the road and then, suddenly, he was sitting, dazed and waiting for the pain. Which didn't come.

Ben waited a little longer, confused by the sudden fury but even in that state unable to accept that no bones had been broken. He had been in many slow crashes on this bike and others, but this was the first at highway speed. He didn't know of anyone who had walked away from something like this completely unscathed. He slowly got up and inspected himself. Dust had been ground into the leather of his pants, jacket and gloves, and the peak of his helmet was ripped to one side, but nothing hurt.

Then he looked back at the bike. The beautiful Beemer. Bought last year with some money left by his godfather in England. His father had told him that it was a waste—that he should invest the money, or at least bank it—but Ben had seen the bike at a dealership in Goondiwindi and knew he had to have it. And now it was lying beside the road with a twisted wheel and forks, and bars that must be bent or broken. The tank was scratched and slightly dented, but the steel bracket that Ben had had made to protect the cylinder heads appeared to have done its job. He doubted that the bike was destroyed. It would need a new wheel and some other parts, and probably some substantial body work, but the panniers attached to the rear had kept most of it off the road.

He lifted the bike upright and slid it backwards onto its centre-stand, which appeared to be undamaged. Like that, it immediately looked better. For lack of anywhere else, he sat on the bike's seat and rested his arms on the bars and drifted into a daze of latent shock.

Twenty minutes passed. It seemed like hours. The last threads of sunlight had disappeared and a blanket thrown across the rapidly-cooling desert. Small creatures made small, furtive sounds.

A heartbroken bird called out to nobody in particular. Something barked, miles away, not quite a bark, as a group of large animals ran, brushing scrub aside and tearing urgently at the sand.

Then, out of the gloom, the bush around him began to be lit with the spotlights of a distant vehicle . . .

CHAPTER 2

'Dombo.'

'Mate.'

We trudged back inside the filthy little Glebe townhouse that Dom shared with a disgruntled and frumpy arts student. The drum kit and PA were packed up and ready to go. We loaded it all into the ute and wrapped it in carpet.

Dom had been sleeping and needed to get changed. I waited outside, worried that some little scrote might try to flog the gear. I took the beer mat out of my bag and looked at it. It was getting a bit frayed from handling. I had called the riding place at Centennial Park that morning and they were happy for me to join in. I told them that I could ride, but wasn't sure that it had registered. I let it go. As long as the horse they gave me could maintain the same speed as Dania's horse, I would be happy. We would probably just be walking—maybe a bit of a trot. I thought I'd take the ute so I didn't turn up sweaty. And maybe we could drive somewhere afterwards. Up to Palm Beach. Or over to Bondi. Have lunch. Like adults.

Dom barrelled out of the house and I snapped back to reality. He stank of the cheap deodorant he soaked everything in. I was pretty sure it was just toilet spray.

'Mate, you smell fucken awful.'

Dom wasn't concerned. 'I'm fat and I sweat a lot. It gets in my clothes. I have to chuck them out unless I take steps.'

I asked him why no-name toilet spray was the only solution, but he pointed out that it was cheap and chicks loved him, anyway. And that was true. They did.

We made our way across to Surry Hills and parked in one of the pub's reserved spots 'round the back, then ferried the gear in and began to get it set up. Scotty and Rick arrived. Rick was smiling to himself. He was a quiet, understated bloke. A bit of a surfer and a pretty good guitarist. Had a penchant for rockabilly. Scotty worked the room, shaking hands. Firm. Eye contact. This was an important skill for a Sydney lawyer, but a bit ridiculous among students in a grungy pub.

I got my bass out and tuned it. It was a nice old Washburn fretless. The smooth neck made for great slides and as I'd played violin as a kid I was used to the idea of accurate finger placement. In pubs, I usually ran the bass amp out through an old five-foot speaker. It sounded brilliant in small spaces. Dom and I had found the speaker one night in a parking lot at the back of one of the university pubs. I put notes up around the university, but nobody claimed it and we decided that it must have been flogged then abandoned.

I unplugged again and played a few scales and riffs to get my fingers working. Rick was doing the same. Dom had some padded sticks and was tapping lightly at his drums and cymbals, concentrating. I sometimes wondered what it must be like inside the head of a genius. He had told me once that maths was like reading a cookbook, inasmuch as every now and then there'd be something a bit different—like putting Tabasco in pumpkin soup—but basically it was just about adding flour to water, mixing it in, adding a bit of butter and a pinch of salt. He couldn't understand how anyone could not get it.

I smiled. There were still fifteen minutes until the start of the gig. Scotty got himself a drink. He sang better half-cut and at one stage had tried to take the cost of it out of our fee. I fetched a jug of water and some glasses. Whatever the season outside, it was always hot in the Shakespeare. Good bands played here. Proper bands. We weren't a good band, but we played good covers pretty well and that made a night in the pub a lot more fun—and where there's fun there's drinking, so the management liked us.

We all plugged back in and set the levels up the way we knew worked well. We generally started loud. Nothing apologetic. It was going on nine o'clock and people were ready to kick loose. The dancing would be mostly pissed chicks and perhaps a few fat blokes. For some reason it was the fat blokes who seemed to dance when they got drunk. The rest would sing where they stood, or perhaps just nod along while mouthing the words. Bodies swaying. Drinking hard. Looking angry.

We had a sheet of songs to work through. About five for each set with a ten-minute break in between. People needed a chance to talk and get more drinks. Have a piss. Scotty had the list. He was the front man, and good at it. No-one could tell he was a dick. He was smiling at the crowd now and waving to a few chicks. Scotty could make jeans and a t-shirt look like a suit.

Rick was chuckling to himself as he pointed at me and moved over to the electric piano. I nodded and felt the strings of the bass humming with passive current. We were going to start with U2's 'New Year's Day'. Scotty turned with raised eyebrows. We each nodded. Then he counted us in. *Two, three, four* . . . and at last the bass intro. The first notes of the night. It's a great riff, and has to be played at full volume, hard and with confidence, and as the driving notes came through I could feel the big speaker behind me buffeting the back of my jeans. Then piano and drums joined in, and finally the vocals. Scotty yelling, his hands over his ears, starting high and climbing down in four steps. And now all of us together with everything seriously loud. Just beautiful. We'd practiced the hell out of this. Each on our own parts, then the timing. Playing and rewinding a tape until we broke it.

Now softer, then Scotty, to the girls he'd picked out. Only to them. All quiet as a world in white gets underway. It's a long song and Rick's version of the guitar solo went on forever. Great in a pub. No rest. Straight into the Hoodoo-Gurus' 'Bittersweet'. The four guitar chords at the start. Everyone knew it. Then vocals. Scotty, with eyes closed. My sword. My reward. The bass and drums came in hard over the top of the guitar, with me and Rick sharing the second mic. Don't cry. Be strong. And then Scotty took the whole thing up an octave. Loud. Belted it out, the crowd singing with him. Cut and bleed.

And the rest. The drumming hard and sharp and bass lines precise. The vocals were bloody good—had to hand it to him—and the guitar then filled in the bits. The crowd was yelling now and a big drunk bloke came over and pressed a rum-and-Coke to my lips. Applause from his mates. Then he stood next to me, head-butting the smoke and noise to the beat of the bass. A bouncer raised an eyebrow but I shook my head. Harmless, and having a good night. We finished and he went back to his table. Happy.

Then we fired up 'The Break-Up Song'. The Greg Kihn Band. Four chords on guitar. Finger-picked. The bass and drums come in quietly with quiet vocals, then steadily more impassioned before the big chorus. I don't think we ever knew the real words. For us it was always 'They don't ride like that anymore'. The crowd was right into it as the song built. It's an easy sequence for riffing and Rick had a go. I had the harmonica on a steel frame around my neck and did some fast stuff, bending the root notes and basically just making a noise. Sliding the bass a lot. No skill really, but it looked and sounded good and kept the crowd of drinkers cheering.

After a few more we finished the set and Scotty thanked the audience for the drinks. He had had a few by then and was loosening up. Pretty much a good bloke now. The rest of us had an agreement not to drink hard until the last set. It didn't matter if Scotty went a bit wild but we needed to concentrate. We had to be able to feel the crowd and respond to it. And to each other. Pull ourselves up out of flat spots or stop the chaotic shit from getting out of hand. Go crazy with riffs, but stay tight and follow the formula.

The second set was more of the same. We started with 'Johnny B Goode'. Classic little riff. Then Chisel, AC/DC, the Angels and Led Zep. More Hoodoos. At the end of it we'd been going for about an hour and the crowd was getting tired, so we decided to do a short acoustic set. Just me and Dom while the others took it easy. Wooden music.

We opened the set with 'Stairway to Heaven'. I picked out the guitar part while Dom played tin whistle and together we did the vocal harmonies. The song has been done to death, but it's such a great piece. When people are pissed and sentimental and have been banging heads for an hour to loud hard rock it always works. There was silence around the pub. Complete silence. For once we nailed it. Probably the best we'd ever played it.

A girl with blonde ringlets had pushed herself to the front. She was skinny and flat-chested and stunning. And staring straight at me with her drink in hand, smiling. We went to America's 'Ventura Highway'. I played the fast rhythm guitar part and Dom came over the top with the difficult lead riff. I could never get it right. The two of us did the vocal harmonies. Scotty was sitting at a table to the side looking bored, but we kept it going with Crosby, Stills, Nash and Young's 'The Lee Shore'. Then Springsteen's 'The River'. Emotive lyrics. A catch in my voice. The chick in the front was still smiling. Intense. Swaying a bit now, as we finished the set with an acoustic version of Chisel's 'Bow River'.

I felt drained and empty and strangely desolate as I unplugged the guitar and started to set things back up for the next electric set. I didn't know if Dom or the others felt the same way with the immediate come-down from the emotion that went into playing and singing. To make it magic, and to purge everything inside— to truly forget—you had to live the words and the music. Every second of it. Follow each song through like a journey and bring the audience with you if it seemed that they didn't get it. It could be easy or difficult, and sometimes it didn't work at all. The music was flat. It was just music. But when it did work there was nothing like it. The release of a week's tension and anxiety in one hit.

I was checking that the bass was still in tune when the skinny girl came over to the little raised stage that we played on. She looked very solemn and was probably pretty stoned. I could see that she wanted to tell me something over the din of drinkers, so I knelt down with the bass and smiled.

She spoke. 'You're beautiful.'

I was a bit shocked. I'm not beautiful. I'm not even very good looking. I stared at her. She had a pen in her hand and pointed to my arm. I held it out and she wrote down a phone number. North Shore somewhere. A rich girl. She kissed me on the cheek and was gone. Nowhere in the crowd. Dom was looking at me thoughtfully. I never liked to think of Dom's brain aimed at me.

I stood up and shrugged it off, and we started the electric set. Mentals' 'The Nips are Getting Bigger'. The guitar chords shuffling, then the sliding bass solo. It always sounded fantastic on the fretless Washburn. Flowed out from the big speaker like a wave, with the crowd almost physically compelled to nod and sway as it washed over them. Scotty's voice was rested now, with perfect intonation and depth. This was a drinking song about drinking and the staff could hardly keep it flowing fast enough. The punters were turning to spirits to cut down on trips to the bar, but that just made them more drunk.

After that, more AC/DC. More Chisel. More clichés. Deep Purple's 'Smoke on the Water'. The Animals' 'House of the Rising Sun'. Another break then the final set was finished and we went through the parody of beginning to unplug and pack up. The crowd was yelling. Hands belting tables. Bar staff nodding encouragingly.

Unplanned, Dom stood up from behind his drum kit. Drink in hand. Bearded wild man. Sweat running down his face. Yelled into his mic, 'DO THE STROLL?'

The crowd roared.

Then he sat down and belted out Led Zep's amazing 'Rock and Roll' drum solo. We let him do an extra loop. It was a virtuoso performance and the crowd went wild. We had never got this one right in practice sessions, but had no choice but to follow him into it. And somehow it worked.

It was a great night. We all knew it. Rick had started hitting the rum hard as we packed the gear up and was now slurred and swaying. Scotty had gone outside with a chick and not returned. Dom and I ferried our stuff back out to the ute. Still buzzing. Exhausted. Dom rolled a joint in the car park. Lit it up and took a long drag then passed it to me. We sat on the tailgate and smoked it down.

I asked Dom where his stash came from.

'Mate back home grows it out in the bush somewhere. Wants me to sell it for him. Fuck that.'

I agreed. Dom got out the pouch and rolled another. 'Probably the best yet, that gig. Funny how it just happens sometimes.'

It was true. And it was always so hard to predict. This was usually a good crowd, with a few yobbos, a few workers and the students, but things could still go either way.

We shared the second joint in silence before Dom remembered the skinny girl who had given me her number. 'That beautiful blonde was keen, mate. Will you call her?'

I shook my head and told him about Dania. About horse riding in the park in the morning. Dom was impressed. 'Well done. And you're actually a bushie. Should be able to impress her a bit. Just go easy on the crazy lost poet thing.'

I chuckled. We were getting a bit wasted now and drenched in smoky calm. I told him that Dania had seemed a bit different. Settled, and somehow older than she looked. More grounded than I was. Might be able to anchor me a bit and stop me feeling like I was floating. Get me to take uni seriously.

Dom was only half listening, but understood the uni thing. It was common ground between us. 'I thought I'd cruise through but I've done fuck-all work and I might actually stuff it up. They want you to learn pointless shit and spit it back at them. Lots of it. I haven't been to any of the lectures. Think I might be fucked, really.' He seemed sincere, but I couldn't imagine Dom failing anything.

We finished the second joint and I stubbed out the butt. Dom was sitting on his hands, looking cold and withdrawn. Smoking sometimes did that to him.

'Let's bugger off, Dom. Get this shit home. Have good dreams.'

He didn't answer but got into the car, still silent. I left him to it and backed the ute carefully out of the car park. Grass always slowed me down, which never seemed like a bad thing, really. We edged out onto Devonshire Street and crept back through quiet darkened lanes to Dom's flat in Glebe.

'That's a mule.'

Silence.

'Seriously, it's a mule. You know, a donkey crossed with a horse. A mule.'

We all stood there, looking at the mule. It had ears like a rabbit. With a saddle. My ride. Dania giggled. The riding school chick looked embarrassed, but thought she should say something. 'It might be.'

'It definitely is.'

Dania poked me and I took the hint. 'No worries. It'll be okay. They're supposed to be smarter than horses. I'll give it a go.'

I checked the saddle and bridle and adjusted the stirrups and led it around a bit, talking quietly. I didn't know whether mules played by the same rules as horses, but it's never a good idea to jump on a horse you've only just met. The mule seemed to be quiet, the big ears flicking left and right as it listened to my voice. I put my foot in the stirrup and jumped up.

'How does it feel to be riding a mule?' Dania was smiling. The other girl had gone to see to the assembling troop.

'Fantastic. At least it's got some height. Where's yours? Or have you got a horse?'

'Mine's ready to go. It's this one's friend, but I think it's a horse. They're always stabled next to each other. Naomi might have thought that would be good for us. She didn't know that you could ride. Will it really be okay?'

I was happier than I could remember being since I'd come to Sydney. 'Dania, honestly, it's great. Get your horse and let's get into it.'

Dania in fact had a small, fat, grey pony with hairy feet, big soft white lips and sad eyes. It would have been lucky to be fourteen hands—practically a dog—but she nevertheless needed to get on with a mounting block. Looked a bit unsteady in the saddle. Stirrups too short. Legs too bent. Funny white hard-hat. Adorable.

'I've only had three lessons, but I love it. Last week I trotted right around the ring.'

I wanted to reach down from my ridiculous mule and hug her.

Naomi blew on a small horn. A call to the hunt. The mule sighed deeply. Pretty sure it said 'fuck'. We moved off.

The track took us over Cook Road and into the park, the riding-school horses unfazed by city traffic. Once in the park, we picked up a wide sandy track that seemed to be following the outer roadway. I walked the mule next to Dania. We pointed at dogs and funny people. She asked me if she was riding properly. I told her she looked perfect to me. She liked that.

Naomi thought we might be ready for a trot and again blew the hunting horn. Dania flapped her arms about like a chicken in the universal gesture of non-riders wanting to go faster. I had a quiet word with the mule and we moved into the most awful trot I've ever sat. I don't think it even had two beats. It was impossible to rise to and I was pretty sure the mule was doing it on purpose. Dania was laughing at my expression.

'This is seriously fucking bad.' I remembered too late that I shouldn't be swearing, but Dania didn't seem to be offended. Still laughing, she'd managed to get her little pony to trot. Its hind feet were overstepping as it tripped over tree roots, rocks, slight depressions in the sand—anything, really—and again, probably deliberate. I was laughing as well now and we pulled back to a walk and let the others get ahead.

'So, are these like the horses you're used to?'

'No. I can say quite confidently that these are not anything at all like any horse I've ever ridden.'

Dania laughed again. I would have to reach out and touch her soon. I couldn't bear it.

'Do you think I've got talent as a rider?' She sat up straight, with shoulders back and both hands on the pommel. I told her that being slim with long legs was a good shape for riding. And that's true. Some of the top riders are short and dumpy, but they're at a disadvantage.

Dania was obviously pleased with the idea of being slim with long legs. 'If you were teaching me, what would you say about how I sit on a horse?'

She was wearing dark blue jodhpurs and a fitted, white polo shirt. It was very hard to look at her objectively and I think she knew it.

'I really don't have much of a clue. I just ride. But I guess what you've got to do once you've had a bit more time on the horse is lengthen the stirrups and take a bit of weight on the balls of your feet. Sit really deep. It's hard to explain, but it's often a good idea to take the saddle off and ride without it. That gives you better balance and helps you to sit right down on the horse. You'll be surprised how different the saddle feels afterwards.'

Dania thought she would just slide off when she went around a corner. I laughed. It was probably true. 'You'd get the hang of it. It takes a bit of practice, but you'd work it out.'

'You look nice on a horse.' It seemed to just come out, and she was immediately embarrassed.

I tried to smooth it over. 'I'm not a great rider but I pretty much lived on horses before I came to Sydney. I learnt to ride when I was about five or six, I think. My brothers didn't like it much, but I loved it. I had a fantastic horse when I was growing up. He was a palomino. Our hair was the same colour.' It always made me sad to think about Topaz. He died when I was in the last year of high school. He was euthanised with end-stage navicular disease, as nothing could be done. He could bow and count and would pick up your hat if you dropped it. While he was still sound, I rode him every day in the hills behind our little farm. I really loved him.

Naomi was telling us all something. We strained forward to hear it.

'Who would like to stop for an ice cream?'

I looked at Dania. She nodded. We put our hands up like kids. An overweight middle-aged woman on a huge old thoroughbred smiled indulgently. The riding school had some sort of arrangement with the ice cream van. With sign language, half a dozen cones were brought over to us by a little girl who immediately told me that my horse had funny ears.

'It's a mule. They're better than horses. Much more expensive.'

'Really? But it's got funny ears.'

'You mustn't say that too loud, or you'll upset it. Then it will buck me off and run home.'

'Oh.'

Dania was giggling. Naomi still looked uncomfortable with the whole mule thing. We ate our ice creams walking along. It was early autumn and the park was beautiful. I was becoming fond of my mule. When the others broke into a trot, we stayed back. Neither of us wanted to get back to the riding school. Neither of us had a horse that could trot.

'Have you always wanted to be a vet?'

I felt a cold wind blow through me. I knew I didn't want to be a vet. I don't think I ever did. I didn't know what I wanted to do but didn't want Dania to know that. Not the full extent of it. The dread. The strange sense of guilt and failure. She liked the idea that I was going to be a vet. She had already told most of the riding school people. But I couldn't lie to her. I tried to find words that wouldn't sound too weak. 'I think I liked the thought of being a vet. My parents are both doctors and I was expected to do something professional or academic. I took a year off before starting uni, trying to work out what I should do. I almost enrolled to be a primary school teacher. Then people kept suggesting vet and I sort of fell into it. But I don't like it. I don't think I'll be a good vet.'

Dania was watching me closely. I chuckled to smooth things over. 'I'll have to sort it out. I'm not doing very well at uni. I don't feel that I'm headed in the right direction. Most of the others enjoy it. They do extra prac work with vet clinics and get right into it. At the moment, I actually think I just want to be a farmer.'

We were again approaching the inner city pedestrian crossing. A cloud had fallen over me. I tried to shake it off, breathing in and out slowly and telling myself that I didn't need to solve this today.

Dania could see I was struggling. 'I'm so sorry, Devlin. I can see I've upset you.'

She was really concerned and I felt bad. I smiled, then saw her hand outstretched and reached down for it. Kissed her fingers. I had never kissed anyone's fingers before. I could taste the ice cream and the smell of horse. I took the hand in both mine and bent down so it touched my cheek. She shuddered, her fingers stroking my face.

Naomi was blowing the little horn and yelling again. We broke away and moved off.

'Hello! I'm Helen! I talked to you on the phone yesterday! I'm sorry you were given Patchy! I meant to tell Naomi that you could ride! You could have had my old dressage horse!'

I stepped back to adjust the volume. She was a large woman held together with frayed upholstery. Big teeth in a long face. Hair three different colours from the roots out and a back end like the boot of a P76. Horsewoman.

'We had a great time. Seriously, it was fine. I liked his ears.' I handed over the money.

We thanked her and Naomi and went out to the car park. I had cleaned the ute up. Vacuumed inside and Armour-All'd the plastic. Polished its cheap wheels and put fresh black duct tape on the back of the bull-bar. Straightened the driving lights. All of which only made it look more ridiculous in a Sydney car park.

She looked at it doubtfully. A small smile. 'I've never been in a ute before.'

I told her it was just a car with a very big back seat. She laughed and looked uncertainly under the tarp. 'You should have some hay bales in it. A roll of wire. Maybe a sheep.'

I chuckled. 'There's certainly been hay and wire in it in the past, but now it just ferries the band gear around.'

'You've got a band?'

I hadn't told her about The Stain. The name seemed a bit silly now.

'There are four of us. We met up in college last year. I play bass. Then there's guitar, drums and a singer. The drummer, Dom, is a good mate. Amazing bloke.'

Dania asked where we played, and I told her about the Shakespeare and the college dances. 'The colleges get several bands, and usually one is a proper band like the Hoodoos or Mentals. Then the rest of us get to use their PA and lights. Sometimes a mixing crew. It's pretty amazing playing through gear like that.'

Dania was impressed. I felt self-conscious. The hand-holding thing still hung between us. I asked her if she would like to drive somewhere and get some lunch. I thought maybe Palm Beach. It was a long way, but supposed to have nice views and good cafes.

'That would be lovely! I've only been to Palm Beach a few times. That was with Mum. Ages ago. We usually go over to Bondi or Bronte.'

'Do you know the way?'

Dania laughed again. She laughed so easily. A really nice laugh. 'I can probably get us to Manly, then we'll just have to keep going up the coast. It would be quicker to go to Chatswood, then across to Mona Vale. But that's such a horrible road. Let's go to Manly. We can have another ice cream.'

With Dania's directions, we got onto the Harbour Bridge then out through Mosman towards the coast. There was a lot of Sunday traffic. These were the wealthy parts of Sydney with Beemers and Mercs everywhere. Small coiffured dogs on string leads and skinny chicks in high heels. The ute ploughed through it all. I didn't drive it much in daylight and was feeling a bit self-conscious about the clichéd country-boy statement, but Dania didn't seem to mind. We had the windows down and arms on the ledges, sharing a packet of stale jelly snakes. I told her a bit more about the band. The guys. Dom in particular. She wanted to hear us. That made me happy. I could picture her in the Shakespeare, with a gin and tonic. Noise and smoke. Huge noise. Noise that picked you up and shaped you like plasticine.

We continued down to the Spit, where the bridge was up to let some yachts through, and sat in traffic with the engine off. The sun was warm through the window. I asked her if she liked music. She gave me that small easy smile. 'Yes. I play the viola. I tried to get into the Sydney Youth Orchestra, but I wasn't good enough. I sometimes play with a string quartet. We do weddings and things. Little recitals.'

I told her that I'd love to hear her quartet—that I'd never known anyone who could play well in the classical sense. Dania thought I would get bored. 'You have to sit upright on school chairs. And you can't drink beer and yell at us.'

The bridge went back down and we moved off towards the outer sprawl of Manly. I parked just off Pittwater Road. We were both a bit shy, but walked close together across the grass to the breakwater and a small footpath shaded by scraggly Norfolk Island pines. There were mothers with babies in prams. Old couples. Lots of girls down on the sand, most of them topless. Dania elbowed me. I must have been staring. I turned to her and took both her hands, and kissed her on the mouth. Her eyes were closed and hands gripped mine as we pressed together.

I felt stunned. She stepped back, smiling. 'Let's walk a bit.'

We held hands again and wandered north along the breakwater. Took our shoes off and went down onto the beach where tiny waves lapped around us like the tongues of puppies.

'Hello, Mrs Mansfield.'

'Hello, Devlin. Very pleased to meet you. It sounds as though you've had a full day. What did you think about Dania's riding?'

I didn't repeat the bit about being slim with long legs.

'Good start. On horses like that it's always going to be a battle to look too flash.'

Dania had already told her a whole lot about me. That I was a vet student and came from the country and had ridden horses all my life. That the Centennial Park people had given me a mule to ride. They had both laughed at that.

Dania was sitting next to me on the couch, holding a fat, scowling cat. We each had mugs of instant coffee and chocolate-topped digestive biscuits.

It was almost dark now. We had had ice creams in Manly, and then went on north to Palm Beach for fish and chips on a secluded bit of grass looking out at the ocean. I took the tarp off the ute to use as a rug. We lay on it and cuddled. Kissed. Sat up again, close together. I stroked her tiny feet till she giggled. We went home around the headland. Dania sat with one leg along the big bench seat and her foot touching me. I held her toes and tickled them again. Ran my hand up her calves. Smooth and warm. We talked about horses. She wanted her own one day. Wanted a little farm, or a bit of land anyway. Chooks. A sheep. Maybe a goat instead. I told her that as a child I'd had a goat called Cuthbert. A huge thing with a wild set of horns. Pulled a little cart and chased the dog. I was the only one who could do anything with him. I used to sit for hours pulling burs out of his angora coat.

We'd turned off the coast road at Narrabeen and followed a wide road back down to the Spit. Dania guided us from there through Sydney's maze of freeways, where every sign seemed to point to the airport. Eventually we got to her house in Randwick. A kid's drawing of a house. Red brick, with two windows and a door. Green grass. Straight cement path to the road. I had no idea how I was going to find my way back to Balmain.

Dania's mum was plump and happy. They lived on a pension from her late husband, Dania's dad, who had died at work many years before. Dania helped her out with money from her office job in the city. It was going to be hard for her when Dania left but she didn't seem to be resenting me.

Unlike the cat.

'You'll probably want to go back to the country when you graduate and treat horses and cattle. It must be a very different job to looking after dogs and cats.'

I reached over to stroke Margie, the cat. I don't like cats at all but felt obliged to do this. To offer the professional touch. Expensive. Learned at university. Its paw shot out with claws extended. Hissed through a row of white needles.

'Margie! You rude, spoilt thing!' Dania's protests went unheeded. Margie was pretty keen to kill me. Mrs Mansfield looked at the two of them speculatively.

I stood up. 'I'd better go. I don't have any idea how to get back to Balmain, but it's got to be easier in daylight.'

'Well, it was lovely to meet you, Devlin. And thank you for dropping Dania home. I hope we see you again soon.' She kissed me lightly on the cheek. It was a gesture from another era. Really nice. Dania put the awful cat down and came outside with me. In full view from the sitting room window, we barely touched hands. But we had each other's telephone numbers. It felt fantastic. Perfect.

Aud was sitting in front of the TV when I eventually got home. Via the airport.

'Hi, Dev.'

'Hi, Aud. What are you watching?'

Aud could watch anything from motorsport to documentaries about the emerging financial power of India. I don't think she registered any of it. Like the sound of birds.

'David Attenborough. It's good. What have you been doing?'

I could hear some urgent and exquisitely pronounced consonants. A bit of growling. I loved Aud. Not in a girly way. Probably like a brother might. She was trusting and completely defenceless and never criticised anyone. Aud had developed a bit of a crush on Dom. This was not a point I was intending to bring up with the Chief Superintendent.

'I'm smitten, Aud.'

She swivelled around in her armchair. Her dad's armchair. I was pretty sure it was bugged. 'The girl from the pub? The one you went riding with?'

I'd only seen Aud briefly since Friday and hadn't had a chance to tell her much about Dania. 'Yes, Dania. Dania Mansfield.'

'Second name terms already?' That was sharp for Aud. Acute. I sometimes wondered whether she might be hiding something.

I chuckled. 'She's beautiful, Aud. I think you'll like her. She plays the viola.'

For some reason this had risen above the more obvious attributes. Where she lived. Worked. What she looked like.

Aud looked at me closely, smiling, then got up to get some toast. Muscled little tubular legs in colourful knitted warmers. She walked most of the way to Glebe and back each day on her dad's orders. Issued from Queensland. Her mum was effectively invisible.

'You're in love? Really?'

'I am, Aud. Honestly, she's just gorgeous.'

'Gorgeous?'

'I can't really think how to describe her. She's really gentle. But assertive. Not girly at all. But wears nice, girly clothes.'

Aud wore nice girly clothes. She spent most of her dad's money on nice girly clothes. And improbable creams. Little bottles and tubes all over her bathroom. Mine had a single deformed bar of all-purpose budget soap.

I continued. 'She's got an office job in town. George Street. Nothing much, but it gives her some money. Lives with her mum in Randwick. Her dad's dead.'

Aud's head snapped back involuntarily. Like I'd told her that Dania had an obscure autoimmune disease.

'Poor thing.' Barely whispered.

I felt like a prick. The evil bastard in me had done it deliberately, but now dad-less Dania had a new friend.

Attenborough was still prattling on in the background. Terribly excited about a tortoise. The tortoise looked bored.

'It happened a long time ago. When Dania was just a kid. She and her mum are very close.'

Aud was never very rewarding on the topic of mothers. Her own was usually spoken of as one might speak of a fading curtain.

'You'll meet her soon. I'll bring her around next week.'

Aud was happy about that. She'd made me toast as well. Without asking.

Everyone loved Aud.

Monday morning was cold and blowy and I had a full day at university. I wheeled the bike out of the shed, checked its tyres, then headed up to Darling Street. The wind felt good against me, but as I finally coasted down past the university's Footbridge Theatre, I could tell from the build-up of morning traffic that I was running a bit late. I got off at the vet building, then wheeled the bike down to the changing rooms where I chained it to a pipe and had a quick shower. There were just five minutes till the first lecture. Genetics. Barely enough time for a coffee.

As I stood in line in the little kiosk, I thought again how much I hated the place. Actually, that wasn't true. I liked the school itself with its ageing buildings and quaint old Oxford feel, but I didn't want to be there. Genetics was a mystery. I had missed a couple of lectures and the notes I had borrowed didn't make much sense. I took my instant coffee and made my way up to the old lecture hall. This must have been one of the original parts of the university, with its beautiful wooden benches arranged as a small amphitheatre with a central lectern and chalkboard. It was exactly what everyone expected to see when they started vet science. I chatted a bit with Toby and Warren as Professor Miller, a crazy bastard who waved a solidified bull's dick about as a pointer and was never without an ostentatiously stained white lab coat, prepared his notes and overheads.

The lecture was about a monk who bred peas in the eighteen-hundreds. Seriously, this bloke bred peas. When he should have been praying. Or chanting. I tried to listen, but I really didn't want to be there. I thought about Dania and the feel of her body held against mine. The way she looked on that funny little pony. It seemed like weeks ago, but was just yesterday. I woke myself up a bit. We were onto rats now and I hadn't written anything down. I looked around. The others seemed to be engaged. A few were even smiling. The girl next to me had a ring binder with all the term's subjects colour-coded. I had a cardboard box of scribbled notes on the floor of my room. I just read textbooks close to the exams and relied on that. But it was still unnerving. The lecture ended and we thanked him, then packed up our things and headed up the road to biometry.

The afternoon was horse anatomy. This was high drama for vet students. The horse cadavers were winched up the outside of the building to a room on the top floor. From there they came out on an overhead rail to the lab itself. In first year, we had been through the anatomy of the dog, and the objective of these sessions was to show us how horses differed.

We went to the cold room and took out the feet and legs we'd worked on the previous week. Each one had been tagged with a group number. I had teamed up with Toby and Warren. We weren't a stellar combination. We retrieved our butchered leg.

Tobe was smart. By unspoken agreement, the smartest in our year. He didn't get great marks, but did even less work than me. Pretty much no work at all. He was very good looking in a James Dean sort of way, and wore tight jeans that tended to make the cleaning ladies nod to each other over their cups of tea. Tobe was an excellent sailboarder and surfer and would go out in any weather. Wild storms. Anything. But he had an evil sense of humour and was very aggressive and easy to anger. Sharky had to throw him out of the Jungle Bar one evening when he got into a fight with a drunk suit. Banned him. Tobe lived in a share house in Paddo surrounded by leather-clad gays in work boots. Paddo was the gay Mecca of Sydney and I think he broke a few hearts eating brekky in a bathrobe on his balcony of a Sunday morning. Tobe wasn't gay. He seemed to churn through a constant stream of identical, pouty hairdressers called Chantelle.

Warren was not much like Tobe. He wasn't very smart and was always untidy. Still dressed by his mum. Huge feet in perpetually brand-new, snow-white sneakers. Warren was pimply and lugubrious, and very calm. Almost deathly, sometimes. He played jazz trombone really well and only ever listened to jazz.

I couldn't really see the point of it. Jazz always seemed to me like high-speed painting by numbers. You asked a jazz musician why something sounded good and they could tell you. They really could. They could dissect a song or riff or something and actually tell you why that particular combination of notes would sound good. It seemed a bit ridiculous to me, given that the whole point of music was that you didn't really know why you were yelling or crying or drinking so much beer. But anyway, Warren loved it and it gave him a bit of unique dimension.

We put the leg on our bench and looked at it. Tobe found the prac notes. Instructions about where to cut. What to cut with. What not to cut. We fucked it up. Completely flayed the thing.

Professor Martin came over wearing the expression you get when you're mowing the lawn and a bit of dog turd gets flicked up into the corner of your mouth. We constantly took the piss out of Prof Martin. He was a Christian with a lot of daughters, and for some reason this made him deeply suspect. Effectively a sex offender. He had a little moustache that twitched like a rodent, and soft, pale hands that he held in front of him like a piece of architecture. No sense of humour at all.

'I went to great lengths to prepare notes that anyone could follow. Even you three. Why is it you can't do the simplest thing?'

'Sorry, Sir. We misread the first part and got a bit confused after that.' Toby. Diplomatic and sincere. And the chief protagonist of the sex offender jokes.

'I think you need to start with a whole new leg. Put this one away and get another. Fortunate that horses come with four legs! Ha ha. Ha ha.'

Something had stuck to the moustache. It looked a lot like a pube. Tobe stared at me with a straight face. I returned the stare. Eventually I managed, 'Okay, Sir. Sorry. The notes are very good. We just got the wrong end of something.'

Partially satisfied, he glided off on silent little feet hidden beneath a gown-length, preternaturally pristine lab coat.

I breathed out and Toby sighed. Together, we looked at the butchered leg, then Toby muttered, 'Wazza, chuck the fucken thing in the bin. I'll get another one.'

The prac ended at three, with a fifteen-minute break before one more lecture. Ruminant nutrition. Caffeine was essential. We gathered down in the kiosk.

The Good Girls already had a table. They made room for us to join them. Warren had a lot of space. Two of them were squashed against Tobe, embarrassed. The Good Girls came from places like Gordon and Killara and Pymble. North. Far north. Somewhere. A whole train line was dedicated to taking people to and from those polar suburbs. Do good works in the city, then return to their two-story white houses. Volvos. Labradors. We liked the Good Girls. There were four of them. All a bit cheeky. I think one, Toni, had a bit of a crush on me. She took exceptionally good lecture notes, which I photocopied with a stolen librarian's card.

Toni was now looking from one to another of us, frowning. 'What did you boys do to annoy Professor Martin so much?'

We looked sheepish. It was hard to be blatantly useless in the face of such goodness.

'Could you really follow his notes?' I was genuinely interested, as I had actually tried. The second time.

The Girls looked at each other, then one volunteered, 'Well, yes, we exposed the deep structures of the caudal hoof. You can really see how the flexor tendons work on a sort of pulley system. I had never appreciated that before. It was very exciting.'

And it really was. They were proper vets. We were just hopeless. After we had buggered up the second leg, Dodgy Martin had lost his temper a bit and split us up. Had to go and watch other groups get it right. Disgraced.

Another of them ventured, 'The fifth years are putting on a keg on Wednesday. Free. Will you be coming?'

The Girls rarely drank more than a plastic cup between them, so free beer couldn't have been much of a drawcard. All four looked at us hopefully—well, at Tobe, mostly—and although we weren't usually keen on these vet kegs, we might have made the effort had it been scheduled for another day.

But Wednesday was Book Club at the Town Hall Hotel. Set in stone. No exceptions. We looked at each other. Ideas?

Tobe swallowed the rest of his coffee. 'We've been asked to go to the launch of a new gallery in Balmain. Veronica has got together a group of people from the Blue Mountains. Very fresh. May completely change the way we look at twigs.'

And this was actually almost true, although I had no idea that Tobe had been listening as Aud had patiently explained it to us in the flat a week or so previously. Veronica, the gallery owner, was a friend of the bloke who ran the bookshop Aud worked in. Aud had a ticket to the gallery opening. The theme for the first exhibition was something like 'structures in the natural environment'. Twigs. But we weren't invited.

I was astonished. Wazza was confused. Tobe looked pleased with himself. The Girls didn't really know what to think, but by then it was time for ruminant nutrition.

The Town Hall Hotel was not the most beautiful of Sydney's old pubs, but had a great top-floor balcony. We sat out there year-round, even when it was raining. And it rains quite a lot in Sydney. Violent rain. Not soothing. Mayhem in the flat and soggy west and in the harbour-side suburbs cascading stormwater drains become death traps for kids and little dogs.

The Book Club met at the Townie every Wednesday evening. It had started on campus as a formal university book club at the beginning of our first year. Me and Toby seemed to be the only non-arts students. Hector was studying philosophy part-time and working for the Balmain Council as a stop-go man. Breast-fed a shovel. Hector was hilarious. He was a big bloke with a big beard and a goat-skin vest with the shaggy wool still attached. In winter, he wore a leather hat with tie-down ear flaps. Hector was a frustrated Viking born into the wrong age. He had even made himself a proper shield, sword and battleaxe, all of which he carried around on the passenger seat of his tiny old Mini Cooper with Jethro Tull or Led Zep at full volume. Hector was an original and basically harmless.

When the campus meetings became a bit shrill with the protestations of neurotically pretentious arties, we formed a splinter group and moved to the Townie in Balmain. Me and Hector were locals. Toby liked to escape boys-only Paddo. Warren liked to escape his mum. The Wild Boys usually gatecrashed. Bill, Will and Billy weren't into reading. Bill was Will's dad and the two of them looked as though they had stepped out of a sepia photograph of colonial timber-cutters. Billy wasn't related. Technically. Although that seemed improbable given that they all came from the same village in the hills outside Wagga. The Wild Boys ran a little cash-only earthmoving business that the tax office hadn't yet discovered. They had a battered Bobcat and truck and a small pre-war excavator. None of it was reliable, but they made a shitload and splashed it around the pub. The Wild Boys thought we were fucken idiots. This was a generic term and covered a lot of bases. But they liked the constellation of girls that generally gravitated to Toby as the night wore on. I think they also liked the fact that we had all the smarts while they had all the money.

We were reading *The Book of Laughter and Forgetting*. Basically, because no-one had heard of it. And the cover had a topless chick. With wings. And because Tobe thought he looked a lot like its author, Milan Kundera.

Book Club didn't follow a formal agenda. We took turns with the jugs of beer and the discussion was pretty much a free-for-all. Tobe was intrigued by the story of Mirek and Zdena—in particular, the notion that you could actually improve yourself by erasing all evidence of the fact that you'd slept with an unbeautiful woman. Although this seemed to us to be the book's main theme, I couldn't let go of the idea of *litost*. In Kundera's words, 'a feeling as infinite as an open accordion'. The anguish of discovering your pathetic self. The inadequate student poet. Pretentious. A facsimile. A failed lover. And love, of course, was important to the playboy Kundera. It was linked to identity. And identity was linked to self-worth. And that was linked to maturity. Or to more *litost*, if you happened to be young. *Litost*, to Kundera, was just an ornament of youth. I was young. But I knew with an absolute certainty that I was immortal. All young people are. And the corollary of this was that I also knew that I could never mature. Ever. It was inconceivable. So *litost* settled on me like the ash of a dying fire. I don't know if the others noticed. It almost killed me.

Holding up the book, Tobe declared, 'One of the surest roads to a woman is through her sadness.'

This deserved some thought. We had been working to the idea that the surest road was Fruity Lexia.

'So how do you exploit a woman's sadness?' This was Tobe again, without a hint of irony.

'Jazz.' A rare contribution from Wazza. Nailed it.

'Roast goat.' That was Hector, who could be difficult to deflect from goats.

'How the fuck do you get at a woman's sadness through roast goat?' Tobe was often irritated with Hector.

'It's a depressant, mate. Candles. Heavy wine sauce. Leeks.'

'Leeks?'

'Symbolic, mate. Can't be too soft.'

'You're a fucken idiot.' That was Will, who was never able to be swayed from this view of Hector. Well, of all of us, really. I don't think he had read the book. And wasn't into goats. Or the sadness of women. Will was my age, but far too mature for *litost*.

By the fifth jug we'd forgotten about the book, as was usually the case, and had decided to call it a night. Wazza had already left. He was an only child and his mum still cooked his dinner and made his lunch. He usually had a bit of a schedule. Will and Billy had been telling us about a really big hole they'd dug that week. Tobe was asking a lot of technical questions, which was really just his way of taking the piss. Old Bill had cottoned on and it was getting a bit dangerous for Tobe.

We scoffed a bowl of hot chips and bailed out. Tobe usually stayed with me and Aud on Wednesday nights. We wandered off down Darling Street, which was generally quiet on a weeknight. Rolled a couple of joints in a side-street then smoked them as we walked. Looked like cigarettes.

'So, serious about this chick Dania, then?'

'Mate, she's just perfect. I tell everyone that, but it's true.'

Girls were pretty much consumables to Tobe. Serious accolades a bit of a difficult concept. No *litost* whatsoever. 'Looking forward to meeting her.'

'There's no band gig this weekend, but I thought I might take her up into the Blue Mountains. Do that walk around the Giant Stairway. Could maybe meet you somewhere back in town afterwards?'

Tobe thought that would be great. He had a barbie at lunch but should be home in the evening. We walked on in silence. The dope slowed things down.

'Still getting stressed about uni?' I'd told Tobe about some of the shit that was going on in my head.

'Yeah, a bit.'

I kicked at leaves that had banked up in the gutter and tried to let it go. But once started, this train of thought always led to the same place. Like Dom, I really did believe that I might fail something. We had exams in every subject—in some subjects, exams in both practice and theory. Failing just one subject meant repeating the whole year. There were no exceptions to this rule and I was terrified of it. I didn't think I could stand the shame of repeating a whole year, but the stigma associated with dropping out was even worse. I felt trapped, as the remaining shreds of control slipped away with each botched lecture or prac class.

Tobe didn't think either of us would fail anything. He was happy to rely on photocopied notes and an ability to spout any sort of rubbish on the spur-of-the-moment. I couldn't do that. And everything mattered too much to me. The stakes were too high. And now getting higher.

'Dania would be so disappointed if I fucked up.'

Tobe was appalled. 'Mate, don't start living some bullshit Czechoslovakian novel. Seriously, this chick's got nothing to do with it. Work if you have to, but do it for yourself. If she stops liking you, she'll fuck off and you'll get over it.'

I had to chuckle. We'd reached the house with the joints smoked down to their butts. 'I'll try. Now, quiet inside. Aud's got a bit of a cold. She'll be in bed.'

Tobe laughed loudly and I hushed him again. He thought I should marry Aud. We made our way up to my loft, where I gave him the camping mattress and sleeping bag. 'You want some toast?'

'Yeah, mate. Feed the brain for another day at the mill. Might have a quick shower first.'

Sunday was brilliant.

I drove over to Dania's mother's house and stayed for a cup of tea. The cat was nowhere to be seen. Her mum knew the Blue Mountains area and I asked if she'd like to come with us. Dania was standing behind her, horrified. Her mum was pleased, but declined. It was a calculated risk.

We drove out through the sprawl of western Sydney to Penrith, then up the hills to Katoomba. Dania again enjoyed the old ute. She said she felt like a country girl in her jeans and walking boots. We stopped for coffee at a cafe with checked tablecloths, somewhere in the hills. It was nice coffee. Good cakes. Both a Blue Mountains speciality. The cafe also sold clever little hessian ducks filled with sand, with bits of felt sewn on as clothes. They were door stoppers and very sweet. Dania liked them. I wished I had more money.

We pressed on to Echo Point and the start of the walk. Incredible views, before the drop down eight hundred steps to sphagnum moss and pretty streams in the rainforest of the valley floor. We walked hand in hand and took up the whole path. A pair of athletic European backpackers huffed past on big, pink legs. We sat on logs and kissed. Then there was the long slog back up to the top. Cycling kept me fit, but Dania struggled a bit. I took it slow and we got there eventually.

We had a late lunch in Katoomba. Complicated pies. Mine was rabbit while Dania had smoked trout, which seemed like an unkind thing to do to a pie. Then more nice coffee and cakes. We found a public phone and left a message with one of Tobe's flatmates to say that there would be a barbie at my place in Balmain if he felt like it. We also called Aud, who offered to take care of the food. Hand-in-hand, we walked back to the car then started the trip back down the hill and across Sydney. I found Crosby, Stills, Nash and Young's live album, *Four-Way Street*, in the box of tapes on the floor, and we talked and sang along to that as the suburbs flicked by.

Back in Balmain, Aud had been busy. Lots of snacks. Meats on skewers. Potato salad. Aud liked to host parties. She welcomed Dania and pressed drinks and nibbles on us and told her nice things about me. Raved about the band. Prattled on a bit too much about Dom. We laughed at her and she got embarrassed. She said she'd go with Dania to the Shakespeare next weekend. Bustled around the house like a happy little colourful beetle.

Tobe showed up just before we started eating. Jeans, t-shirt and leather jacket. Standard uniform. Dania was impressed. A bit of meat fell off the end of her skewer. Aud was pretty much

Toby-proof. We all drank a fair bit. Just beer and wine. Happy. Then Dania had to get back home, so we took a ferry to the Quay and a bus out to Randwick. Tobe was with us. We left Dania at the gate to her Lego house and waved goodbye as her mum opened the door. We were still a bit pissed and didn't want to embarrass her. Shared a joint as we walked back to the bus stop.

I was almost teary. 'Sensational day.'

'Great chick, mate. Very cute. And she's hooked on you. Doesn't stop touching you.'

I had noticed that, too. It was fantastic. We talked about the gig the following weekend. Tobe would try and get the evening off work. 'It'll be a hoot. I'll look after little Danny for you. Predators out there, mate. Sharks. Can't be too careful.'

We both chuckled, then Tobe remembered something. 'Chantelle was there last Saturday. She should have said hello to you. Thought you blokes went off. Just amazing.'

I wasn't sure that I'd ever met this Chantelle.

'Yeah, you know, dark hair. Sort of. Usually. Came with us to that uni dance. She loved your acoustic guitar stuff.'

'Right. Yeah, last week was probably the best ever. Usually it works pretty well, but every now and then the whole thing just goes off.'

'That's what Kundera thinks, too. Read somewhere he said you have two or three thousand roots in a lifetime, but only two or three of them really matter.'

Kundera was now Tobe's hero.

'Two or three thousand?'

'He's an old bloke. Been around.'

'He's completely full of shit.'

We got a bus to Paddo. I left him there and went back into the city and over the water to Balmain.

We were setting up when Tobe arrived with Aud and Dania in tow. He had borrowed his flatmate's old beaten-up lime-green

Daihatsu Charade. I always found it hilarious to see James Dean get out of a Charade. Tobe had done a lot of driving that night. He'd picked Dania up from Randwick, then gone over to Balmain to get Aud. Dania said that her mum had seemed flustered and had forgotten to say goodbye. Tobe was good with mothers. They said things like, 'he's such a nice boy', but God knows what they were thinking.

Everyone had drinks. I had reserved them a table with my guitar case and stacked some chairs up behind our speakers where no-one could flog them. These were extreme measures, but I wanted Dania right in front. I also wanted Aud to be able to watch Dom. I knew she'd like that.

Aud seemed oblivious to the grunge of the place. The drunken yobbos and sudden anger. Half-naked girls and spirits dispensed by the gallon. She was wearing tight little jeans, a pink top and faux cowgirl boots and seemed to be very happy. Dania appeared a bit nervous. Surrey Hills on Saturday night was an experience. And I guess I looked different. Thin and introverted. I wasn't sleeping well and my eyes were hollow, but the prospect of playing music always made me feel in control and I think it showed. I watched her, talking to Tobe. She looked good in jeans and a black leather jacket. Completely without warning, I realised I loved her.

We finished getting things organised and did some little sound checks. I was a bit distracted. Dom saw it and talked to me, then got hold of Rick and the three of us went quickly through the set. How we'd play it. The crowd. Scotty wasn't interested. Our chick-slaying front-man still up at the bar. Dom had noticed Aud tapping the table with two beer mats. Went over and gave her his spare sticks and showed her how to hold them. Told her to help him out. She blushed, smiling. Tobe looked uncertain. He always seemed a bit wary of Dom, and I sometimes wondered if he had become too used to being the smartest bloke in the room.

We were going to try a different approach tonight. Start soft, with a bit of soul. Most of the crowd had been there two weeks ago so we couldn't do a repeat performance. Never worked anyway. We were going to have a crack at Chisel's 'When the War is Over'. We hadn't played it in public before, although it seemed to work well in rehearsals. We got ourselves organised with Rick at the electric piano again, the guitar on its strap across his back. Scotty, me and Dom would sing the intro.

We took a final look around the room. All was quiet now. Then Scotty counted us in. Just the piano with our three harmonised vocals. Scotty fantastic on the high part. No-one could steal his heart away. The crowd loved it. Chisel was the best pub band the country has ever produced and this was beautiful music.

Rick played a few more bars as Scotty moved off to the side. The shade. I took the centre mic, as we needed the vocal contrast, the lower pitch. He would take over again later. It was still just the piano. I was standing alone at the mic, holding it tightly with my right hand while the left gripped the neck of the bass. My eyes were closed and the crowd went silent. I couldn't remember ever feeling such tension. Not nervousness, but just raw explosive tension. Everything was shut out. No lights. Just the beautiful music. I finished the passage and stepped back, eyes open. Unsmiling and intense. Blown away. Dom came in with a roll on the drums. I added the first bass notes. Rick was still at the piano, with quiet gentle chords.

I moved forward again and flicked the harmonica up on its hanger and leaned into the mic. My eyes were closed again now, as I eased out the first notes. Slight bending and tremolo. The classic Ian Moss guitar solo played on harmonica. Rick had tried it with the guitar but couldn't get the sound right. It was just too difficult. I had had a go with the harmonica at one of the rehearsals. It was much easier and sounded good. Sort of followed Mossy's lyric but didn't need to be identical. There was so much soul in this song.

I flicked the harmonica back down. It was still my song. Eyes closed and everything blacked out. Except the music. 'You and I had our sights set on something.' I opened my eyes and Dania was in front of me. I could see tears on her cheeks. The sound was everywhere. I stepped back and Scotty took over. He lifted the mic out of its cradle and went right up the register. It seemed like a full octave, but may just have been a fifth. Very clever signing. Fantastic voice. No doubt. Clear. Right up high. The crowd breathed out. Still just piano, bass and drums, but then they came in with us. The chorus. Full bore. Again and again until it ended. Banging on tables. Yelling.

I was smiling now and caught Dania's eye. She was smiling, too, her face dried, shaking her head. I felt one of Dom's sticks hit me in the back. Dania laughed. I picked it up and gave it back to him. We went into the next song.

Tobe came back with another round. 'Mate, that was sensational. Seriously, such a great sound.'

We had packed the gear up and were sitting around the table. Free drinks till closing time. Rick and Scotty had gone to a club in town. Just me and Dom and the others. It had been another good gig. Two in a row. We had done an acoustic set that opened with Led Zep's 'The Battle of Evermore'. I played mandolin and Dom guitar. Vocal harmonies. Dom had dedicated the song to little Aud. Everyone cheered Aud.

I took the beer from Tobe. 'It does work well, but I reckon I'm a bit of a fraud really. Dom's a great drummer, Scotty's a great singer and Rick can play guitar pretty well. But any Wally can keep things going on the bass.' I wasn't playing things down—this was pretty much true, really. The acoustic stuff needed a bit of skill, but it wasn't hard to be a reasonable bass player if you knew the music well.

Dom disagreed. 'Mate, you really feel the music. You live it. Every song. I get it every now and then, but it's like a drug for you. It doesn't matter what you're playing. Gets everyone into it. I reckon that's a big part of our secret.'

And it was a drug for me. An escape, really. Magic. I felt drained again, but completely free from the anxiety that was otherwise so much a part of each day.

I squeezed Dania's hand, then noticed the bar staff beginning to close the place down. 'How we going to do the cars?'

Tobe looked shagged. 'Mate, I'm going to leave the hairdresser car here tonight. I'm pissed and there's too many cops in the inner city. I talked to the bloke behind the bar and he's okay with that. Get it tomorrow arvo.'

Tobe had had a late night on Friday as well. He said goodnight and wandered off to get a bus. I asked Dom if he wanted to cuddle up to an amp in the back of the ute. It would just be fifteen minutes. We could drop him at his place then head back to Balmain from there.

Dom shook his head. 'Thanks you get for drumming your heart out. Cringing in the back of some bush-pig's ute.'

'You'll be right. Just lie back on the carpet and smoke a little joint in peace and quiet.'

Aud giggled. Dania looked surprised. I bit my tongue and ushered everyone out to the ute. I hadn't drunk anything much. Just little bits and pieces. I wanted to be able to get the ute and gear and girls home without any problems.

We packed Dom in. He had a joint ready to go and gave Aud a puff, then I fastened the tarp over him and drove quietly through the backstreets to the university. I wanted to show Dania and Aud the vet buildings and ovals, and the big main quad with its sandstone spires and turrets and floodlit arched windows. Dania loved it. Dom seemed to have gone to sleep. We dug him out at his place in Glebe and ferried in the gear. Said goodbyes. Dom would be up all night, drumming quietly with headphones. Playing guitar. Sometimes he just walked around the streets, restless. Huge brain trying to get out.

We took more small streets back to Balmain. Aud made coffee. Very happy. Humming Led Zep.

Dania looked shy. 'Can I call Mum?'

'Go for it. It's a bit late, though. She won't mind?'

'She wanted me to call and let her know what I was going to do.'

'What are you going to do?'

'Stay here.'

Aud came in with the coffee. My hand shook violently and I was suddenly terrified and trying to breathe. Dania didn't seem to notice as she took a cup and pulled the cable of the phone out into the hallway to make her call.

I lay on my side, propped up on an elbow, and ran my fingers along her thigh. Across her tummy. Around one small breast. Kissed it. She smiled, her hand in my thin blond hair.

'No more.'

I chuckled. Insatiable. So beautiful.

She looked at me, serious. 'You seem sad.'

I was surprised. I didn't think I was sad.

'I don't mean right now. Right now you seem to be as happy as a little rabbit.' She poked me in the chest. I smiled and kissed the other breast. She continued. 'I mean generally. You seem to have so much on your mind. You get so moody so easily, as though something is eating at you.'

I rolled onto my back and stared at the wood-panelled ceiling. 'Uni is really getting to me. I don't feel right about being there. But I don't want to fail and let everyone down.'

'Who's everyone?'

'You.'

She elbowed me softly. 'Why do you think you'll fail?'

'I'm not doing any work. Tobe can get by like that, but I can't remember all the stupid bloody Greek names and stuff. None of it makes sense. I sort of resent the people there who like it. It's not fair on them, but I can't help it.'

'Can't you just do some work and turn it around?'

'I feel like I've left it too late. We've got exams in a month or so.'

Dania thought that seemed like a long time to study—that I should be able to make it through if I started now and kept at it. I knew I could give that a go, but I still felt uncomfortable. I couldn't shake off the feeling that every day at uni brought with it some sort of darkness and anxiety.

'What else would you like to do if you stopped training to be a vet? You said once you almost enrolled to be a primary school teacher, but I think you might get bored.'

I squeezed her hand and held it against my chest. In school, I had mostly just wanted to be a teacher. We had some good ones and they had made such a difference. I had also wondered about marine biology at one point, and palaeontology, but for some reason these never seemed like real jobs.

Dania was watching me. 'You just have to do something or other until you get a bit older and can think more clearly. Can't you approach vet like that? Just as a stop gap. Whatever you do later, it can't hurt to have a vet degree.'

I knew that made sense. I also knew that all my objections to just getting on with it sounded a lot like a spoilt kid, when so many others would have loved to have had the chance I had to get this degree. 'It wasn't so bad last year. Everything was new.'

'I'm new.'

'You're brand new and you're very beautiful. And I love you.' It was out before I could stop it. I had never said that to anyone before.

'I think I love you, too. I loved watching you play. I've never seen anything as erotic as that. You completely lose yourself.'

I chuckled. Dania looked thoughtful. 'I wondered about relaxation when you were talking before. I think maybe you do need to relax more. Everything you do is so highly charged. It seems casual. But it's not. I bet you time yourself riding to university.'

I rolled on top of her, laughing. Kissed her face and hair. 'How did you know that? I only met you two weeks ago.'

'You're transparent. To me. That's a good thing. But tell me what you can do to relax.'

I kept kissing her hair. It was getting more urgent.

'Other than that.'

I rolled off again. 'There is a thing that I do, and I think it really helps, but you'll probably laugh if I tell you.'

'I won't laugh, I promise. What is it?'

'I tell myself a story. It's strange, because I almost speak it out loud. To begin with, it's like reading from a book, but the book is in my head and I read it to myself. After a while it becomes more like directing a play or a movie, as the characters speak their parts and I can feel the world they're in all around me.'

I risked a look at her face. I thought I might have gone too far. I had never told anyone about this before. It was a bit crazy, really. There was probably a name for it.

But Dania didn't seem to be horrified. She sat up and looked at me. 'Can you really do that? Can you think through a story, as though you were reading a book?'

'Yeah, I can. I really can. I actually started to write it down. Everything is real. The voices are real, but it's not like crazy people hearing random voices. The voices are following the script. And I control that. But I get completely lost in the detail of it. Sometimes whole hours go past. It tires me out, but seems to push the anxiety away.'

She lay down again and snuggled up against me. 'Could you show me what you've written?'

The pages were in a folder under the bed. 'It's just the opening. I was going to keep going, but it felt a bit weird.'

Dania read about Ben's crash in the desert. It suddenly seemed paltry and insignificant. But she was smiling. 'I don't think anything that you keep in your head will be helping you much right now. I think you need to get this and everything else outside your head and let it have a rest. Could you write the rest of the story down?'

I looked again at the ceiling and thought about that. It was true. My head was running full steam from the moment I woke, and that was getting earlier and earlier. 'I think I could do that. The story is quite long, but I think I could do it.'

In truth, the story scared me a little. Although set in that parched and arid country on the edge of the desert, it seemed to have grown from something that had happened on the logging place up in the mountains near Nundle. The place where I worked for a while during the year I had taken off after school. I remember that the boss had become crook with the cold that came after a big dump of snow. I couldn't do much work without him, so took the rifle and tent and followed the Barnard River down through the wild country at the back of a couple of neighbouring properties. On the third day, something strange happened. I never told anyone about it, and never thought about the forests afterward. It was after I had left Nundle and travelled west through inland New South Wales, then north to the cattle stations in Queensland, that the heat and sparse enormity had swamped me and it was in that setting one night that the story first emerged as a dream.

I told Dania this. She was intrigued. 'Is this like a mystery?'

I chuckled. 'You'll have to wait and see. Each chapter can be a long letter, so the story builds up to a little book.'

I began to feel excited about the idea. I would make myself do a few hours of studying, then take a break and try to write some more of it down. I kept thinking about this as I kissed her hair again. Then her ears and the back of her neck. But by then her breathing had changed and she was sleeping. Her eyelids fluttered and a small smile played around the edges of her mouth.

I eased myself down next to her and gently pulled the duvet over us both. The candle had died, and without our voices the complex rumble of the city returned through the open windows.

But I could see the stars from where we lay and let them take me away to the baked silence of that other place. That open and endless blue of the sky. The huge birds, drifting. Always watching. A place where stories like this one could unfold. A place without *litost*. A place I had always called Warkon.

Dear Dania,

I hope this will work okay . . .

It felt a bit strange writing things down, knowing that you would read them.

And I seem to have filled up a lot of pages

Anyway, first chapter 1—from where we left off

I hope you like it . . .

Love, Devlin xxx

It's still Thursday

. . . Then, out of the gloom, the bush around him began to be lit with the lights of a distant vehicle. Ben lifted his head and followed its progress towards him. The road was long and flat, and the vehicle was still at least a kilometre away when Ben gratefully registered that this was a car and not one of the predatory road-trains that terrorised Australia's inland highways. As the car drew closer, Ben could make out the shape of what looked like roof racks, which then materialised into the distinctive rectangular outline of a police beacon.

. . . Then, out of the gloom, the bush around him began to be lit with the lights of a distant vehicle. Ben lifted his head and followed its progress towards him. The road was long and flat, and the vehicle was still at least a kilometre away when Ben gratefully registered that this was a car and not one of the predatory road-trains that terrorised Australia's inland highways. As the car drew closer, Ben could make out the shape of what looked like roof racks, which then materialised into the distinctive rectangular outline of a police beacon.

The driver turned on the beacon and rotating lights, pulled off the road in front of the bike and cut the motor. Leaned forward to peer at Ben's ragged figure hunched across the seat of the broken bike. Strains of Deborah Harry seeped out into the punctured opera of the desert night.

The driver's door opened and a figure emerged. Then paused. Hands raised, hips still, shoulders jutting in flawless staccato synch to the one-two-three-four of 'Heart of Glass'. Sent a small yelp up into the night sky, before reaching back to switch off the stereo, tucking in his shirt and moving into the beam of the driving lights.

Stepping forward, the figure called out, voice like a frog in a drum, 'Mate, what the fuck are you doing?'

Ben wasn't sure how to respond to this. He looked down at his bike, then up at the silhouette, which now seemed to be scratching furiously at the back of its pants. 'Crashed the bike. Roo or something hit me from the side.'

'Be an emu, mate. Maybe a pig. Could be a roo, I guess. Sometimes jump after the light goes past. Kill it?'

'I don't know. Probably not. I think it just jumped into me and sort of bounced off.'

'Sounds like an emu.'

'My bike is fucked. Can you help me get it somewhere?'

'Not a pig, if it came from the side. Some big roos out here. Move about as quick as a car. Or a bike.'

'I'm not hurt, but I need some help to get the bike somewhere I can fix it.'

'Emus move quick as a car, too. Sometimes. Bastards for suddenly swerving sideways. Bad on dusk. Hit a couple'

'For fuck's sake, are you even listening?'

The figure stepped back. 'Mate, calm down. Must be in shock. Give you a lift back into town. Organise someone to come out and pick the bike up.'

Ben slid off the bike and had to balance himself against the bars to stop from falling sideways. He wondered if he was concussed. He had heard that it was delayed sometimes. That your brain could swell with blood and kill you, hours after the injury. It was probably bullshit. He managed to remove the panniers and backpack from the bike and staggered over to the car.

Away from the beam of the powerful lights, he could see the driver more clearly. He looked to be a few years older than Ben and although only several inches taller, it was his width that was so striking. Head like a medicine ball, and slouching as though trying to make himself look smaller. Ben wondered how he got himself in through the door of his car.

'Can I put this gear in your boot? It's a bit grotty.'

'Mate, don't worry about it. Had old Cecil spewing in there last night.'

Ben placed the panniers and backpack carefully on the back seat, avoiding small patches of crusted vomit. 'I think you might have missed a few bits here.'

'Yeah, well, didn't know I'd be picking little girls up off the road. Get yourself inside and we'll head back to town.'

Ben sat back and directed the heating vents onto his face. It still surprised him how cold the arid inland was once the sun had gone. The cop moved around to his own side and Ben felt the big Ford list to the right as it adjusted to the weight.

Ben looked at the array of police switches on the dashboard. He still felt dazed and a bit confused, but thought he should say something light to break the ice. 'Can I turn on the siren?'

The cop chuckled. 'Fuck off.'

Ben relaxed a little. 'My name's Ben. I'm not really a dickhead.'

'I'm Duncan. And mate, you were sitting by yourself on a dead bike in the middle of the desert making vroom vroom noises so I think you probably are.'

Duncan started the car, switched on the stereo, and lifted the radio's handpiece from its bracket, still chuckling to himself like a small tractor. 'Warkon mobile calling Barker base. Over.'

'Dunc. Over.'

'Jane, can you call Byron at the Warkon garage and get him to pick up a damaged bike from the Corner, near to Watson's mailbox? Over.'

'Rider is where? Over.'

'Got him here. Take him back to Warkon and get him somewhere to stay. Over.'

'He's okay, is he? Over.'

'No, Jane, he's a dickhead. Over.'

'Dunc, is the man injured? Over.'

'Don't think so. Says that something jumped on him. Crashed the bike. Skidded down the road a bit on his arse, but doesn't seem to be suffering too much. Over.'

'Well, Dunc, he's in a small closed space with your good self, so I don't think that last bit can be quite true. What jumped on him? Over.'

'Topic of some debate here, Jane. Touchy. Ben, mate, what jumped on you?'

'Questing beast.'

'Says a questing beast jumped on him. Over.'

'A literary allusion. Arthurian. Perhaps not a stupid man, this traveller. Over.'

'You'd be surprised, Jane. And I think it was probably a questing emu. Maybe a roo. Probably not a questing pig. Over.'

Jane seemed to consider that for a second, then, 'And Dunc, tell me that's not Blondie in the background . . . not when Trev has specifically asked you not to play it in police vehicles. Over.'

Duncan, in a surprising soprano, 'Once I loved and it was a gas . . . Over.'

'Dunc, no, for the love of God, no. And you've been dancing again, haven't you? In the headlights? Duncan, you know you shouldn't— '

'Fuck off. Out.'

The car pulled away, and Ben caught a last brief glimpse of his bike before the powerful lights swung out across the saltbush.

'You were definitely dancing back there. Little shimmy.'

'Fuck off.'

Ben smiled as Duncan replaced the radio handset and fastened a fully-extended seatbelt. The cabin seemed too small.

'Out of interest, what would happen if I told you to fuck off?'

'I'd shoot you.'

'Okay.'

The big car surged forward, a myriad tiny flying creatures parting in the lights, like krill.

Ben was still lightheaded. 'So, Duncan, we're headed to Warkon then, are we?'

'Yep. Where I'm based. Was on my way to see a mate in Barker. Nothing much happens in Warkon of a weeknight. Goes off on the weekend, when blokes from the properties 'round here come into town to get on the piss.'

'My tent and stuff are still on the bike. Is there somewhere I can stay?'

'The pub. About it, really. Some flats out the back.'

'Sounds good. I'm rooted. I think I've got concussion.'

Duncan was not noticeably concerned. 'Mate, had an idea. Can you pull a beer?'

'Sort of, I guess. But not tonight. I think I've got concussion.'

'Chloe at the pub is looking out for someone to help. Filling in for her uncle. He's crook. Some sort of old blokes' disease. Fucken prostrate.'

'Prostate.'

Duncan looked pained. 'No, mate, the bloke's *prostrate*. As in lying down. Sick. Not running his pub.'

'Right.'

'Think you might have concussion, mate. Not focussed. Anyway, she's getting a bit snowed under. Asked yesterday about someone to take some shifts. Could probably do that for a week or so while your bike's off the road. Might give you free board.'

'That would be brilliant. I haven't got much spare money. I'll have to try and get Mum to help out with the bike. That's going to cost a shitload. Parts from Germany. What's Chloe like?'

'Chloe's the goods, mate. Great chick. Everyone loves her. Got to tell you, though, you can put a bit of shit on me and get away with it, but not Chloe. Off limits. Every bloke in the district after you with a gun. Some of them can shoot. Some have planes. You'd be fucked. You and your questing beast.'

Ben registered that something else had been said. Duncan leaned forward and inserted a new tape with fingers that were meant to be used for shoeing Clydesdales. Hammering in the nails. Without a hammer. Cold Chisel's 'Khe Sanh', volume down.

'So, Duncan, what's in the gun case on the back seat?'

'A gun.'

Ben closed his eyes and felt the movement of the car over the hard gravel road. The song ended. Another one started. He tried again. 'Yeah, but what is it?'

'Long thin one. Know a bit about guns?'

'A little. I was a roo shooter in Queensland for a while, before getting away on the bike.'

Duncan ejected the tape, cutting Jimmy off mid-sentence in an undignified garbled squeal. 'Fair dinkum? You were a roo shooter? Fuck, I never would have picked that. Pretty serious shooting. Where in Queensland?'

'I was working for a bloke based in Goondiwindi, but we travelled a fair bit. Did a lot around Roma. He was a great shooter, really amazing, but he couldn't stay off the drink so we sort of switched roles a bit towards the end. He'd drive and I'd shoot.'

'Wow. How did you get to be good enough to shoot roos?'

'My dad was a bench-rest shooter. He went to the Commonwealth Games. He taught me about rifles and shooting and loading ammo. It's a science to him. He's never killed anything at all. Not even a rabbit. But he was bloody good up to a thousand metres. Not anymore, his eyes are rooted.'

'What were you shooting with in Goondiwindi?'

'A gun. Long thin one'

Duncan chuckled. Ben continued. 'We had a whole lot of guns when I was a kid and they were all constantly changing. I mean, he'd be swapping out barrels and receivers and sights and whatever. We had a range of calibres. I had a .308 with a heavy target barrel that I used a lot. I took that to Queensland. The old bloke I was working for loved it. I left it with him, but I'll get it back one day.'

Duncan pointed over his shoulder. 'The case. Back seat. Sako .243 with a Zeiss scope. Second-hand, but bugger-all use and it looks new.'

'Wow, that's about as good as it gets for a production rifle. What do you use it for?'

'Only had it a week. Haven't fired it yet. Bought it for pigs, mostly. Maybe scare some goats. A bit light, but not bad with hollow points.'

'.243s a good all-round calibre, I reckon. Similar trajectory to a .308, really. Not as flat as the smaller guns, but hits a lot harder. Do you load your own ammo?'

'No. Mate showed me how, but I can't be bothered. Just go shooting. Not that good, really, but that just means there's more left to go after next time.'

Ben smiled and settled deeper into the seat, intrigued by the police paraphernalia and stickers. Police work-instructions in a grubby ring binder had been shoved into a pocket in the door.

Scuffed police maps that had spilled from a glove compartment that no longer closed. A ridiculously large police hat lay among disposable coffee cups on the floor near his feet. On the dash, incongruously, a book titled *Working with Difficult People*.

Duncan didn't seem to be paying much attention to the road as he hummed along happily with Jimmy Barnes. One thick arm lay on the door ledge and across the top of the wheel, while the other occupied the padded rest between the seats. Turning to Ben, he said, 'If Chlo can spare you at the pub on Saturday night, how would you feel about camping out near the escarpment and having a go at a few pigs? Bloke last week reckoned he was checking a tank out that way and saw a whole lot. Do the place a favour and get rid of some of them.'

'Mate, I'm in. Aren't there supposed to be some cave paintings out there?'

'Yeah. One main site, and a lot of little bits scattered around. Weird country. Can see why they reckoned it was sacred. Magical, I guess.'

Distracted, Duncan flipped the sunshade up and down with his spare hand and looked out at the darkened scrub. 'Hard to say what it is, but the place can be sort of deafening. Doesn't make sense because, really, it's dead quiet— just the birds and insects— but there's some sort of intense thing happening all around you that feels like noise. Wouldn't want to go up there by myself at night. Freak you out a bit. We'll leave the car in a little gully at the base and sleep there. Walk a big circuit over the top during the day.'

An ageing flatbed truck approached. Duncan flicked his lights and the driver of the truck did the same. Duncan nodded towards the mirror. 'Byron. Off to pick up your bike.'

'Thanks, be good to get it off the road. He'll be okay lifting it onto the truck?'

'Has the NRMA contract out here. Got a little crane on that truck. Winch as well. Byron's a biker, too. He'll be gentle with it. Got an old Norton in his garage. Gets it out a few times a year. Not heaps of him, but he's a hard man, Byron. Locals don't give him any shit. Got some sort of problem from the war. Vietnam. Him and a few others from 'round here get together at the pub every now and then. Sit and drink in silence. Probably remembering shit they don't want to remember.'

The road had seemed dead straight, but Ben could see that they were now rounding a wide, slow bend. Up ahead on slightly skewed pipe-steel legs a hand-painted sign proclaimed, *Welcome to Warkon: a Tidy Town.*

Duncan chuckled. 'We're here, well-read traveller. Now, got to tell you. Take it easy with the locals. Don't rile 'em up. Look to me to keep the peace. Don't want to have to lock up my new camping buddy. And don't forget what I said about Chloe. They're going to be watching you.'

And so will you, Ben thought.

In the meagre light of a dozen straggly streetlamps lay a wide dusty street and a handful of defeated buildings. A power pole marked the edge of a parking area. Two white utes were parked side by side, each with a pig-dog cage on the back. Behind the utes was a long, low veranda with tables and chairs and some coloured Christmas lights around the rafters. The pub. The interior was brightly lit and Ben could hear strains of what sounded distressingly like John Williamson. Opposite was a striking red brick building and, as far as Ben could tell, the only solid structure in the town. A lighted Police sign hung from a pole at the gate.

Duncan pulled over and pointed. 'My place. Keep an eye on you. Flat around the back, next to the cells.' He leaned forward to peer out the windscreen, hands on knees the size of small sheep. 'Byron's garage. Up there on the right. Can't miss it in daylight. Don't front up too early if you want his good side. And don't pat his dog. Prick of a thing.'

Duncan turned, the seat groaning as his weight moved on strained springs. 'Just back from there on the other side of the street is the shop and post office. Get a bit of takeaway there, but I'd eat at the pub if you can. Town locals, mostly retired farm boys who still do a bit of work around the place. Prop up the pub. Wives get together and make quilts. It's all go.' He chuckled. 'But you'll be surprised tomorrow night. Get a bit of a band in, sometimes. Street here is chockers with farm utes and fourbies. Reckon I could cut back to just two nights a week and go and live in Barker, but there's always some dickhead stacks his bike in the middle of nowhere and needs a bit of help.'

'Evening, boys.'

'Dunc.' Four old blokes in a dribbly and unconvincing *a cappella* chorus.

'Found a stray pup by the road. Looking for its forever-home. Not housetrained. Where's Chlo?'

'I'm behind you, Duncan, but I admit that term encompasses a fair bit of real estate. None of it prime.'

Duncan was transformed in the presence of Chloe to a self-conscious little fat boy with long socks and trousers pulled up too high. But happy, anyway. And loved.

Chloe smiled indulgently.

Chloe had never been told to fuck off.

'Chlo, this is Ben. Travelling through. Stacked his bike out near the Corner. Byron's gone out to pick it up. He needs a place to stay and might help you out behind the bar.'

Gorgeous girl. Slim. A small hand offered to shake. Assertive. Smiling. 'G'day Ben. Have you worked in a pub?'

Ben took her hand. Warm and dry, the skin hard. 'Hello. No, I haven't. But I can work a tap and add up okay. Be great to get the job for a few days, to help out with accommodation and that. I've got bugger-all money and the bike's a bit stuffed.'

'Wondered whether Ben could stay in one of the flats till next week. Maybe work it for the food and board?' It was impossible to ignore Duncan, who occupied a large part of everyone's immediate and peripheral vision, but Ben had the feeling that he needed to be noticed.

'Well, that would be great. But don't worry about tonight. There's nothing happening and you must need to take it easy if you've just crashed your bike. I'll show you the flat and you can settle in and get cleaned up.' Chloe turned and opened a door that led out from the public bar. 'We've got soup and casserole cooking. If you're okay tomorrow morning, I'll explain how the place runs. What I really need is someone to stick behind the bar, so I can run the rest of the show. If it's quiet, just clean things and talk to the living dead. We don't open the door till after midday so there's a bit of grace there to get organised.'

Part of Ben wanted to keep talking to Chloe, but his head had started spinning and he knew he just needed to get clean, have some food and lie down. He wasn't aware of fainting, nor of Duncan's surprisingly agile lunge to stop him hitting the floor.

'Do you think we need to get him back to Barker, Chlo?'

'Not just yet. He looked fine walking in here. I think he's just in a bit of shock. Might have some concussion. Take him to the first flat and I'll organise some food.'

Ben had started to come around even as he was lifted over Duncan's shoulder. Staring down, he could see only an enormous blue arse in trousers held up by a complicated webbed police belt with a whole lot of pouches on it. And a holstered gun, which in context looked tiny. Ben's gear was in Duncan's other hand.

The flat was tucked away behind the kitchen. The roof sloped to the outside, suggesting that it had once been a veranda. The floor was polished boards and the furniture a collection of Formica and steel. An ageing air conditioner had been wedged into one window with lengthy instructions on a laminated card hanging from a chain. A double bed was hard against one wall, covered in a patchwork quilt that looked as though it had been made by the local women. A porcelain electric jug sat on the sideboard of a small sink. Everything was clean and neat, and a dream compared to the tent that Ben had become accustomed to.

Ben's head had cleared and Duncan had left him saying that he'd be back in half an hour to check. He stood under the hot shower, enjoying the feel of the water until noticing a sign warning of restrictions. Dried himself and changed into the cleanest of his clothes, and returned to the flat.

Duncan and Chloe were waiting for him, and looked relieved when he smiled.

'Had us a bit worried there. Give me your washing and I'll get that organised. If you're going to be working here, you'll need some clean clothes.'

Ben noticed his bag on the bed and handed it to Chloe. 'Thanks. Pretty much everything here has been worn, so it should probably all go in the wash. Some of it might be a bit feral.'

Chloe thought she'd cope. 'There's some bread and soup on the sideboard. Should still be warm. You look very tired, so why don't we leave you to sleep things off. I'll stick my head in before closing to make sure you haven't slipped into a coma.'

Lovely smile. Ben thought he could drown in that smile. 'Thanks again. And Duncan, thanks for picking me up and organising the bike. I think I'd better just take it easy now before I pass out again and you have to carry me back over the threshold.'

Duncan turned back towards the quiet pub, chuckling. 'Mate, next I'll time leave you where you fall. Take it easy. We'll see you tomorrow arvo.'

CHAPTER 3

'I didn't know you liked motorbikes.'

We were having breakfast in Ernie's cafe. I had managed to clock up six hours of credits. Dania was eating pancakes with fresh fruit, bacon and maple syrup. I could never go past the big cholesterol bolus—eggs, bacon, sausages, mushies, tomatoes. The whole lot. The deal was all you could eat. I didn't abuse it too much, but Ernie maintained that blokes my age were supposed to put away about three or four kilos at a sitting.

Dania was enjoying her pancakes, but thought they might make her fat. I told her I wasn't really into fat chicks and she'd have to go. She told me Tobe might be keen. Might whinge a bit less about uni. Might have more money. I tickled her and told her she wasn't fat.

'I love bikes. Always have. Used to have a PE250. Suzuki.'

'Is that a bike?'

I chuckled. 'I'll have to tickle you again. Yes. It's a bike. A trail bike. Two-stroke enduro.'

'A bike, then.'

'You really are very cute. And you look especially nice eating an expensive breakfast. I reckon cafes are really just put on streets so that cute chicks like you can look good in them.'

'By "like me" you mean whom exactly?'

'Just you.'

'Good.'

'And the "whom" was impressive.'

She smiled and carefully assembled another forkful of pancake and fruit. Small piece of each. Layered. It took some doing.

I closed my eyes, smiling. 'Lovely coffee.'

Dania finished her mouthful and dabbed at her lips with a napkin. 'When you say "lovely" like that, I'm led to wonder whether you might have some breeding. You know, people who don't wear jeans and cowboy boots and drive old utes.'

'I am in fact exceptionally well bred. Imported English bloodlines. Stayers.'

'I thought all English people were inbred and neurotic.'

'Well, maybe that's something you could discuss with my mum. Little icebreaker.'

'Don't you dare.' Laughing now. Kicked me under the table.

Ernie came over with fresh rolls. He had found a white dishcloth to drape over his arm. Almost like a real waiter. 'Now, little children. No squabbles. More bread for you. Devvo, your lady is too much skinny. Looks like a French photograph, no?'

'Thank you, Ernie. A true gentleman.'

'Yeah, thanks, Ernie. Lovely coffee. And you really should stop looking at those French photographs.'

Ernie huffed and put his hands on plump little hips. 'You cannot take anything this boy he says seriously, no? Everything is his little joke, no? I think you need to make a lot of fun of him for a change. Good that you are a tough girl.'

We both chuckled. 'It's all fantastic, Ernie. Really. Beautiful breakfast. No joking. Best ever. Thanks, mate. And I like that dishcloth.'

Ernie huffed again and went off to clean tables.

'So, tough girl.'

'Yes, funny boy?'

'What are we doing today?'

'I'm sunning my gorgeous fat body on a beach somewhere, and you're getting your textbooks out and working.'

'Okay.'

I walked Dania down to the ferry and we said a long goodbye. Lots of kissing. We didn't care what people thought. We had talked a little more about the letter. I had felt a bit self-conscious giving her such a big bundle of paper, but it wasn't until I started writing the story down that I realised how much detail there would be. Dania said that she'd enjoyed it and was looking forward to reading about what happened to Ben and Duncan and the others, and then putting the whole thing together as a book. She asked if it was violent, but in all honesty, I couldn't tell her. Regardless of how many times I had told it to myself I could never see the middle part of the story very clearly until it began to unfold in front of me.

But I had promised that there would be no story-telling or letter-writing today. There were only two weeks left now until the start of the university's designated study vacation, or 'stuvac'. And after that, the exams. Dania had helped me to organise my subjects a bit and to work out what I needed to do to pass. Just thinking it all through made a big difference. I was still waking up early, and still getting periods of anxiety, but I could rationalise it a bit more easily now. Aud was also pleased. Aud told me she had been getting worried.

Today was going to be genetics. Fucking genetics. Ridiculous monk with his ridiculous fucking peas. I wondered how you actually went about breeding peas. The books seemed to leave that bit out.

I thought it unlikely that Tobe was spending the day studying pees. Tobe was in love. Brand new woman. He had met her in a pub in Paddo. His description actually sounded a lot like one of Ernie's French photographs. She was a fully qualified lawyer and a few years older than us. This was brave new ground. Rich, and apparently happy to pay for everything. Had told Tobe that he was cheaper than batteries. Straightforward. They were down in Victoria this weekend on a wine-tasting thing with a corporate client. Five-star hotel. Tobe had hit the jackpot.

I had to focus. I took the books and the course syllabus and went downstairs. Aud was out somewhere. She had become a bit mysterious, but I was too preoccupied to follow it up. I arranged the books on the couch, made some instant coffee and set to it. Reading and highlighting. Note taking. And somehow it became a bit interesting. Hours passed. Whole hours. The warmth of the day wore off and a cool breeze came in off the harbour. I made a snack and went back to reading. Eventually Aud returned home. Looking vague. Alarm bells sounded, but they were distant. Underwater. I mumbled pleasantries, engrossed. I had worked out the whole inheritance thing. Alleles. Dominant and recessive genes. The monk was really a bit of a legend.

Uni had started to feel a bit better. I had put a fair bit of work into most subjects and a lot of it made more sense. Horse anatomy had become intriguing. I felt annoyed that I couldn't revisit some of the practicals. I had also done a lot more photocopying with my stolen card. I still tended to use the textbooks for learning and revision, but it was useful to know what the lectures had actually been about as I had no memory of most of them. It was as though I had been wandering around in the wrong building. Dania was a bit scathing about the bulk photocopying of the Good Girls' notes. She thought she might have charged me a fee to borrow hers. I told her Toni thought I was cute. Might even be a bit keen. She thought anything would look cute after staring at the leg of a dead horse all day.

We were gathered at the Townie on a beautiful winter evening. Dania was with us. Management had set up some gas-powered patio heaters, possibly to encourage the Wild Boys to stay out on the balcony.

'*Superb Country, Superb Parrot.*' Tobe had returned from his road trip to Victoria and was appalled by the stupidity of Australia's rural road signs. 'Seriously, what the fuck does that mean?—sorry, Dania.'

'Superb parrot is a fucken parrot.' Will came from down that way and couldn't see the problem. 'Fucken green.' As though that would clear things up.

Tobe wasn't convinced. 'But mate, if you don't know that it's the name of a parrot, it's a stupid fucken sign. Seriously, it's like saying *Superb Country, Superb Dog*—or *Superb Goat* for fuck's sake. Sorry, Dania.'

'But everyone knows it's a fucken parrot, you dickhead.' Will seemed to be working up for a fight. Technically, you couldn't have a fight over a road sign—but if you insulted the other bloke enough then that might be okay.

Tobe ignored him. 'Then there was this other one, out in the middle of a fucken paddock somewhere, said *Sorry, No Pumpkins*. Like what's going on out there? Are there really blokes just driving around all over the place looking for pumpkins?'

I had a chuckle at that. 'I like the one that says *Caution: Concealed Driveways*. It's like they do it on purpose. And Danny, what was that dumb sign we saw in the Blue Mountains?'

'*Falling Rocks Do Not Stop.*'

'That was the one. I know it means don't stop or you'll get hit by a falling rock, but there wasn't any punctuation so it was like having a road sign warning people about gravity.'

Tobe laughed, but Will was still annoyed about the parrot. 'Fucken idiots.'

Hector arrived with a tray of jugs and fresh glasses, keen to get us back to the Book Club topic. 'I reckon it'll be proven one day that all us whiteys have Neanderthal blood. You know, that the whole "white" thing is from the Neanderthals. Big fucken irony with the whole white supremacy thing.'

It was Hector's turn to select the book and he'd gone for *Clan of the Cave Bear*. Hector liked fantasy novels and particularly those with animal skins. The book was about a Cro Magnon human child who is adopted by a clan of Neanderthals and then grows up looking very different, and with a very different sort of brain. Tobe had jacked up a bit—in his view it was all just girly horseshit—but I was actually quite intrigued. It seemed a shame that dinosaurs and human evolution were generally considered topics for kids and esoteric academics. And people like Hector.

'I reckon Hec's right. Apparently, the Neanderthals did have pale skin and red hair. People are saying now that it's possible that they introduced these genes into the Cro Magnon people. Those of them who left Africa and went across to Europe where the Neanderthals lived.' I took a mouthful of the over-sweet, cheap warm beer. 'The Cro Magnons lived alongside the Neanderthals in Europe for a few thousand years. That's a long time. Plenty of opportunity for interaction.'

'Interaction?' Tobe wasn't convinced.

'Rooting.'

'Devlin!'

'Sorry, Danny, cultural exchange. But, you know, five thousand long ice-age winters with lots of nice little furry women in the cave up the road . . .'

'Devlin!'

'Sorry, Danny, cultural exchange. Fireside seminars on cooking with bear.'

Hector was looking dreamy. Will had moved on from the parrot, and was extracting a bit of bubblegum from between the slats of the table with his pocket-knife. Tongue coming out the side of his mouth. Heavy brow. Focussed. It was a compelling theory.

'So how is your revision going, Toby?' Dania asked in earnest, her fine eyebrows knitted. I squeezed her knee under the table.

'My what?' This was not a term that Tobe used with much frequency.

'Revision. For the exams.'

'There's all next week for that—stuvac.'

'Haven't you done anything at all?'

'No. Been a bit busy.'

Dania was confused. I helped her out. 'Lawyer chick.' I don't think any of us knew her name. Toby may have. He was looking defensive.

'Dev's got himself in a bit of a tailspin, but you don't really need to do any work until stuvac. That's what it's there for.'

'I've been working. I've done a lot the last month or so.' That was Warren. Always quietly following. Never said much.

I was relieved. 'Good on you, Wazza.'

Warren looked pleased. He had dropped a whole lot of guacamole dip onto a snow-white tennis shoe, then removed it with a grubby handkerchief, and had been trying to put the handkerchief full of guacamole back into his pocket.

Tobe shook his head and turned back to me and Dania. 'Mate, you got through okay last year. You'll be right.'

'Do you photocopy notes as well?'

'I just photocopy Devvo's photocopies. That card's had a hiding. Might need a new one soon. University will begin to wonder about Tangia Nakumara.'

'Don't think she works there anymore. She was that chunky chick with a head scarf. Agricultural arse.'

'Devlin!'

'Beeped when she backed up?'

'Toby!'

'That's the one. Have to take your word on the backing up bit, though. Didn't do that for me.'

'Devlin!!'

'Drinks, boys and Dania.'

'Thanks, Bill. How's that hole going?'

'Fuck off, Toby.'

'Okay.'

Hector and I went back to *Clan of the Cave Bear*. Dania was talking to Tobe and Warren, while Bill and Billy were discussing some land they thought they might buy, back down near Gundagai. Will was half-listening to them, and driving a cold, greasy chip around the table. Wheelies over the fork. Broadies round the corners. Sound effects. For a while, Dania had looked as though she might try to smack his hand, pull up his shorts and sit him down with a colourful book about a caterpillar.

Hector got out some more articles about human evolution that he'd found in the university library. He had gone berserk with a highlighting pen. Scribbled notes all over the margins. The story was that while the Neanderthal's huge brain and prodigious memory had served them well in the predictably awful ice-age, the Cro Magnon's imagination was a far more powerful asset when the climate changed and the ice retreated and the world around them was reborn.

I had often wondered about the evolution of imagination. How its purpose might have altered since Cro Magnon times. How close it was to madness. And to magic. Would a Neanderthal have been able understand why a Cro Magnon might watch a film or read a book and feel anguish or happiness or even cry? Could a Neanderthal kid join in a game with Cro Magnon kids, where they were all sitting in a cardboard box on the living room floor and completely convinced that it was a boat in a storm on the ocean?

I thought about the crazy flatmate of my friend Jilly, from the Jungle Bar. He believed that the TV was talking to him. Following him. But how different is that really to kids in their cardboard box? As we grow up, do we just learn to manage our imagination? To turn it right down? And if we can exert this sort of control, can we also turn down reality? Can we recolour a memory to the point where it is effectively invisible? Or re-badge it as fiction? A story? A recurring dream?

Hec and I were just getting going, but the others were winding down a bit and looking tired. Will had worn out his potato chip, then thrown it off the balcony at someone he recognised on the footpath below. They were down there now having an argument that looked as though it might get ugly. Tobe was yawning and

Dania was leaning against my shoulder. We picked up our bags and made our way out through the kitchen, keen to avoid whatever brawl Will was trying to line up.

Tobe took the camping bed and sleeping bag and set it up downstairs. I had some toast with him then went up to the loft.

Dania was lying on her side. Her tartan skirt had ridden up, showing lots of stocking. I sat on the edge of the bed. I couldn't get used to thinking she was real. She was way too good for me. She was looking worried.

I stroked her thigh. 'Sorry about the dissertation on cave men.'

Dania wasn't worried about Neanderthals. It was the other stuff. My fragile stability and frequent dark and silent moods. 'I'm not sure about this university thing now. You've always said that letting it slip and feeling like you don't belong is the problem, but sometimes I wonder whether those are just symptoms of something else.'

'What do you mean?'

'Mum gets depressed sometimes. She has to take things for it. I hope I don't get it, but I guess I might. I wondered whether you might have got in a bit of a hole. Trying to keep your head above water is all part of it.'

I lay back on the pillows. I had thought that, too. But also wondered whether the uni stuff was a trigger for some other demon that had been lying there waiting, just below the surface of the pond.

Dania looked down at me. 'Do you think you should go and talk to someone?'

'A psychiatrist?'

'Yes. I could go with you if you like.'

I rolled over and kissed the top of her head. Undid her white blouse. Red bra to match the undies. She stopped my hand. Held it. I sighed. 'Let me try and get through these exams first. Maybe next term, if things are the same.'

I wanted help, but also feared someone poking around in my head. 'It would be nice if you came along. I don't ever feel like a loser when I'm with you.'

'You're not a loser on your own. You're exceptional in so many ways. But sometimes you burn all your matches at once. It makes a beautiful flame. But then you feel cold.'

I had told Dania about the matches metaphor in *Like Water for Chocolate*. I kissed her again. 'I've written another chapter of the story for you. It's in the package on my desk. But be warned, it's another tome.'

I enjoyed writing the long letters and thought that the process might be helping. She smiled. 'Thank you. And now perhaps you can burn some matches. Just a few. And not all at once.'

Dear Dania,

I have finished another day.

We're still just in Warkon, getting to know the people a bit.

The adventure starts tomorrow . . .

Anyway, next chapter—Friday.

Love, Devlin xxx

Friday

Ben awoke to a still-dark room. Months spent sleeping in a cheap translucent tent had left him attuned to the coming dawn. The bed was unbelievably comfortable compared with his thin foam roll-up and while the warm, hand-stitched quilt scratched his chin, it also comforted him in a way that a sleeping bag never could . . .

. . . Ben awoke to a still-dark room. Months spent sleeping in a cheap translucent tent had left him attuned to the coming dawn. The bed was unbelievably comfortable compared with his thin foam roll-up and while the warm, hand-stitched quilt scratched his chin, it also comforted him in a way that a sleeping bag never could.

A rooster began to crow. Ben had never heard a rooster's morning crow. He thought it was myth. But this one was in full swing and probably a bit of a danger to itself if anyone in the pub or surrounding houses had a hangover. The rooster was joined by a kookaburra, and then another, and soon a third somewhere along the street or perhaps high in the red gums that he had seen clinging to pockets of moisture at the edge of the desert's ephemeral creeks and rivers. By the time the currawongs had added their hydraulic gargling to the mix, thin streaks of daylight had appeared around the faded, pull-down blind.

Ben moved around in the bed to feel for injuries. His neck was sore, but it was only muscular. He recalled the damage to the helmet, which would have to be replaced when he could afford it. His back was also a bit painful, as was one wrist. He looked at his jacket on the back of a chair in the little kitchen area and even in this light could see the long scratches from rock and gravel. The pants and gloves would probably be the same. It was all second-hand gear, but nevertheless expensive and bought mostly to placate his mother. At the time he would have been happy to ride in jeans and work boots.

He got up slowly. The jug was empty and its element caked with salts from the hard local water. Ben was surprised that it still worked, but soon had a cup of instant coffee to take back to bed. He lay there thinking about the night before. Chloe was definitely a cutie. He could see why the local blokes loved her. She was just a girl, really, and probably about his own age, but she had an air of innate maturity that suggested that she could probably have run the place at the age of ten. Ben wondered whether Chloe came from Warkon or whether her uncle had moved here from somewhere else when he took on the pub. In places like this the true locals were often treated like aristocracy, even though they shared way too many genes.

He could hear a radio in the pub and realised that Chloe must now be up and having breakfast, so dressed hurriedly in clothes from the night before and padded out into the corridor.

In the daylight, the old building's decay was more evident. Countless oscillations of searing outback heat and freezing winter nights had warped the wooden boards on its walls and floors, so that each step was accompanied by a soft shifting and sighing. It was like walking through the entrails of a living animal. Pictures on the walls told of days when men seemed to stand up much straighter and smile less. Long-dead horse teams and bullock teams were frozen in time, along with their stiffly waistcoated drivers. Women in bustles stood in front of the pub, with carts and buggies to one side. The *Warkon Hotel* sign that still rested on the veranda roof was fresh and sharp. The blurred figure of a child running could be seen in one corner.

Life out here would have been hard in those days, without cooling in summer or even cool water to drink. Ben had heard that most people died before their fifties—a lot of them just worn out—and that many more died young from injuries and illnesses that were now so easily treated. Appendicitis was a killer. Wound infection was a killer. Childbirth was too often a killer. Depression was definitely a killer. Horses killed. Wild cattle killed. These rigid men and women in their rigid clothing must have had a different outlook on life. It must have seemed like a brief gift, and less awful when snatched away as that was just how things were.

The corridors of the pub were full of the old pictures and as Ben made his way towards the sound of the radio he wondered whether Chloe's uncle had hung them there to decorate or authenticate the place, or whether he had wanted to tell people something about Warkon and its past. There was almost no joy in any of them—just the sadness of hard lives lived briefly in the white light of the bush and now reduced to two-dimensions of faded brown.

Further on, the old photographs were mostly of aboriginals, and presumably the tribes-people of this area. One showed a group around a series of humpies. Blankets and other European affectations could be seen, including clothing and some bottles that must have held alcohol of some sort. The people were slender and their faces were ancient in a way that only Australian aboriginal faces can be. But again, none were smiling. Not even the children. Ben wondered what the occasion of the photograph might have been—perhaps the last picture of a camp on a nearby station before they were moved off to the escarpment or some less productive bit of bush.

By now Ben had reached the kitchen, where Chloe had her back to him, reading a novel. He could see that her shoulders and neck were slim beneath the folds of a cashmere shawl. He coughed and she dropped the book with a start, even though he was sure she had known he was there, and turned to face him through a pair of over-sized horn-rimmed reading glasses.

'How did you sleep? Have you found any breaks from the fall?'

'I slept like a fat little pup. After a few months in a tent, that bed and quilt were just unbelievable. And no injuries! I really can't explain it, because the bike is pretty much totalled.'

'That's definitely good news. You can have some cooked breakfast if you want, or there's muesli and cereal.'

'Cooked breakfast would be great. I can't think when I last had one. But I can make it if you show me where things are.'

'A handy man. This I will enjoy watching. Eggs and bacon are in the fridge there, and bread also. Proper coffee if you want it, from that little stove-top doover, or you can have some tea.'

'I'll go the whole hog with good coffee. I had one of those little cookers, but someone flogged it from my pack. What are you reading?'

'*Anna Karenina*. Duncan lent it to me.'

Ben stared. Chloe smiled. 'I'm serious. I bet you wouldn't have guessed that our Big Duncan is a bookworm?'

'I was actually going to say "fuck off".'

Chloe laughed, spilling some coffee on the book and her jeans.

'Seriously, Duncan lent you *Anna Karenina*?'

'Yes. And you should see the walls of his bedroom.'

Ben was again silent. Chloe's hand came to her mouth as she laughed louder.

'Sorry, that didn't come out as I had meant.' She stood and walked over to lean on the windowsill. 'I went into Duncan's one room, which happens to have a bed in it, to browse his bookshelves. He asked me to, and he waited outside like the very large gentleman that he is. He's got everything from Tolstoy to *The Lord of the Rings*. Who was the guy who wrote *Sons and Lovers*? DH Lawrence? He's got a whole lot of those. And the *Poldark* series. Can you believe it? Twelve of them, I think. One wall is completely covered in books. Things like *A Hundred Years of Solitude* and the Toni Morrison books and *The Unbearable Lightness of Being*. And he's even got the whole *Dune* series. It's pretty amazing.'

'Wow. If there is a merciful god, I'll never ever ever see the inside of Dunc's bedroom. But I'm impressed and a bit amazed. So is the big pig dog thing just an act, then?'

Chloe returned to her chair and bent down to pull a loose thread from a faded cowboy boot. 'Part of it is, but let's face it, Duncan is pretty much a big pig dog. It's just that he's a very smart pig dog, and probably the best bloke to have on your side in this town.' Sitting upright again, she added, 'I think he likes you. He's usually much more distant and less bullshitty. He only tells people he likes to fuck off.'

Ben was smiling to himself as he started trying to get eggs and bacon organised, aware that he was providing some entertainment in the process.

Chloe took another three quick mouthfuls of coffee. 'He's just a big gentle bear, really. One who reads DH Lawrence, can you imagine it?'

'Actually I can't, and I'm not sure if you're just pulling my leg. Last night we talked about guns and pigs.' Ben stopped as an image came back to him. 'But does Duncan, like, do weird dances sometimes? In the headlights?'

Chloe laughed. 'Well, I haven't seen that but, yes, it does sound like something he might do.'

Ben told Chloe that they had planned to go camping and shooting on the weekend and was hoping that she'd give him the night off.

'I thought it was too good to be true. A worker who works. The great Australian myth. But no, that's okay, I can get Byron to help out on Saturday. He's always happy to do that in exchange for a bottle of something. Now there's a bloke you really don't want to annoy.'

'Duncan said the same thing. Said he has some Vietnam War mojo going on.'

'Yes, I think that's right. And then there's his disgusting dog. It's an awful vicious bloody thing and he never goes anywhere without it. But really, I don't know much about Byron. He keeps to himself. But he's definitely got a switch, and you don't want to push him and flip it.' She got up to rinse the empty cup. 'He nearly killed a couple of fencers in here a year or so ago. He'd fixed their four-wheeler and when they got drunk they started telling him he'd ripped them off. Wouldn't leave him alone. He actually showed a fair bit of restraint, but must have snapped in the end because one of the locals found the two of them on the veranda a bit later covered in blood with broken bits of chair all over the place. One was unconscious and took three days to come around. The other had an arm and a leg broken. Apparently, it looked a bit systematic, which freaked out Cecil and the other old blokes who'd been propping up the bar.'

'Good to know. I've got to go up there a bit later and talk to him about the bike. Duncan said to give him a few hours to wake up.'

Chloe smiled. 'Yes, they say he's not a morning person. When you've finished stuffing around with that stove, I'll cook you some breakfast then we can go through the bar routine.'

Ben piloted the immaculate black Norton tentatively down the dusty main street. He had delayed visiting the garage until late morning, concerned about the warnings, but Byron had been up early and by that time had stripped the bike down to its frame and motor. Tank, wheels, swing-arm, bars, controls and a whole lot of other bits were strewn about the garage, and the supposedly maniacal local hard-man was flitting from one pile to another while humming contentedly to a Credence solo that seeped softly from a speaker high up on the garage wall.

'Hello!' Ben, from the door.

Continued humming. Falsetto.

'Hello!!'

Air guitar now. A short riff, kneeling in a grainy shaft of light from the garage skylight. Balletic.

'Hello!!!'

Byron was a lot taller standing than he had looked in a crouch. Lean, with the long arms and the huge cracked hands of a shearer. His face was complex and contradictory. Like a bad portrait. In profile, the clichéd laconic Australian droop. Long, narrow jaw. Perpetual smoke, hanging. But there was nothing laconic about the eyes, which were intense and fearful. Bloodshot. Virtually varicose, with sclera the colour of weathered putty. It was clear why people avoided Byron. Conceivable that he broke that chair over a couple of drunk fencers.

Then, without warning, it was all gone. A dam braking. The ruined eyes lit up and the deep lines that had mapped out a relentless haunted isolation drained away to a smile.

'Mate!'

Ben was relieved. Immensely. And smiled back, pointing towards the dismembered carcass on the garage floor. 'I see you found my bike.' It was a poor joke, but he was still a bit nervous.

Byron didn't seem to notice. 'Mate, I did. And I'm glad. Wanted to get my hands on one of these boxers. The mighty R80GS. Fucken ridiculous concept, but geez they're clever. See why it works so well. What's it like to ride?'

'To tell you the truth, it's the first decent bike I've owned. I got left some money and bought the bike to travel with. I've ridden a lot of farm bikes and trail bikes, but nothing much. But I love this thing. I really hope you can help me get it back together.'

'Mate, we'll get it sorted. Never know it's had a bit of a sleep on a hard dusty road. Making a list of parts. Go through that with you when I'm finished.'

He moved across to a bench and rested against it. Arms folded, with a hand around each bicep. Singlet and baggy pants. No gut. A still-life pose from the 1920s.

'Courier out of Sydney, owes me some favours. Saved his fat arse more than once. Bring the parts out on Monday or Tuesday. Not going to be cheap. Parts, I mean. Help you out with the work. First decent bike I've had in here in about five years. Pleasure to get into. That's my old Commando behind you. Been riding bikes since before the war.'

Ben turned, wondering which war, then remembered what Duncan and Chloe had said about Vietnam. The Norton was propped up on a milk crate to save the suspension. It was the only shiny object in the dusty carnage of the garage. 'Wow. That's beautiful. Duncan, the cop who took me into town last night, said you had one of these.'

'Good bloke, Dunc. Asset to this God-forsaken turd of a town. Some good laughs with the big fella over the years. Not many blokes out here you can laugh with. Fucken mouth-breathers, most of them.' Byron levered himself upright and off the bench and moved over to where the shell of the BMW was suspended from the garage beams. 'Wish that chick Chloe would get the hots for him, but doesn't look like she will. They'd make a good pair, you know. Anyway, the bike. You hit the ground pretty hard, I reckon. Amazing you don't look a bit the same, really. Seen plenty of blokes busted up well with less damage to their bikes than this. What do you reckon, Hoots?'

Apparently hearing the conversation for the first time, an aged red heeler lifted his head from a large cushion on which he had been sleeping away the morning. He regarded Ben with angry, liquid eyes, before shuffling over to his master and dropping down protectively at his feet.

'That's Hoots. Hooty. Getting on a bit now. Still has a bit of snap in him. Don't touch his ears. Or his head. Or his stiff leg. Fuck's sake, don't touch his tail.'

Ben resolved not to go near Hoots. Hoots, on the other hand, gazed up at Byron with unguarded love and was rewarded with a vigorous scratch of his ears and head. Which he seemed to enjoy.

'Great mate, this dog. Get old too soon. Such a fucken shame.' Byron looked down fondly at the curled scurfy ears. 'Never did get on with my ex-missus, though. Couldn't really see the point of her. Follow her around the house making sure she behaved, which pissed her off a bit. He'd tolerate her coming into the kitchen every now and then, and eating off the bowls, but hated her getting on the furniture. Sad, but in the end we had to let her go. Happens like that sometimes. Think a family in Sydney took her, so it ended okay.'

Hoots had obviously heard this story before, but smiled appreciatively before starting to lick his balls.

Ben looked away. 'About the crash. I don't really understand it either. There's some scuffing on my jacket and the helmet is probably rooted, but I'm completely okay. I must just have skidded or rolled and not really hit anything hard.'

'Well, tank took a hit, mate. It's over there near the wall. Beat that out and respray it for you. Bars a bit bent and I reckon should be replaced. Not very strong. Can get some harder bars in the same bend from a mate in Sydney. Steel you had around the motor did a good job, but not pretty. Bloke did that doesn't ride nice bikes. We might take it off for you and replace it with something that does the same thing but looks less like your mum made it.'

Byron walked forward to see the bike from a different angle. One arm across his chest. The other pointing. All sinew. Mechanical. A long hard lever. 'Your panniers saved the back end. One frame's a bit bent, but easy to fix. Controls pretty much fucked. Get those from the shop in Sydney. Big motor's fine, but I'll give it a service for you. Valves and all that shit. Tune those lovely carbies.'

Ben could see that this was going to be the biggest bowl of ice-cream Byron had had a go at in a long time. 'Sounds great, but let me make sure I can get some money together before you get into it too much. I'll have to borrow some of it from my mum. Chloe will let me work a bit in the pub while you're getting it all sorted, so I shouldn't be spending too much. But I'm not very wealthy at present. Going to get some fruit picking in WA, when I get there.'

'Mate, no worries. As I said, going to enjoy getting this thing organised for you and don't want much for the work. Nice change from fixing fucken utes and tractors. Might need some wheels while you're in town. Take the Norton for a few days. Good to get it running a bit. Take it easy on the dirt, but. Cafe racer not a trail bike.'

'Really? You're okay for me to ride the Norton? I've shown what I can do to a good bike.'

'Yeah, mate, honestly. Like to see it chugging around. Like to hear it, too. Don't get that when you're on it. Nothing sounds like a Norton. It's a '75 Mark III. 850 plant. Big turd-on-a-stick, really, but there's something beautiful about it.'

'That would be fantastic. I'll be careful with it. Daylight only. And I'll keep it round the back of the pub. There's a bit of an annex next to the flat Chloe put me in. It'll be safe in there.'

'No worries. One thing about this town, not much thieving. Not much to thieve, I guess. But if you did flog something, what would you do with it? Everyone'd know where it came from. And for some reason, locals seem to think I'm a scary bastard and not the one they want after them for lifting his pride and joy. Very much doubt anyone would touch the bike, even if you parked it with the key in right outside the pub. But the annex sounds good. Keep the dew off it.'

Byron gently extracted the Norton, filled its tank and showed Ben the complicated starting routine. 'Listen to that, mate. Fucken beautiful. Tell you to pop Chloe on the back, but might break the big bloke's heart.'

'I've been warned off. And honestly, I just want to get over to the other coast. I don't want to stuff around.'

'Good man. Now piss off and leave me and Hoots to enjoy this nice music and this big beautiful German goddess.'

Ben backed the little Norton gingerly into the annex, then stood to the side and looked at it.

So unlike the Beemer.

The road to Warkon was gravel and usually Ben would have enjoyed it. But this Norton was something so completely different to the big R80GS. It was faster. No doubt about that. But it wasn't as smooth. Vibrated at even modest speed, and any tiny change in his position resulted in a sudden shift in the bike's direction. Definitely a road rider's bike. Completely sexy. A totally British bike, in the traditions of Matchless, BSA, Triumph and the other great names.

And parked right outside his bedroom window. Just needed a pouty chick in tight black jeans, perched on the back. Chloe really would look great on this thing. But he understood what Byron had meant about Duncan. When Ben's bike was fixed and he'd gone to Western Australia, Duncan would still be here and he didn't want to think about him agonising over some sort of idea that Chloe had betrayed him. They might get together one day. Byron didn't think so, but Byron might not have seen some of the stuff that passed between them.

Anyway, Chloe didn't seem to be very interested in him so it was probably all okay. He looked at the time and realised he'd have to start his first shift behind the bar very soon. Didn't know what to expect of a Friday night in Warkon, but it was reassuring that Duncan would be there to keep the peace.

He found a half-reasonable shirt and some jeans among the clothes that Chloe had cleaned, had a quick shower and made his way through to the public bar. Duncan was already in the bar and Ben had a chance to observe him from a distance. Jeans, and a shirt that had probably been cut from a small and colourful sail. Riding boots. All the stuff that had been going on the previous night. Laughing loudly, throwing his bull head back. Schooner glass in hand. Not beer. Maybe lemon squash? Ben had wondered whether the local policeman would be drinking. Technically off duty. He caught Ben's eye. Waved and winked. Ben felt he'd been let in on an intricate joke.

He made his way in behind the bar. Chloe smiled at him and pointed at a couple of locals straining forward to place orders.

'VB, mate. Schooners. Four.'

'No worries.' He took chilled glasses from the fridge and pulled four half beers. Repeated the process to top them up. Perfect heads all.

'Good man.'

'Cheers.' Took the money. Bloke not interested in the change. Big jar under the counter. Chockers.

And so it went. The bar had VB, Fourex, Reschs Draught and Tooheys New on tap. To cater for the few more discerning clientele, the same beers were offered in bottles. Boutique beers. White wine was dry or sweet and kept in the beer fridge. Red was of an uncertain provenance but something like a shiraz. Cheap whisky, gin, white rum and Bundy stood in opened bottles with plastic pourers fitted. Coke, tonic and squash were served using an ancient trigger gun connected to a small carbonated barrel beneath the counter. Good whisky sat up on the top shelf, symbolic and rarely noticed. A small sign on the back wall read *No Cocktails. No Martinis, No Margaritas. No Pimms Fruit Cups.*

Ben tried to blend in, but in a place like this he knew that his hair was too nice, his hands too soft and voice too quiet. And that made him nervous, and a bit sullen. He breathed deeply and tried not to overcompensate. 'Cecil, mate. What do you need?'

Old Cecil seemed to be taking the piss. 'Ben, mate! Top-o-the-evening to ya! Big beers. Me and Keith. Usual fucken goat piss'll do.'

'No worries.'

Ben poured the beers and took the money. Cecil pointed. 'Shirt, mate. Collar. Always wear it like that?'

Turned up. Fuck. He'd forgotten. It was the trend in Sydney and looked sharp there. Do it here and you might as well front up in your sister's undies.

'Sorry. Put it on in a hurry. Thanks. Didn't realise.'

'Too easy. Save you from the fucken riff raff. Usually here by seven. Not subtle, those blokes. Probably try to kiss ya.' Wet laughter strained through old brown pegs. Bits now on Ben's shirt. On the bar.

'Appreciate it, Cecil.'

'Worth a free beer, you reckon?'

'No, mate. Chloe's told me. Not under any conditions.'

Cecil chuckled. 'Got you in the grip, mate? Well, worth a try.'

'Cheers.' Ben was pleased with his resilience.

Chloe returned with a big plate of hot wedges and sour cream and deposited it in front of a bloke at a table near Duncan. Duncan looked at the bloke. He was new. Unsure. Duncan leaned over and took a handful. Eye contact the whole time. Straight face. No comment. The bloke shat himself. Chloe slapped Duncan's wrist and took a swig of his drink. Laughs all round. Introductions. Big bloke's the local cop. Softy. Labrador. Duncan, behave yourself. Woof.

Chloe returned to the bar. 'You've turned your collar down. I liked it.'

'Cecil didn't.'

'Cecil's got the fashion sense of a cane toad, Ben. Tell him to piss off.'

'He thought the next lot of locals would give me a hard time. Wanted a free beer for his wisdom. I told him no.'

'Good on you.' She looked pensive. 'It's good now. Wish it would just stay like this. When the truck gets here, the whole thing changes. Some of these nice blokes leave. They don't want to fight anyone. Duncan has to earn his free drinks keeping the peace. Remember what I said, no-one else drinks without paying.'

Chloe had explained the system. Ringers from half a dozen of the bigger stations were taken into Warkon in a horse truck, then returned on Saturday morning. Swags could be rolled out overnight in the rubber-cushioned horse stalls. The process was repeated Saturday evening and Sunday morning. The arrangement had been engineered by Duncan a year or so earlier to cut back on drunk driving and the scores of alcohol-related accidents. The ringers paid a fee that covered the truck's diesel and gave the driver a small income. Everyone benefitted, including the pub.

But it did mean that with the truck's arrival the bar was immediately inundated with cowboys panting for a drink. Most stations were dry and weekend binge drinking the norm.

A lot of them got drunk quickly and discovered themselves to be hilarious. There would be jokes and ribbing. A few might even try to challenge him in some way. Without batting an eyelid, she had added that they were for the most part just dumbos and no-hopers, while he was exotic and good-looking and had blown into town on the best bike anyone had seen. Ben had barely registered this compliment as he'd been distracted by her bra strap which had become visible as the t-shirt slipped around a bit. For a terrifying second he had actually thought he might reach out and touch it. He didn't think she'd noticed and recovered in time to hear the bit about a great bike.

'Above all else,' she told him, 'don't try to compete with these flogs. Even if you win and they lose, you lose as well because they'll get the shits and leave and I'll have to fire you.' Chloe smiled. 'And stop staring at my bra strap.'

The truck arrived in a pall of red dust. Its rear door was lowered hydraulically and a crazed mob emerged. Chloe had told him that occasionally they started drinking during the trip. This wasn't part of the agreement, but bottles of Bundy could be secreted back to the stations in swags and saved for the next trip into town. Duncan turned a blind eye. This lot looked to have had about half a bottle each.

Ben positioned himself behind the bar and tried again to look comfortable. He realised that he'd failed when some clown wolf-whistled and his mates packed up laughing, but was then too swamped pulling beers to notice any further jeering. The frenzy went on for about forty minutes, until everyone had downed three or four schooners. Most were friendly, leaning across the bar to shake his hand and yelling shit and spittle into his face. But then he got an order wrong. It was a little wizened and ageless bloke with a big buckle and tall boots. Smutty. Real name unknown. Travelling horse-breaker, legendary buck jumper and sour little prick. And pissed because he'd ordered rum-and-Coke and been given beer.

'What the fuck is this?' Appalled. Face like a sunburned puckered arse.

'Sorry, mate. Not yours?' Ben was looking around for the bloke who had ordered beer. An older man. Sandy hair.

'You so fucken stupid can't tell beer from fucken rum?'

'Mistake, mate. Bloke ordered these, but he's wandered off somewhere. So what were you after?'

'I fucken told you, mate, rum-and-Coke.'

'How many?'

'Just one, mate. Get one fucken drink right, blondy?'

Duncan appeared. 'Smutty. Easy, mate. Ben here's had a hit on the head and we're trying to rehabilitate him. Starting with simple tasks. Pulling beers. Working up to rums. Baby steps, mate.'

Duncan took the tray of beers from Ben. 'Who owns these, Ben? I'll take them over.'

'Tall bloke. Reddy hair. Bit older. Blue shirt, I think.'

'Playing pool next door? Back in a sec.'

'Thanks, Duncan.'

Ben poured a rum-and-Coke and slid it across to Smutty. Told him the price.

'Got to be fucken kidding, mate. Going to charge me after waiting here half the fucken night? Fuck off.'

Ben misread him. Should have let it go. 'No free drinks, mate. Sorry. Chloe's orders.' Hand extended for the money.

'Fuck you, mate.' Threw the drink in Ben's face.

Then Duncan was back. Instantly. Grabbed the back of Smutty's shirt. Dragged him outside.

The bar went quiet, then a few chuckles.

'Normal procedure, mate. Get used to it.' An older voice, from somewhere in the crowd.

More laughter.

Conversations resumed, shouting face-to-face to be heard.

'You okay? Need to change your shirt?' Chloe. Concerned.

'Thanks. No, I'm okay. It washed off some of old Cecil's spittle.'

'Sorry, but this is how it often is. Friday is the worst. They've usually sorted things out a bit by Saturday.'

The pace kept up. Checked shirts with shiny cowboy buttons, three-deep at the bar. Beer, rum-and-Coke, scotch-and-soda. Young faces lined like fence posts. Hard and battered hands. Only respite from a week of work. No girls out here in the bush anymore. Just drink and bullshit. A dead end.

Then Duncan was back. And with him, Smutty. Both laughing. 'Ben, mate. Let's have that rum-and-Coke again. Charge him for two.' No break in his smile. Huge arm across Smutty's shoulders.

Smutty paid. Twice. Eyes down. Then scurried back over to the blokes he'd been working the week with.

Duncan poured himself another lemon squash. 'So, mate, enjoying yourself?'

'No-one else to enjoy, Dunc.'

Duncan chuckled. 'Like that. Use it. And mate, go a bit easy with Smutty. I've taken his knife, but he's been known to break bottles. Should be okay now, but hard to tell. I'll park myself here for a bit, I reckon.' Duncan's broad arse consumed a bar stool. 'Send over a few peanuts, mate. Pour yourself a drink and sit down for a bit. Tell them to fuck off.'

'I'm okay, Dunc. Better keep watering the horses. Shit-scared of Chloe. She'll turf me out of my flat. Some nuts for you.' Ben tossed him a couple of packets.

More chuckling. Duncan's natural state. 'Thinking about the trip tomorrow. Tent and bedding. Warm clothes for overnight. Backpack. Don't worry about food or cooking gear. Boots you can walk in. Hat. About it, I guess. Maybe change of socks and undies. Don't want to scare the pigs.'

'No worries. Got the panniers off the bike today. Tent and all that. Thought I'd be late finished here tonight, so did some packing. All sorted. What time do you want to start out?'

'Want to sight that new gun in on the way. Then a full day's walking up on the escarpment. Have to start out at dark o'clock, mate. I'll come over and get you. Don't be naked.'

CHAPTER 4

I made it through the mid-year exams. I even managed a credit in genetics and nutrition, and a distinction in biometry. It was a huge relief ahead of the four weeks' break. I needed to get some of the mandated practical work done, so spent two of the weeks with a horse trainer in the Hunter Valley and the remaining two weeks staying with my mother and working on a big intensive piggery up near Tamworth.

Joan, the horse trainer, had a small business helping to prepare thoroughbred yearlings for sale. Basically, just halter breaking and manners. We worked long days, but it was great to be out in the sun and handling horses again. The piggery, however, was appalling. I like pigs. They are very smart and personable—at least as smart as dogs. It has always seemed wrong to eat them. And these poor bastards lived their whole lives in enormous high-biosecurity sheds with the minimum possible time on earth before the chop. I fantasised about releasing several thousand Fielders Hybrids out onto the Liverpool Plains. It would be like the baby turtles. One or two would make it into the bush and at least get the chance to run around for a few days. I really hated the job, and the place stank like you wouldn't believe. The smell got right into my skin and hair. It was worse than the Jungle Bar.

At the end of the four weeks, Dania caught the train up from Sydney. She wanted to meet my mum. It was nice. Mum could see how much strength and common sense Dania had. Not just a pretty little thing. I think Mum feared for me a bit. I was a clever kid but floating around and likely to hit a rough spot and go belly-up.

But back in Sydney things became a bit difficult again. I started uni on the Monday, full of beans and enthusiastic after getting over the exam hurdle. But everyone else was also enthusiastic and most of them had done better than me. Even Tobe, on about three days and nights of solid work and a carton of No-Doz. Lectures were immediately stressful again. Not the topics. Just being there. I have never felt comfortable in crowds and started getting anxious and a bit panicky sitting down in a closed theatre with people on either side and in front and behind. I became convinced that others could sense this and were laughing at me.

At first, I missed a few lectures here and there. I just sat on one of the ovals and read a novel. I generally slipped back in during the breaks for coffee and a chat, but felt self-conscious. Like an interloper. Every now and then I went home early and then, gradually, that became the norm. I tried to read textbooks on my own, but with no real idea of the focus of the lectures it didn't work very well.

I could hide this from Dania to begin with, but I was getting a reputation at uni and this filtered through to her by way of Toby and Warren. I tried to reassure her, but I think she was getting pretty worried about me. Once again, she brought up the idea of seeing a psychiatrist, as she thought her mum's periodic depression had some bits in common with my own moods and deterioration. I didn't disagree, but it seemed like a huge step to take. And beneath that I still felt some uncertainty about letting someone get too close to my thoughts and memories.

During the term break, I had lent my microphones and other bits of PA gear to Scotty and Rick. Scotty had dug up another drummer and bass player and they had played a couple of gigs while me and Dom were out of town. Apparently, it was a bit of a flop, but nevertheless made me uneasy and now that we were all back in Sydney I was keen to get in as many gigs as possible. We had another couple of good nights at the Shakespeare and a cracker at the Women's College Formal. Dania had loved that one. The black tie dress code and the pompous college scene. There were a couple of good professional bands and an amazing PA with synched lighting. Free drinks for the band. I gave Dania my tokens and she got a bit plastered, but it was great fun.

On the strength of that, I managed to convince the others to make a trip up to Armidale to play at the University of New England's notorious Rural Science Ball. I had already been to one of these as my brother was studying up there. The balls were held in woolsheds, in the best and worst traditions of Bachelors and Spinsters, or B&S, balls. I thought Dania would get a kick out of it and wanted to try to get Tobe to come along as well.

At the same time as this, we had a major development on the home front. Dom and Aud had started seeing each other in earnest. At first, I was horrified, but in fact they made a great couple. Aud came out of herself a bit and Dom settled down. He was attending lectures again now and sleeping at night— sometimes in the house, which was a bit disconcerting. Aud focussed all her maternal ambitions on Dom and he blossomed. Got fatter and went to arty dos around Sydney and helped out at the Glebe book shop. Aud bought him expensive deodorant, after-shave and body spray and he no longer smelled like the council bogs.

On a Friday in early August, we all set off for Armidale.

The plan was to stay overnight at the pub in Nundle, then do the last bit on Saturday morning. I took Dania and Tobe in the ute while Dom and Aud travelled separately in a car that Aud had borrowed from her boss. Aud was on fire. She had bought a whole new country wardrobe from a saddlery shop on Broadway. She looked fantastic. Just glowing. We went up the Putty Road, stopping for coffee and cakes at a little place in

Wollombi, then headed across the Hunter Valley to Glenbawn Dam and up to Nundle through Barry Station and Hanging Rock. I knew the road through Barry Station from my time on the logging place near Nundle. It was gravel, but well graded, and the twenty-odd river crossings had a solid base so as long as there hadn't been too much rain upstream it was passable for two-wheel drive vehicles.

Nundle itself has always been one of my favourite places—a quiet little collection of tidy weatherboard houses, nestled up in the beautiful cold forest country. Something about my time on the logging place had left a taste in my mouth, but that didn't seem to detract from my memory of the village and the hills around it. I told Dania that we could perhaps live up there when we were old and doddery. Help each other down to the shop for the morning paper, stopping to let our fat little Jack Russell terrier piss on mailboxes. Dania wasn't convinced.

Nundle also has a great old pub, which sits at the crossroads in the centre of the village. Huge verandas and wood fires. Our rooms were a glimpse back to the last century with paling cream paint, creaking brass beds and oval gilt-edged mirrors.

The plan was to have showers and change, and a bit of a rest, then meet up in the dining room for dinner. Dania carried her bag in ahead of me and parked it in a corner. I put my old rucksack down next to it and left the car keys on a faded wood-veneer dressing table. Next to them was a Gideon's Bible and a box of tissues. Seemed to cover all bases. We held hands and kissed. This was one of our few nights away from the Balmain house. Although I had visited Dania many times at her mum's place, I had never stayed over.

Dania squeezed my hands, then turned away to look out the window. Below us was a courtyard that served as a beer garden in summer. The browned winter bones of an enormous wisteria reached out across one side and over the trellised roof. Its trunk was like a tree.

'We should come back in spring. That thing would be beautiful.' I was standing behind her now, with both arms around her neck.

She reached up and stroked my sleeve. 'You seem really shaky, honey. Is it all the driving? It was so lovely coming through those hills.'

I let her go and sat on the edge of the bed with my face in my hands. I could feel the tremor and the heat of my palms. It had been there for an hour or so. Then I realised that my hands were wet, and that tears were running in little rivers down to my chin.

Dania sat down next to me and again stroked my arm. 'What's wrong?'

'I don't know, Danny. I really don't know. Sometimes everything is okay, then I just seem to get all this pain and fear. I can't push it away, and I feel really panicky.'

I knew what was coming.

'Honey, you have to see someone. This has gone on too long now. You said you'd do something after the exams, and that's now.'

I nodded. I had hoped that the new term would be a new start, but things were getting worse each week. I had never been insecure about girls, or jealous of other blokes, but I found I was beginning to obsess about this as well. Whenever Dania wasn't with me, I became terrified that she was with someone else. Someone stable. Better looking. Easy going.

Dania seemed to sense this. 'You're not trying to handle this on your own because of me, are you? I've told you I want you to see someone. It doesn't bother me. I just want someone to be able to help you to get better.'

'Why are you with me, Danny? Seriously, why do you stay with me?'

But I knew the answer, and we just lay back and cuddled a bit and eventually we both slept.

I woke with a start when I realised that the sharp sunlight had gone and the room had grown cold. The anxiety had disappeared completely and I felt light. Powerful. The sting of dried tears at the edge of my eyes seemed incongruous. I drew myself up on one elbow to better see the beautiful mountains and forests. I knew now that there was something dark there. Something I had left lying in the snow-damped magic of a cold, hidden valley.

I got up and closed the curtains, then turned on the archaic oil heater. I could hear a pair of crows calling urgently to each other in the last of the evening light. Or to me. I shivered as I knelt by the bed and kissed Dania. She opened her eyes. I smiled. 'It's almost dinner time, baby. We'd better have showers and get down there. The others will be waiting.'

Dania could see the change in me and smiled as well. 'Don't forget what we said. You must see someone. Please, Devlin, do it for me.'

We met the others in the wood-panelled dining room. Ancient studded-leather couches had been arranged in a semicircle around a huge slow-combustion heater. Toby was playing with the vents, trying to get it to flame up a bit. Dom was patiently telling him what he was doing wrong. Aud was shushing Dom. A bottle was open on the coffee table. I poured glasses for myself and Dania.

Tobe had been out for a run up the hill towards Hanging Rock. He thought Nundle was the best place on earth. I told him that Dania wanted us to come back here when we were old and had a fat little Jack Russell terrier that pissed on everyone's mailbox. Dania punched me playfully on the arm. Tobe thought that the two of us would look great sitting out on the veranda with our feet in slippies, enjoying our small bowls of soft food.

Talk of food woke up Dom and Aud and we moved a table close to the big heater. The pub had a long menu, but I had told them how good the roasted home-made sausages were so we all had those with peas and mashed potato and about a litre each of onion gravy.

'So Devvo, two years ago you used to eat and drink here with the loggers?' Tobe nodded towards a noisy group in the public bar in flannelette shirts, heavy boots, and tannin-stained jeans.

'I did. One evening they taught me how to play poker and I won all their money. Then after that I won every week. I never got paid by the bloke I worked for and that was really my only income.'

The others chuckled. Glancing through the open doorway, Dania said that she couldn't picture me drinking with those blokes and stealing their money. I couldn't either. I had wondered earlier whether anyone might remember me, but it was two years ago and clean-shaven and with shorter hair, I think I looked quite different.

We shared another couple of bottles of red. Dom wanted to ask the staff if we could play some quiet, acoustic music as he was keen to get in a bit of practice. Dania knew I was exhausted and said that she needed an early night. I squeezed her knee and she held my hand. Aud cottoned on and stood up, declaring that an early night would be wonderful. Dom stood up as well, music forgotten.

Tobe thought he might go and see whether any of the blokes in the public bar felt like a game of poker.

After breakfast on Saturday morning, we continued on to Armidale, sticking to the gravel roads up in the ranges. We met up with Scotty and Rick at a cafe in Armidale, early in the afternoon, and after a bit of a chat went out to the campus college where my brother was staying and got directions to the woolshed where the gig was to be held.

The woolshed was on a sheep station about forty kilometres out of Armidale. The organisers had pushed up three shed-sized piles of wood to make bonfires. It was mid-winter, and in the hills outside Armidale the temperature overnight was likely to be well below freezing. Might even be snow. Already there was a marked chill in the air and low, scudding, angry little whiffs of cloud blowing around the bare bluffs.

I rigged a small dome tent in the back of the ute and unrolled a thick foam mattress with sheets and a heavy duvet. I had thought that Dania would probably like some warmth and comfort. Tobe had borrowed a mate's high-tech expedition tent and sleeping bag. He'd be okay, and in any case probably not alone. Rick and Scotty had a flimsy looking thing and bugger all bedding. We thought they might be huddled around one of the fires later on, and especially if a bit of weather came in.

We met a couple of the students who were coordinating the ball and moved the gear into the shed. We were on first this time, with three other bands after us. The woolshed had rough showers for the shearers, which were not ideal for struggling into ball gowns and assembling complicated hair, but better than nothing. Aud emerged looking like an extravagant little Christmas decoration. Dania had an amazing fitted bronze-gold gown with ruffles all the way up one side.

Dom and I fetched drinks for everyone, then started to get the gear organised on stage and test the levels. It was another brilliant PA with a good mixing board, and even came with a geeky computer science student who knew how to get it all working. There was a barbie running and once we'd got ourselves organised for the gig we joined the girls and Tobe for a bit of dinner and a little wine. Everyone was excited. Tobe just loved the whole ridiculous feel of the thing. It was like a country race meeting from somewhere in the eighteen-hundreds.

By six it was dark and most people had arrived. The place was now roaring. The big fires had been lit with a mix of petrol and diesel and five-metre flames climbed out into the icy winter sky. Inside the shed the noise was building, and the organisers were getting twitchy. Pointed at the stage. We kissed Aud and Dania and left them with Tobe, then climbed up and got ourselves together.

We wanted to make this one as much about Australian pub rock as possible. Not to the exclusion of other stuff, but to focus at least on the covers and new music that had been playing around Sydney and Melbourne. We had decided to open with Australian Crawl's 'The Boys Light Up'. Rick counted us in and I leaned into the mic for the classic harmonica riff. Everyone knows it. Crisp drumming and rhythm guitar off the beat. The crowd were calling out to us. Hand claps above their heads. The bloke on the mixing board had the PA ramped up several notches above the Shakespeare. It was a big woolshed, but on that still winter night the sound must have bled out right across the district.

Scotty brought the crowd in with him. He could look a lot like James Reyne. Chicks fell like flies as he told them about his mountain home. It worked beautifully. The bass line wasn't difficult and I could look around at the crowd. Smiles everywhere. Drinks in hand. Mostly spirits. It was good to be playing before they got themselves too hammered. Aud was clapping and singing along and catching Dom's eye through his nest of drums. Dania was swaying with a glass of wine. A sophisticated lady. Tobe was dancing with a very tall, slim, good-looking girl. It had taken him all of one-and-a-half minutes. I nodded in his direction and Dania smiled, shaking her head.

Scotty was at the chorus now and the crowd were ready for it. The singing was deafening, then back to the harmonica and the next verse. The filthy lyrics. The rugby players were loving it and Scotty played to them. Dania was looking around her. A wry smile. We had hardly got going but it was clear this was going to be huge.

When we'd finished with the song, one of the organisers climbed up onto the little stage. He had been talking to my brother, but got the wrong end of it and thought we were all vet students. 'LET'S HEAR IT FOR SYDNEY UNI VET SCIENCE!' A few chicks cheered. The rugby players booed. Scotty looked put-out. A Sydney lawyer slumming it. Dom laughed. Budding astrophysicist and mathematical genius who didn't know one end of a sheep from another. And then the irony of my own conflict. At least easy-going Rick fitted the bill.

We moved on to Midnight Oil's 'Beds are Burning'. The classic guitar chords climbing up in three steps. One. Two. Three. Wait a beat. The crowd cottoned on. Repeat. One. Two. Three. Then the chugging rhythm guitar, down low and driving hard through the big PA with the bass and drums underneath it and Scotty doing the Garrett drunk-puppet dance. Feet anchored. Swaying. Arms everywhere. Everyone was still yelling. Mostly good, but a few shouts of 'fucken greenies'. I chuckled. I had warned Scotty.

After that, a whole lot of Angels, Hood Gurus, Mentals, Rose Tattoo. Even AC/DC. All the pub anthems. Finished up with Chisel's 'Flame Trees'. Drums and bass. Rick on electric piano again. Chicks swaying. Big blokes teary. Then with gear packed away, we went outside to stand around one of the big fires. Dom and I had swapped into our tuxes. It seemed a bit silly at this point, but the girls wanted us to. Pissed people were milling around us.

'Great fucken band, mate.' A big, red-faced rugby bloke in a torn, too-small dinner jacket.

'Ta.'

'So what's vet like?'

'It's great, mate. Love it.'

Dania elbowed me, giggling.

'Little brother wants to do it. Probably won't get in.'

'Tell him to work hard. Best time of his life. Thank you forever.'

'Cheers, mate.'

'No worries.'

He ambled off happily to another fire, probably to see if anyone wanted a fight.

Dania was looking a bit unsteady. 'I think I'm drunk.'

I hugged her. 'Good. You go off when you're drunk.'

She let that go. Might not have heard.

'What if I'm sick in the tent?'

'Then you'll have to go. Find another ute. Lots of them here to choose from.'

She let that go as well. Definitely slipping. But looked happy.

'Seeing you out here I can see why you feel funny in Sydney. These people sort of look a bit like you.'

The second band hadn't kicked in yet and I stared around at a whole paddock full of drunken rednecks with shirts untucked and imitation bowties hanging from torn collars, sunning themselves by enormous bonfires.

'You're kidding.'

'I don't mean literally. You don't really look like anyone I know. But the image you give off. It seems more comfortable here.'

I chuckled. 'I want to get inside that amazing dress. How do you undo all those ruffles?'

She giggled. 'You could just lift it up at the back.'

I coughed a mouthful of horrible, flat beer into the fire.

She smiled. 'I think we should go back to the car for a bit. It's nice and dark there.'

I stumbled after her. Obedient. Coloured party lights glinted across the bronze taffeta. Bottom taught against sheer fabric.

We went back to the party a bit later. The second band was winding down. It had sounded okay from the car park. Not as loud, but maybe someone had had a word to the bloke on the mixing board. We couldn't see Tobe anywhere. Shook his tent and called out, but he wasn't there. God knows. And Rick and Scotty's car had gone. They must have decided it was going to be too cold and bailed out back to town.

Dom and Aud had found some chairs and were sitting by a fire chatting to a tattered and earthy-looking group. Dom was plucking at his guitar. Laughing easily. Aud was telling them a story. She looked fantastic. We sat down.

Dom handed me the guitar. 'Mate, sing us 'American Pie'.'

'I think I might be too pissed, Dom. Can't really play when I'm pissed.'

Dom looked around at the group. 'I reckon collective powers of discernment are low, mate. You'll be right.'

I played the song. Dom helped sing it. We cut out a couple of verses, just so we wouldn't still be going when the sun came up. People smiled. I started playing a bit of blues. Dania had her hand on my knee. Dom handed me a joint. Dania was used to it now. I took it and smoked while I played. I gave Dom back the guitar and got the mandolin from the woolshed, and we messed around for what seemed like hours. The big fire went down and we drew in closer. The cars were all frosted up and the ground hard and icy. It was beautiful by the fire. Dania leaned into me.

When I felt her slipping we called it a night. Locked up the gear and went back to the tent. It was cold at first, but our bedding was warm and we went to sleep to the sound of a wild party in a big open paddock.

It was still going at sunrise.

We drove home to Sydney late Sunday morning. Everyone was quiet and pretty hung-over. Said a quick hello to Mum on the way through. I was tired, and found the driving difficult, so Tobe took over for a while and I snuggled up to Dania on the big bench seat and closed my eyes.

We dropped Tobe off in Paddo and went back to Balmain. Aud and Dom were already there. We had showers, then took a plate of toast to bed. Exhausted.

'Honey?'

'Yeah, Danny?'

'That was such a lovely weekend. I'll never forget it.'

I hugged her and snuffled into her hair. It still smelt faintly of smoke. 'Even with the bullshit in Nundle?'

'I don't care about that.'

I had been thinking about Nundle during the drive. Not about the tears and anxiety. I felt that something had drawn me back there—then reached out to me in the evening when I woke in that cold dark room. There had even been a sound, or a call. A bird, or was it two birds? Maybe crows, but I couldn't now be sure. I held Dania hard against me and waited for the memory to die again. Willed it to die, and to disappear. Disappear completely. I thought about my story, as I always did when I felt like this, and mumbled to Dania that I had put another two chapters in her bag. They were big chapters. A lot of pages. The story had flowed out of me like water. And as things turned out, there was some violence.

But she was already asleep.

Dear Dania,

I have written out both Saturday and Sunday.

Once you get into it a bit you'll see why the two go together.

Things start to get a bit gnarly here.

I hope you can get through it okay . . .

Love, Devlin xxx

Saturday

Ben was woken by a rough shake and a blinding light of a police torch.

'Get up, gorgeous. Pigs to shoot'. . . .

. . . Ben was woken by a rough shake and the blinding light of a police torch.

'Get up, gorgeous. Pigs to shoot.'

'Fuck.'

'Brekky in the car. All set to go. Put your panties on and we'll hit the road.'

'Fuck.'

'Stop saying that. Sound like a Queenslander.'

'Okay. I'm getting up. Have you got coffee?'

'Yep, just brewed in Chloe's little machine. Goes bitter in ten minutes, so you better move.'

'How long have you been here?'

'Mate, I live twenty metres away in a limitless arid wilderness. "Here" is a relative term. I've been here all night.'

Ben pondered that as he slid out of bed and pulled on his jeans and shirt. 'Okay, my gear's by the door.'

'No, mate, it's in the car. Just you we need. Let's go.'

'Fuck.'

'If you say that again, I'll have to take you in. We can't have tourists impersonating Queenslanders wandering about and upsetting the locals.'

It was still dark as they pulled away from the pub and back up the road that Ben had been travelling on when he had crashed his bike.

'So we're not taking the blue-and-white out shooting, then?'

'No, it's the mighty WB's turn today. The blue-and-white doesn't enjoy paddock-bashing and my boss is not a man to take the wanton abuse of state property lightly.'

'Does anyone in this town not own a ute?'

'Why would you not own a ute?'

As they followed the river northeast through the saltbush lowlands, the sun began to move above the horizon. Duncan pulled down the shade. 'I thought we'd suffer a bit once dawn came.'

Ben squinted against the sudden glare. 'It's going to be blinding in a few minutes.'

'We'll pull off on the stock route up the road a bit and sight in the rifles. Better to do it here than the escarpment where the sound echoes all over the place. Pigs aren't stupid.'

Duncan eased the car off into a gravel lay-by and backed it up so that the tailgate was facing out into the scrub. 'Got a few posts to set up. I want to test that new gun and make sure the other's scope hasn't moved at all. You might have done something a bit more professional, but this should be okay.'

'No worries. I'll put up the posts while you get organised. What range do you want to use?'

'Put one at seventy-five metres, another at a hundred, then one-fifty and two hundred metres. I can't hit the side of a shed at more than two hundred metres, so that'll do. Both scopes should be sighted for a hundred.'

Ben took the steel posts and dolly off the back of the ute and started pacing. The ground was lightly frosted after the cold, clear night with thin wisps of blue mist clinging precariously to the sandy channels.

Back at the car and Duncan had arranged a bag of fertiliser and the ute's tarpaulin into a stable rest. 'Start with the Sako. You might as well shoot, since you'll be using it.'

'No worries.' Ben extracted the lovely Finnish rifle from its case and lay on the canvass with the stock wedged into the fertiliser bag, quietly feeling the weight and balance of the gun and its fit against his shoulder.

'It's not loaded.'

'I know it's not loaded, Dunc, I'm just getting to know it a bit. There's a way to do this that can't be hurried.'

'Mate, here's the bullets. Stop rooting the thing and see how it shoots.'

'Okay, okay.'

Ben propped himself on one arm and loaded the rifle, inspecting each shell as it went into the magazine. He then laid the gun carefully back on its rest and positioned himself next to it.

Duncan seemed amused by the performance. 'So, Ben, out of interest, how does a proper marksman go about aiming a gun?'

Ben chuckled. 'I'm not a marksman. I'm just a target shooter and failed roo shooter. But what I do is to stare down through the scope straight at the bull.' Ben settled in again against the bag of fertiliser. 'Don't be distracted by the crosshairs. Just stare at the bull—hard enough that you feel you can reach out and touch it. It's right in front of you and there's thin bit of string connecting you to it. Breathe in deep, then let half of it out as you bring the crosshairs up into place. Never break that line of sight, though, straight on the bull. You know almost subconsciously when the crosshairs are in place, but you never stop to look at them. Keep your focus on the bull. Then squeeze the trigger, reaching forward with your mind to touch the bull.'

The shot startled Duncan, who had thought that Ben was still just messing around. Before he could recover, he heard the bolt work and within a second another shot. And then a third. Then silence.

'At this range, it's pulling about one-and-a-half centimetres to the left. And a touch high.' Ben said, without looking up from the scope.

Duncan reached into the cab to retrieve the binoculars. He managed to locate the one-hundred-metre target and could see what looked like one large ragged hole to the left and a little bit above the bull.

Ben sat up. Stretched. 'It's a good gun, Dunc. That's a nice tight group for factory ammo.'

Duncan's eyes were still pressed against the binoculars. 'Mate, that's not a group. That's three bullets on top of each other.'

'No, if you went up to the target you'd see where the three bullets have torn the cardboard. But it is a good group to start with. The gun feels fantastic.'

Having adjusted the scope and repeated the process, Ben moved to the remaining targets to work out the trajectory of the factory ammunition. He then went through the same for the Remington. 'Dunc, this 700 has a beautiful action but it's not as close as the Sako. Not with this ammo, anyway. Sometimes you have to play with the loads a bit. Seems like some receivers cope better with more or less grains. And different barrels like different projectiles.'

Duncan was feeling uneasy, but was unsure why. 'Good enough for me. Only .243s. Can't take any heroic long shots at big, tough pigs.'

'True. They should be fine though, with hollow points. I'd go for heart shots really, as long as the front leg's not in the way.'

'I just aim for the pig.'

Ben chuckled. 'Okay.'

They unloaded, then swapped to double-check that the rifles were safe before returning them to their cases and resuming the journey. The sun was well above the road now, and slightly to the north, which made driving easier.

Duncan yawned, rubbing his face to clear the fatigue. 'Any of Chlo's coffee left?'

'Is this Chloe's coffee? I thought you just made it with her machine?'

'Mate, I can't drive that faggoty little Italian thing. Just drink instant.'

'So Chloe was up early, too?'

'Reluctantly. Sort of. Whinging a bit. Still in her jarmies. We thought you weren't old enough to see that.'

'Okay.'

'Didn't have her teeth in.'

'Okay.'

'And she's got these little pink pony slippers. You know, like a horse's head with a nose where the big toe goes?'

'Fuck off.'

'Steady on. Impressive shooting back there.'

'Who do you usually shoot with?'

'Generally, just yobbos from the pub. I ask around Friday night and try to pick ones who aren't getting too wasted. Locked a bloke up once, so he'd be in good shape the next day. Wasn't happy at the time. Had to cuff him to the bed. Thanked me in the morning.' Duncan looked thoughtful, then added, 'Hard to find an Australian bloke who'll thank you in the morning. No sensitivity.'

Ben shuddered, but let it go. Thought about the Sako. A beautiful gun. Stock from the factory, but not your usual factory. Scandinavians are a bit passionate about their hunting rifles.

A small squeak, but loud in the ute's cabin. Duncan looked away. 'Sorry mate, strong coffee always does that.'

'Fuck.' Ben wound the window down and leaned out as far as the belt would allow.

Duncan was unperturbed. 'If you can hear with your head out the window, that stuff about staring at the bull. Is that what all proper shooters do?'

Ben tried to talk with wind whistling around his head, but it wasn't working and the air in the cabin seemed to have cleared a little. 'Can I ride the rest of the way in the back?'

'Not legal. Won't do it again. Hear my question?'

'Yeah. But I don't know what most people do. To tell you the truth I think I got that from some bullshit Wilbur Smith book. Or maybe Tom Clancy.' Ben was tempted to say *Poldark*, just to test the waters, but wasn't quite brave enough. 'It works for me, though. It's easy otherwise to focus on the crosshairs and then try to somehow juggle those onto the target. And, you know, the gun's moving a bit, even on a rest, and the target can be several hundred metres away, and it all falls apart. You end up squeezing the trigger when you get sick of juggling and just sort of hope the gun's in the right place. But if you concentrate only on the target and let the crosshairs just move up between it and your eye, it's much easier. Well, I think so.'

'Makes sense. Actually, I think I probably do what you're saying I shouldn't. Look really hard at the crosshairs, then try to find the pig.'

'You don't really just shoot at the whole pig, though, do you?'

'No, mate. Being an idiot. I don't like wounding anything. Really hate it. No, I go for the heart. Head with roos. That's back home. Queensland. We don't shoot roos out here. They're mostly the big reds and their numbers don't seem to build up like the eastern greys.'

'Roos are beautiful animals. I really hated shooting them, but we used to see mobs of maybe five hundred or more greys in one paddock and nothing else was keeping them down. I don't really like shooting pigs, either, but it's true they bugger up the environment. I used to shoot a lot of foxes as a kid. That's a good way to get some long-range practice.'

'Yeah, Dad used to have a thing about foxes. But wouldn't let me near a gun till I was seventeen. Reckoned I'd shoot the house. Or one of his prize fucken horses. Older brother had a gun as soon as he could walk.'

Ben sensed this might be a difficult topic and turned back to the wakening bush. The frost remained in small protected pools of shade, but the exposed red dust and rocks now had a glow like fresh-baked terracotta.

Within an hour they had arrived at the campsite. It lay at the foot of the ancient escarpment and was accessed by a small dirt road that led off the main Barker-Warkon highway.

The rock itself was sandstone that had been laid down in the Devonian, almost four-hundred million years ago, as tiny grains of quartz washed away from the granite ranges of eastern Gondwanaland—sand that held in each perfect crystal a memory of that time when life on earth was born, and magic was everywhere.

Vascular plants had appeared and had spread across the empty ground, with vast forests eventually covering both Gondwana and its smaller northern neighbours, Siberia and Euro-America. Enormous primitive scorpions, and other arthropods, had made the transition to land, but it was in the world's primordial oceans that life first peaked. This was the earth's 'age of fishes'. Trilobites, the mollusc-like brachiopods, and the great coral reefs, were common, as were the clumsy bony-plated placoderms and the tentative, primitive sharks of an even more distant time. Pressure to survive in this highly-charged marine environment had forced some fish up into tidal swampy wetlands where they began to hop or crawl between ponds on primitive fin-like legs. In this period, oxygen in the air was much lower than it is today, but as the Devonian gave way to the utopian Carboniferous, breathable oxygen soared and life on land exploded.

And magic was everywhere.

The Carboniferous marked the end of the overarching Paleozoic, and the commencement of the Mesozoic and later Cenozoic periods, when life evolved through a cascade of increasingly complex orders and the previously limitless geological time became compressed into units that could be conceived by living creatures. Most significant of these were the *Homo sapiens* and their now-extinct cousins who had left the ancestral home of Africa in successive waves and, with the exception of the frozen wasteland of Antarctica, colonised and subsequently dominated all of the earth's rapidly changing continents.

The first of the new humans to arrive in Australia were dark skinned, and the direct forefathers of today's aboriginal peoples. No-one knows exactly where they came from, although it may have been across Asia and over a land-bridge from what is now Papua New Guinea, or by boats across the Timor Sea. By human standards, they are an ancient people and their progenitors probably among the first to have left Africa.

And somewhere between forty and, perhaps, seventy-five-thousand years ago, these people discovered the escarpment. Its elevation above the flat and arid plains gave a point from which to view the harsh new land, and its porous rock provided sweet, clear water in times of drought, when the river below had dwindled to muddy holes and the waters from the great artesian basin had receded. But it was something else that made the escarpment so special to these people and their descendants. There was magic here. The ancient magic that had been breathed into the tiny souls of a trillion primitive life forms and then trapped in the mountain's sands like the pages of a scrapbook—the magic that now compressed the silence around the bare rocks and gullies so that the air was like a drum, and lay dreaming in the reflective sediment of small, green, shaded pools.

'Old people reckon that Baiame came through here. Important place on one of the local songlines.' Duncan's broad back was advancing with surprising speed along a narrow path. 'You know, mythical things that link places where heroes from creation touched the earth. Some stretch right across the country. Connect a whole lot of different tribes and languages. Baiame himself was the Sky Father, or creator. Appears all over Australia. Sometimes different names, or names that sound a bit different.'

The sandy scrub of the lowlands and foothills had given way to red gravel, with boulders interspersed. Duncan had stressed to Ben the importance of staying only on the track. Ostensibly, this was to preserve the fragile environment, but it also seemed to underscore an unspoken imperative that they interact as little as possible with the mountain.

'Tribes used to gather here in the old days. Before we buggered it all up for them. Stone people from the hills around here, as well as the river people. Separate tribes, apparently.' Duncan stepped carefully around a fallen boulder. 'Lot of sacred sites. You know, quarries for tools, ceremonial sites, burial sites, camp sites, scarred trees and shelters where they put their paintings. But a lot of the old history has been lost. Went right back to the time when our own ancestors were running round the Baltic with the Neanderthals. This is one of the oldest cultures in the world.'

'Can we see any of this stuff?'

'Mate, I don't go looking for it, to be honest. I reckon it doesn't belong to us. More people know about it, the more likely some idiot will come up here with a spray can. I've been through the place quite a few times after pigs and have stumbled on a fair bit. Pigs shouldn't be up here snuffling around in those places. Thought I'd killed most of them off, but those blokes the other week reckon they saw some more and I wouldn't mind putting your sniping skills to a bit of good use.'

'Happy to give it a go. I know what you meant the other night about the weird feeling here. It's like that scene in *Picnic at Hanging Rock*. You know, where the fat chick, Edith, wakes up and sees the others floating off through the gap in rocks?' Ben tried a wavering falsetto. 'Miranda! Miranda! Come back, all of you! Don't go up there. Come back!'

Duncan chuckled. 'Great movie. And you're right, that's the feel of this place. Strange thing is that after the aborigines got booted around the district and their tribes broke down, they started getting leery of it. Wouldn't come up here. Too scared of something. It's changing now, apparently. Some of them are coming back and a few barriers been put up around some of the paintings. Like the place has forgiven them. But I don't know, maybe too much has been lost.'

The trail was winding steadily through a series of switchbacks towards the top of the escarpment's first major ledge. The drop down was in places precipitous, with little substantial vegetation to grasp or break a fall. The mountain appeared in parts as though made from enormous sandstone boulders. It was in reality a continuous structure, but erosion from wind and water had left innumerable cracks and fissures that had widened in places to give the appearance of a disintegrating dry-stone wall.

Duncan nodded towards a shadowed space near the base of some rock at the edge of the trail. 'Snakes should be in bed this time of year, but need to be a bit careful. Browns like these holes.'

The bimble and red box of the lowlands and open plains had given way first to stately bloodwoods, with their long finger-like leaves, and then to the scrappy cypress pine and mallee. Mulga were interspersed throughout the escarpment, but clustered more tightly along a hidden network of ephemeral waterways. On top of the ledge, where grazing had exacerbated the erosion caused by wind and water, the small, tough, woody shrubs began to dominate—principally turpentine, with local stands of budda, emu bush and hop bush. Red rock scree lay thick in pools between dislodged boulders.

From this height, the seemingly endless plains faded to a pale blue haze on the horizon and the course of the big river could be seen in the distance, picking its thin and torturous path through the scars of the now-dry river valley. In flood, it would be astonishing, Ben thought. The whole valley would be one single river, with the surrounding country turned to wetlands and endless wildflowers. It was hard to know how accessible this area would be with the gravel roads turned to red mud, but if you could get in by car or bike then the view from up here would be brilliant.

Duncan thought it was probably time for a break. Sitting on some smooth rocks, he brought out sandwiches from a pink plastic lunchbox, carefully wrapped first in greaseproof paper and then in foil. 'Got tuna and ham here, I think. Bit of mayo, looks like. Leaf of some sort. Then another lot for later that's mostly recycled chicken parmigiana.'

'You made chicken parmigiana sandwiches?'

'Mate, I don't make food. This lot came blessed with the lovingkindness of little Chlo.'

Ben seemed happy to let the incongruous Biblical association pass. 'Chloe made us lunch? Even though we're just wandering around out here in the bush while she tries to run the pub on her own?'

'She's a gem. A princess among publicanesses. And she always makes my lunches. In return, I throw the drunken yobbos out of her pub.' Duncan looked thoughtful. 'I hope she'll be okay with Byron tonight. Refuses to leave his dog behind. Last time the fucken thing wouldn't let anyone in the place.'

'Reminds me, what did you tell Smutty? When you came back, you were best buddies. And he even said "please" when he asked for his drink.'

Duncan chuckled. 'No fucken way Smutty would have said "please". And I can see you're smiling. But I did have a bit of a chat with him.'

'Why do you bother? Couldn't you just kick the shit out of him and shut the door?'

Duncan looked pained. 'Mate, need to understand that people can have different values out here. True, Smutty is a mean prick who feels bad about his stumpy little legs. But he's shit-hot with horses, and you can't run these places without horses. Or the blokes or women who can break them in and train them. Plenty of riders, but not many horsemen. Or women. Never have been, even in the old days when everyone was riding everywhere. And Smutty's not vicious when he's dealing with horses. See a different side to him. Doesn't speak at all, really. Just touches them and somehow gets them to do things. He's worth more to the blokes who run these stations than probably the rest of that lot in the pub put together. Can't be too hard on a bloke like that. A bit special. Needs special treatment.'

'So what did you tell him?'

Duncan sighed. 'Told him you were Chloe's cousin and running away from some problem with a pretty boy in your home town. Sad story. Tried to gut yourself, but too soft to finish the job. Chlo wanted to give you a break. Everyone loves Chlo.'

Ben looked horrified. 'You told him that? So now, that's what all those blokes will think?'

'Mate, it's better than them thinking you're moving in on Chlo. That would be really bad. I can only throw one out at a time. Maybe two. Perhaps three little ones. Anyway, brought out the soft side of Smutty. Think he probably likes blokes, too, to be honest.'

'I don't like blokes.'

'Okay.'

'I'm serious.'

'Okay.'

'Fuck.'

'Don't start that Queenslander thing again. Neck's way too not-red. But probably good not to go to the little room same time as Smutty. Just, you know, safe side.'

'Fuck.'

Duncan decided that they'd better start moving again. His plan was to continue up to the top of the second ledge, then follow the crest around to the eastern side of the escarpment. 'It's a fair way, but once you're up on top it levels out and the walking is a lot easier. Should get there by about midday, I reckon. Then wander down to the bottom and follow the track around the base of the rock back to the cars. Even if we run out of the light, the last bit is easy to follow.'

'Where did those blokes see the pigs?'

'All along the track running down from the top. The country's a bit softer at that end and there's a bit more standing water. I reckon they're probably moving from the top to the bottom and back each day. Might see them from this next ledge onwards so better keep the talking down. Hard to follow pigs on foot once they've had a fright.'

'Fair enough. Have you had any problems with them? I mean, having a go at you?'

'Not here. At home, I have. One bailed me up on top of the ute. I was standing on the roof and had to keep kicking it off with my boot. Wasn't even a big pig. Just some angry little turd that didn't want to get shot at.' Duncan chuckled. 'Little Smutty of a pig, come to think of it.'

Ben smiled. 'I heard of a sow chasing a bloke I knew once. But you never know with some of these stories.'

'Well, don't shoot at a sow with piglets and miss. Probably would have a go at you. Can't count on me saving the day.'

They moved off in silence, Duncan easily negotiating the endless rocks and ledges and pausing every now and then to allow Ben to catch up. As he had thought, it was close to midday when they reached the northern tip of the escarpment and the start of the downward path. There had been no sightings of pigs, although clear evidence of their rooting around in the low scrub. They had also noticed a lot of droppings, and Duncan was beginning to view the trip as a first pass with a need to return for several more circuits to shoot out the herd, or at least scare it back down onto the plains.

But then they saw the bikes.

In fact, they saw the glint of midday sun off something metallic in a small clearing at the end of a long but minor access track that ran from the highway back towards Barker on the eastern side of the escarpment. Duncan was concerned that rifle fire might upset any hikers who had ventured into the area from this side. It would mean a bit of messing around, but they might need to try and locate those hikers and let them know that they were shooting feral pigs, and that care would be taken.

Ben raised his rifle, so as to see the clearing through its scope. With magnification, the bikes themselves were apparent. There also seemed to be a small van of some sort. 'Dunc, you'd better have a look.'

Duncan was still squinting at the clearing and swearing quietly under his breath at the thought of what might be a thwarted day's shooting. But when he raised his own rifle and looked through its scope, he could see what Ben meant. Even from this distance the chrome on the bikes was distinctive, and clearly the cause of the reflective glint that they had seen.

These were not trail bikes, or even touring road bikes, they were Harleys. Bikers' bikes.

'What are bikers doing out here?' asked Ben, the new Sako still focussed on the clearing.

'Mate, whatever bikers are doing anywhere isn't generally good works for the community.'

'I really meant the bikes themselves. How would you get those fat pigs over gravel roads without scratching them up?'

'I don't know what it's about. Gangs from Sydney been pushing a bit of dope out into the bush lately. Drug squad boys from Sydney have been giving us little talks about it. Testing the market a bit, they reckon. Maybe moving surplus shit. Last thing the poor bastards hanging on at the edge of these places need.' Duncan lowered the gun and stepped back from the ledge, then sat down on some low rocks.

Ben was excited. 'What do you want to do about it? Head back down to the car and call it in?'

'Better have a good look first. We've got the scopes and can stay out of sight. Just be careful with any reflection off the lens. Stick your hand above it if you can. And cover up the scope while we're walking. Don't want to stir those vicious pricks up. Whole different animal to your harmless drunken cowboy. Basically nothing to lose.'

Ben nodded, pointing down towards the base of the escarpment. 'If we follow this path to the last ledge we'll be out of view. It goes behind that ridge, and the sound won't travel either.'

Duncan agreed and they moved off carefully. Duncan was wearing heavy hiking boots but walked almost soundlessly. Ben found the rapid downhill passage easy at first, but soon struggled to keep up without risking slipping and possibly alerting the bikers below with a small avalanche of rolling rock. In less than half an hour they had circled back to the lowest of the remaining ledges, no more than a hundred metres from the clearing.

Duncan motioned Ben down behind the rock ledge and they both paused to catch their breath.

'I'm going to have a quick look. Just stay down here out of sight for a second.'

'Okay, Dunc. No worries.' Without consciously thinking about it, Ben reached into his pack for the first of the pre-loaded five-shot magazines and slotted it into the Sako.

Duncan had crawled forward over the ledge and was now concealed behind some turpentine bushes and staring through the rifle scope. After a few minutes, he crawled back down.

'Fuck fuck fuck.' Duncan's face was pale.

'What's going on there? Are they making a sale?'

'No, mate. Worse than anything you could imagine. Don't know what they were doing there to start with. Maybe it was a sale. But they've got hold of a couple of campers. Looks like they were staying in that white van we saw. Bit of a table set up outside, and an esky. Bloke's on the ground. Might even be dead. There's blood all over the place. Chick has no pants on. Tied to one of the bikes.'

'Jesus, you're not kidding?'

'No, Ben, I'm absolutely not kidding.'

'How many are there? What are they all doing?'

'I counted four of them. I think that's it. It's a pretty open area. One's having a go at the chick, or about to, and the others are lounging about. One's sitting on his bike. Might be asleep. Two shotties that I can see. One's leaning against a stump and the other's next to the bloke with the chick. They're all probably pissed and stoned. Almost guarantee, it really.' It was a torrent of words spoken through the fingers across his face.

Ben could see where it was going. 'You can't walk in and arrest them. You couldn't say what they'd do if they're pissed and stoned. And they're vicious pricks, anyway, as you said yourself. Maybe if we had a car we could do it, but even so you'd probably get shot at.'

'Got no choice, mate. Can't leave that chick there like that. And the bloke on the ground might not be dead, but the poor bastard will be when they've finished. No way they're going to leave witnesses. Not to that sort of shit.'

'Dunc, you can't walk down there. Seriously, mate, they'll kill you. You won't achieve anything, because then they'll just kill the other two anyway and piss off.'

'Don't have a lot of options. There's a chance, and sometimes you just have to take that chance. With your sharp-shooting to cover me I might get away with it.'

'I can't let you do it, Dunc. Think of Chloe. She wouldn't get over it.'

Duncan began to look less decisive. Ben went on, quietly. 'Look, mate, there's another way. We're sitting up here with two high-end .243s loaded for pigs.'

Duncan could see what Ben was going to suggest. 'I can't do that. Thought about it while I was checking them out. Be easy enough, but can't do it. Doubt you could either mate. Cold-blooded killing. Not many blokes could do that to anyone, even to those scum. Sounds good but this is reality.'

'Well, I guess we don't have much choice, then. You're going to have to go down there. But do it with a gun pointed at them. I'll be up here with the Sako but if anything happens, you can't rely on me to knock them all out. They'll be running around and might be shooting those shotguns. There could be other guns, too.'

Duncan's head fell back into his hands. Knuckles white. Bush noises surrounded them. A small flock of galahs peeled past in a fluid cloud of high-pitched chatter.

'Have to work this through a bit, Ben. If they were just some random sickos then that would be one thing, but the gangs are vindictive. It's their creed.' Ben leaned forward to catch Duncan's voice, muffled again through his fingers. 'Thing is, mate, they've got informers in the Sydney police. Well known. People they've threatened or blackmailed. Maybe just paid. They'd tell the gangs that another bloke was involved and even if your name is suppressed somehow, it won't be too hard to find out who you are.'

Duncan looked up. Eye contact now. 'They'll come after you, Ben. And your family. Seriously, these bastards won't just stop at you. I might be okay. Just a cop doing his job. They probably don't want to cross that line. But you and your family would be fucked. Seriously, they'd find you and kill you. You're not going to get your whole family in witness protection and whoever's left they'll go for.'

'What are you really saying, Dunc?'

'Mate, what I'm saying is that if you give me some cover and it all goes to shit, then our lives change. Completely change.'

'Yeah, well, if we're going to do this then we'd better get into it. That poor chick is still down there.'

Duncan looked at him. 'A commitment, mate. Life changing. You understand that?'

'Doing nothing would be, too, Duncan. Neither of us could do nothing. We've got no choice. Really, there's no choice.'

Duncan looked around at the escarpment. 'Last minutes as normal people, mate.'

'Just do it, Duncan. No time now.'

'Okay. You're loaded. Good. Get that second magazine ready, too. I'm going to duck down the hill on this side of the ridge, then go across to that big tree. Be about twenty metres away there. Hopefully surprise them a bit. Trouble is, I'm easy to shoot.'

'You are, Dunc. Very. A target even you would have no trouble hitting.'

Duncan chuckled. Ben added, 'I'll have the group in my scope the whole time. I'll try and see who you're going to find it hardest to get a line on and focus on them.'

'Thanks, mate. Be careful. If I point to you and bring my hand down like this, just fire one into the tree above their heads. Let them know you're there.' Duncan paused. 'And seriously, if I go down and they look like they'll get the upper hand, don't fuck around up here. Bolt back over the hill and take the car into town. Barker, I mean. Cop shop there.' Duncan threw him the keys. 'They won't know the terrain. Probably not fit. Hopefully still pissed or stoned or both. You should be okay, but just get out of here quickly.'

Duncan didn't wait for a response as he began moving as quickly and quietly as possible down the last part of the trail.

Ben watched him briefly, then eased himself over the ledge and into a prone firing position. He was aware of the danger, but equally aware of an intense thrumming silence pressing in around him through the tiny detail of branches and insects. A thin spider's web. The hard red rocks. There was too much clarity. And in the background, something like tinnitus.

He felt completely calm and detached as he brought the rifle up to his shoulder and stared down through the scope. He could see the scene below clearly and it was just as Duncan had described. The woman was straining against the bike and away from one of the bikers, who was undoing his belt and laughing. A shotgun was lying in some leaves nearby. Ben panned the rifle slowly across the group. Another biker was resting on his bike, head cradled on his arms, while the third was seated on a log in the shade at the edge of the clearing. The fourth biker seemed to be pissing into the dust on the opposite side of the clearing, his back to the group.

Ben registered movement to the right and in the foreground, and watched through the scope as Duncan crept forward, in a crouch, from the track to the big bloodwood, just in front of the clearing. Ben chuckled to himself at the sight of such a big bloke trying to sneak along. *What we really needed here is little Smutty*, he mused, still smiling incongruously through the rifle scope. It didn't occur to him that he should be nervous, or filled with dread. He felt nothing other than the warm sun on his back and the beautiful thrumming of the bush all around him.

Duncan looked up towards him. Gave a guarded signal. He then sprang up to full height and walked quickly towards the gathering with his rifle raised but looking like a toy against an enormous shoulder.

'I'm a cop! Just stay still! Don't touch those fucken guns!' Duncan knew he was speaking too loud and too fast. Adrenalin. He tried to calm himself. 'I'm a cop, okay. I'm a cop from the town back down the road. Don't want to fuck with a cop. Whole lot of them come after you. Just stay still for a minute. Tell you what's going to happen.'

Duncan found it difficult not to be distracted by the woman, who was now screaming hysterically in a language that might have been German, or something Scandinavian.

The biker who had been about to rape her stood still, but straightened up and motioned with his head towards the shotgun lying near his feet. The biker sitting on the log to the left nodded almost imperceptibly and motioned to the second shotgun leaned against the nearby stump.

Duncan saw it. 'Don't be fucken stupid, mate. This thing is loaded with hollow points. Shooting pigs. They'll knock a hole in you the size of a football.' Duncan nodded towards the escarpment. 'Mate's up there on the ridge with another gun. He's a fucken pro roo shooter and very pissed off about this chick. Covering those two shotties. One of you might get close, or even get a shot off, but you won't fucken live.'

Duncan moved closer, instinctively turning side-on to the group to minimise the target offered by his huge body. 'No-one has to get hurt here. You'll go down for attempted rape, and maybe bashing that bloke, but that's not too bad. Be out again in a few years. Don't blow it by doing anything stupid.'

'You got some balls, big fella.' It was the one who had been about to rape the woman. Calm. A lazy voice. One leg cocked. 'There's no-one for a few hundred miles, and you come in here alone and threaten a whole group of us bad men. You reckon you can take out four of us with a bolt action rifle? I doubt it, mate. That friend of yours has to be a hundred yards back, if he exists at all. And there's a few logs and things here for us to hide behind.'

He started to move slowly away from the other group, making it harder for Duncan to cover them all and Duncan began to realise that the man was probably not as drunk or stoned as they had hoped.

The biker continued. Tall. Deep voice. An easy drawl. 'Mate, the best way for this to end is for you to fuck off slowly back into those hills. We've only got shotties, so you'll be pretty safe. I might even let you go without any aggro, in appreciation of the fact that you've had a bit of a go. We like blokes who'll have a go. Admire it. That's what we're about, really. That's what the patch means, just having a go. Fuck everyone else.'

Duncan could sense that he was losing ground. The tall biker seemed to be the leader, probably trying to distract Duncan while his mates thought about how to get to the shotguns. The biker kept talking. 'I can see you're getting a bit flighty now, mate, and that's a good thing because you need to understand that if you don't back slowly into the bush and piss off up the hill then you're going to get hurt. You don't have much time left. Just back out slowly till you think it's okay, then run into those rocks. You'll be right. We'll get on our way and your cop mates can have a go at finding us. No-one gets hurt.'

The voice was almost hypnotic. To lead a group of bikers you needed to be tough and decisive, but also smart. And manipulative. This bloke was used to talking and Duncan knew he had to try and regain ground. Assert enough authority for the rest of the group to question their leader.

'Okay, mate, you've had your say. Now move back towards the others.' He nodded at the barrel. 'You're right, this is a bolt action rifle. But I can work the bolt quick enough to put three rounds in you and your mates. And in that time, the bloke on the hill will have taken out anyone still standing. I've told you these are hollow points. You know what that means. Shoulder wound and your arm will be hanging on by fucken skin. Bleed to death before I can help you. Gut wound, you'll be holding the shreds of your liver in with two hands. Alternative's a bit of time for attempted rape and battery, or a bit less for watching and doing nothing. Fuck all. Just have to stay calm and keep away from those shotties.'

This approach would probably have worked. The bikers were at least partly stoned or drunk and must have known it. But then the screaming, which had subsided to mumbled sobs, recommenced and as Duncan's eyes went involuntarily to the woman the man in front of him lunged for the shotgun.

Simultaneously, a rifle shot rang out from the ledge and a wound flowered on the back of the man's jacket. He collapsed soundlessly, then crawled for a second or two in the dust, an already-dead hand opening and closing as it sought out the shotgun. Duncan kicked the gun away and looked across to the group, and as he was doing so the bike behind the woman roared into life as the man who had been sleeping on it leaned close to the tank in an attempt to bolt from the clearing. Duncan followed the bike with his rifle instinctively, while trying not to lose his focus on the man still seated on the log and on the fourth biker who had been returning from the bush on the far side of the clearing.

A second shot rang out and the tank exploded in flames. There was again a moment of silence, before the man on the log moved for the second shotgun. Duncan fired this time without thinking, hitting the man in the hip. He reloaded immediately, and shot him again through the chest as he began to stand. The man returning to the clearing had lowered himself into a crouch and was moving sideways towards another bloodwood when a further shot rang out from the hill and the back of his head flew off in an awful shower of red.

Duncan moved quickly to the nearest shotgun and scooped it up with his left hand. He turned towards the hill where Ben lay and tried to motion 'no' to him with his head, but even as he was doing that another shot was fired from the escarpment. Duncan looked down at the wounded man beside him and saw that most of his face was now gone.

Duncan gazed in horror at the scene around him. The clearing was silent. There was no movement on the hill. The woman had stopped screaming with the first of the shots, but now began to cry softly, saying something again and again in a language that Duncan couldn't understand. He dropped the two guns and sank to his knees, burying his head in his hands.

The woman's crying continued unheeded and then, for the first time, Duncan noticed a sound from the man who was presumably her husband or partner. He had been too preoccupied with the bikers to pay the man any attention as he entered the clearing and had thought he was probably dead. Duncan leaped up and went to the man, who motioned weakly with one hand towards his wife. Duncan left him again and moved over to the woman. She had been tied down to the bike's frame. Her hiking shorts and underwear had been cut away and there was a small cut on her leg where the knife had nicked her. He freed here and she ran immediately to the man on the ground and collapsed against him. The two consoled each other, sobbing.

Duncan stood still and again surveyed the scene in horror, then turned slowly and looked up towards the hill where Ben lay concealed.

Ben had heard the woman scream and had seen the man lunge for the shotgun. He had been panning his rifle slowly between this man and the one seated closest to Duncan, who seemed the most interested in the second shotgun. He couldn't hear what the standing man and Duncan had been saying, but could see that Duncan had begun to look less confident. Ben gasped when the man lunged, as he had been focussed at that instant on the other, but with the smoothness acquired from shooting a thousand kangaroos at night, he moved the gun to his right and squeezed off a round. He didn't for a second look at the crosshairs, but found the man in the field of view and stared hard at him as the man dived diagonally down and to his left. And the gun fired almost of its own accord.

Ben was still calm and unmoved as he reloaded and swung the rifle back to the group. The man who had been sleeping on his bike was now quietly and surreptitiously lifting the stand, switching on the controls and easing the matt-black skull-cap helmet onto his head. At that moment the bike roared and the man crouched low to make his exit. Light flashed from the moving tank as Ben changed his plan, then watched through the rifle scope as the bike exploded and the rider's burnt and torn body cart-wheeled lifeless into the scrub.

Ben was surprised when Duncan twice shot the third man. He had seemed too hesitant. The man returning from pissing hadn't looked as though he would do anything rash and was crawling towards some scrub. Ben shot him in the face. This left only the man whom Duncan had twice shot and wounded. Ben was uneasy about this man, seeing the fear and wonder in his face as he felt around his chest and lower abdomen to try and stem the bleeding. But the uneasiness passed, and he fired.

And then there was silence.

Duncan seemed to be falling apart. Or falling down at least. He then freed the woman and she ran across to her partner, still lying on the ground. Ben could feel the silence building and now a screaming in his ears. He dropped the gun and looked wildly at the sticks and branches around him, then rolled onto his back grasping at the brittle air. The sun shone down hard on his face and he could make out a trio of wedge-tailed eagles circling in the endless blue above him. *Why three?* he wondered irrelevantly, his mind still confused. Then suddenly, the screaming was subsiding and the quiet and softness of the bush descended. And he almost fell asleep. Only the sharp light and a sudden call from one of the eagles prompted him to sit upright and look back at the warm gun beside him.

Duncan was calling, he could hear that now. He must get down there and help him. Ben hardly trusted his legs as he rose gingerly and looked around on the ground for the empty shells. They were lying close to each other. Controlled shooting. One each for the four men lying dead below. The enormity and horror began to sink in as Ben bent to gather up the shells. Bits of broken twig and red gravel still clung to his clothes. He straightened again and looked out through the scrub, seeking an easy route down through the moraine of broken rock.

In a few short minutes, Ben had reached the bottom. Duncan strode out towards him. Ben didn't trust his own face or expression and closed his eyes. Part of him was confused by what had happened. Unsure of the details. But another part still held a memory of the scene and every tiny detail of how the killing had unfolded. He couldn't yet believe that he was involved in it, much less that he had affected most of it.

Duncan was standing in front of him now, eyes also on the ground. 'That was bad luck about the scream. I reckon I almost talked them out of it.'

'No, mate, I was always going to kill him.' It was out before Ben could stop himself.

'What do you mean?'

Ben was confused. He didn't really know what he meant. Only that it was true. 'I don't know. It was like I was stoned. But I was basically up there killing people and the scream only brought on the inevitable.'

Duncan looked hard at him, then back to the clearing. 'Mate, I guess we're both in shock. It's gone to shit.' Duncan seemed to be struggling. 'Ben, we've got two choices here. We call this in and fess up, and try to keep you safe from the rest of this gang. Or we cover this up and bolt.'

Ben was stunned. 'Dunc, we should call it in. Do it right. I'll take my chances. We can't hope to get away with this.'

'Disagree, mate. I think we can. We can clean this place up a bit and move our camp. Pretend to do some shooting there. You got the shells?'

'Yeah, I picked them up. And had a good look around up there. It's all clean, but you can see where I was lying if you look hard enough.'

'Can't help that. Hopefully animals will be interested in the smells. Scuff it all up a bit. I've got my two shells, so let's put them together and keep them safe.'

Ben wasn't convinced. Nodded across to the two campers. 'What about them? They've seen us both. You'd be easy to describe—pretty distinctive. Your mates in the police will join the dots.'

'True. And that's the weak link. Guess we can either ask them to walk away from it all quietly, or we can think of a story and train them up with it. Ask them to take it to the police in Barker.' Duncan thought about this for a second. 'But you're right, if they don't want to do anything dodgy then we'll just have to call it in.'

'Do you reckon they're also at risk from the gang?'

'I hadn't thought about it. But yeah, probably. Gang might see it as important to come back and finish the job. Light of what happened to their mates.'

'Then I reckon we should try to convince them to let it go.' Ben watched the woman and man lean their heads together, the man crying. 'Maybe we could get them to go to Sydney, then leave the country? I could drive their van down there with them in the back. You could follow in the ute and meet me somewhere in Sydney tomorrow morning. Take at least nine hours from here.'

Duncan was also watching the couple. 'Mate, I'm really struggling. Can't imagine how they must be feeling. Going to be hard to get them to think about this practically.' He sighed, swearing under his breath. 'But what you're saying makes sense. I could duck up over the hill and be back at the ute before dark if I didn't stuff around too much. Don't like to split up, though. You reckon you'll be okay after all that shit?'

'I don't know. I've got to tell you about it, but that can wait. Maybe give me a chance to work things out a bit.'

Duncan nodded. 'Once we get back, we'll have to find another campsite. There's a place on the other side of the highway that would work. Back towards the river. Pigs like it. Should set up camp then take it down again. Make food and a fire and do all that stuff. Find a good place to shoot from and throw away the shells. Be some evidence, anyway. Then head back to Warkon in the evening and try not to talk to anyone before morning.'

Ben was relieved that Duncan seemed to be taking control again. 'Okay well, let's go talk to these two.'

'Don't touch anything around the clearing. Especially not the bikes, but really anything. In fact, let's walk around the clearing and get the two of them to meet us near their van. That way your footprints won't be there. I'll go back in there when it's all done and you're on your way and try and wipe out mine. Distinctive bloody boots, but.'

Ben chuckled. 'Those ridiculously enormous boots might be our undoing, Dunc, but at least you'll have a good idea of what the police will be looking for.'

They made their way carefully around the clearing and over to the white Toyota van and, with hand signals, motioned to the couple to join them. The man moved with a lot of difficulty. He was blond and very tall, and now that they were closer Ben could see that the woman was also tall. At least his own height and solidly built. They were obviously both strong and robust people, and hopefully that would help them. The four sat down on two sawn logs. Ben and Duncan on one and the couple on the other.

The woman reached forward to Ben and squeezed his hand. 'Thank you.'

The man nodded painfully.

Ben looked away. Toward the hill. He couldn't see the eagles. Just an empty sky.

Duncan handed them his warrant card. 'I'm Duncan and this is Ben. I'm a policeman, but we were just out shooting some pigs when we saw the bikes and came down for a look. Can you understand me?'

They both nodded again and the woman said, 'I am Hilde, and this is Andes, my husband. We can follow the English okay, but speaking, you know, is not always so good.'

'These men,' Duncan gestured behind him, 'are from a biker gang. Do you know what a biker gang is?'

Hilde attempted a smile. 'Yes, we have such gangs in the Netherlands, and in Sweden in particular. I think Sweden maybe invented the biker gangs. They sell drugs and bring girls to the country for prostitution. And they sell guns. They are bad people all over the world.'

'Sounds like you get the picture. Problem we have over here is that the gangs avenge killings. If they find out who was involved here, they'll kill them. And they'll kill their families, too. I'll probably be okay. They don't often touch police. But they'll find and kill Ben here, and probably his family. And I think they'll try and do the same to you. They'll think you were somehow involved.'

'How will they know if we go to the police?' Hilde asked.

'The gangs know people in the police. They will find out. They'll be patient. They won't let it go, and eventually they will find out.'

'So what do we do?'

'Right thing to do would be to take you to the police in Barker and tell my boss what happened. Ben would have to go to court. Me, too. But I guess you would hope that we could explain the situation and would get off okay.' Duncan paused. 'But like I said, I think that doing that would result in Ben's name coming out. And then the gangs would turn on him and his family. And yourselves. They might even be able to follow you back to the Netherlands. Either in person or through other gangs over there.'

Duncan had stopped. Seemed reluctant to continue. Ben nodded his encouragement. 'We think we should say nothing. Try to cover this up. We think Ben should drive your van to Sydney, with you in the back. We can get you some simple medicines from a chemist. The trip will take about nine or ten hours, but you should be able to sleep for some of it. I'll go back and get my car, then drive to Sydney as well and meet up with Ben somewhere tomorrow morning. You'll have to sell the van to a car dealer in Sydney, then book a flight back to the Netherlands. We'll come back up here and cover everything up as best we can. I'm a cop and can do that pretty well. I know what they'll be looking for. But if we're found out, then we promise never to tell the police about yourselves. You will be safe.'

The couple spoke to each other for a few minutes in Dutch, while Ben and Duncan looked around at the clearing. Then Hilde beckoned them over. 'We agree that this is the good plan and will do what you say. The chemist is not necessary. We have first aid pack in the car. Andes laughed at me for buying such a big pack, but now he will be pleased. We are rich people really and we will give you money to help you make it okay.'

Duncan was relieved. 'Thanks. Really, thank you. But, no, we don't need any money. Money won't help us. In fact, the police may look at me and Ben quite closely and the last we want them to find is money that they know neither of us should have.' He smiled. 'They know they pay me bugger-all, and Ben here keeps crashing expensive motorbikes into mythical creatures. We're both broke.'

Ben smiled and glanced at Duncan. Pointed at the watch on his wrist.

Duncan nodded. 'True, mate. You and Ben had better get going. Get lots of food at a servo, but otherwise drive straight through.' Duncan paused, then added to Ben, 'When you get to Sydney, find a motel and leave Hilde and Andes there with the van. Then get a train out to Penrith. I'll meet you at the station there at about seven in the morning. Hopefully. If I'm not there, just find somewhere to sit and go back to the station every couple of hours through the day. It's a pain in the arse, but I can't see it working any other way.'

'No worries. You'll be okay getting back to the car?'

'Yeah, I know this trail pretty well. I'll clear things up here a bit then head back across the top. Harder walking, but quicker than around the base. Should only be about three or four hours behind you, and then I'll be travelling quicker. Another thing. Obey every conceivable road rule and don't freak out if anyone stops you. Just tell them you were hitching and the pair in the back wanted to sleep while you drove. School them to back that up.'

The dusty twin-track ran for about five kilometres before merging with a larger gravel road and after another half an hour they were out onto a highway. The van was virtually new and managed a good pace and in a little over an hour they had cleared the peri-urban mess of Barker.

Hilde made her way forward to the passenger seat. 'We will stop somewhere soon. Somewhere we can be away from the road. There is a shower for camping, here in the van, and we must wash.'

Ben was dismayed. He had settled into the rhythm of driving and was aware of the length of the trip ahead. 'Do we really have to, Hilde? I know it's grotty, but can't we just drive on through and clean up in Sydney?'

'I think you do not understand. We have to stop and wash. I have to wash. We have to be clean.' She saw his concern. 'It is better we do this, anyway. We look bad now. It would not be good if we have to get out of the car.'

Ben could see the sense in that. Hilde was now wearing a filthy pair of Andes's shorts. Andes himself still bore the dust and leaves he had been lying in on his clothes and in his hair.

'Okay. Look, we'll pull off at the next little road and you can take some time to get cleaned up.'

He saw a gravel farm road ahead and turned in over a broken grid. The road followed a low ridge around to the left and was soon beyond view from the highway. He stopped the van and stared ahead.

Hilde thanked him, her hand on his shoulder. 'You please leave for ten minutes. We will use the horn when we are ready.'

Ben nodded and trudged back up the track towards the highway. A small dead tree stood out above the brush. He sat on an exposed root and looked down at his boots. The sun was beginning to slide towards the west but was still warm on his thighs and, in the silence of the afternoon, thoughts of the killing clamoured. He didn't understand what had happened on the escarpment. He had felt at a distance from everything. Dissociated. Almost stoned. His memory of those few minutes was still blurred, as though it had happened sometime in his childhood.

Ben heard a short blast of the horn and walked back down to the van. Hilde and Andes had both had showers and were now dressed in clean jeans and t-shirts. Hilde had her head to one side, combing out the knots in her wet hair. 'We can go again now to Sydney.' She smiled.

'Okay. You look much better, Hilde. That was a good idea. I should have thought of it.'

Hilde and Andes returned to their bed in the back of the van, talking quietly to each other. Back on the highway, Ben returned to his thoughts and was startled some time later to hear Hilde speaking behind him as she climbed back into the passenger seat. 'Andes is sleeping. He is feeling very bad about this thing.' She drew one foot up underneath her, then turned as she wiped away tears with both palms. 'I think it will go, but he is feeling he should have protected me from those men.'

Hilde stroked the dashboard, searching for the words. She seemed to need to talk. 'It was not good at the start. We were about to go walking when the bikes came. We could see they were bad people. We should have run, but there wasn't any time. They stood around us in a circle making fun. One made to hit Andes, and he hit back. But another hit him behind his head, and then they all hit him until he fell down. Then they kicked him a lot. I think he has broken ribs and maybe collarbone. I don't want to talk about what happened next. What almost happened. It was all very bad. I will never be able to forget it.'

Ben nodded, staring ahead, and felt her watching him.

Hilde went on. 'I can see you are also feeling very bad now, too? You should think to yourself that you have saved our lives, Andes and me. We won't forget you and Constable Duncan Morris. My death would have been very hard, and Andes was awake enough to know what they would do to me. You are my hero.'

Ben turned to see her smile. It was a pretty smile, like an advertisement for butter. He nodded again and Hilde persisted, 'Do you want to talk about this thing that you are feeling?'

'Maybe I need to. I feel a bit confused about it. Me and Duncan will have to pretend a lot when we get back to Warkon. I'm afraid all the shit inside me is going to be really obvious.'

'What part of it is very bad for you now?'

Ben was silent as he chewed his lower lip. He felt close to tears.

She kept going. 'Is it the shooting? That they were people, even though they were very bad people? Or are you worried that the police will know it was you and Duncan?'

'It's not the shooting of those bikers that worries me. And we should have a reasonable chance with the police. Duncan thinks so, and he should know something, I guess. It's hard to explain, but it's the fact that the shooting didn't bother me at the time.' Ben paused to look out the window of the van, as the last light of the afternoon's winter light played across the vast open landscape. Then he asked, 'Did you and Andes think there was anything strange about the escarpment. Did you feel anything?'

Hilde surprised him by laughing aloud. 'The spooky thing you mean, I think? I will tell you this, because you ask and because it is somehow part of what you are feeling. Me and Andes, we were in the tourist place in Barker yesterday and the person, the girl, in there I think she thought Andes was nice. Anyway, she was making lots of talk with him and telling us things to see. She said it was good aboriginal paintings on the escarpment, if we could walk on rough tracks and over rocks. But she told us we should camp at the bottom because the mountain was haunted. That is right? Haunted? Ghosts?'

Ben nodded, intrigued. 'Did she say anything more about that?'

'She said there had been lots of stories. That some aborigines still would not want to go there. It was once a special place for them? She said a man was found about five years. He was dead. He had fallen off a rock and broken his neck. But she said he had no shoes, and his feet and hands were very cut up.'

Hilde paused, fluttering her hands in the global symbol for ghosts. Ben smiled, despite himself, as Hilde continued. 'Police, they think he had been chased without his shoes for a long way and had been breaking branches with his hands. He must have been very scared. But there was no-one else up there then. It was a big mystery for a while, I think. Andes said we should camp at night on the escarpment to find out about these ghosts. He thinks it would make me feel very sexy, you know?' Hilde laughed lightly at Ben's discomfort. 'Andes was then having some serious ideas about it. He said that some gas could come out of the rock? It is the sandstone? With little holes? And people lie down and breathe it and go a bit crazy. He tell me we should be careful about that.'

Hilde paused again to look at Ben. 'Andes, he did not think there were ghosts. You understand, there is nothing in the Netherlands that is very ... spiritual? We have lots of churches, but they are just for religion. Everything in life is very controlled. There is no magic.' She paused again, then added, 'So you think the ghosts somehow made you not notice the shooting?'

Ben was astonished that she had been able to see it so easily. 'Is that really dumb? Do you think I'm just trying to find an excuse for killing those blokes?'

Hilde seemed to need to talk. 'I don't know, Ben. I am, I think you say "open minded" about things. I am not so simple as Andes. I tell you, my job in the Netherlands, I am an advocate. You know, a lawyer, in the courts? I see a lot of people who have done bad things. Some of these are just little things. Like they steal something they want or they get drunk and fight. Other things are in-between. Like they hurt a woman a bit or they rob a shop with a knife. Then there are big things. Like they rape or they kill someone.'

Hilde stopped, her jaw tight as she realised what she had said. She looked out at her side of the plain and seemed to collect herself. 'You know the thing that is most strange to me is the way many of these people, they behave when they come into the court. You think some will be sorry and some won't care. And others, they didn't really do the thing and will be angry and defend themselves. That would all be normal?' She turned to face him. 'But you know what most of them are like, Ben? They are very confused. They don't know why they are in this court answering my questions. They think there must be mistake. They have somehow forgotten what they have done. This is most common in house crimes. Like hurting a woman. But also it happens for crimes that this person had thought about before. You know what I am saying?'

Ben nodded again.

Hilde smiled sadly. 'I am surprised by this when I first see it because I think, how can they be confused when they know they really did this thing? But it is true, and sometimes you have to think then that there is a reason why people are like this. I think maybe a lot of people can do more bad things than they know. That this is easier than they know. They think it is impossible, but it is not impossible. They have conscience, but that does not mean they are not able to do the bad thing. And this surprises them a lot, I think.'

Ben nodded, as Hilde added. 'The thing I must say to you Ben is you are a good person for killing those men. That is what I think. They would have got very small jail time. Some maybe none? And then they would have done more bad things.'

Hilde looked pained and wiped her eyes with the palms of her hands. They sat quietly, listening to the patient thrum of the diesel motor and steady hiss of tyres on smooth tar. Then Hilde turned back to Ben, and when she spoke he could hear the tears behind her words. 'I think in some way I maybe caused it, you know. Your friend Duncan, he was talking to them. He is such a big man, and he is a policeman, and he had a gun. They were listening to him. He was telling them that they would be arrested, but they would not have a big punishment. He wanted them to let him arrest them so there would not be shooting. I heard him say these things and I screamed loud. I wanted them to die or me to die. It was after my big scream that the shooting it starts. I think the leader, he tried to do something and you shoot him from the hill. Then everything it happens very fast.'

Ben was horrified. 'It's not your fault, Hilde. God, don't start thinking that.'

'I don't think bad about that, Ben. I am pleased that they are dead. I tell you now, I will follow this case from the Netherlands and I will come back here to help you if the police find it was you and Duncan.'

'No, Hilde. You mustn't do that. I don't know what the penalty would be, but there must be some crime in knowing about a killing and helping to cover it up. You and Andes must get away from this free so that there is some point to it all. Honestly, that's what Duncan would say, too. If we get found out, we'll probably get treated leniently. We can play up the fact that they were armed and say that they were going to start shooting. Like self-defence.

And the jury will sympathise with us. But at the end of the day, we've got to know that you both got away free.'

'I will think about this. Even if this is true, I will give you money to pay for the good lawyer. I will also find this good lawyer. I know some people here.' She smiled. 'You tell me if you are feeling tired? I can drive for a while if this is what you need.'

'Thanks, Hilde. I'll let you know, but I feel okay now. We'll be in Dubbo in an hour or so and from there the driving is easier. More corners, and little towns if we need to stop for food or something.'

'I like this name, "Dubbo". Andes and me, we laugh at this name as we drove to Barker. It has a nice outside zoo?'

Ben chuckled. 'Dubbo is known for that zoo. I haven't been there, but they say that the animals are kept in big pens and paddocks. Plenty of room. Not like a lot of city zoos.'

'One day you should go to this zoo and see these happy animals.'

'Okay, Hilde. Go and get some sleep. I'll be fine. I'll think about happy hippos.'

Duncan sat down on a stump at the edge of the clearing and looked first at his boots, then out across the carnage to the three beautiful bikes parked up in the shade.

Fuckers always look after their bikes.

The bones of the fourth bike were blackened and twisted, with bits strewn all over the scrub. Its rider had been flung across the bars and into some turpentine. The remaining three bikers lay in the dust and leaves, in varying degrees of awfulness. The man closest to Duncan was the leader he had tried to reason with. Duncan stared down at him.

Triggered it all, you stupid fucken idiot. Could all have been okay. Arrests, then a bit of stuffing around to get everything secured. Ben could have taken the van to Barker and dropped the Dutch couple at the hospital, then gone onto the cop shop.

Duncan put his head in his hands. The sun was starting to slide to the northwest, leaving the shadows longer and a little cooler. There was quiet everywhere.

I would have stayed here looking after things and keeping this fucken idiot from rallying up his mates. Probably gag the prick. Throw bike keys into the bush somewhere. Maybe even blow the bikes up to compensate a bit for the shit-fight and grief. I'd be back in Warkon tonight. Celebrating. Chlo would have been happy. Don't know what the fuck is going to happen now.

Duncan looked at his watch and decided he had better begin to mess up the scene of the shooting. He still had to walk back over the escarpment to the car. If he was running late he could perhaps call ahead to the railway station in Penrith from a town somewhere and get them to put a message out to Ben, but he wanted to be down there by seven if he could. They would still have the long drive back, and then the second campsite to setup and take down.

Hope he's okay with the other two. She looked like a strong chick, but Andes was pretty much fucked. Have to be hard on a bloke, watching that.

Duncan moved out into the clearing a little and looked at the scene systematically as he knew the investigating police would. He could see where he had walked and stood and moved about as the shooting unfolded. There were clear hiking-boot prints in the dust, with a different pattern from the bikers' smooth-soled long leather boots. And the hiking boot prints were huge.

Should leave these. Start a fucken Yowie myth.

He took a leafy branch and worked systematically around the clearing, scrubbing away the marks. Anyone could see what he'd done, but it would be difficult to get a reliable print or indent and whatever might be left of the exploded hollow-point bullets couldn't be linked to their rifles. Dark blood was congealing in the dust and leaves around each body. The slow winter flies were gathering. The ants would be next.

He examined the clearing a final time, then moved to where the van had been and repeated the scrubbing. With everything cleared as well as it could be, he picked up his pack and the two rifles and set off back up the escarpment.

The plains had gradually given way to low hills and stringy eucalypts now lined the road. The light had completely gone and the trunks of the hungry trees flicked past like the struts of a tunnel as road markings caught fragments of the van's bright lights and threw them back in a staccato, hypnotic rhythm. The warmth and quiet felt like a submarine. To the left and right there were tiny rapid glimpses of the dark bush. The glint of eyes, occasionally, and generally low down among the scrub, but sometimes something taller and always moving towards the night. A long way ahead a soft shape crossed with exaggerated movements. Sudden, but not scurrying. Then gone, and they were alone again.

As they approached Nyngan and the Bogan River, the country began to change again. First there were the wide-open river flats, and then the beginning of fenced paddocks and grazing country. Farm gates and mailboxes loomed up and every now and then they could see the lights of buildings set closer to the road.

A big roadhouse was coming up. Ben turned the van onto the access road, then slowed and pulled up alongside a rack of high-flow diesel bowsers. Ten or fifteen trucks and road-trains were camped close by in a pull-out with showers. Hilde and Andes seemed to have been sleeping, but slid the side door open and came out into the garage lights as he started to fill the tank.

'Thought we could stop here for half an hour or so. Doing okay for time.' Ben pointed towards the parked trucks. 'There's toilets on the left over there. Showers, too, if you want another. Hot water. Then we'll get some more food to keep us going through the night.'

Hilde was pleased. 'A hot shower would be very nice, I think. We will meet you in the food part. Here is some money for the petrol.'

The food was rich and fatty and tasted good after driving. Andes was still quiet, but spoke a little with Hilde in Dutch and attempted some simple English sentences. The roadhouse saw a constant stream of long-distance truckers and travellers, as well as the local town and farm people. No-one would remember the trio in a nondescript white van.

They bought more coffees then went back out to the parking area.

'You can keep driving okay?' Hilde asked.

'Yeah, I think it'll be alright for another few hours. But if you get bored back there, come up front and tell me some Dutch jokes.'

'Andes is usually the one for telling jokes. Women are not so good with jokes, I think. But Andes is not remembering lots of jokes tonight. I will come and talk to you about other things.'

'Thanks, Hilde. But sleep as much as you can. Tomorrow you'll need to sell the car and get organised to fly home. You'll want to have had some sort of rest.'

As it turned out, Hilde and Andes slept almost all of the remaining journey, waking only as Ben was pulling into a small all-night fuel station in Lithgow.

'I'm sorry, Ben. We didn't wake up. We had some sweet drink in a little bottle. It is not far from morning now and you have driven all this way.' She reached over and hugged him, holding onto him for several seconds.

'It's okay, Hilde. Really. It's sad this happened to you in Australia. It is really such a quiet country. But you must hate it now.'

'No, no, no. Not at all. And we will come back. We have promised ourselves this. When everything has been finished with the police, we will come back. We will want to see you both again. And we want to continue our journey. We were going to go up into the Northern Territory and then to Queensland and down the eastern coast. We want to see the big reef and Kakadu. Lots of things we want to see.'

'I hope so much this will all blow over as some sort of biker gang thing. I want to keep travelling, too. I was on the way to Western Australia when I crashed my bike and had to stop off in Warkon. That's how I met Duncan. He picked me up by the road and got me a job in the pub. A bloke in Warkon is fixing my bike, and then I want to keep going. But what you said before is true. I should stick around in Warkon with Duncan at least until we see how the investigation is panning out.'

'How bad is your bike broken?'

'It's pretty bad. I'll have to get Mum to help me out with the money.'

'How did you crash this bike?'

'I don't really know. Something bumped into me from the side. It was soft and quite big. Duncan reckons an emu, most likely. It was just near to the escarpment.'

Hilde was smiling her butter-advertisement smile. 'You are thinking now it was a magic thing that jumped on you?'

Ben glanced at her.

'Ben, it was just an emu. That Sesame Street Big Bird thing? It runs along by the road very fast and would knock you off a bike very easy. We saw lots of them. Don't be silly, it was definitely this emu.'

Ben smiled at the Big Bird idea as he got out of the van. Hilde had given him some more money and she and Andes had gone off to use the toilets. They met again inside and bought some lukewarm rubbery pies and thin instant coffee, then continued on into the Blue Mountains. Hilde pointed at a sign to a car parking area. 'We stop here for some days last week or two. There is a beautiful walk down a big cliff into the forest. And you can get coffee here like in Europe. Very nice. But they put a trout in a pie. That is a really horrible idea. Yuck.'

Ben chuckled. It was cold and a heavy frost visible already in the pre-dawn winter dark. Hilde sat in the passenger seat with Andes in a small fold-down seat behind her. They talked mostly in Dutch, translating small snippets for Ben. Andes could understand English reasonably well, but wasn't able to speak more than very simple sentences.

Having left the pretty mountain towns and suburbs they turned down towards Penrith and then to Parramatta Road. Soon they passed St Marys and Westmead, and continued on towards Silverwater. Car yards and motels lined the road and Ben thought it a good place to stop. He saw a motel that looked slightly larger and cleaner than most others and set back slightly from the traffic. He pulled up beneath an overhang that marked the office. A light was on and the motel appeared to be open.

They were silent for a few moments, then Ben turned to face them. 'You can take the van to any of the car dealers we passed. Maybe just Hilde, so no-one sees the both of you together and links you to the van. Tell them you split up or something, and that Andes has already gone back home. Then just call the airline you've booked with and get them to change your tickets. The hotel can get you taxis to take you around Sydney and then to the airport.'

Ben noticed an elderly woman in the office looking out at them curiously, and got out of the car. Hilde took her purse from the glove box. 'You should go now, Ben. You are looking very tired. Let us book into this ugly little hotel and get a taxi for you. And we also want to pay for the taxi all the way to where you are meeting Duncan. And give you more money for food there. And for Duncan's petrol down here to Sydney and back again. We owe you very much.'

Duncan was walking fast now and thinking about how he'd handle his boss, Trevor. It was going to be difficult lying. Trev was a good bloke. A mate, really. And Trev knew him pretty well. He was a good watcher. It would be important not to say too much, or to appear to know too much, but it would also be important to be curious. To have ideas. That's how he would normally behave, and what Trev would expect.

He was almost at the summit now, and thought he could probably stretch it to a trot along the ridge as the footing was good and there was plenty of light left in the cold winter afternoon. Overhead an eagle, so high in the paling sky that it seemed almost motionless.

Always eagles up here. Amazing eyesight. This one would already know about the dead men lying in the clearing at the foot of the escarpment.

But when Duncan looked up again the eagle was gone and the sky was empty and the old mountain slept among the last shallow breaths of winter warmth.

Duncan glanced left and right as he trotted along the familiar ridge-top trail, and thought about the mystique the escarpment seemed to hold for a lot of people. He liked to retell and embellish the bullshit he'd heard about it as those he was with then seemed to become convinced that something alive was all around them. One bloke he'd taken shooting had panicked a bit and insisted they go back to the car. Pretty much ran back. A tough bloke. A ringer. Ben had also heard some stories and had said that he felt something. But Duncan had primed him a bit, too, when he thought about it.

Duncan loved the place. Every hidden chasm caught the light in its own way and seemed to shelter its own tiny ecosystem. You didn't get that down on the plains. He paused at the rocks where he and Ben had eaten sandwiches. Little Chlo's sandwiches, always so thoughtful and nicely wrapped. He loved opening his lunches. It was the best part of the day. And he loved the pink lunchbox, which was hers but always in the fridge for him first thing of a morning. Duncan never really talked about stuff with Chlo. He knew he should do, but it was difficult. The shit from his childhood seemed to get in the way and the lunches had become a sort of shy, unspoken symbol for them.

Duncan was still smiling to himself as he made his way down the final descent to the car. It was a long way to Sydney but the ute had a motor made for Australian roads and he had a lot of music in the car. He could stop for food and coffee when he got tired. It would be a strain, but a good opportunity to really think through the inevitable police investigation—the different ways it might pan out and the strategies that might help to protect him and Ben, and the Dutch couple.

Sunday

'Dunc!'

It was seven o'clock and cold and the station car park was beginning to fill with early-morning commuters. Ben had wondered how he might find Duncan once the crowds built up, but Duncan was not easily missed. He looked fresh and seemed to have changed his clothes . . .

'Dunc!'

It was seven o'clock and cold and the station car park was beginning to fill with early-morning commuters. Ben had wondered how he might find Duncan once the crowds built up, but Duncan was not easily missed. He looked fresh and seemed to have changed his clothes . . .

'Had a shower at a servo, mate. Stank like old Cecil.'

'I might grab a quick shower and change of clothes on the way back, while you're filling the car or something. I'm feeling pretty grotty.'

Duncan nodded. 'Good thing there's two of us for this next bit. Car's in the back corner there. Talk inside.'

The ute was coated in fine red outback dust and with its beaten bull bar and big lights, was no less distinctive than Duncan. 'Full tank. Couple of jerries in the back. Get five or six hundred kays at least.'

'That's good. We stand out a bit down here. Should aim for a stop back in Dubbo. Or maybe Nyngan. We passed another big roadhouse there.'

Duncan unlocked Ben's door, then walked around to the driver's side. 'You seem okay, considering. Not cracking up? Not about to go on a rampage? Shoot people?'

Ben smiled and put his backpack at his feet. Looked at his hands. The cab felt too small, his clothes greasy. 'No, I think I'm alright. If you can get us out of Sydney then I can drive for a bit.'

'No worries.'

Once out of Penrith, the V8 pulled smoothly upward towards the mountains. Cluttered commuter traffic was heading to Sydney and the road west virtually empty. Ben turned towards Duncan. 'So you got the place cleaned up a bit? No tracks?'

'It's okay, I think. Looks like someone cleared up after themselves, but they'll expect that. Haven't touched the bodies.'

Ben stared out at the grotty peri-urban outskirts of Penrith. 'Can you believe what happened yesterday? Does it seem real? We killed four blokes, Dunc.'

'Mate, I don't know what to think. Bit I find hardest to believe is the fuckers themselves. Would have taken it in turns with Hilde. Mates sitting around drinking. Passing the bottle, with Andes probably dying on the ground. Completely fucken evil.' Duncan glanced across. 'But to answer your question, no I don't feel bad. You? Feeling guilty?'

'No, not really. I should, but I just feel a bit buggered by the whole thing. And then the drive.'

Ben stretched out and felt the tiredness coming on, but thought he should try to stay awake for Duncan. 'You know, Hilde is amazing. She was keeping me going most of the way down here. Andes has broken ribs and a collarbone and he's a bit screwed up inside. He was conscious most of the time, I think. In the clearing. Must have been terrible for him. Must have wished they could both just die.'

'Good that Hilde is okay. Would have been difficult, her falling apart. Have to go to a hospital. Cops would get involved. Reckon they'll sell the van and get a ticket home?'

'Yeah, I left them at a motel on Parramatta Road in the Silverwater area. There are car dealers right along there. She'll sell it sometime today and then they'll change the ticket over the phone.

They've got a lot of money and can make things happen. Actually, that reminds me, Hilde gave us some cash for petrol and stuff.'

Ben reached into the pack for the envelope. Duncan looked at the fanned notes. 'Mate, that's got to be five-hundred dollars!'

'She really is fantastic. Andes is probably a good bloke, but he hardly said a word on the trip down. Hilde is a lawyer. Andes inherited his father's business. Don't know what that is. But anyway, Hilde says she'll buy the Australian papers in Amsterdam and stay in touch with the investigation. If we get found out she's going to pay for a good defence.'

'Mate, that's very good to know. We took a bit of a risk coming down here, although there wasn't much choice, really. Couldn't expect the two of them to get themselves organised after what they went through.'

They drove on in silence through the Blue Mountains and then on to the western hills of the Dividing Range. Ben tried to fight it, but dozed on and off as the morning sun warmed the rear window and the back of his head. He was faintly aware of Duncan humming along to a Dylan compilation as they continued through Lithgow. Outside Bathurst they stopped for coffee and food.

Ben stretched in the cool morning sun. 'I'll drive for a bit, Dunc, and you can have a sleep. We can get fuel at that truck stop outside Nyngan. It's probably about three-and-a-half hours from here.'

Duncan nodded and went around to the passenger side. Slid his seat right back against the cab and tried to stretch his legs out. Failed. Curled up instead.

'Dunc, you need a horse float.'

Duncan grunted. 'Take it easy, okay? No speeding close to towns. Should get into Nyngan just after lunch. It'll be dark by the time we get to that campsite, but that can't be helped.'

Ben was nervous at first with the big car, but it floated along effortlessly once out on the open roads. He wondered how many people could have done this trip twice in twenty-four hours.

Truckers, perhaps. It had to be halfway across the state. He barely noticed the country as the small towns and villages grew further apart and they continued northwest towards the arid inland. Duncan looked peaceful and unbothered and Ben relaxed. He felt a lot better after his talk with Hilde. Hours passed and the country flattened out.

Duncan stirred as they slowed down through Dubbo. Ben looked across at him. 'Probably an hour and a half from here to Nyngan. You get some sleep? Seemed to be dribbling a bit.'

'Fuck off.' Duncan wound down the window. 'How are you feeling?'

'I'll be okay till we stop. But you might have to take over for a while after that. I'm rooted.'

'No worries. Should probably have a bit of a chat about what will happen from here on.'

Duncan looked out the open window for a few moments and Ben wondered whether he'd lost his train of thought. At last, he spoke. 'Campsite's the first consideration. No evidence back where we parked yesterday morning. That's all okay. When we get to this new place by the river we'll need to set up the tents and roll around in them a bit. Flatten down the scrub. Get a fire going as soon as we get there so there's some coals to leave. I don't usually leave rubbish, but we'll put something from the car near a bush somewhere.'

'Okay, you just tell me what do and I'll do it. You'll know what the police will be looking for.'

'Mate, wish I knew more. Don't think Forensics will go to the campsite, but my boss, Trev, might. He always starts by cementing the facts. His little motto. Good bloke, Trev. He's helped me a lot. It'll be hard to fuck him around.'

Duncan continued to look out the window, now closed again against the cold. 'Anyway, that side is okay, I think, but we need a reason for getting back to Warkon so late. Maybe stick a knife in one of the tyres, change it over, then bugger up the jack a bit?

Might look convincing?' He rubbed his face with both hands. 'Probably too complicated. I'll look at the map. We'll say that we were trying out a new track and the going was slower than we thought. Late back to the car. That would sound better.'

Ben agreed. 'When we get a chance, you'd better get the map out and tell me what it looks like in different places. Maybe we better think about a fictitious schedule for the whole day?'

'Okay. Probably do that back in Warkon. Come over to the cop shop and we'll go through it.'

Ben nodded. 'Who will lead the investigation? Will it be you?'

'No, not me, but I want to try and be the first one out there. Tricky if it's called into Barker. They're not that much further away. Don't want to have to try and look surprised. Harder than lying, I reckon. I'd like to be the one showing the scene to Trev and the others.'

Duncan was silent again while he thought about the call out, then added, 'Blokes will probably come up from Homicide in Sydney and take things over. Might also be the Drug Squad, and maybe Organised Crime. The gangs cover a lot of bases. Hard to pick. Not sure what Sydney's priorities are now, or how excited they'll get about a country shooting.'

'Where do you reckon the biggest risk is? For us, I mean.'

'Well, best thing is really that the truth is almost unbelievable. Seriously. It's a ridiculous fucken scenario. Trick will be to behave right, and not like actors. It's surprising how people pick up on unnatural behaviour, even without training.'

'How do you think you'd react, if you hadn't been involved?'

'I've been trying to work that out. Truth is, I think I'd be full-on excited and all over the crime scene. Showing people the mountain. Where you park. Where the trails go. Where you could shoot from.'

'A grassy knoll?'

Duncan smiled. 'I think I'll need to use excitement as an excuse to bugger up the scene a bit. Reckon I'll find the place where you were lying, but add my footprints to it in case I missed any yesterday. Then try to drag the mob back over the hill to where we parked the car. Walk ahead and look again for prints then scuff them out a bit. Carry on about the spooky stuff and get them riled up a bit.'

'Chloe?' Ben asked, leaving the question open.

'Nothing at all, mate. Not a word. If she knows she'll have to lie. Accessory after the fact. Stay in the background a bit this week. She won't like it, but we've got to be smart about it.'

It was nine o'clock when Ben walked into the bar. Chloe looked worried.

'Sorry, Chloe. We were trying out a bit of a different track, and got lost.'

'Duncan never gets lost. Where is he?'

Ben groaned inwardly. 'He's tired and went straight to the station. He was going to get a sandwich then go to bed.'

'Duncan doesn't make his own sandwiches—ever. I make them. And he doesn't get tired, either. What's going on, Ben?'

Fuck, fuck, fuck. 'Sorry, Chloe, it's like I said. I'm really knackered, too. I reckon I'll just have an early night.'

'BEN.'

Fuck, fuck, fuck.

Hands on hips. Young girl going on forty. 'Go over the road now and fetch Duncan. Tell him I want to know what's going on.'

Ben tried one last time. 'Honestly, Chloe, it's all okay. He won't want to come over here.'

'He will if you tell him I want him to. NOW GO AND GET HIM.'

Ben could see there was no point arguing. He dropped his gear against the bar and made his way to the police station. Duncan was cleaning out the back of the ute.

'Duncan, it's no good. Chloe's angry. She knows something's wrong and wants to talk to you. And when I say "want" I mean she pretty much demands that you go there right now.'

'You haven't said anything?'

'Mate, I barely got in the door. She's smart and she knows you. We're going to have to tell her something. I reckon we're going to have to tell her the truth. No other way.'

'I'll talk to her. Do me a favour and look after the bar while I talk to her?'

Ben returned and took over from Chloe at the bar. Duncan shuffled in, looking beaten. He didn't say anything, but pointed towards the kitchen.

There were only two old blokes drinking. Ben put a Neil Young tape into the player then made himself busy cleaning tables and packing glasses into the dishwasher. Duncan emerged and beckoned him to join them. Ben gave the drinkers a five-minute signal and followed Duncan into the kitchen. Chloe had been crying.

'Mate, I've told Chlo the whole thing.'

Ben got a cup and poured himself some tea from the pot on the table. 'What do you think, Chloe? Do you think we did the right thing?'

'I don't know. Honestly, how can I answer that, Ben? I thought you'd had a flat tyre or something, but now you're telling me that you've just killed four people. What do you want me to say?'

She got up and paced the kitchen, then switched the electric jug on again. Duncan stayed hunched in a toy chair at a little table with a tiny cup of tea. He reached out and caught her hand. It looked like a child's in his.

'We've still got a choice here, Chlo. We can call in the killing. Fess up to it. Just tell Trev that we agreed to urge the couple to run for it. Say they didn't want to get involved. Didn't want to give evidence against bikers. Particularly dead ones. Tell Trev we swore to keep their identity quiet.' Ben looked up at Chloe. Duncan continued. 'Problem is that the gang will come after Ben. Guarantee it. His family, if Ben himself goes into witness protection. I wouldn't trust protection either to be honest.'

Chloe squeezed Duncan's hand, then moved away and stared out at the dark yard. 'Would they come for you, too?'

'Probably not. I'm police. But it's hard to tell. They might do something a few years down the track. Drive a truck into my car. Accident. Something like that.'

'If you get found out, if Trev sees through it, would he understand why you tried to keep it quiet?'

'I really don't know. Trev does everything by the book.'

Chloe turned to face them again, arms folded across her chest. She walked back to the table and put her hand on Duncan's arm. 'Okay. Look, I don't think you should tell Trev anything. Just stick to what you've decided.' She softened. 'And I'm sorry I barked at you. Really, I am. You must be completely exhausted. Both of you. Ben, do you know how long it will be before your bike is fixed?'

Ben thought it could be the end of the week, if the parts could be found and delivered to Warkon.

Chloe nodded. 'I can see you did a hard thing. You could have walked away and just reported it to Barker.' She looked at them both. 'I should be telling you you're heroes.'

'Hilde already told me that, so I'm okay. You could tell Dunc maybe.'

They both looked uncomfortable. Ben realised that he'd strayed into difficult territory. 'Or just make him a sandwich. I'd better get back to the bar.'

'No, leave that to me. You both go and get some rest.'

CHAPTER 5

'Dev, you can't be fucken serious.'

'Mate, I am. That's what he said.'

Dom and I were at the house. Aud was out somewhere. Dom was staying there so much now that he had effectively moved in. So far, it was working well.

Scotty had called. Rick was with him. They had hit a roo on the way back to Armidale from the woolshed. They could have been a bit pissed, but even so it's hard to avoid a roo. They just appear out of nowhere. The problem was that Scotty wanted to use the band fee to pay for the damage. The fee had been paid to me and I had already divvied it up between us.

I had told Scotty to fuck off. Scotty then got the shits and said that he and Rick wanted to start their own band with the drummer and bass player who had stood in during the uni break. I could picture quiet Rick in the background tuning it all out and thinking about the surf. But Scotty was his mate, so that was that.

'No more band, Dom. That's it.'

Dom sat down and looked out at the little garden. He had even done some gardening the other day. A changed man. 'Well, fuck it. Way it is, mate. We had a good thing, but it wasn't going to last forever. Nothing ever does. Great that we got that Armidale gig in.'

He and Aud had also had a brilliant weekend. Little Aud was unstoppable these days. Her dad had called the other night and when I told him that Aud was out, he had explained that it was me he wanted to talk to. I had shuddered, unsure what unspeakable detail he might have found out. But he just wanted to know why Aud was so happy. Was she okay? Was there a bloke hanging around? I fessed up straight away and told him that Aud was seeing a friend of mine. Told him how smart Dom was. Physics student. Heading towards astrophysics. He asked what Dom's parents did. I told him and he was impressed. You could hear it in his voice. He told me that Aud never talked to him about things like this. Thanked me.

I sat down next to Dom. The band had probably meant more to me than it did to the others. I got a real kick out the way we could light up a pub or hall. Make people dance. Cheer. Drink. Everything else seemed to be sliding. Everything except the band. And Dania.

Dom sensed it. 'Mate, you've got to try to get around this uni thing. If that's still what the problem is. You can do it. You're smart. Just need to try and stabilise a bit. Avoid the highs. Always lead to lows.'

'I've hardly been there the last ten days or so. I do the pracs— you have to do those—but I don't go to lectures. I've been doing some work from textbooks, but it's hard.'

Dom stopped drumming on the arm of the couch. He looked concerned. 'You seem to be drinking a lot now, and smoking a fair bit of weed. Don't do that. Save that for when things are good. It'll fuck you up for sure.'

'I know. Danny doesn't like it, either. But some days I find it really hard to do anything. Can't even get out of bed.'

'Wouldn't do anything stupid, would you, mate?' Dom was always black and white.

'Tell the truth, I don't know. Sometimes with Dania, everything feels fantastic. But then sometimes I just seem to panic. Lose confidence. I feel like something inside is eating away at me. Dania's been great, but she must be getting sick of me.'

'She's not. She really loves you. Dania's the one thing you don't have to worry about. Seriously, mate, just get rid of that thought.'

We could hear Aud coming up the path, then the key in the door.

'Talk again. Take it easy, okay?'

'Thanks, Dom.'

'Hello, boys! I've got some chicken! We'll have a curry for dinner!' Big kiss for Dom. Little kiss for me. Bounced into the kitchen. Humming.

We looked at each other. Dom smiled. I smiled. Nothing much wrong with Aud.

The following morning, I got myself organised for the ride in to uni. It now seemed like a huge effort. I didn't know how I was going to get on. I didn't ride as much these days. Not much at all, really. I was becoming unfit.

I pushed the bike up from the garage and out onto the road, then headed up Darling Street. I felt very anxious and watched the traffic incessantly. Did a whole lot of unnecessary braking and swerving. Then up near the Bowlo some bloke pulled across my lane, and I veered off into a metal garbage bin. It made a loud noise as the bin fell over and the lid rolled off across the road. The car stopped and the driver jumped out to see if I was okay.

I stood up and looked at myself. Then the bike. Blood was running from a cut on my leg. Probably the metal on the bin. And the bike's bars were a bit bent. I felt lightheaded, dizzy, then suddenly furious. I grabbed the bloke and threw him against a parked car. Swore at him. His wife started yelling. She was standing back at their car. The bloke was terrified. He wasn't young, or big, and I was obviously a raving madman. I let him go and he managed to get his wallet out with shaking hands. Tried to press notes on me. I turned away and picked up the broken bike, then dragged it back down Darling Street. I could hear him yelling apologies behind me.

Ernie was on the footpath, cleaning tables. He looked up and said something but I hardly acknowledged him. Just stumbled past and kept going down the hill to our street. I think I was crying a bit now and walking faster. Beginning to panic. I had to get home. I didn't feel safe. I had to get off the street. I left the bike unchained by the side of the house and ran upstairs to my room. Had a long shower and tried to relax. Got changed and lay down in the bed and somehow slept. I woke up at lunchtime, disorientated and shaky. I thought I should eat something but wasn't hungry, so went back to bed and listened to music and tried again to relax.

It wasn't working, so I got out my story and started writing. And that settled me down a bit. It almost always did.

There was a knock at the door. It was Ernie, with some food from the cafe. I guess I must have looked bad, as he flinched when I opened the door. He gave me the food. 'Some pastries and pies. Make you feel a bit better, no?'

I couldn't speak. I didn't know why anyone would care about me.

'You want me to call your lady? You give me her number and I get her.'

I was jerked back to reality. Realised I was crying. 'Thanks, Ernie. I'm sorry. I'm really fucked up. But no, I'll be okay. Aud will be home in a couple of hours. She's only working the morning today.'

Ernie looked desperate. 'This thing, it is not the drugs, is it? Fucking drugs killed my boy. You must not go near drugs, Devvo.'

That broke through. I had forgotten about his son. He had died of an overdose the year before. 'No, mate, it's not drugs. I've got a bit messed up and I'm not sleeping. I think there's something else as well, but no, it's not drugs.'

Ernie seemed to relax a little. I took his arm. 'Thanks so much, Ernie. Honestly, thanks so much. I'll come around and mow your lawn sometime.'

Ernie smiled. Wiped an eye. Ernie was soft and sentimental. 'You can just work at the cafe anytime. Okay? If you can't do uni, then you come and work at the cafe. Okay?'

He patted my shoulder and shuffled off up the path. One day I'd have to try and find a way to thank him.

'What happened?'

'I don't really know, Danny. A bloke cut me off while I was riding to uni and I crashed into a bin. Then I lost it a bit. I didn't hit him, but I pushed him around and yelled at him. He was really scared.'

'Oh, Devlin, this has gone too far. Please see someone. Please. I'll come with you.'

'I'll do it, Danny. I'll find someone. I promise.'

Dania had been crying. She was convinced that my moods and the stupid obsession with university were symptomatic of something else.

I felt exhausted. Momentarily exhilarated, but somehow completely gutted at the same time. I knew my moods were swinging pretty wildly now and that left me with no self-confidence. None at all. I had come to recognise these fragile little highs and knew it would only be twenty minutes or so before the slide and the panic started. I also understood that even though it was nice to have Dania here fussing over me, I was probably better off alone. Aud was downstairs. She was also worried, and wanting to do something. Aud was a natural carer. I guess she knew that the old version of me would have been horrified if she had seen me like this.

Dania had brought clothes with her for work tomorrow. I didn't know what sort of ridiculous measures she'd had to take to get so quickly from her work to her house, and then over to Balmain. We had some food upstairs and went to bed early. We sat up in bed like old people. She asked me about the two long letters. Saturday and Sunday. Dania had enjoyed the bit about the escarpment—she had grown up in Sydney and had never seen the outback—but was concerned about the murders, and what was happening inside my head.

I tried to laugh it off. It was only a story and it helped me to write it down. I had told her at the start about the camping trip along the Barnard River, near Nundle, but now that we'd been there together, and seen the country, she wanted to know more about it. It was only two years ago but seemed another lifetime. I repeated what I could remember.

The logging place I was working on was in the Hanging Rock area, up on top of the range on the eastern side of Nundle. The country up there is very steep and wild and beautiful, but I knew that as long as I stuck to the river, I couldn't get too lost. I had the rifle with me and had shot and cooked a small hare on the second day then carried some of the meat with me to have the next night. I also had some fishing gear. I was surprised when I saw the clearing, as I had thought that I was in the middle of nowhere, but a rocky and rutted twin-track wound down from the ridge above and followed the river to a flat open area that repeated flooding had left bare of trees.

At the far end of this clearing, and around a bend from where I had first seen it, was a group of bikers and their bikes—chromed Harleys. I was probably about seventy-five metres away when I saw them, and higher up, making my way around a series of large boulders. I ducked back out of sight, then crawled forward through some thick bracken to a place where I could look at them more closely without much risk of being seen. The rifle was old, but had been fitted with a good scope, and I used that to see them better. There were four of them, all wearing black and big boots, and all with the same patch across the back of their jackets. I remembered that at the edge of the clearing, and at some distance from the group, was a stump, and perched on top, a shiny black crow.

When I looked more closely at the bikers, I could see that one of them seemed to be crying and was being consoled by two of the others. The fourth biker was angry and kept lunging at the crying one and being thrown back by the other two. Bottles were being passed around. Eventually, the angry one left to build a small fire, then lit it with a rag soaked in fuel from the tank of his bike. The others found logs to sit on and they all seemed to settle down a bit.

Evening was coming on by then and the remaining light diminishing. I pulled my oilskin coat more tightly around myself and snuggled deeper into the leaf litter and snowy bracken. I must have fallen asleep as when I next looked up it was fully dark. I raised the rifle again and from the little I could see with the light of their campfire, the four bikers seemed to have drunk themselves to sleep. I remember thinking it was odd that the fire itself was raging now, as though recently stoked.

I felt hollow and drained and strangely dream-like, and thought I might have been getting close to hypothermia. As quietly as I could, I crawled back through the bracken and in behind the boulder, then used a small torch to follow my trail back up the river for an hour or so to a place I had thought might make a good camping spot. I was still quite vague and disoriented as I set the tent up in the dark, then slept dreamlessly without food or a fire.

Early in the icy dawn of the following morning, I packed the camp away again and began the trip back up to the logging property. Walking quickly, I arrived later that afternoon. The old bloke was still ill and in bed, and now struggling with an infection that seemed to have settled on top of his emphysema. He told me that a nurse would be visiting that evening. I didn't tell him anything about the trip, or the bikers, but decided to get a lift with the nurse back down to Tamworth and after that headed off to look for work on the big cattle stations in Queensland.

Dania was interested in the story and could recall some of the wild forest country we drove through near the top end of Barry Station. She asked if I had seen anything about the bikers in the local papers. Fights or drugs. Things like that. I hadn't, but then I had left straight away and was only in Tamworth a day or so before starting the long trip west. She wanted to know more about what they were doing in the clearing but I couldn't remember much. I clearly recalled the one man crying, and the other furious, but aside from the patched jackets and boots, I couldn't even tell her what they or the others had looked like.

Dania didn't think I would make a very good witness and asked if the story I was writing had any more violent bikers. I didn't really know, but thought it unlikely, and told her that I would have to go back to find out. She smiled and squeezed my hand, and when I felt her slide gently into sleep I got up and dressed quietly and walked down to the wharf. It was too late now for ferries and I had the place to myself. I sat down in the pale streetlight and closed my eyes, then leaned back against a pylon. It took a few minutes, but gradually I could feel the heat of Warkon. The dryness and shimmering horizon. And then the voices came back to me. Not clamouring or garbled, just conversation. I was invisible, but watching and listening as the story unfolded and the remnants of our talk of cold forests dissolved into the night-time harbour mist.

Time passed, and I was startled back to reality by the horn of a party boat out in the harbour. I realised that Dania would worry if she woke alone, so got up and stretched and started back up the hill to the house. In the background, the voices were still faint and I felt distracted, longing to lie down and let them take me over again. I climbed the stairs as quietly as I could.

Dania stirred as I got back into bed. 'You okay honey?'

'I couldn't sleep. I've been sleeping most of the afternoon. I'm sorry.'

She squeezed my hand again, only half awake. I closed my eyes and snuggled against her and let myself drift lightly west again across the plains to the escarpment. The voices were quiet now. There was only the warm sun and huge sky and the tiny noises of the bush. I found a soft place among some dense grevillea and lay down. Far above in the deepest blue, three beautiful birds circled slowly, watching. Always watching.

Dear Dania,

Monday, and just a short chapter.

I'm sorry that the last two upset you a bit—hopefully that's okay now.

Anyway, Ben and Duncan are back in Warkon, but no-one's found the bodies yet. Ben's a bit nervy about the escarpment and the feeling that he wasn't in control of events. He wants to go back there and see the place again. Test it.

You'll have to read on to see what happens . . .

Love, Devlin xxx

Monday

'Byron.'

'Mate.'

'Just thought I'd pop by to see if I could help you with anything.' . . .

. . . 'Byron.'

'Mate.'

'Just thought I'd pop by to see if I could help you with anything.'

'Well, that's a very kind thought. Matter of fact, I hate sharpening chainsaw chains. Know how to do it?'

Ben thought he could do that, as long as it was just a file and jig.

'No electric sharpener here, mate. Lazy pricks come into town and hand over about a hundred rooted chains. Charge em' five bucks a chain. Adds up. Be surprised. Now, know the biggest secret with old chains?'

'Are you going to say that you need to file down that little guide link thing?'

'Man's a genius! Only fucken bloke in this region I reckon who knows that. Thought I'd have to tell you for sure.'

'Dad was always on about it. Practically wouldn't let us eat dinner unless we could show that we'd filed the bloody thing.'

'Well, that's the big secret. And seriously, be amazed how many dickheads just sharpen the teeth, then whinge about the fucken saw not cutting wood.'

Byron spat out into the dust. Hoots went over to inspect it.

'Anyway, bucket of chains sitting in the corner. Each has a name tag. Need to make sure we don't lose that. Pricks don't turn up again to get their chains for maybe three or four weeks. But they know exactly how many they left here.'

Hoots carefully scraped dust over the offending gob of spit, then returned to his cushion. Byron looked at him critically. Hoots huffed and closed his eyes.

'So, the chains. Take them out and clean them up in some two-stroke fuel. Little can of it made up over near the forty-fours. Ice-cream bucket and wire brush there, too. Fuel dissolves away the wood and grease and shit and the oil stays on the chain. Lubricates. Stops rusting. You clean those chains up and make a bit of a start on the sharpening, I'll keep going with your bike.'

'No worries.'

Ben positioned a small stool just outside the shed and started cleaning. Hoots was curious and wandered over. Looked up at Ben, panting.

Ben recoiled.

Byron chuckled. 'Breath's a bit ordinary. Bottom jaw's too short and his teeth don't line up. Don't clean themselves, apparently.' Side-on, Hoots did look a bit like a shark. Or an enormous rat.

'Had it looked at once. Young vet. Child really. Came out with a little rubber thing on his finger. Bristles on the end. Said he was going to put his hand in there and scrape some of the shit off. Couldn't tell him anything. Too fucken smart.' Byron had picked up a piece of Ben's bike. Wire hanging out of it, and leaking something. Chuckled at the memory. 'Mate, seriously fucken hilarious. Silly prick had to run off to hospital to get his hand stitched up. And called Hoots a kelpie. Can you fucken believe it? A kelpie. Do they teach these fucken kids anything?'

Hoots was obviously enjoying the story and panted happily, filling the air around him with the fetid fug of his rotting teeth.

'Tell him to fuck off.'

'Don't think I'll do that, Byron.'

'Hoots, come over here, mate. Stop hassling my workforce.'

Hoots looked at Byron reproachfully, and went back to his cushion. Opposite direction.

Byron smiled. 'Sulk now. Hates being told what to do. Work things out for himself. Independent. Been that way since a pup. They're so fucken smart, these red dogs.' Hoots let out a long, damp fart, moving his scurfy arse about on the cushion to get out the last bits. 'But not good in society. Need your whippet for that. Mate had a whippet once. Broke it somehow.'

Ben turned away from Hoots and continued to clean the chains, thinking about the morning. Chloe had been guarded at breakfast and had looked as though she hadn't slept well. He had helped her to get the bar in order for midday opening, then visited Duncan in his police station across the road. Duncan was sitting behind his desk, looking at nothing in particular.

'Dunc, not disturbing great thoughts, am I?'

'No, mate, got rid of those in the little room out the back ten minutes ago. Want to look at some maps?'

They spent half an hour looking at the trails and talking about where they might say they had taken a wrong turn.

'Shouldn't come up, really. That story was just for Chlo. How's the little woman this morning? Perky self?'

'Pretty quiet, Dunc. Didn't say much. I thought she'd want to go back through it all again but she just told me to clean the bar.'

'I'll go and see her soon. Want to give her a bit of space, though. Get her thoughts organised before any shit hits the fan.'

'I'll stay in the background and let you steer this boat. Might duck up the street to see Byron. Maybe help him with the bike for a bit.' Ben had been tempted to take the Norton, but it seemed a bit pointless to go through the lengthy starting procedure for the five-minute ride to Byron's garage.

He was now looking at the parts strewn across the garage floor. 'Byron?'

'Mate.'

'How do you know when it's time to stop pulling things apart and start putting them back together again?'

Byron was at that point bearing down on the starter motor, one of the few bits that Ben still recognised. He had the body of it held to the bench under a hand like a ham and was lining it up with a screwdriver.

'Mate, difficult question. Probably one of those Zen things. Get a feeling that it's time. Like Gough, poor fuck.'

'Gough?'

'Whitto. Never stood a chance.'

Ben wasn't sure how Gough Whitlam was linked to his starter motor. Now gutted. The confusion must have shown, as Byron began singing in an improbably feminine voice,

> *It's time, for freedom*
> *It's time, for moving*

Ben chuckled. He remembered the campaign song although been a child at the time. His dad had liked Gough. Everyone had liked Gough. To begin with.

Byron was laughing. 'Fucken kid in a candy store, Gough. Give everyone money. Fucken free services. Education. No fucken long-term plan. Inevitable he got the arse. Good bloke, but.'

Hoots let out a short, high-pitched red heeler bark. Enough frivolity.

Byron went back to the workbench. 'No, mate, look, I'm just working through a bit of maintenance while the thing's apart. Starter motor has a whole lot of dust in it. Fuck it completely in time. Needs a good clean.'

'Thanks, but just keep in mind the labour cost thing. I can sharpen a few chains for you, but I can't pay to have the whole bike rebuilt.'

Byron put the parts of the starter motor aside. Went over to Hoots. Prodded him with his boot. Could have been a tender moment, but Hoots was still sulking.

'Ben, I wasn't going to tell you because I was told not to. Fact is, you don't need to worry about payment. Call this morning from a bank in Sydney. Wanted my details. Said they had a cheque for two thousand. Put towards this bike. Balance to go to you in cash. Big secret. Sorry.'

Hilde.

Byron continued. 'Must have been shagging the right woman, mate. Bank kept talking about "her" and "she" when they forgot to say "our client".'

Ben recalled that he had told Hilde about the bike, and how the payment was going to be a struggle. But it was going to be dangerous if the spotlight was put on him in an investigation.

'Byron, look, that's great about the money. Seriously, I wasn't sure how I could pay you. But can you do me a favour? If anyone comes asking about me and the bike, can you leave this bit out? I mean, just not say anything about the money? Or maybe tell them I was going to work it off somehow?'

Byron stopped stroking Hoots. 'Not bullshitting, mate?'

'No, Byron, I'm really not.'

'By blokes asking questions, you referring to the big fella?'

'The big fella is the one person who definitely won't be asking questions. But his mates might.'

'Something happen on the weekend?'

'Just please don't say anything. Don't bring it up with Duncan, either. The money in particular, but really anything about what I've just told you, too.'

'No problems. Hoots, you got that?' Hoots growled and looked meaningfully at Byron's boot. Go either way. Byron moved his boot. 'Mate, when you've had a go at those chains, why don't you take the Norton out for a spin? Look a bit rooted, to be honest.'

Ben thanked him and went back to cleaning and sharpening.

Ben eased the little bike out of its annex and onto the red dust in front of the pub. Byron had given him a five-litre jerry can that fitted to a steel rack behind the seat. The rack could easily be removed but, as Byron had explained, the Norton had been designed to run down to the cafe and back. It wasn't a touring bike, but with a full tank and the additional five litres Byron thought he could probably get a comfortable two hundred kilometres. There was a cattle station part-way to Barker that sold fuel on an as-needed basis and could be used for the trip back.

Ben wanted to return to the escarpment. He wouldn't go to the clearing where the bikers' bodies lay, but wanted to ride to the place where he and Duncan had parked the ute. Walk up the rock a bit and see if there was anything in the air—or seeping out of little holes in the rock.

The Norton started easily, which was unusual. Byron had explained the lengthy but apparently failsafe procedure that might need to be followed if it wouldn't turn over when he was out of the town somewhere. This was not a BMW. Ben put on his damaged helmet and gingerly steered the bike through the loose dust at the edge of the road.

Once out of the town, the bike stabilised and Ben's confidence grew. There were very few bends or corners on these outback roads, with minor changes in the underlying road base the only real difficulty. The Norton felt a lot lighter than the BMW and seemed to elevate itself quickly above the looser dust. He let the throttle out a little and smiled at the beautiful engine, then relaxed for the first time since the incident with the bikers.

Time passed and he almost missed the turnoff to the escarpment. He slowed the bike and turned onto the rougher twin-track. This would stretch the Norton's urban suspension and he compensated by keeping the bike just above idle and letting it lug up the track.

Ben stopped when he reached the car park, switched the bike off then pushed it into some dense scrub and stowed his helmet and heavy leathers nearby. Keeping his eyes on the mountain and the sky above it, he began the ascent. He didn't want to retrace the whole length of the track that he had taken with Duncan—just the stretch that would take him to where they had stopped for a sandwich. That was where the oppressive feeling had started. The jokes about fat Edith and beautiful Miranda.

Ben looked closely, but couldn't see any evidence of his or Duncan's passage over the rocky ground. He wasn't a tracker but there didn't seem to be any obvious prints. The stark beauty of the terrain was familiar, with its small canyons and pools and the fractured rocks that lay discarded among the sparse scrub, and Ben seemed to reach the first ledge more quickly than they had previously. He continued along the top of the ledge, following a low ridgeline, then sighted the rocks where they had sat down to rest. He recalled Duncan's little pink lunchbox, and the stupid stuff Duncan had told Smutty, and it occurred to him that he hadn't had the chance to try the chicken parmigiana sandwiches.

Ben sat down on the rock and gazed slowly around, trying to feel for something in the air. But there was nothing at all. Small birds clamoured in the scrub behind him, with an occasional flash of colour. A troop of ants moved resolutely across the gravel between his feet. The sky was wide open and empty and the sun was warm against his back.

He lay down on the rock and closed his eyes, willing the feeling to return. He had to be careful not to drift off to sleep, but kept his eyes closed and listened to the tiny sounds of the bush. It was truly beautiful. And completely calm. After some time, Ben sat up and looked out again across the landscape towards the dry riverbed and the endless plains. Everything was as it had been. Almost everything. He picked up his small day-pack and trudged back down to the bike.

Back at the car park, Ben extracted the Norton from its hide in the scrub, retrieved his helmet and gear and emptied the spare fuel into the tank. Once again, the bike started effortlessly.

The cattle station Byron had told him about was close by and accessed from a farm track that led off the road that he had come in on. There were several sets of gates, then a low-set building nestled in among a stand of aging bloodwoods. Corrugated iron clung to the roof and walls and to the small sheds scattered about. Everything was bone dry. A broken chook run and tennis court. Red dust and midday silence.

An old woman came out of the house, bowed almost double, and bustled quickly towards him. 'What do you want here? What do you want?' Her eyes were impossible to see in a deeply creviced and drought-stricken ruin of a face.

Ben nodded towards the bike. 'Just some fuel. Byron from the garage in Warkon told me to stop here and fill up the bike.'

That seemed to reassure her a little and she pointed to a forty-four-gallon drum with a hand-pump, just inside an open shed. 'How much you need?'

'Not much. Got a small tank. I reckon about twelve or fifteen litres all up.'

'Give me the money for fifteen.'

Ben sighed and counted out the sum she came up with, which seemed to be quite arbitrary. 'Thank you.'

But she had already turned and was stamping angrily back up the path to the house.

Ben filled the bike and the little jerry can and replaced the pump handle in its makeshift wire cradle. A mummified rat lay against his foot. He stood still. There was no noise at all. Nothing. Not even a clattering windmill somewhere down in a paddock, sucking artesian water out of the ancient ground. Complete silence.

Haven for snakes in summer, all this dead iron.

He got back on the bike, happier now about the feel of the road tyres in the dust and sand and the easy but predictable slide. He set his weight back a bit to lighten the front and pushed it up into a higher gear, then let the bike stretch out a little as the road to Warkon came into sight. At the turnoff he stopped to check that the empty fuel container was still secure, then followed the dry riverbed back into town.

CHAPTER 6

The following day I had to go in to uni. I knew I couldn't get out of it, even with a doctor's certificate. My bike was unrideable after the incident with the garbage bin so I went with Dania on the ferry. We were both sombre and subdued. I had promised to look for a psychiatrist. I thought Mum might know someone. Mum knew I was struggling and would be pleased that I was trying to do something constructive about it. Dania looked lovely in a black office skirt, snow-white blouse and tartan stockings, and her hair tied back in a tortoiseshell clip. We had an expensive coffee at a cafe we knew in The Rocks, then I caught a bus up George Street to the university.

I slipped quietly into the vet building. Tobe had flu, but had struggled in for the same reason as me. Pracs were not negotiable. He was sitting by himself in a corner of the cafeteria, bundled up in about four heavy coats.

'Fucken sick as a dog.'

'Me, too.'

He laughed. 'Well, which one of us is going to make it through the prac, do you reckon?'

'Not a betting man, Tobe. On that road lies only unhappiness.'

I got a Styrofoam cup of the crappy cafeteria coffee and sat at a table near to him. But not too close. He was shaking with cold. And sweating. On the survival question, I thought I might have had the upper hand. He coughed again. 'Seriously, mate, I don't know when I've ever felt this crook. Just want to lie down on fucken Parramatta Road.'

'Lawyer Chick would be disappointed. Probably sue your corpse.'

He chuckled. 'Lawyer Chick has dumped me for one of the partners. Hope the poor fuck is fit. Bloody hell. Reckon I'm only sick because she ran me into the ground.'

'Ran you? I obviously had the wrong end of this one.'

He chuckled again. 'Piss off and leave me alone. Want to die in peace.'

I made my way up to the prac room. Microbiology. Bacteria and their tiny microscopic mates. I quite liked it and talking with Tobe had lightened things up a bit. I found the bench and microscope that I'd used the week before and got some books out.

Little Fat Man was out the front, busying himself with the overhead projector. These blokes supposedly had brains the size of God's underpants, but not one of them could work any sort of technology. He had the spool in a complete mess. One of the Good Girls went over to help him. Had to unwind the whole thing. He had it completely inside out. She was laughing it off. He seemed to be looking down her shirt.

Everyone else had arrived now. I found it helped to get there first and settle in a bit. Relax. There were people all around me now, but I tried not to think about it. Tobe had struggled in and had his head on a bench in the corner.

Little Fat Man coughed and started his lecture. Gram-negative bacteria. I knew about them as I had done a bit of reading at home. These evil buggers have an outer membrane that forms a toxin when they die off or are killed. And that helps to produce septic shock. They affect humans, as well as most pets and livestock. Little Fat Man was on a roll now and visibly excited, chaotically unravelling his overhead projector notes and gesticulating wildly with pink pudgy hands. Prodigious puddles of sweat had appeared on his chest and under his arms. It was a shame Tobe was missing this.

I watched, amused, and listened closely for twenty minutes or so. But then I began to be more aware of the people around me. Too many people. Too close. I should have taken a short break—maybe sat in the toilet for a few minutes—but I stayed, and quickly the stress started to build. At first, I was just squirming a bit in my seat, pretending discomfort or boredom. Yawning ostentatiously. But then I realised that I was starting to sweat as well, and found it hard to breathe deeply. I sat on my hands and tried to calm down.

The girl next to me looked nervous. I turned to her. 'Getting flu. Sorry.'

She smiled tightly. I wiped my face with my sleeve. It was dripping. I blinked a few times, willing the lecture to end so that I could get outside. But Little Fat Man was droning on and I now had no idea what he was saying. I was only trying not to panic. It seemed as though everyone was watching me, so I closed my eyes and rested my head on my arms and feigned sleep. I could feel the sweat on my back soaking through my shirt and I began to shake a bit.

And then I realised that I really had to get out. It would be embarrassing, but I just couldn't stay there. I stood up slowly and tried to gather up my books. One slipped and fell to the floor. Little Fat Man heard it.

'Bored already, Mr Mack? Too clever for microbiology?'

'Fuck off.' It was out before I realised. Growled. Loud, and with a lot of menace.

He was a bit shocked and just looked at me. Didn't say anything.

I picked up the book and bundled everything together, then stumbled out into the corridor. Tobe was fast asleep and missed the whole thing. The corridor was empty and instantly I felt the weight and pressure diminish. But I kept going—almost running—out of the main doors and over to the oval where

I knelt down in the shade with my head on my knees. I was breathing deeply. Panting really. I felt the tears on my face, but it didn't seem like crying.

'Devlin. You okay?' Two of the Good Girls had come after me. They had their books and bags. They weren't going back. I looked up at them. 'Feel a bit fucked. Sorry.' Even completely rooted—as in potentially end-stage rooted—you couldn't say 'fuck' around them with a clear conscience.

'Don't worry about it.' They smiled and talked quickly to each other, then turned back to me. One, Toni, added, 'My brother is at home sick. Everyone has this flu. I'll call him and get him to come in with Mum's car and he can take you home.'

I couldn't believe it. People kept doing these outrageous things when I was basically just some sad, broken, useless prick. 'Really? But don't you live, like, up there somewhere?' I pointed vaguely towards the north. New Guinea. England.

They both laughed. 'What is it with this north shore angst? Yes, we live at Killara. Yes, there are roads there. And yes, my brother can get in the car and come and get you. He's not that sick. Bludger, really.'

Toni went off to use the phone in the vet school office. The other, Mary, sat down next to me. Stretched out her legs. They were very nice legs. She looked at the sky. 'You need some help with this.' She said it quietly.

'I know. I'm going to get some names from my parents. See if someone will take me on.'

'Good. We've been a bit worried, really.'

I thought about that. 'Sorry. I know it's been going on for a while now. Getting worse. I let myself get distracted a bit by the band and my girlfriend. I thought it might just go away.'

Mary picked a blade of grass. Studied it. Turned to me. A lot of force in her eyes. She had nice eyes, too. 'It won't. I got sick when I was at school. I stopped eating. Mum and Dad got scared. I wasn't even allowed to walk to school by myself.'

I was staggered. 'Really? How did you get over it?'

She reached out and squeezed my hand. 'You don't get over it. It becomes a part of who you are. But it goes into the background.'

Toni joined us. 'I said we'd meet him at the Ross Street entrance. We've got some time, but do you feel like walking?'

We only had to wait at Ross Street for half an hour or so before a deep blue Volvo arrived. A blue so deep that it was almost black. Polished to a mirror. And brand new. With P-plates. The younger brother was at the wheel. He was very tall with fashionably long blonde hair and unblemished clothes that seemed to have been deliberately ruffled. There were no visible symptoms of flu.

We piled into the car. The seats had a lot of short, white hairs on them. Definitely Labrador. I chuckled, despite myself. The kid turned in his seat and offered a hand. 'I'm Greg. Mate, I saw you blokes at the Women's College ball last term. Grouse, man. Best band ever. You hurt yourself?'

Greg had not been briefed.

'Thanks, Greg. Think I ate something. Bit of pain when I talk.'

The Girls chuckled and told Greg where I lived. I had no idea how they knew.

We left Greg in the car outside, double-parked, and went through to the living room. The Girls looked around. 'Lovely house. I had pictured you living in a wheelbarrow under a bridge.' She saw my face and looked horrified. 'I'm so sorry, Devlin. I was only kidding.'

She sat me down and put the kettle on. Immediately found cups and biscuits. I had no idea that we had biscuits. 'Do you want us to stay with you until your flatmate gets back?'

'Thanks so much, but no. And Greg looks like he might succumb to that flu pretty soon. Better get him off to casualty.'

They both laughed. 'Lazy little bludger. It's his last year at school. And he wasn't supposed to be at the Women's College ball. He's not old enough. I think he did it for a dare.'

The other added, 'We'll get you copies of our notes, so you can keep up.'

'Really? You don't mind?'

She shook her head. 'Just don't tell Toby. He doesn't need any encouragement.'

'I'll get you my dodgy library card so at least the copying won't cost you anything.' I said it without thinking, then looked ashamed.

She smiled. 'It's okay, we've got our own.' And held up a laminated card on a frayed lanyard from which the thin, mousy face of Muhammad Saleem, postgraduate student in veterinary parasitology, peered hopefully.

Once the Girls had gone I called Mum. I told her what had happened and asked if she knew anyone in Sydney. Mum said she'd ring back. I got another biscuit, wondering again where little Aud had hidden them. She was trying to get Dom to eat less sweet stuff. Dom loved her little round body. Couldn't stop cuddling her. Chased her round the flat.

Mum rang back in about ten minutes and gave me a bloke's name and number. 'Now, Devlin, you'll need to tell him everything. Okay? Don't just paint one of your pictures. And ring me if you get in a fix. Please. You'll do that?'

'Thanks, Mum. Yeah, I'll do that.' I looked at the name and rang the number.

'Doctors rooms.'

Open book.

'Dr Gidleigh's rooms?'

'Yes. Please hold the line.'

I'd had my chance, and was now going to be punished with elevator music. She came back three minutes later. It sounded like she was sipping tea. 'How can I help you?'

'Could I make an appointment to see Dr Gidleigh, please.'

'You'll need a referral.'

I told her that Mum was a GP and knew Dr Gidleigh, and was writing him a note. She thought about that. 'We'll need to have that note, or the doctor won't be able to see you.'

I formed a picture of a doctor fumbling around in the waiting room, blind without his note. 'Okay. I'll make sure she gets onto it today. Can I make that appointment?'

'When did you want to see the doctor?'

'This afternoon? I could be there in half an hour.'

Silence. Obviously not used to dealing with nutters. 'Dr Gidleigh is fully booked today. Is this really urgent?'

'I'm not bleeding, if that's what you mean.'

'Are you in distress?'

There were no more biscuits. Possibly. 'Yes, I am. Yes. Very. Distressed.'

'Okay, well there's a slot tomorrow morning at eleven. You'll need to be here a few minutes before that so the nurse can take a history.'

'Okay. Thanks.'

'We'll see you, then.'

'Bye, then.'

I hung up. Take my history in a few minutes? Born. Went to school. Went up into the hills. Went north. Went to uni. Went off the rails.

I went upstairs. I lay on my bed, but felt agitated and somehow unclean and got up again. I noticed my writing pad on the desk and took it downstairs. A lot of things had happened at Warkon last night. Important things. I made a coffee and lay on the couch with the notepad rested on my thighs.

Dania went with me to see Dr Gidleigh. She had taken the day off work. Mum had called her to get some more details for the note. There were tears on the phone, apparently. Mum had also called Dr Gidleigh and talked him through it. I had given Dania another chapter of the story, but she was too distracted to comment. Dania was really worried about me.

We sat in an expensive waiting room in St Leonards. Mum was paying. Everyone looked completely normal. It was as though we had accidentally gone to the rooms of the dentist who shared the building. I held Dania's hand. Her eyes were red. A woman opposite looked at her with sympathy. I wanted to tell her that it was me who'd gone crazy, not Dania. Perhaps she knew.

We had seen the nurse and had given a brief history. This had turned out to be for relevant medical details. I didn't have any. I hadn't been to a doctor for about three years.

A short, compact bloke in his thirties stuck his head into the room. Clipboard. Neat beard. 'Devlin Mack?'

I guess if it had been Monty Python, everyone except me would have got up and walked in. But no-one in the waiting room seemed to be suffering delusions about their identity, and Dania and I picked up our things and followed him obediently down a corridor to a small consulting room.

'Have a seat, please.' He was courteous and contained. He sat behind a desk while we took the two small armchairs facing it. I crossed one leg over the other. Dania sought my hand.

'So, Devlin, how's your mum?'

'Pretty sane, I think.'

He thought this was amusing. Dania nudged me, and I stopped smiling. 'She's well, thanks. Sends her regards.'

'Thank you. Yes, we had a chat a little earlier this morning. She's very concerned about you. And you must be Dania? I'm John Gidleigh.' He leaned across the desk and held out his hand. We both stood and shook it, then sat back down.

'So, tell me about what's been happening.'

I had expected this and had prepared a summary that went back to last year, then told of the more recent and dramatic events. Dania was silent, but nodded to herself. Dr Gidleigh watched each of us in turn, and took occasional, scant notes. These seemed almost to be single letters. He brought his pen to the paper, made a mark, then sat it back on the desk again. It might have been code, or maybe he was just filling out a lottery coupon.

I stopped. I had got as far as yesterday. The big fuck-up. End of the story. He didn't seem perturbed. 'So what do you think, Dania? Is that an accurate depiction of events? Anything important to add?'

Dania bit a nail and looked at the floor. She wasn't as comfortable with doctors as I was. Her mum wasn't this bloke's friend and colleague. When she spoke, it was to a print of an impressionist's painting of a duck on the wall behind Dr Gidleigh's desk. 'Everything Devlin has told you is true. I don't think he's left out anything in terms of what's been happening. But he hasn't told you what he's really like now.'

Dr Gidleigh sat forward. Arms on the desk.

Dania squeezed my hand again. 'He's a bit special. He can do things that other people can't do. His friends are all brilliant. One's a genius. They don't realise they're not normal people. He gets passionate about things. Too passionate. When he's playing a song he likes, it sort of takes him over. He's not there anymore. And it drains him. He doesn't see it, but there's nothing left after a big night with his band. Nothing left at all. Sometimes he can't even talk properly.' She glanced at me quickly. 'He's worried about university, but I don't think it's the main problem. I don't think he would be worried if the problem wasn't there. Or he'd be a bit worried, like the others, but do a whole lot of work at the last minute and get through it all.'

She paused.

'Go on. Please.'

'Something has got hold of him. It seems to me that he used to be able to bounce back from his down times, but now he just can't. He stays down. And he wakes up really confused and scared. Mornings are really bad. Almost all of them now.' She sniffed. Ran a hand across her eyes. 'When we first got together, we had lovely breakfasts. Now he never eats before midday. He goes off to university all confused and upset, and he hasn't had any breakfast.'

I didn't know how much more of this I could take. I would have eaten breakfast if I'd known it was upsetting her.

Dr Gidleigh seemed to sense this. Put his hand up. 'Thank you, Dania. That's a much better picture. Thank you very much.' Passed her a box of tissues. They had small rabbits on them. It occurred to me that he must churn through a few boxes in this line of work.

He seemed to be thinking. I took Dania's hand. Kissed her cheek. She smiled.

'You're an exceptionally lucky bloke.' Almost to himself. Wasn't even looking at us. Dania put her other hand over mine.

'Devlin, I confess I had quite a long chat with your mum about this. I hope you don't mind. She told me you were close, but wanted you to know that nothing would go back to her from this point onwards without your permission. You understand that? Completely confidential.'

I nodded.

'Your mum felt, and I have to agree from what I've heard from you both just now, that you are now clinically depressed. Do you know what that means? In medical terms?'

I nodded again. 'I've done some reading in the library.'

'Okay. So what I need to understand is whether this is what we might call "endogenous", or a result of persistent exposure to a stressful or otherwise difficult situation.'

'Can it be both? I mean, can one predispose the other?'

He sat back again. Smiled. 'Yes, it can be both. Tell me why that has occurred to you.'

'It was Danny's thinking, really. I mean, I do find the uncertainty associated with uni really stressful, but I don't really understand why it has worn me down so much. Partly, I think, it's because I can't control anything.' I paused, wondering how to explain this. 'You know, when I was working on the big stations up north,

I was independent. Everyone was. Blokes told me what to do, and I could take it and get paid or leave and work somewhere else. I was in control. Down here, I can't control anything. Even myself.' I looked at Dania. 'Dania is working full time. It's not a job she loves, but it's okay. She's a great musician. She could be a professional viola player. But she's in control of her life. She's happy. I'm not. But I shouldn't be this buggered by it all.'

Dr Gidleigh considered this for a bit. 'It's very hard for me to know, having only just met you. On the one hand, you can't overestimate the effect of prolonged negativity of the sort you describe. People can become worn down to the point of a chemical imbalance in the brain—to put it simply. Alternatively, it can be argued that someone who's brain is prone to such imbalances will be more likely to find themselves in this position.' He paused, and looked directly at us. 'Ultimately, we may not be able to answer this one in the short term. It may be something that only becomes clear when you have been through another ten years or so.' He stopped again, and this time seemed to consult his strange notes. 'But look, underneath both theories is a third issue. And that's the way you've taught yourself to respond to life's stresses. And perhaps an underlying condition, if there is one there. Have you got destructive thought habits? Are you able to relax effectively? Are you carrying a whole lot of "baggage", for lack of a better word?'

I started to speak, but he held up his hand. 'No, I don't want to try and answer those questions now. What I want to do is decide how we're going to deal with this in the short term.' He pressed clean chiselled fingers against his temples. 'Devlin, your mum really is worried about you now. And I can see that Dania is also. I'm not going to beat around the bush here. No-one wants you to come to any harm. And young blokes like you who feel everything so deeply are always a risk, in my view. I think you should accept an invitation to spend a couple of weeks in hospital so we can try out some medicines and I can get to know you a bit.'

I wasn't prepared for this. Dania was. Obviously, Mum had broached it with her. She looked at me. Imploring.

'Where?'

'Here in St Leonards. Just a few doors up the road. It's a small private hospital. A very good one. You'll be safe.'

Dania was starting to cry. I turned to her and gave her some more of the rabbit tissues. 'What would you think, knowing I had been in one of those places?'

'I just want you to get better honey. I don't care what it takes. Honestly, I don't care. I'll be proud of you if you really try. That's all I want.'

I looked at Dr Gidleigh, as something else occurred to me. 'Is this actually optional?'

'At the moment, yes, absolutely.'

'You mean, until I say no?'

He chuckled. 'Look, Devlin, just listen to two nice women who love you. Okay?'

I looked at the duck on the wall behind his desk and wondered how anyone back in the eighteen-hundreds could have convinced a duck to stay still long enough to paint it. 'Alright. I'll go in. When do I do it?'

'I would like you to go home now and get some things. Any books you want. Washing things. Here's a pamphlet that will help. Then go straight to the hospital. I'll call them and get the paperwork organised. Your mum will handle the account.'

I looked at Dania. She was biting her lip. 'Can I bring a guitar?'

They both laughed. Dr Gidleigh stood and gestured towards the door. 'No, Devlin, you absolutely can't.'

Dear Dania,

Tuesday, and now things in Warkon get exciting . . .

The bodies are found and Duncan's boss Trev starts an investigation.

What can Trev find out from carnage at the clearing?

Can Duncan and Ben keep themselves clean?

You'll have to find out . . .

Love, Devlin xxx

Tuesday

Duncan was doing paperwork when the call came in. A local farmer had been up in his ultralight checking tanks and troughs, and thought he might look at the escarpment and take some pictures . . .

. . . Duncan was doing paperwork when the call came in. A local farmer had been up in his ultralight checking tanks and troughs, and thought he might look at the escarpment and take some pictures. The glint off the bikes' chrome had caught his eye, just as it had Ben and Duncan's. He had brought the tiny plane in as close as he dared, mindful of the danger from unexpected thermals. Through binoculars he had seen the bikes, and what looked like bodies, and had radioed in to his wife.

His wife was distressed and was now on the phone with Duncan. A fraught little voice. 'Constable, you must go out and see what has happened. But don't give anyone our name. We don't want to be mixed up in any bike gang thing.'

'I'll do that, Meg. Straight away. Tell your husband to come down out of the sky. And to stay away from the escarpment. And tell him not to talk to anyone about this. That goes for you, too. I don't want a whole lot of rubberneckers fronting up in their utes.'

'I'll tell Ronnie. And we'll keep it to ourselves.'

'Thanks, Meg. I'll get back to you sometime later in the day and let you know what's going on.'

Duncan stared at the opposite wall, then picked up the phone again. 'Jane, it's Duncan. Get Trev, will you.'

'That would be Senior Sergeant Bolan, then?'

'Not feeling funny, Jane. Soonest.'

A cough and a gruff voice. 'Duncan, what's up?'

'Boss, something big might have happened at the escarpment. Eastern car park area. Local cocky in an ultralight reported bikes and bodies. Lots. Chrome bikes, like bikers. I'm heading out there now.'

Silence, then, 'Reliable bloke? Know him?'

'Met his wife. She's okay. Local station owners. She sounded stressed. Had the wind up for sure. Definitely worth a look. These blokes check out their stock water from the air. Good at looking. I believe it.'

'Okay, well, look, go straight there. The eastern car park, you say? I know where you mean. Get back to me when you're out there and have had a chance to see what's happened. And Duncan. . .'

'Boss.'

'Don't get anywhere close to any bikers if you think they're alive and kicking. I know most sensible folk are more scared of you than the other way round, but this lot might be armed. And might not want to be disturbed. Just stay right back at first, and make sure it's safe. Okay? Jane here would be very distressed if anything happened to you.'

Duncan could hear muted protestations from Jane, whose phone Trev must have been talking on. He couldn't be taught how to get his own phone on and off hold and took most of his calls standing behind Jane's chair.

Duncan stared again at the opposite wall.

First lie. Fuck. How many more before this shit-fight is over?

He stirred himself and got up to get some things together. These included the hiking boots that he had worn the previous weekend, and a police shotgun, which he thought might look convincing. *A cautious man preparing himself.* He packed the car then went across the road to see Chloe and Ben.

Duncan found them chatting in the bar. Ben looked good with her. Same size. He let it go.

'Shit's hit the fan. Cocky's seen the bodies from his plane. Called it in. I've told Trev, my boss. He wants me to check it out. That's good news, as I'll be the first on the scene. Put some fresh boot prints all over the place.' Duncan was distracted, and thinking aloud, 'If I bring Trev back here afterwards, be very careful, okay? He notices the little things.'

Ben nodded. 'We will, and good luck. Hope the animals have made a bit of a mess of it.'

Duncan agreed. After three nights it would be surprising if the bodies were undisturbed.

Chloe took his hand. 'Take care, Duncan. We'll find a way to talk to you quietly when you get back.'

Duncan stopped the car several hundred metres back from the clearing and turned it around, then proceeded carefully in reverse, thinking that this was probably what he would have done if he had been concerned about live, angry bikers with firearms. He stopped again closer in and got out of the car, then kept going on foot. He had the shotgun with him. Everything as it would have been.

As he came up to the clearing, he paused, listened, then walked up to place where the van had stood. The scene had been interfered with but not as much as he had hoped. Two of the closer bodies had been dragged around a little, with limbs no longer exactly as they had fallen. Their eyes had been taken, and faces lacerated. That was probably birds. Maybe an eagle. The leader's shotgun remained where it had been. Good. He looked further and saw the second gun was also where it should have been.

Duncan went back to the car and lifted the radio's handset. 'Warkon mobile calling Barker base. Over.'

'Hang on, Duncan, I'll get the boss. Over.' Jane's voice, contrite now.

'Duncan, what have you found? Over.'

'Boss, everything as the cocky said. Four dead blokes here. Two guns. Three bikes, another one blown up. Parts. All bikers. Jackets, patches, tatts. Major shit-fight. Over.'

'Okay, look I don't need to tell you not to disturb the scene. Just sit back in your car and I'll get there as soon as I can. Over.'

'Boss. Out.'

Duncan looked up at the hill. He thought he should probably walk around the area a bit in his hiking boots, just in case he'd left any prints or other evidence on Saturday. Trev would be annoyed, as he had told Duncan to stay in the car. Maybe he could tell Trev he'd wanted a better look from a vantage point.

Duncan took his binoculars and skirted the scene, looking for bruised scrub or broken branches and old prints that looked like his. He couldn't see anything at all, so turned away and walked up to the place where Ben had shot from. Forensics would know that the bikers had been killed with rifles, and probably from a distance. That meant the hill. A police tracker would cast about systematically and almost certainly find this place. Duncan himself would have done, and might still be given the task of looking. He reached the spot and looked carefully around. There was a slight indentation where Ben's body had lain, but nothing that would link the site to Ben specifically. Satisfied, Duncan made his way back down the hillside and returned to his car.

Duncan heard a car in the distance and realised that he must have dozed off in the warm sun filtering through the windscreen. The engine note was uneven, as though churning through loose sand.

Had to be Trev. Clever bloke, but a complete fucken idiot behind the wheel.

The car appeared with both wheels deep in the ruts and its belly dragging noisily across tufts of saltbush. Duncan smiled protectively, shaking his head.

Get out of the fucken holes, you dickhead.

It came to a stop several metres away and the engine raced with the clutch in, then stalled. The door opened and the car rolled forward. The door then closed again and Duncan could hear a muffled curse as the handbrake was applied. The door now reopened and Trev got out.

Duncan walked over. 'Senior man like yourself should have a driver, Boss.'

'Bugger off.'

They shook hands.

'You look surprisingly calm, Duncan. Show me the damage.'

Duncan flinched at the remark. *Fuck. No flies on this bloke. Don't forget it.* They walked together towards the clearing.

Trev stopped just short of the scene. 'My word.'

'Yes.'

Trev then moved around the clearing systematically, like an airport beagle. Duncan began to feel nervous and tried to distract him. 'I've had a quick look around in the scrub and up the hill. See if there are any others. Nothing.'

Trev was annoyed, as Duncan knew he would be. 'Duncan, I specifically asked you to stay in the car. We must preserve this scene for Forensics. I've organised for Rob, Andy and Geoff to get hold of the caravan and join us. They'll secure the area and stay here overnight. Hopefully the ghosts won't get them.'

'Probably be too busy holding hands and singing camp songs, Boss. But thought you might have had me in mind for that job. Relieved, though. Wouldn't really like to be out here after dark.'

'Well, I thought it likely that you would be needed to show people around. I know you like to hunt pigs up here, so you probably know the trails.'

Trev bent to examine some small broken branches. 'I suspect we're going to be overrun with clever Sydney people by the morning. Homicide obviously, I've already had a word to them. They'll run the investigation and may want to involve their Drug Squad comrades given that these are bikers.' He stared over to the body of the leader. 'This man has his fly open. And his underpants have been pulled down a bit.'

Duncan flinched again. *Fuck. Fuck. Fuck.* Why hadn't he seen that? He could see now that whatever had been pecking at the bodies had rolled this one over a bit.

'Maybe taking a piss?'

Trev didn't answer immediately but continued to step carefully around the edge of the clearing. 'Doesn't look like it. And there's some blood on the ground over there, but there's no body.'

Andes's blood.

Duncan grunted, still flustered and not fully trusting his voice.

But Trev appeared not to notice, still looking thoughtfully at the bloodstain. 'Odd that. The rest would have died quite quickly. Except perhaps that one, but he also stayed where he was.' The gut-shot biker. Later executed from the hill.

'Maybe one of the killers, Boss? Must have been more than one to knock this lot off so quickly. Might've got hurt in the process. Could be gold, this blood.'

'Good thinking, Duncan. I like that idea.'

'Or maybe one of the bikers got away? Maybe there were five. Played dead. Left when the killers had gone.'

'Possible, but you'd think the killers would check.'

'If one did get away, there will be reprisals.'

Distract him. Too close.

But Trev couldn't be distracted. 'Shot with a high-powered rifle, by the looks of things. All of them. That seems a bit odd to me. You would think they would go for shotguns or handguns, wouldn't you? Maybe the killers weren't bikers?'

Duncan was beginning to feel light-headed. Surely it couldn't unravel within twenty minutes? He remembered his resolve to be excited and helpful. To act naturally. Have good ideas. 'Might have been an ambush? Planned hit? Maybe hired shooters?'

'Could be. But this looks to be more complicated than a big brawl with guns. There are bottles lying around, so they were probably relaxed. But why did they come out here with those bikes? They don't usually like to get dust on them.'

Duncan recalled Ben asking the same question. 'Could have been meeting a local pusher. Got into an argument. Pusher had mates in the bush with rifles. Cockies or ringers. Use hollow-points for hunting.'

'You might be getting close to the truth there, Duncan. It is possible that this is all about bikers, but it doesn't look right. Why would they choose this place and not gun each other down in Sydney somewhere?'

'Nice and quiet. No witnesses. But you'd think it would have a local angle. And that would have to mean the pushers. Do you know them?'

'Some of them. And we suspect some others. But they're all pretty hopeless. I honestly can't imagine them planning something like this.'

'Maybe they just took some precautions. Some mates parked out in the scrub with rifles. When everything went bad, that lot started shooting. Some good shooters around here. No trouble hitting pigs and roos. Probably no trouble hitting bikers, if they had to.'

Trev nodded, then headed back to the car. Duncan stayed with him, trying to stay focussed. 'Some vehicle tracks here, Boss. Look a bit recent. Bit more blood on these bushes.'

The van. More of Andes's blood.

'True. Well spotted.'

'Maybe the killers arrived in this vehicle, Boss. Ambushed the bikers. Or maybe it came to pick them up afterwards. Including the bleeding one.'

Suggest. Distract.

'All possible, Duncan. Perhaps the vehicle arrived first and one or two of the killers went off into the scrub with their rifles. Then the remaining one—or maybe more—was responsible for whatever negotiations were to take place. That went pear-shaped and his friends started shooting.'

Duncan began to relax. 'Be interesting to test these theories out on the Sydney boys. Should have a good feel for it.'

'Forensics are generally silent, Duncan. And don't count on good manners or inclusive behaviour from the Homicide fanatics either. If I'm honest, I don't relish the thought of babysitting that lot while they try to get to the bottom of this. Hopefully it won't take them too long.'

They had reached Duncan's car, and sat together facing back down the track and waiting for the arrival of the second group from Barker.

Trev looked uncomfortable. 'This seat isn't very good, Duncan.'

'Just a seat, Boss. Standard Ford seat.'

Trev grunted, still squirming. 'What music have you got?'

'Case near your foot, Boss. Most of it from this century. Sorry about that.'

Trev chuckled. 'Duncan, Duncan, Duncan. You may be surprised to learn that I attended the Aquarius Festival in Nimbin in 'seventy-three.'

'Busting hippies, Boss? Perving on topless chicks?'

'Presumptuous, Duncan. Cheeky. No, I was there with some friends. Chilling out.'

'Chilling out, Boss?'

'That's right. Very chilled. Listening to righteous folk music. None of which you seem to have here.' Trev was rummaging in a dusty case of cassettes. 'Although I note that you haven't burnt this Blondie tape, as instructed. I trust there's been no more dancing? Police image, Duncan. Do I have to send you on a course?'

Duncan looked across. 'Sorry, Boss, the other case. That one's for when Rob, Andy or Geoff are in the car. Short attention spans. Chorus in the opening line. No more than four chords.'

'Like, *No way, get fucked, fuck off*?'

Duncan chuckled. 'That's the one, Boss. And many others just like it. Look in that other box. Full of righteous shit. Some of it's so righteous it doesn't even have words.'

Trev found the second box and began sifting quietly through the tapes, intermittently emitting grunts that seemed to indicate approval or dismay. After a few moments he looked up, eyebrows raised. 'Brother Leonard? Several collections thereof. My estimation of Constable Duncan is on the ascendance.'

Duncan smiled. 'Too late, Boss. Here's the cavalry. Wasted no time getting here. Clearly didn't spare the blue-and-white horse.'

Trev inserted a tape, anyway, and pressed Play. Cohen crooned. Trev smiled.

'Hot dog.'

Duncan flinched. 'Boss, please don't say that to the others. Ever. Wouldn't survive.'

'We always used to say Hot Dog. I should be able to say what I want.' Trev sounded petulant.

'You can say what you want, Boss. Privilege of rank. It's what happens next. When you're not in the room.'

'Okay, cool.'

'Fuck.'

'What?'

'Nothing, Boss. Boys, welcome.' The car had pulled up alongside them. Windows down. An argument audible. Rob was driving. Duncan leaned out and shook his hand.

'Dunc. What's with the hippie shit, mate?'

'Cohen, mate. Boss's choice. Andy, Geoff, greetings.'

The others nodded. Geoff leaned across from passenger's seat. 'Been out killing people again, mate?'

Duncan choked, then recovered. 'No, mate, not this time. Too professional, this one. Long range. Shooters who can shoot.'

They all got out and followed Trev back to the clearing.

'Fuck a brown dog!'

'Rob, I don't care what you say when you're around other children but please attempt something approaching the decorum of a police officer when I'm standing right beside you.'

'Sorry, Boss. Horrific. Can I touch one?'

'No, you can't.'

'My kid would love that jacket, Boss.'

Trev looked pained. 'Enough. Now put the caravan in that pull-out up the road a bit and get your gear organised. There should be posts and crime scene tape in the van. I want that right around this clearing. And while you're doing that, decide how you're going to break up your protective duties. I want one of you out on the highway, with a car parked across the track. And another down here near my car—again, with your car parked across the track. The third can be resting.'

Trev looked hard at each of them. 'This is a serious business. The press will try to get their noses in. I want a firm but polite police presence. No-one gets past any of you without showing ID. And without verbal confirmation from me. No-one at all. Period. Do you understand?'

They understood.

'You've got your side-arms and I want you to make sure that those are ready to fire. There is no reason to think that either the killers or the rest of this gang will come back, but anything is possible at this stage. You've got shotguns in the car. I want one of those to be handy down at this end.'

Another pause.

'I know I'm generally quite lenient. That's just my way. But every now and then something matters. This matters. It really does. Do all three of you register that?'

They did.

'You will not under any circumstances approach this crime scene and risk contaminating it. That includes the surrounds, and the hill behind, all of which Duncan has already trampled over. There will be no discharging of firearms at wildlife, or any other form of hooliganism. I will make sure that you have food and non-alcoholic drink.'

A final pause. This was a very long speech for Trev. Probably a record.

'Do you all understand what I have said? If you do as I have asked, I will be grateful. If any of you disappoints me on this job, he will be looking for employment in another town. And just in case you haven't noticed, there aren't any other towns.'

'Okay, Boss.'

'Boss.'

'Boss.'

'Good. Now get to it.'

Rob, Andy and Geoff moved off purposefully, talking among themselves. Rob tripped on a branch. Thought he might have been pushed. Punched Andy. Andy punched him back. Trev sighed and turned back to Duncan. 'You and I will go to Warkon. I want the two Homicide people to stay there, and I will, too. Just until we have a better idea of how this is going to pan out. I have overnight gear with me in the car. Forensics will hopefully just be in and out, but I'll organise transport for them from Barker. Others we'll have to play by ear.'

'Sounds good, Boss. Let's get back to Warkon then and I'll get you some maps of the area to have a look at.'

'Right-on.'

Duncan saw flashing lights in his mirror. They were just halfway down the track back to the main road.

Shit. Maybe he can't work out how to turn on the aircon.

He pulled over and walked back to Trev's window. 'Boss, what's up?'

'Occurred to me, Duncan, are there any homesteads nearby?'

Duncan was surprised. 'There is one actually, but access is off the other road. The Warkon side. West. We can go down the highway a bit and cut across. Think they might have seen something?'

'It's possible.'

'The place I mean sells a bit of fuel. Not sure it's legal, to be honest. Important back-stop for a lot of locals, so I've never looked too closely.'

'Let's go there on the way back to your station.'

Duncan always liked the sound of that. Your station. 'No worries, Boss. You can drop back a bit out of the dust. I'll stop at every turn off.'

Duncan smiled to himself. *Distract. Ask questions. This new diversion could only be good news.*

Having taken half a dozen local farm tracks and minor gravel roads, they arrived at the track leading to the station homestead. Duncan got out to help Trev to close the first gate, then did the rest himself. Soon they reached the broken, dying house.

The old woman barrelled out into the hard light, slamming the screen door behind her, and scurried down the path towards them. 'What do you want here? What do you want?'

Trev looked back at the two police cars, then drew himself up, hands clasped behind his back in what he appeared to think the correct pose for a senior officer taking a polite line of enquiry. Duncan closed his eyes. Trev took a step forward.

'Good afternoon, Ma'am, a few minutes of your time.'

She looked up at him sceptically. 'What did you call me?'

'Ma'am?'

To Duncan, 'Your mate sounds like a fucken sheep. What's he saying?'

Duncan could see that he would have to intervene. 'Mrs Folten, we're just here to ask whether you have seen any strange people lately.'

'Apart from you lot? No.' She faltered and thought for a moment. 'Well, yes, actually.'

'Yes?'

'Bloke here yesterday, on a bike.'

Duncan choked. 'A bike?'

'You planning on repeatin' every fucken thing I say, son?'

Duncan was flustered. 'Sorry. What did he look like?'

'He looked like he rode a bike. Leathers. Boots.'

'Can you describe the bike?'

'Black. Two wheels. Motor. Shiny. A fucken bike.'

Duncan was genuinely astonished. *So perhaps there were more of them?*

But she hadn't finished. 'Probably a poof.'

'What?'

'Not bright, you lot. I said, probably a poof.'

'Why did you think that?'

'You know, blondy hair.'

Duncan considered the logic. 'Reckon three quarters of Norway might be gay then, Mrs Folton?'

'Don't get smart with me, Yogi. This bloke had that blondy hair that blows around in the wind without getting messed up. Not tall. Tight trousers. Nice manners. Said please and thank you. Fucken poof.'

'Mrs Folten, is there anything else you can tell us about this man? This poof?'

'Fucken stupid. Too stupid to breathe. Charged him enough to fill a fucken road-train. Didn't blink.'

'Okay, thank you for your time.' Duncan turned away. Then, as an afterthought, turned back again. 'And if you ever swear at me like that again, I'll shoot you.'

'Now I'm horny. Piss off, big fella.' The old woman ambled off, laughing.

Duncan smiled and turned back to Trev, who still appeared to be standing to attention. 'Yes, well, the hot dry weather gets to a lot of people, Boss. Sorry about that.'

'That's okay.' Trev stood easy.

'Interesting about the man on the bike, Boss.'

'The poof. Yes, it is. Sounded like a cultured person. Not a typical biker. I wonder if this could be our killer?'

'Can put out an alert, Boss. Maybe leave the poof bit out. You know, police image and that.'

Trev agreed. 'We'll do that when we get to Warkon. I'll get on the radio and call the boys back at that clearing. We need them to be aware that there may be another biker.'

Duncan was thoughtful as he drove. *So there was another biker. What might he have seen or heard? Why was he alone, and why did he not look and act like a biker?*

They parked in the police yard and walked over to the pub. Duncan carried Trev's gear.

'Chlo, you remember my boss, Senior Sergeant Trevor Bolan? Boss, Chlo.'

'Hello again, Trevor.'

'Trev. And yes, I do remember you, Chloe. You've had your hair done. It looks wonderful.'

'Thank you, Trev. And I can honestly say that you're the only bloke in a thousand square miles who has noticed my hair.'

Duncan looked at his boots. Filthy. And far too big. He had noticed.

Trev, in control. 'Now, Chloe, I'm sorry to intrude, but we've got an investigation underway at the escarpment and I would be grateful if you had a room. Actually, two rooms. Myself in one, and two colleagues from Sydney who will be arriving tomorrow morning, in another. Hopefully just for a couple of nights.'

'That would be fine. Ben—the temporary barman—is in one of the flats, but he can move into the spare room in my apartment.'

Duncan didn't like the sound of that.

'Sorry to put you out. Full peak season rates, of course.'

Chloe laughed. 'There isn't really a peak season in Warkon, Trev. But thanks for the thought.' Then to Duncan, 'Could you take Trev through to the second apartment? I'll talk to Ben and ask him to move his stuff out of the other one. I'll clean it this evening.'

Duncan nodded and led the way. Boards groaned under his weight. Trev stopped to look at the old pictures, then, apropos of nothing at all, 'Lovely girl, Chloe. Always thought you should spend a bit of time in this pub.'

'Do that, Boss. Toss out the drunks. She makes my lunches.'

Trev was peering closely at a horse and dray. 'Her hair looks good like that, don't you think?'

'Wish I'd noticed, Boss. The hair.'

'Well, you noticed some very small details out at the escarpment today, so perhaps bring those powers to bear on the domestic front and you might get dinner as well.'

Silence.

'Maybe even breakfast.'

'Working on it, Boss. Long-term strategy. Flawless.'

'Forgive me, but in my experience long-term strategies are not generally effective. Think short-term, Duncan. Think of a term short enough for flowers to wilt.'

'No worries, Boss. Appreciate the advice. Your apartment.'

'Hot Dog. I'll change my shirt and socks and meet you back at your station.'

'Your boss is lovely, Duncan. Isn't he, Ben?'

'Really lovely.'

'Fuck off, both of you.'

'Duncan!'

'Dunc!'

'Don't push it, Ben.'

Chuckling all-round. Ben asked, 'So what did it look like out there?'

'Not much change. Disappointing. Bit of pulling around. Probably eagles. Doesn't look like dogs have got in there. Or pigs. Surprising, really. There's three of our blokes out there now in a caravan, keeping an eye. So no chance from here on.'

'Is lovely Trev suspicious at all?'

Duncan chuckled again. 'No, I don't think so. Strange thing is that the harpy out at Polka station saw a biker yesterday. He stopped there for fuel. Described him as a poof. Apparently said "please" and "thank you". Tight trousers. Nice hair.'

Ben put his hands over his eyes and sat down. 'Fuck. That was me. I took the Norton out there for a spin.'

'YOU WHAT?!!!' Duncan exploded as he leapt to his feet, tipping the chair over and terrifying both Ben and Chloe. Duncan stood still for a minute, still furious, then noticed the little hand over her mouth—eyes wide—and put the chair back and sat down heavily.

'Sorry, Chlo. But, Ben, mate, what the fuck did you do that for?'

'I wanted to look at the mountain again. See if it still felt evil.'

'What?!!!' Duncan was incredulous.

'Seriously, it's been on my mind. I wanted to get a feel for the place. But there was nothing there. It was just a mountain.'

'Of course it's just a fucking mountain. Oh, Christ.'

Chloe was visibly angry now. 'Duncan! Stop this right now! It's not just you involved here and your language is upsetting me!'

Duncan started shaking. He knew that he was still tired from the weekend and would have to be careful. 'Sorry, Chlo. Sorry. But honestly, Ben, what's Trev going to think when he works out that you were at the mountain the day after the killing?'

'Two days. And why should he know? No-one knows except that old lady. And her description is hardly going to point Trev at me.'

Neither Duncan nor Chloe said anything.

'I'm not a poof!'

Silence.

'I'm not!'

Duncan smiled. 'Okay. Don't pout. But keep that bike hidden and take it back to Byron when Trev's out of town. And tell Byron not to say anything.'

'Alright. But I might actually move it tonight. It's in the annex behind the pub and Trev might see it if he's staying in the apartments.'

'He's in there now. Be out in a sec. Better move it then. Byron leaves the gate to his yard open. Stick it around the back. No-one will flog it.'

Trev looked pained. 'There's something wrong with this chair.'

Ben stooped to examine the chair.

Trev persisted, 'It doesn't feel quite right. Can I swap it for another one?'

Ben swapped the chair with the one opposite. Trev looked relieved.

'Thank you. So you're the young man who crashed his bike last week and is taking refuge in this beautiful pub?'

'I guess that's me. Something jumped into me. I wasn't hurt, and the bike isn't insured, so I didn't report it. Officially. But Duncan picked me up and brought me back here'

'I was in the garage this afternoon. The bike looks like it's a mess. Bits of it everywhere.'

Ben winced. 'Byron was keen to pull everything apart. He hasn't worked on a BMW with the boxer motor and I think he wanted to look at everything.'

'Well, he's certainly doing that. I hope he's got a good memory. Or a map. There are bits of it from one wall to the other. Very small bits.'

Ben was still uneasy about the dismembered bike, but at least it was a safe topic. 'Byron seems to know what he's doing. Chloe's letting me stay here rent-free if I do some work behind the bar and in the dining room.'

'Yes, and I'm sorry that we've turfed you out of your flat. There will be a couple of detectives tomorrow, up from Sydney. Hopefully we will be out of your hair by Friday, so you can have the flat back if your bike is not fixed.'

Trev stretched his long legs out under the table. Inspected its construction. Apparently fascinated. Picked up a fork.

Ben was again uneasy and thought he should keep Trev talking. 'Thanks. Byron was getting some more parts this afternoon and tomorrow. We're hoping to have it back together on Friday.'

Trev stopped prodding the table's joints with his fork and turned back to Ben. 'You'll be pleased not to have to go near that dog again. What's wrong with it?'

'Hoots?'

'The damn thing bit me for no reason at all.'

'Did you touch his head?'

'No.'

'His ears? His stiff leg?'

'No, neither.'

'Not his tail? You didn't touch his tail, did you?'

'Well, no-one told me not to. I thought he would like it. I was only being friendly. I gave it a tug.'

Ben looked at him in disbelief. 'You tugged Hooty's tail?'

'Bloody dog. Should be put down.'

Ben fought down a smile. 'Well, good luck with that.'

'Anyway, I understand you've been out hunting with Duncan. Good trip?'

Ben was immediately on guard. 'Good, yes. But we got a bit lost on Sunday. Late back. I think Chloe was worried.'

'Got lost? With Duncan? Duncan never gets lost.'

Ben cursed Duncan quietly. *The flat tyre idea was better.*

'Well, I think we were trying a new track and it didn't end up where Duncan thought it would.'

'Did you shoot anything?'

'I shot a pig. Duncan shot at one, but it was a long way away.'

'Really? How far is a long way?'

'Probably two hundred metres, I reckon. Hard to see it in the scrub. Completely missed.'

This was getting too specific. Much too specific. Ben was terrified he'd say something dumb, or forget something important that he'd need to tell Duncan.

'Oh, well. Probably an entertaining couple of days, anyway. So, what do you recommend for dinner?'

Thank Christ. 'The chicken parmigiana.'

'What else is there?'

'Nothing.'

'Excellent. And a wine?'

'Well, there's the house white or the house red.'

'Or the house beer.'

'Yes, you're getting the picture.'

Trev chuckled. 'I am, Ben, I am. Getting the picture. Yes, and I'll have a glass of the white, thank you.' Trev paused, looking suddenly thoughtful. 'Is this chair taller than the other one?'

Ben left him to study the chair. Chloe was in the bar, having asked Ben to look after Trev for the evening. 'How are you getting on in there?'

'I've waived my right to remain silent. Couldn't help it. You just find yourself talking. I don't know if he's doing it deliberately.'

Chloe smiled. It was a cute smile. 'Duncan reckons he's just the best interrogator. Others lose their tempers or try to scare people, but Trev just makes friends with them. Be careful.'

'Didn't make friends with Hoots. Byron's dog. Tugged his tail.'

'He tugged Hooty's tail?!!!'

'Apparently. He's got some bandaids on his fingers. Wants him put down.'

Chloe laughed. 'Byron or Hoots?'

'Have to be a job lot, I reckon. I'd better get him his dinner.'

'You okay to do that?'

'Yeah, I'm a poof, remember? Poofy hair? Tight trousers? All poofs can cook.'

She chuckled, shaking her head. 'Give him a huge glass of wine. Then maybe another, on the house. Hopefully he'll run out of steam and go to bed.'

CHAPTER 7

'Peas?'

I held the phone close against my head to better hear Dom. Chuckled. 'Yeah, mate, peas. You've got a whole room full of disturbed and shaky people, and they serve you peas. Should have seen it. Everyone trying to spear peas on bendy little plastic forks. Peas everywhere. All over the table. The floor. Debacle.'

Dom was laughing. Aud was on another handset in her bedroom, but didn't really get it. 'But peas are nice.'

'They are, Aud, but they're hard to catch when your hands don't work very well.'

'What would be easy to catch?'

'A big bit of spud. Or maybe a sausage.'

'Okay.' Aud was still unsure.

Dom was enjoying himself. 'So mate, anyone think they're a chicken?'

I'd tried to make a joke of this when I went back to the flat to get clothes and things. 'No, and so far I can't see Jack Nicholson. Might be sticking to his room. Scared of the matron.'

Dom laughed again. Aud still didn't get it. Aud was still worried about the peas. 'So was there something else you could eat? If you couldn't eat the peas? Do you want me to bring you some easier food?'

'Thanks, Aud. But, no, it's all okay. Honestly, I was just being silly about the peas. The food is fine. It's a bit weird having to eat at fixed times, but that's okay. I'll get used to it.'

'Dania is coming around to pick up your car. I've made some more biscuits for you.'

'Thanks so much, Aud. That's fantastic. Thank you. There's a small gym here. I'll have to work them off.'

Aud was happier. She liked the idea of people getting fat. Except Dom. He was now on a diet. She hand-fed him. Literally. It was pathetic.

I had told them and others that I didn't want visitors. Except Dania. I didn't want to have to deal with people seeing me in there. Dania had used the ute to move some of her things from her mother's house in Randwick to our place in Balmain. She wanted to be a link for me back to that life. I thought it was really nice. Her mum was okay with it. Dania could take the ferry to work and back, then drive the ute to St Leonards in the evening every now and then. Not every day. A few times a week.

The hospital seemed almost new, but was perhaps just newly refurbished. Pale pastels throughout, with most of the fittings a de-sexed and antiseptic shade of peach. Lots of plastic. Lots of rounded edges. Heavy objects fixed to the floor, as they are on yachts. And in prisons. The staff wore smart grey uniforms. The doctors had white coats. It was very quiet. At night you could hear the steady pulse of the airconditioner. Warm. Almost *in-utero*.

I was a low-risk patient and could wander about the place. It was a private hospital and most of the other patients looked to be quite affluent. Middle aged. Cardigans. Quietly spoken. Some were wearing slippies. But there was also a sprinkling of waif-thin, furtive girls with hooded eyes. I had counted at least three of those, although they were not easily differentiated. Goths. They didn't seem to eat in the dining room, if at all. Troubled kids of wealthy parents. Like myself, I guess.

The first night was very difficult. Dania had helped me to settle into the room. She had arranged my books and writing things and put my clothes away, then fetched us cups of coffee from the lounge area and put a photo of us on the desk. It was one she had kept near her bed at her mum's place. I looked relaxed and happy. She just looked like a girl in love. It was a beautiful photo. I stroked her face through the Perspex cover. We sat on the edge of the bed and I made silly jokes about the squeaky rubber under-sheet. There was another one on the pillow. Under a peach cotton pillowcase. Catch the tears. A lot of tears in this place.

Dania left at dinnertime. I wanted to have it in my room and share it with her, but she thought I should meet people. She picked up the little leather handbag I'd bought her at the Paddington markets. We hugged again and I went with her to the exit. We said our goodbyes. She was teary and put on her big sunglasses. I told her not to worry about me. I said I'd take it seriously. Get myself better. It must have been awful for her to leave me there and drive away.

I wandered down to the cafeteria and lined up for dinner. Had a quiet chuckle about the peas. Seriously, who would put peas on the menu in a psychiatric hospital? I sat next to an old bloke. He turned away from me, angry and muttering, so I ate quickly and went back to my room. I could hear people talking in the lounge but didn't think I could face it, so got out my little cassette player and headphones and lay on the thinly-disguised piss-proofed rubber bed and wondered what the fuck I was doing there. Then I recalled the outburst at uni and the bloke who had knocked me off my bike. The panic that descended sometimes when I was close to Dania. Feeling like I was nothing. A shell. Worthless. And underneath that, the sense that an unbearable shame had been gestating and was now struggling to be born. I wanted to get rid of it all. Everything. I wanted to die, basically. It was true. I really did just want to die.

I curled up on the bed with the cassette player held against my chest and pressed Play. My head filled with the opening bars of Icehouse's 'Walls'. I blacked out the hospital sounds and let the music wrap around me. The endless heartbeat, on the inside. I felt myself crying. Urgent sobs now, as well as the tears. I curled up tighter and the music continued. Sound, crawling through the walls. The starch in the sheets felt like ice-cold brittle fronds of bracken. In the corners of the room I could sense the gnarled and twisted forest gums, weighed down with snow. Eventually I slept, but then woke again in the dark. Someone had turned off the light and put my cassette player and headphones on the table. My head was almost clear. I had a dream-memory of darkness and snow, but a series of silent doors seemed to be closing against it, one after another.

I sat up and got out Aud's biscuits. Ate a couple. I smiled, then retrieved the cassette player and lay back down again and put on the second side. First track, 'Great Southern Land'. I often found myself humming this when I was writing the Warkon story. I could picture the flat, dusty roads out in western New South Wales. The colours. The urgent movements of a lizard on a hard road. I loved the way the song floated along on that clicky, precise beat. Then the synthesiser. Simple chords, but really effective. And nicely resolved. Nice harmonies.

I played it through a couple of times, feeling the music and singing it quietly to myself, then got out of bed. It was almost five o'clock and effectively morning so I pulled on some jeans and a t-shirt and wandered out to get a coffee. Said hello to some of the early-morning staff. There was a muted sound of someone yelling upstairs. I took the coffee back to my room and found the spiral-bound notepad. The dreams in my mind were still warm. It was all still real.

I started writing.

I had an appointment to see Dr Gidleigh at eleven that morning. He wanted to start me on some drugs. Medication. Drugs sounded better.

'So, Devlin. How do you like the place?' He had the same compact composure but I felt at a disadvantage now. An officially-certified nutter. Without my beautiful girlfriend. Dania had insisted I bring only good clothes to the hospital. She said it would make me feel a bit better. It did. A bit. But I still felt like a nutter.

I tried for a joke. 'The rubber pillow's a bit novel.'

He smiled and I could see now that he was very tired. 'Yes, it is a hospital. We try to make it feel more like a hotel, but at the end of the day it is a hospital.'

I was contrite. 'It's okay. Really. No complaints. The food is fine. The bed's comfortable. I've been to the gym. It's all okay.'

'That's good. And yes, I can't overstate the importance of exercise. Twice or even three times a day. Hard aerobic exercise. Not just weights. Get your heart-rate up.'

I told him about the clever exercise bikes that had a heart-rate monitor in the handlebars.

'Excellent. I ride a pushbike to work. I couldn't keep doing the long hours if I wasn't fit.'

He looked at his notes. I noticed that he had a box of tablets with him. 'Okay, Devlin. This is Prothiaden. It's one of the tricyclics. Have you done any pharmacology yet?'

'No, that's next year, I think. Well, maybe.'

'Definitely, Devlin. You're not going to fail.'

'Okay.'

'Alright, now I'm going to start you on a reasonably high dose of this, given that you're young and fit and we have you in here under observation. I'll ask the nursing staff to take your blood pressure each day.'

'Okay.'

'Now, the way things work is that the nurses have your treatment schedule and will hand out the medications. I consider you to be one of the lowest risk patients in the hospital, but we don't hand out boxes of tablets to anyone.'

'Okay.'

'Prothiaden has some side effects. Not purple elephants. Medical side effects.'

'Okay.'

He took the folded pamphlet out from the packet. 'Side effects are very individual. Most people tolerate this group of drugs quite well. But then occasionally we find someone who doesn't tolerate them at all and we need to look at other medications.'

'Okay.' I knew I wasn't helping him, but was struggling to think of anything else to say.

'With the tricyclics, the most common side effect is a dry mouth and constipation. Then I guess sweating, followed by drowsiness.'

'Fantastic.'

He smiled. 'And not infrequently, sexual dysfunction.'

'Excellent.'

'By that, I mean a generally lowered sex drive. This one is complex because sex drive is also often affected by the depressive illness itself. How have you found that side of things?'

Australian blokes don't go there. Ever. Especially given that he had met Dania. I thought he ought to have known that. 'Okay.'

He sighed. 'Right. Well, just give the Prothiaden a bit of time to do its work. We generally find the side effects to be worst at the start, and then decline. Whereas the anti-depressive effect is the opposite. It takes some time for the chemical balance in your brain to normalise. I generally say about ten days to two weeks, but it's very individual. And we're starting on quite a high dose. Let's aim for an effect in about a week.'

'Okay.'

'Alright. Have you got any questions about the drug?'

I didn't have any questions.

'Good. Now I should explain that Prothiaden interacts with alcohol. As you know, there is a ban on alcohol within the hospital but some people nevertheless sneak a bit in. Don't do that. All right? You might be able to drink a little once you've got used to the drug, but not during the next two weeks at least. Promise me that?'

I promised. I told him that Dania was not the smuggling type.

He chuckled. 'Good. You know, you are very lucky to have her.' He seemed to reflect on that a bit. 'Look, I shouldn't say that. Partly because it's just a feel-good thing to say. But fundamentally because it's not true. You're not lucky to have Dania. She's with you because of who you are. Look around you. Look out on the street. How many of the blokes that you see could attract a young woman like Dania? It's not your looks. It's who you are. You've got to keep reminding yourself of this. So, what I meant was, you're lucky you have what it takes to have Dania.'

It was a big speech and it seemed to cost him a bit. I helped him out. 'I don't take that for granted. Really, I don't. I struggle a bit sometimes, but mostly I can see that there's something good to build on.'

'Good man. Now, there are some people working in this place who can help in background ways. We've got psychologists, and I'd like you to talk to one of those. I've made an appointment for a few days' time. We've also got therapists who specialise in relaxation techniques. I'll leave you to make your own arrangements there. The girls at reception have a schedule of individual and group sessions.'

He explained some of this a little more, then asked if there was anything I wanted to talk about. I couldn't think of anything, so he told me to settle in for a couple of days and then he'd see me again.

I left Dr Gidleigh's office feeling good. Very much better. I wanted to call Dania, but had vowed to myself that I would not contact her at work. She had told me that I could but it seemed like the thin end of the wedge.

I took myself around to the nurses' station for my first tablet. I thought of it as a dog-choc. A chubby little thing was manning the post. She reminded me of Aud. I told her who I was and she fetched my notes, then went into their pharmacy and retrieved the tablets.

'Now the doctor has talked to you about the side-effects?'

'Yep. All bad.'

She smiled and giggled a bit.

I felt encouraged. 'He told me it was okay to go out and get really drunk. Parking meters would start talking to me. Said it was completely hilarious.'

She shook her head, smiling. 'Now, you must take this stuff seriously. Okay? He wants me to take your blood pressure, so sit down there and I'll bring the machine around.'

I sat down. My blood pressure was fine. I took the dog-choc and a small plastic cup of water, and swallowed it in front of her.

She could see I was going to make fun of something else, so waved me away. I went around to reception and got hold of the therapists' schedules. If I hurried, I could see Angela for half an hour before lunch.

It was a bit like being on a very strange cruise ship.

Tobe would have liked Angela. The tiny part of me that hadn't been colonised by Dania liked Angela. I kept that part in check. Isolated. No postal service. Economic sanctions.

Angela wore tight dark clothes and was probably a nutter. At least that was the conclusion reached by another tiny part of me. The part that had not been utterly crushed by the experience of walking around a psyche hospital wearing the wrong sort of name tag. But Angela was also undeniably a bit hot in a skinny, older-woman sort of a way. Black velvet jeans. Masses of jet-black hair. Stretch top over pert little breasts.

But Angela looked tired. And a bit fraught. She was perched on a stool at her computer's keyboard, pecking at it angrily with long thin fingers. I wanted to do something to help her.

She heard me, and looked up. 'Can I help you?'

I sighed and told her why I was in hospital. And that my doctor thought I should learn how to relax. Angela looked physically pained by the prospect of teaching someone how to relax. She ferreted around briefly in a cardboard box and found some tapes, then asked me if I had a player. I told her that I did. With expensive headphones. I was keen to explain my own method with music, but she was already looking at her watch and at the same time scratching frenetically at something on the other wrist—which had started to bleed.

Angela told me to try out the tapes and come back in the afternoon if they didn't work. I took the tapes and left quietly, then went back to reception for another look at the therapists' schedule. Someone else would be free after lunch. I thought I might shop around a bit.

The first tape I tried was brilliant so I didn't bother with the others. This one told you to picture a quiet place. A nice place. I thought of the hill above our place in Tamworth, where I used to ride my horse as a kid. It then told you to focus on different parts of your body in turn, blanking out the rest. As you did this, you sort of worked your way inwards. The voice was hypnotic. The tape went on for about thirty minutes then moved into some hippy music before ending with a reversal of the first part. The very first time through it seemed to work. I decided to do it several times a day.

There was a knock at the door and the little chubby nurse came in with my second tablet. She explained that tomorrow I would have the first one earlier in the morning. I took the tablet and drank the water, then looked out into the corridor. People seemed to be going to lunch. I put on shoes and locked the door. The staff had keys to every room, but it made you feel better.

A happy old bloke came barrelling along. 'Friday's a hot lunch! Lasagne! Highlight of the week!'

I joined him, quietly wondering how much worse my life would have to become before this could possibly be true.

The lasagne turned out to be excellent. I had three helpings. Then chocolate self-saucing pudding. But no-one talked much in the cafeteria. Just ate and passed condiments as needed. It was a profoundly sad gathering. Easy-to-manage food. Soft. I went back to the room with a cup of coffee and had a bit of a nap. Then took myself off to see the second therapist.

This one was a big, slobby, gentle-looking bloke with a red beard and a moist handshake. Alan. An overgrown spaniel.

I showed Alan my relaxation tape.

He thought it would do the job and we spent a productive forty minutes or so talking about the technique. He said he always got up to the bit where you had to focus on your gut. But then it made him feel sad. So invariably he got up and ate something.

We talked that through a little and established that eating for him was a sort of paradoxical, nihilistic urge. I thought that was an interesting conclusion and a good place to leave the day's session. We agreed to meet again in the morning.

I wandered off to look for the bingo room.

The second night was much better.

The rubber sheet seemed to squeak less, but maybe I was less restless. The room felt less like the inside of an aircraft at midnight, halfway to Bangkok.

And Dania was going to come to see me in the morning.

I wrote a bit more of the story and listened to my tape. The drugs were making me drowsy and I almost dropped off at the desk. I got into bed and stretched out happily. Slept like a pup.

I woke up to screaming. It was a woman. I was disorientated. My mouth was dry and eyes were itchy. The drugs again. Something slammed against my door. Then the walls of the corridor outside. There was more screaming. Several voices. Hushed. Urgent. A struggle going on. A benevolent struggle, hopefully. I stayed inside anyway.

The place went quiet again.

A little later a new nurse knocked on the door with my morning tablet and the small plastic cup of water. She offered no comment about the uproar. I tried a tactful raised eyebrow. Nodded towards the corridor. No response. If no-one hears the tree fall down in the forest, then apparently it doesn't. I thought that might be worth remembering.

'Honey bunch!'

'Baby, I missed you!

Big hugs and kisses in the reception area. The staff frowned. I took her down the corridor to my room. She thought I looked better. I told her that the surgery had gone well. She laughed. We locked the door. It was a pointless exercise, but if someone barged in anyway then they had at least been warned.

'You don't seem to be suffering too much.'

I had told her about the drug. Well, warned her. I didn't want her to be worried if I started molesting her less.

'No. Fit as a fiddle. Look out.' I was pleased. I had feared some sort of unspeakable complexity.

And everything did seem to be working well, except for one detail. 'I just can't finish.'

'You're going to have to finish, because otherwise I won't be able to walk out of here.'

We were both laughing. But it was impossible. Go till you run out of energy. Then go again. And again. And again. No relief. Apparently, this was one of the less common side effects. Something that might disappear once I got used to the drug.

Dania was pushing me away. 'Perhaps Dr Gidleigh can tell you what to expect.'

I laughed. 'No fucken way I'm talking to him about this.'

We got up and shared a shower. I loved washing her under a hot shower. We got dressed again. She told me to sit at the other end of the bed. I grabbed her and cuddled her. Her hair smelt fantastic.

She wanted to know how things had been going. I told her I was concerned about Angela, but making some good progress with Alan. She laughed and poked me with her finger. I told her about the thrice-daily dog-chocs. How you had to put your hand up on the nurse's knee and stare at her intently. Fetch a rolled-up newspaper. About the good food. Lots of time in the gym. All things considered, it was way better than Long Bay.

Dania was visibly relieved. Glowing. She told me about her plans for the weekend. She would take the ute home to Randwick for the day and see her mum. Maybe take her out to lunch. She'd probably stay there tonight then go back to the flat tomorrow. She said it was strange without me, but working well. Dom and Aud were worried. Aud particularly. Actually, Dom just kept making jokes about me. I laughed at that.

Dania had also told Tobe. He'd asked if I needed anything. I told Dania he should get in touch with Angela. She laughed and poked me again. We had another coffee, then I told her she should go and not be late for her mum. We kissed again in the reception area, and then she was gone. I took myself back to the gym.

Things went well for a few more days. I think I was just so relieved to have no pressures at all. There was nothing I had to do and no-one minded if you weren't sociable. Everyone seemed to be working to their own little plan.

Then we heard about the suicide. A woman had electrocuted herself in her room. The staff obviously tried to keep a lid on it, but everyone knew. Everyone was talking about it. It affected us all. The staff must have blamed themselves to some extent. It was inevitable, really. And for us it was a reminder of the thin line. A dangerous precedent. The sheer craziness of killing yourself puts a lot of people off, but when it happens just up the corridor you start wondering whether it really is such a ridiculous idea.

I think the staff were used to this phenomenon. A few patients were reclassified. I wasn't, but Dr Gidleigh did want to talk to me about it.

'What did you think when you heard about Mrs Ipswich?'

I considered this for a moment. 'I thought it was sad. And heroic. And enabling. But I don't want to do it.'

'Why heroic?'

'Because ultimately, it must take such courage. Even when you're desperate.'

He nodded. Wrote something down. Then out of the blue, 'What do you think is wrong with you?'

I replied without hesitation. '*Litost.*'

'*Litost?*'

'Yes, *litost.*'

'That sounds like something the French might have for breakfast.'

I kept a blank face. Stared at him.

He went on. 'You know, please pass *litost*. And *le marmalade.*'

I screwed up my face and pressed my temples, so as not to smile. 'It's a Czechoslovakian word. The overwhelming realisation that you're shite, basically. In a nutshell.'

'Right. Technically difficult concept, then.'

I chuckled. I couldn't help it.

'How do the Czechoslovakians think you get over this *litost?*' He asked.

'By getting older. Or not. Killed a lot of people over the years. Not all of them Czechs.'

'You think maybe Mrs Ipswich had it?' He said that quietly. Mrs Ipswich was in her early thirties and had a small child. I had met the child. A little girl. Neither of us spoke for a few minutes while Dr Gidleigh made some coded notes. His next question again surprised me. 'Do you think there might be anything else wrong with you?'

'I hear voices.' I hadn't told him about the story telling. Or the letters. I hadn't told anyone except Dania.

'No, you don't.' He was smiling now.

'How do you know that I don't?'

He thought about that and made another few marks on his pad. 'Because although I don't know exactly what's wrong with you, I do know what isn't. You are not schizophrenic. I'm sorry if that disappoints you.'

I smiled as well. 'I've read a bit about schizophrenia. The flatmate of a friend has it from smoking too much dope, and no, I don't think that's me. But I honestly do hear voices. I can close my eyes and bring them close, then it's like the people are standing in the room with me. And I can make them part of a story.'

I told him that Dania had suggested I write a story down as a series of letters. But I didn't tell him that there was really just one story and that writing it out was now the only way that I could keep the cold at bay.

He looked hard at me, to see if I was pulling his leg. 'That's unusual, but I still think it just qualifies as an overly effective imagination. Broadly. A very powerful version of daydreaming.'

'You don't think it's crazy, then?'

'No, I don't think it's crazy.' He looked at his notes and frowned. 'But out of interest, has being here in hospital altered things? The voices, I mean. Are you still able to feel the voices and the story, and write it all down?'

I looked around the room. The sterile furniture. The sterile pastel prints. The small empty rubbish bin. 'It was okay at first, but I think it's getting harder. Sometimes I can hear the talking but I can't quite tell what they're saying. And sometimes when I try to feel the place I'm in, it's sort of like looking at it from the window of an aeroplane.' I realised I was biting my lip. 'I really hate that. I feel like half of me is pulling away. Like I'm losing something. In a way I'm also scared that I can't now control the story. It just seems to be going on without me. Somewhere else.'

Dr Gidleigh was staring hard at me now. He took some time to speak. 'I think the change is probably your adjustment to the drug. The Prothiaden. Your affect seems a bit flattened now. Less acute. I think your imagination is being dulled. I honestly don't think there's anything more complicated happening inside you.'

But he seemed preoccupied, and a bit less certain. He wrote some more code down on his pad, then crossed it out. 'Apart from that side of things, how does the Prothiaden seem to be working? Can you discern any change in your moods?'

I told him that I had been okay for a few days, but had then started to become a bit agitated. It was probably worse than I let on. I was having nightmares regularly now—even when I tried to rest after lunch—and they always seemed to leave a feeling of darkness. An anxious desolation. Failure. Shame. I had asked Dania to bring in a torch that I could keep by my bed so that I could turn it on when I needed to and lie in a warm and well-lit cave beneath the duvet.

But again, I didn't want to tell Dr Gidleigh any of this so asked instead if the agitation could be another side effect of the Prothiaden—or perhaps just an artefact of doing time. He chuckled. 'Doing time will certainly get to you eventually. And hopefully we'll have you out of here before that becomes a big problem. The agitation might be the Prothiaden. Are you sleeping?'

Again, I was evasive. 'I wake up very tired. And I'm tired during the day.'

'That sounds like Prothiaden. We have put you on quite a high dose and we can probably bring that down in another few weeks. During that time, you should adjust to it to some extent.'

'Okay.'

'Have you got any university work to be going on with?'

I told him that I had a mountain of photocopied notes and some textbooks.

'Alright, well, look, just hang in there with the drug's effects. Keep exercising. Keep eating. Try to establish a good routine and stick to it. That will all help.'

I asked him how long he thought I would have to stay in hospital. He leaned back against the chair. 'I can't tell you precisely, but I think we can review things in another ten days or so.'

I thanked him and left. I hadn't bothered going back to the therapists. But I had an appointment with Anna, the consulting psychologist, later in the day.

Anna turned out to be a busy, no-nonsense redhead. She sat me down and read some of the notes from Dr Gidleigh. Made little 'hmph' noises every now and then. Quite a lot of them, actually. I started to look around the room.

She glanced up from her reading. 'Right.'

'Okay.' I wasn't really sure what else to say.

She went back to the notes, then again looked up abruptly. 'So Dr Gidleigh has started you on Prothiaden. That's good. It's not a perfect drug, but it's one of the best we have at the moment for this sort of illness. How are you feeling?'

'The side effects?'

'Yes, sorry, I was meaning physically. How do you feel physically?'

'Not too bad. I think I'm feeling a bit tired and strung out. That's new. And different to feeling anxious. My mouth is dry, but that's okay. Going to the loo is a problem. The nurse gave me something for that.'

'Yes, that's commonly a problem. Easily overcome. Nothing else? No sweating?'

'I did wonder about the sweating. I've been exercising a lot. So much spare time. But I do seem to be sweating more than I was.'

'Yes, well hopefully that will pass once things stabilise.' She continued to scan the notes, then added, 'I won't comment on the drug treatment, because that's Dr Gidleigh's responsibility, but I would like to talk a bit about some of the other sides to the sort of problem you've been dealing with.'

Anna talked with me for more than an hour. It was all very sensible, but I wasn't really listening. I was still concerned about the drugs. I could feel my mind fighting them, and fighting to keep some sort of control. To keep the doors closed. All of them. Hospital had at first seemed to be a safe place to heal, and a respite from the real world, but I was now beginning to feel that the real world had been keeping me alive and that, without it, there was only the story left to keep the cold away. And the story was getting harder to find.

I was starting to lose track of time and realised too late that I should probably have been making little post-and-fence marks on a wall somewhere. Dania had been back for evening visits and would be here again soon. I did some exercise on the bike in the gym, then had a shower and tried to get myself together. I found it very difficult now to sit still. I was irritable and there were flashes of temper.

I sat on the bed and tried to calm myself, but it didn't work. I felt as though I had been up all night drinking coffee. I picked up my little porcelain statue of Jesus, sitting on a rock, and smiled at the memory it invoked. Dania and I had been waiting in line in the small pharmacy attached to the hospital—my knee was sore from too much gym work and Dania thought that a stretchy neoprene brace might help. The bowed and tentative shade of a woman ahead of us was taking a long time counting and recounting tiny change and, while waiting, I noticed on a shelf behind the counter a row of religious icons. For some reason it struck me as a strange thing to sell in a pharmacy.

Eventually it was my turn and I put the knee brace on the counter. 'Could I have this brace, please. And a Jesus.'

'Devlin . . .' Dania recognised the tone and was immediately on guard.

'Which one do you want?' The girl looked bored, and not very bright, and was already reaching for an icon.

'Which ones do you find work the best?'

'Devlin!'

'What do you mean?'

'I'm just wondering whether perhaps the sitting ones might work better?'

'DEVLIN!'

The girl was now confused. 'Why?'

'I don't know—they just look more composed. More powerful.'

But Dania had had enough, and as punishment she made me buy a sitting Jesus. I actually liked it. I have never been religious, in the sense that I have never really trusted the motivation of people and institutions. But the little statue was nicely made and well painted. The only problem with it was that his face sometimes looked a bit like Tobe—with a beard.

There was a knock on the door and the nurse called out. Dania was early. I jumped up and opened it. My eyes must have been bad, as Dania stepped back involuntarily and the nurse looked concerned. Then everything went out of me like a balloon. Dania said it was okay. We went into the room and shut the door, then sat beside each other on the bed.

She held my hand. 'You're not well, baby.'

'No. I don't know why it's like this. I can't turn it off.'

She took her shoes off and got me to lie down next to her. 'Tell me some more things about horses.'

I smiled. We'd done this before. Talking always helped me. Dania was still learning to ride at the place in Centennial Park, and before I had been admitted to hospital I had been going along to watch. She was getting a lot better. She could canter around okay now.

'What sort of things?'

'Tell me about training horses. Anything. Something I'll be able to use later.'

We talked for twenty minutes or so and I started to feel a bit less wound up. I looked at my hands. There was still a fine tremor in all fingers.

'Do you really think I'll be able to sort this out? Really?'

'I do. I think you're going to have to change some things, but I think eventually you'll be pleased that this whole business forced you to look at yourself. I think it will be a good thing.'

'And you'll still be there?'

'I will—as long as you don't ask Angela to help you relax.'

I tickled her, then lay back and looked up at the strangely perforated ceiling. 'I want to get out of here, Danny.'

'Just give the drugs another week or so. Keep talking to Dr Gidleigh about the agitation. Keep exercising. I like you nice and fit. And keep writing my story. I don't mind all the pages. I like Trev. And I like Hoots.'

'Hoots is a shocker.' I chuckled at a memory. 'But it's getting harder to write, Danny. Sometimes I can get there but can't hear anything. There's just the sky. And sometimes I can't get there at all. It's like the magic is dying.'

She stroked my damp hair. 'Nothing's dying, hon. Your body's just trying to cope with that drug. Be patient with it. Have you been able to write anything at all?'

I smiled. 'Yes, if it doesn't work I do some vet reading then try again later. And there's lots of laters in here. There's another little bundle for you to take home.'

Dear Dania,

It's been a bit difficult to write this one. Sometimes I couldn't get back there, or I could but was then unable to hear or see what was happening. I had the feeling that things were unfolding without me. I think it's just the drug, which Dr Gidleigh says I'm still taking at a high dose.

Hopefully things will clear up a bit soon.

Anyway, the next chapter, Wednesday, and Duncan and Ben start to feel the heat now as Homicide detectives from Sydney join in the investigation.

Love, Devlin xxx

Wednesday

'Pulled his tail. Can you fucken believe it? Nice bloke, that Trev. Apparently smart. But fuck me, what can you say?'

Ben told Byron that he and Chloe had had a laugh about it . . .

. . . 'Pulled his tail. Can you fucken believe it? Nice bloke, that Trev. Apparently smart. But fuck me, what can you say?'

Ben told Byron that he and Chloe had had a laugh about it.

But Byron wasn't finished. 'Tried to tell me I should tie him up. Public menace. Fuck, some people.'

'Unbelievable.'

Hoots was not having a good morning. He was lying on a fresh, clean cushion with his head on his paws and breathing heavily. Ben could see that he wasn't well.

Byron knelt by him. Stroked his huge bear-like head. 'Had a bad night. Probably upset.'

Ben didn't think Hoots was upset about biting Trev.

Byron got up and went to an ancient rounded fridge that served as a cupboard and took out several boxes of tablets. 'Small green one makes him piss more. Gets rid of fluid in his chest. White one strengthens his heart. Other white one helps his back legs. Trouble getting up now. Poor bastard was never that fit really.'

Byron took the tablets over to Hooty, who eyed them sceptically. 'Have to put them in little bits of roo meat. Won't take them otherwise. Not a model patient.' Each tablet was carefully inserted into a small slit in a piece of roo meat. Hoots looked on approvingly. 'Here you go, mate. Get that into ya. Much better in half an hour or so. Top up in the arvo. Not really a morning dog.'

Ben couldn't ignore the pain in Byron's face as he administered the treatment.

'Get old too fucken quickly.' Byron wiped dust out of his eyes. There was a performance about it. Ben wanted to leave.

'So, mate, your bike. Some progress. Yes.'

Ben was relieved. 'I can see that. Looking good.'

'Made up some new engine bars. Improvement. Controls arrived. Box on the bench there. Cleaned and serviced the whole thing. Start on the tank today.'

'Thanks. Let me do some more chains for you while I'm here.'

'Good on ya. Bucket's over there. Know the drill.'

Ben got himself organised with a pile of old chains. 'I returned the Norton yesterday afternoon. Put it in your yard. Duncan thought it would be okay there.'

'Saw that. No worries. Trev asked about it.'

Ben's heart stopped. 'Asked what?'

'Wanted to know if I still had it. Taken it out anywhere recently. Told him yes and no.'

'Right.'

'Mate, what the fuck is going on here? That Trev may do some stupid fucken things, but you can see the little cogs turning. Doesn't miss much. You tell me the big fella's mates will be around here asking questions, and sure enough, they are.'

'I don't know what to say, Byron. Maybe best to talk to Duncan.'

'Thing is, you blokes go away for the weekend. Shooting. And some biker pricks get shot. And you're walkin 'round like you ate the icing off the fucken cake and don't want your mum to find out. Elementary maths, mate. Applied it.'

Ben concentrated on a filthy chain.

But Byron wasn't finished. 'Mate, up to you. I'm not going to say anything to anybody, but some chick in Sydney was grateful. Very grateful. Ask myself what might make the big fella actually hurt someone. See he's not like me. I'm a mad bastard. Enjoyed 'Nam. Never got over it. Fucken ride of me life. The big fella, different kettle of fish. Gentle as a kitten. Pissed cockies have a go at him in the pub, wraps them in cotton wool and places them outside. I'd fucken axe the pricks. But now there's a whole lot of dead blokes up on the hill, a grateful chick and a couple of fucken fugitives with icing on their fucken fingers.'

Ben slumped. 'Is it that obvious?'

'Well, mate. I guess I got some additional information. I know you blokes a bit and I know about the money. I'm not saying anything to anyone. But wouldn't hurt to look a bit happier. Chloe know?'

'Yeah, she knows. She's not really talking to Duncan.'

Byron sighed. 'Well, mate, let's get this bike back together and put you on the road to the other side of the fucken desert. Good start.'

Hoots barked, smiling. Byron knelt down in front of him. 'Better already, mate? You want your hammer?' Byron produced a small, yellow, plastic hammer with a squeaking valve in it. Hoots sat up. Byron placed one end in Hoots' mouth. Held the other. Hoots bit down. It squeaked. They both laughed. Ben wept.

'John, Phil, this is Constable Duncan Morris who runs the Warkon station. Duncan, this is Senior Sergeant Beale and Sergeant Mitchell.'

Hands were shaken. Pressure applied. Eye contact.

'Senior Sergeant Beale will be running the investigation now, Duncan. Our task is to help him and Sergeant Mitchell here with local knowledge.'

'Starting with who's the piece runs the pub?' Mitchell wore a cheap, grey polyester suit with sweat stains in the armpits and faux-Italian slip-on tasselled shoes. A big man with a big chest, and once strong, but running prematurely to florid fat.

'Sergeant, please.' Beale, small and sparse with unnaturally black eyes set deep in the cadaverous face of a poet. Rapid, fleeting expressions quick to extinguish. A lonely and unhappy child, but a hard man now.

Mitchell smirked and Duncan turned away, looking dangerous. Trev caught it. 'Well, gentlemen, you've had a freshen up and some coffee so shall we head out to the escarpment?'

'Yes.' Beale, economical.

'Duncan, you've got some food and drink for us from Chloe?'

'In the car, Boss. Blue esky.'

'Chloe, then.' Mitchell, now chortling. Beads of moisture caught on the blond stubble around his mouth.

Duncan put the car in gear and drove off too quickly, spinning wheels in the loose gravel. Trev sat beside him. The Sydney boys were in the back. Trev tried again to smooth the waters. 'It's about an hour to the site. We're closer here than at Barker, which is why I thought you should stay in Warkon. At least for one night. But we need to take some gravel roads to get there.'

Beale nodded, his eyes half-closed. A likely insomniac. Mitchell was hot and uncomfortable and seemed annoyed by the promise of more heat and flies. Kept scratching uncomfortably at his groin. Shifting about on the hot vinyl seat. Dabbing at the sweat and spit on his upper lip. 'So you look at this shit every day then?'

Duncan knew that Trev felt proud of his huge outback beat and would feel he had to defend it. 'It can be harsh. But also beautiful in different light. The view from the escarpment is quite stunning.'

Mitchell chuckled from the backseat and wiped his face on the slippery sleeve of his jacket. Beale remained silent, eyes still part-closed. Duncan drove quickly, letting the weight of the big car move it through the gentle corners.

Mitchell seemed to need another distraction. 'Any snacks in that esky?'

Duncan looked back at him in the mirror. 'Not in the car, mate. Police policy.'

'Sergeant to you, Constable. Police policy.'

'Bring walking boots, Sergeant? Might head up on the escarpment later. Rocks. Snakes. Long walk.'

'I'll be right.'

Duncan smiled. Thought he might actually enjoy the day. A complicated expression settled briefly on Beale's closed face, then vanished. Trev sighed.

The rest of the trip was tense and quiet. Duncan tried to think through the range of possible scenarios they might encounter at the escarpment. Beale and Mitchell discussed a burglary-homicide they had attended the previous day, and which Beale thought might have been staged. Trev hummed his way patiently through a chain of long-forgotten folk anthems.

As they slowed down for the turn off to the escarpment, they saw that a police car had been parked across the track, precisely as Trev had requested. Trev and Duncan shared a look, eyebrows raised. Rob stepped out and saluted smartly. Trev smiled. 'Good work, Rob, but no need to overdo it. Anyone try to get in?'

'Some journos from Barker, Boss. Looked unsure. Had some information but not much. Someone in Warkon or Barker must have heard something.'

'It'll be out on the wire during the day. Prepare yourself and the others.'

'Will do, Boss. Need me to move the car, Dunc, or can you get around?'

'We'll be right, mate. Chocolate brownies from Chlo.' Duncan reached into the esky and handed him the neatly wrapped package. The whole lot.

'Thanks, mate.'

'No worries. Give some to Geoff and Andy. We've just had brekky. Not hungry.'

Trev sighed as Duncan drove the car up a small bank and back onto the track. Soon they saw the second car. Geoff got out to greet them and waved Duncan around.

Trev turned back to Beale and Mitchell. 'I've got three men here around the clock. My plan was to increase that to six today, when the news starts to filter out. We have the area cordoned off, but I'm expecting some news crews to try and hike in. Either from the road we've just taken, or the track over the escarpment, which Duncan will show you later today.'

'You boys have done well, Trevor. Appreciate this is a bit out of the ordinary.'

'Thanks, John. Well, let me show you the scene. One of my people will guide Forensics out here. They should be with us soon. And I think a couple will come up from the Drug Squad?'

'Yes, I asked them to send someone. Probably two. Very likely this is drugs related. Gangs making a move into country towns, setting up networks of pushers and dealers.'

'We've seen a bit of it already and it can only get worse. This does look like some sort of disagreement or turf war. But there are some complexities. Let me show you.'

They made their way to the clearing. Beale was careful. Effectively soundless. Mitchell was left behind, balanced on one leg while picking burs from a damp nylon sock.

Trev continued. 'You'll want to go over this yourselves but, Duncan, would you like to give us your thoughts?' Duncan was surprised. Beale also. Mitchell had caught up and was looking up at the escarpment. He didn't appear to be listening.

'Sure, Boss. From a distance, looks like a big biker brawl gone wrong.' Duncan stopped and coughed, thinking, 'But doesn't really stack up like that. Shot with rifles for a start. Forensics will confirm this, but looks like hollow-points. I shoot a lot of pigs. These exit wounds are the same. You blokes will know more about bikers than we do, but it doesn't seem right.' He paused again, 'When you think about it, wouldn't try and shoot out a group of bikers with rifles at close quarters. Hard to aim quickly. Slow to reload with the bolt action. Closest decent cover is up the hill there.' He pointed to the escarpment behind them. 'I reckon I found where one shooter was lying. That's a hundred metres, give or take. Not a hard shot for anyone who shoots a bit, but there's more.'

Duncan turned back to the clearing. 'Look at the bodies, you'll see the shots have been placed accurately. One gut shot, and that looks to us like closer work, but then the back of his head is missing. Pull off a shot like that in a hurry, along with all these others, takes a bit of skill. Fair bit of skill. Another was blown up when his tank was hit. Bike was moving. It's right away from the others. Need a bit of confidence, that. Most people would just have shot him in the back. Big target. Maybe finish him off later.'

He needed to pull things together now. Not too smart. Careful. 'Me and Trev reckon this was probably done by an accomplished shooter, or shooters. Not necessarily a professional, but good with a rifle and cool-headed. Maybe that includes some bikers, I don't know.'

He looked to Trev, eyebrows raised.

Trev nodded. 'Keep going, Duncan.'

'Other points. Some blood near that stump. Not close to any bodies. Might be one of the shooters. Maybe trying to negotiate, while his mate or mates covered him from the hill. Also, car tracks over there near the tree. Car might have brought the killers, or maybe just picked them up afterwards.'

'Good.' Beale was impressed.

But Duncan hadn't finished. 'And you'll see two shotguns. Sawn-off pumps. More like a biker weapon. But neither seem to have been fired in this incident. Magazines full. No shells. No pellets around the place. Two blokes close by, and one was reaching when he died. You can see that. Hand grasping. Suggests quick shooting with the rifle. Seconds. Less. These blokes wouldn't have messed around once they were threatened, but they didn't get to their guns. Final thing. Boss noticed that bloke over there has his fly open. Might just be pissing, but his undies are pulled around a bit. Looks more like sex.'

'Excellent, constable. Really excellent. And thanks, Trevor. Phil, I hope you caught all that?'

'Boss.' Mitchell, grunting. Now sitting on a log, with one shoe and sock off.

Trev looked relieved. 'Well, look around and see what you think. Forensics should really be here by now. Duncan, can you go to one of the cars and call Barker to see where they've got to?'

'Boss.'

Beale moved over to Trev, beckoned him away from Mitchell. 'Good man, that Duncan. Lucky.'

'He is. And well respected around here. Knows all the locals. He's thrown most of them out of the pub at one time or another. But he never hurts anyone. He's a gentle bloke.' Trev looked away for a second, then back to Beale, smiling. 'But it might be good to warn your man Mitchell about slights to the girl at the pub, Chloe. I'm not sure that Duncan's good nature and gentleness is limitless, and you'll agree he's not a bloke you'd want to push too far.'

Beale laughed. His face transformed. 'Understood, mate. I can see there's a bit of friction. Maybe let the two of them have a big hike around the hill later?'

'I think that would be an excellent idea.'

Duncan returned. 'Boss. Forensics on their way. Rented a minibus. Bit slower. Should be here any minute.'

'Thanks, Duncan. Well, let's leave these two gentlemen to their work.'

'Cup of tea in the caravan then, Boss?'

'Awesome, Duncan. Awesome.'

Forensics were going to take the rest of the day to finish their tasks, and following that the autopsies and lab work, but Beale had been able to convince them to draw some tentative conclusions.

'Hard to get the overalls to commit to their own names, but we can tell you a few things.'

Beale, Mitchell, Trev and Duncan were having lunch at a fold-out card table that had been set up outside the caravan.

Beale continued. 'Forensics agree about the use of rifles. And the hollow-points. They'll confirm that in due course, but the wounds are distinctive. No chance of matching any exploded projectiles we might find to particular rifles. And the shotguns haven't been fired. Very interesting. Now, the man with his fly undone: no semen stains in the area. Spare you the detail, but not urinating and no evidence of recent sex. Prostitutes? Groupies? A rape to be? Interesting possibility that last one. Can of worms. Blood on the ground is AB. That's rare. Only about three percent of the population and excludes the four dead men. So you were right about that, Duncan. The bleeder is a person of interest. Curious sandwiches, by the way. Is this chicken parmigiana?'

'Yes, Sir. Chlo makes them with leftovers from the restaurant.'

'Hmm. Anyway, some options here. One of the men has the AB blood on his shirt, so there was probably a fistfight. Three of them have what look like freshly abraded knuckles. Again, a fight. On face value, it does look like a negotiation gone wrong—with the bikers then gunned down by a hidden shooter or shooters. Perhaps there were some prostitutes to sweeten the deal? Hard to know. There's certainly no evidence of anal sex on any of the bikers.'

Trev looked pleased to hear that their initial assessment was panning out. 'Okay. Well, shall we take a walk up the track here and Duncan can show us where he thinks one of the shooters may have lain? Everyone had enough lunch?'

'All okay, Boss. After that, maybe Sergeant Mitchell and myself can stroll on over the escarpment and see if there is any evidence of activity?'

'Excellent idea, Duncan. And I think you should try to convince one of the Forensics people to accompany you. It will be helpful to have some eyes trained for signs made by creatures without small cloven hoofs.'

'Don't think a faun did this then, Boss?'

'I don't, Duncan. Or a satyr. But I was actually referring to *Sus scrofa*. See if you can locate a Forensics person who looks as though he or she might be reasonably robust and ambulatory, and perhaps a good arbiter of violent disputes between children. It is a long way.'

Ten minutes later, Duncan rejoined Trev and Beale, who had located the place where Ben had lain.

'Best I could find, Boss.'

They looked back down the slope to where Mitchell laboured alongside a petite technician named Jenny. She had removed her disposable paper overalls and was now wearing small pink denim shorts and a pretty pair of low-cut tennis shoes. She seemed to be picking flowers.

'Sometimes, Duncan, I'm not convinced that you're altogether a good person.'

They gathered at the rise and looked down at the flattened grass.

'You're right, Duncan, it does seem that someone or something has lain here. What are your thoughts, Jenny?'

'Sir, I'll just take some photographs and poke around a bit then we can talk about it.'

'Poke around.' Mitchell, chortling.

'Sergeant!'

Jenny knelt down and carefully inspected all aspects of the small clearing. She noticed the indent made by Ben's boot and took some measurements, then sat back on her heels, pencil in mouth and eyebrows raised. A parody of someone thinking. Trev and Beale shared a look. Jenny caught them. Smiled.

'I'll need to run this past my boss, but I think it's very likely that this was where one of the shooters lay. Possibly the only shooter, if he was good enough. He could see the whole clearing from here and wouldn't have been obvious from below. There isn't really any cover down there that he couldn't get through, except maybe that log. But it probably wouldn't be big enough to completely shield anyone. This would be an excellent location.'

'What do the measurements tell you?'

'Oh yes, sorry, Sir. I think the shooter was not very tall or heavy. Maybe five-foot-ten or eleven, medium build.'

'A poof perhaps?' Trev, with eyes closed.

'What? Sorry, Sir?'

'Apologies, Jenny, I was thinking aloud. Please carry on.'

A moment's silence, then, 'Well, that's about it really. Although some of these other marks are interesting. It almost looks as though he was rolling around a bit.'

'Laughing, perhaps? Hilarious occasion. Who knows? Anyway, thank you. Senior Sergeant Beale and myself will secure this site and have a bit of a look around for any others. Would you like to accompany Sergeant Mitchell and Constable Morris here on an inspection of the rest of the track upward, and along the ridge?'

'I'd love to!' Jenny gave a little squeal. Hands together in a silent clap. 'I hardly ever get out into the bush, and this place is so beautiful. Are the ghost stories real?'

'I'll let Duncan talk to you about that. He hunts things up here and knows all about the place. In your hands, Duncan.'

'Boss. Sergeant, got your breath back?' Without waiting for an answer, he moved off to join Jenny who had already started up the narrow track. And seemed to be skipping.

'He wants to make an official complaint. I'm sorry, Trevor.' Beale looked uncomfortable. He and Trevor were back at the cars.

'You can't talk him out of it?'

'I'll try again. And yes, probably. But I thought you should know.'

'Thank you. I'll speak to Duncan.'

Beale went back to the clearing to locate Mitchell. It was late in the afternoon. Jenny had returned rosy-cheeked and apparently in love with Duncan. Duncan had not noticed this, being preoccupied with needling Mitchell.

Trevor beckoned Duncan over. 'Duncan.'

'Boss.'

'What happened?'

'He tried to shoot an eagle, Boss. Not lawful.'

'Did he actually fire on it?'

'Well, no, Boss. I convinced him not to.'

'He says you threatened him.'

'Don't recall doing that, Boss.'

'Was Jenny nearby?'

'No, she was looking at wildflowers, Boss. Nice girl. Not dedicated to catching bad people.'

'Apropos of bad people, Duncan: Mitchell claims you told him that if he discharged his pistol he would not live through the balance of the day. His words. As conveyed to me. By way of explanation, he says you then threatened to throw him off a cliff.'

'Again, don't recall, Boss. Hazy. He might have been feeling a bit unwell. Erratic. He was upset about his shoes.'

'His shoes?'

'Ruined. Leatherette ripped. Little tassels gone. Soles flopping. Basically fucked. Boss.'

'And this caused him to lose his mind?'

'Last straw. Pretty much knackered. Not fit. Jenny does aerobics. She handled the walking no problems. The sergeant kept wanting to stop for a smoke. Tried to just leave him behind, but he kept calling out.'

'Like Edith, Duncan? Calling to Miranda?'

Trev was peering at the horizon, distracted. Duncan seemed uncharacteristically strained. 'Interesting allusion, Boss, but not much like that. Except for the fat bit.'

'I think you were unkind to this man, Duncan, because he said something rude about Chloe almost nine hours ago. That is not good behaviour. I expected more.'

'Sorry, Boss. He was too far from the cliff. Next time.'

'You are not making me laugh, Duncan, whatever my face may be doing. He wants to make an official complaint about you.'

Duncan became upset. 'Bullshit aside, Boss, the man's a prick and I'll just deny whatever he says. I'm sorry, but he really is a prick. But I won't provoke him again.'

'Alright, well, hopefully Beale can talk him out of it. And you seem to have made quite an impression on young Jenny.'

'Who?'

'Noted. And I will pass that on to she-who-waits-behind.'

The journey back to Warkon was tense.

'So, an interesting day I would say.' Trev seemed keen to break the ice. Duncan looked away. Beale looked hard at Mitchell.

Trev pressed on. 'Duncan, I have told our colleagues about the strange woman on Polka station who provided petrol to a lone biker on Sunday. They are interested in this man, and so am I. Ostensibly he might fit the physical profile of the shooter, whom Jenny believed to be not tall. What do you think?'

Duncan had the feeling that Trev knew exactly what he thought. 'Boss, it is interesting but I'm not sure what we can do about it. When you think it through, if this bloke isn't a real biker—as in a gang biker, because he's polite and has nice hair—then how relevant is the fact that he rides a bike? I mean, isn't he just a bloke—as in any bloke—with a bike?'

'Yes, that's true, Duncan. But, existential motorcycling issues aside, how many people can there be out here who ride shiny black bikes? The roads are no good for them. If you lived out here and had a bike, then presumably it would be something like whatever that lad at the pub rides—some sort of BMW he said?'

'Well, yes. But Ben's bike is actually black as well. To us it would look very different to a Harley, but to old Mrs Folten it might not. Just a black bike. And most blokes wear leathers of some sort.'

'You may be right. And perhaps this is just a red herring. But to be quite frank with you, I have never much liked fish.'

'I'll ask around, Boss. Maybe go back out to Polka and get a better description.'

Trev wouldn't let it go. 'Byron has a black bike. An old Norton, I believe. But I don't think anyone would describe Byron as polite. Or a poof.'

'No, Boss. No-one would do either of those things. And he's tall. And he doesn't have nice hair. Or tight trousers. And he would not pay any more for anything than he absolutely had to. Byron is not a person of interest for us, Boss. And in any case, he was working on Ben's bike all weekend.'

'Ben's bike. Yes. So we come back to Ben and his bike.'

The four of them sat in silence. Watched the red desert blow past on warm puffs of breath. Beale leaned forward. 'Trevor.

I would like to go back out to the escarpment with Mitchell tomorrow. Can someone get him some new shoes?'

'Certainly. Duncan's are probably not going to work. Unless we gave him some small wheels and a motor, so he could make them into a little car. Look I'll give him a pair of mine. Size eleven any use to you, Mitchell?'

'Thank you, Sir, that sounds perfect. Sturdy shoes?'

Trev seemed pleased to hear Mitchell perking up a bit. 'Boots, lad, boots. You can't tramp all over those rocks in shoes.'

'Well, Sir, I guess that we don't usually do a lot of nature walks. Bit of a surprise, this one. Bit different.'

Trev sent Duncan a warning look. 'Yes, well, I'll get one of the Barker people to pick them up from my house. Another team will be coming in to help out the men that I have there now. I suspect we're going to be inundated with newshounds before too long.'

'Newshounds, Boss?' Duncan, trying not to smile.

'Isn't that what they're called?' Trev, an eyebrow raised.

Beale leaned forward again. 'Trevor, I have been talking to Mitchell and we think that there would also be something to be gained from a day or two in Barker. I'm keen to understand the local drug dealing and pushing network a little, just to help us to judge whether these people might be capable of something of this scale.'

'Okay, well, look if I'm not around just ask one of the boys out there to get Jane in my office on the radio. Jane will fix you up with accommodation and will take care of washing and anything else you need.'

'Thanks. Jane. Okay. Will do.'

'I'll run you out to the scene in the morning and give you one of the local cars. You can take that back to Barker when you're done. Keep it till you leave. We'll make sure you've got some maps.'

'That would be appreciated. Thanks again. And we'll shout the two of you dinner tonight.'

'Looking forward to it. Now, Duncan, you'll join us? Chicken parmigiana? Suspect Chilean house wine?'

'Wouldn't miss it for the world, Boss. I'll drop the three of you off first and take care of a few things back at the station. Join you for a drink before dinner.'

'Super.'

Duncan was seated again at his tiny desk. Head throbbing. *Too fucken stressful. Just want to tell him what happened.*

Ben appeared in the doorway. 'Heard you were over here. How'd it go today?'

'Well, Trev thinks it was you on Byron's bike filling up with fuel at Polka station. Good start, mate. I reckon he would take you out there for confirmation, but doesn't see how it all fits together, or why it's being covered up. And I reckon he can't honestly see you as a vengeful slayer of four bikers.'

'Be surprised. Us poofs with nice hair can do great things. And it was only three really. Well, three-and-half.'

Duncan tried not to smile. 'Really not joking, mate. Head's killing me. Nearly axed that dickhead Mitchell up on the escarpment. The stupid fuck wanted to shoot an eagle. Reckoned it was watching him. Lost it.'

Ben went cold. 'What do you mean, lost it?'

'Got all panicky. I was with one of the Forensics people. Little chick. She was fit and loved the place. Virtually fucken skipping. Embarrassing. Anyway, we pulled ahead a fair way and the fat fuck couldn't keep up.'

Duncan got up and walked around, his head in his hands. 'Thought he'd be okay just sitting down having a smoke, but got all upset, shouting and whatever. Anyway, went back to get him and he had his gun out and was lining up an eagle. Told him I'd throw him off the cliff if he pulled the trigger. Now he wants to make a complaint against me, but I'll deny it.'

'How is he now, this bloke?'

'Still a bit rooted, I think. Very quiet.' Duncan twigged. 'But don't go and talk to him, okay? I know what you're thinking, and don't do it. I'm dead serious, Ben. Hurts to say it, but he can't be completely stupid to be in that Homicide unit. He'll cotton on and tell his boss. And that dude scares me even more than Trev. Like a fucken raven. Watches everything.'

'Okay. You're right. I'll keep a low profile. Might be good if Chloe could look after dinner. Trev keeps wanting to talk and it's bloody hard to fend him off.'

Duncan found the energy to chuckle. 'I know. He's like that. Means he's interested in you, which is bad. Yeah, try and get Chlo to look after dinner. Tell her not to rise if that fool Mitchell tries anything. But I doubt he will tonight. I think he's a bit fucked, really. Scared him.'

'Just quietly, you're scaring a few people at the moment Dunc. Not like you. I know you're under pressure, but try to lighten up a bit.'

Duncan sat back down. Breathed out slowly. 'You're right. Sorry. Hey, Byron wanted to talk to me this arvo. Didn't have time. What's that about?'

'He knows, Dunc. And before you start, I didn't tell him anything or do anything stupid. Apparently, Hilde wanted to pay for my bike and got a bank in Sydney to call him and wire through some cash. Two thousand. I told him not to say anything about it if people came asking him questions about me. Then Trev came asking questions. He put two and two together, Dunc. He knows that a chick somewhere is grateful. And that four blokes are dead. And that I look guilty and you're becoming scary. He's not dumb, Dunc.'

'Fuck. Oh, fuck. Is this all coming undone, mate?'

'No, I don't think so. Byron told Trev that the bike was in the shed and hadn't been used. Trev's got no reason to doubt that. Byron's got the world's straightest face. The rest is just how we thought it would be. I've thought about it a lot. We've got to keep telling ourselves the truth of this thing. We're not trying to evade justice. We just know that if it came to a trial, then the gang would take revenge on me and my family. And possibly you, too. Maybe even Chlo. Trev would understand that, if we ever had to explain to him why we've been lying.'

'You're right. Look, I need to get a couple of things done here. I might not see you this evening, but take it easy, okay?'

'You too, mate. Remember, don't scare people. Think small. Cuddly.'

Duncan smiled. 'Fuck off.'

'Okay.'

'So, Chloe, tell us what culinary delight awaits.' Trev was folded sideways into a small paisley armchair that he'd found in the pool room, but then discovered to be too bulky to fit under the dining table.

'Chicken parmigiana.'

'Lovely. Three of those please. And a bottle of the house white.'

'Doesn't actually come in a bottle, but I'll get you some glasses and a carafe.'

'That's like a jug, Duncan.'

'I know what a carafe is, Boss.'

'Thank you, Chloe, we're in your hands.'

'Pleasure.'

Chloe turned to Beale. 'Will your friend be wanting any dinner?'

'That's very kind, Chloe, and yes, could you please take him a plate and add it to the tab? He's not feeling well, but he should eat.'

'Certainly. Shall I take him some wine as well?'

'Not too much wine for Sergeant Mitchell, please. Maybe just a glass. He's having visions about eagles that we don't want to encourage.'

'Understood. I keep thinking I should call you "Sir".'

Beale sat up straight in his chair. 'My name is John. And the day a pretty girl feels the need to call me "Sir" is the day I give her permission to shoot me with my own gun.'

Duncan looked at him, astonished.

Chloe blushed.

Trev coughed. 'I've been thinking about the scenario, Duncan.'

Duncan turned to him. 'The scenario, Boss?'

Trev closed his eyes. 'Yes, the scenario. That's what I'm going to call it. Now where's that lad, Ben?'

Duncan cringed inwardly. 'He's probably in the bar, Boss.'

'Could you fetch him for me, please?'

Duncan could only get up in a dream and walk next door to the bar, where Ben was serving a group of ringers. A resigned nod of Duncan's head towards the dining room told Ben all he needed to know.

'Ah, Ben. Now, have you met Senior Sergeant Beale?'

'No. Hello, Mr Beale.'

'John.'

'Okay.'

'Now, Ben, we've got a conundrum. I understand you're a marksman, is that true?'

'No.'

Trev feigned surprise. 'Oh, I'm sorry, I had the impression that you were a kangaroo shooter and a competition bench-rest shooter. One of the best in northwest New South Wales. Under 19 champion. Have I got that wrong?'

Duncan closed his eyes. *Fuck. Fuck. Fuck.* He checks things. Everything. Ben didn't seem fazed. 'No, that stuff is basically true. Sorry, I just don't consider myself to be a marksman.'

'Good, well, that's very humble, but I think for our purposes you fit the bill.'

He doesn't want to fit the fucking bill.

Ben noticed Duncan's discomfort. 'Okay.'

'Now, have a look here. Pretend this salt shaker is a shootist.'

'A shootist?' Ben, not actually taking the piss.

Duncan groaned.

Trev sighed. Pressed on. 'A shooter. And this placemat is a clearing with lots of bikers in it. The distance between the two is about a hundred metres. The bikers start running about, looking for shotguns.' Trev searched for items that might serve as bikers. Duncan gave him some peanuts. Trev continued. 'The shooter up here has to hit all these peanuts. Bikers. Accurately. In the head, mostly. Blow up a bike for the fun of it. And this all happens before they reach their guns. How good is this shooter, in your opinion? Could you do that?'

Ben now seemed anxious, and Duncan could see he was trying to steady himself. 'It would be difficult. Each individual shot would be easy, but the timing would be difficult. And you would be shooting at people, not peanuts. That would count.'

'But could you do it?'

'Yes, I probably could do it. If I had to.'

Silence. Trev looked up at the ceiling, then down at the table. Picked up a peanut and ate it. 'Why would you have to do it, Ben? Why would you have to make these men and their bikes just shining artefacts of the past?'

Ben looked confused.

'It's a quote mate, Leonard Cohen.' Duncan, his voice flat. *Everybody Knows.*

Ben seemed to recover a little. 'Thanks, Duncan. I don't know.'

Beale's eyes darted from one to the other. Duncan could see that he'd sensed things had taken an unscheduled turn, but couldn't read it. 'Leave the kid alone, Trevor. I think you've scared him.'

'I'm very sorry, Ben, it's just a practical problem we're trying to solve. I'm a bit tired. You've been very helpful. Thank you.' Trev was conciliatory, but smiling, his legs stretched in front of the little armchair, crossed at the ankles.

Ben watched Trev eating the peanuts. 'No problems. Can I go back to the bar now? Cecil will be wanting a fill-up.'

'Thank you, yes, sorry to have kept you.'

Beale was blinking now. Duncan thought he could hear the cogs straining to get traction. 'That was harsh, Trevor. Poor kid.'

'Well, I want to know what sort of person or people we are looking for here. How exceptional they are.'

'And what's your conclusion?'

'I think he was alone on the hill and his friend was in the clearing. And he was very exceptional. And there was a woman. And this exceptional man became very angry.'

'Boss, can I say something here?'

'Of course, Duncan, what's on your mind?'

'Have you thought about what happens when we catch these blokes?

Trev was caught off-guard. 'What do you mean?'

'What I mean is that if it's not gang members, the gang itself will retaliate. They'll kill these blokes, or their families if they can't find the shooters themselves.'

'Are you suggesting that we ignore this shooting because we want to protect the killers?'

'No. What I mean is, often these things will just be about violent pricks killing each other. As they do. The police step in, but really we're just punctuation marks. There's always more killing until some group is dominant.'

'What is your point?'

Beale remained silent and watchful.

Duncan continued. 'Well, have you considered that this one might be different, Boss? Maybe this isn't a simple killing. Maybe the killers are not just violent pricks. Maybe they're not even bad. The dead here are bikers. Gang members. Evil bastards. Sex was involved. A woman, or women. This might be complicated and all we'll end up doing is signing some death warrants.'

Silence.

Duncan looked across the table in time to see a placid smile spread across Beale's face as his eyes closed and his head began a slow, metronomic nodding.

Trev had seen it also. Carefully unfolded his long legs. 'Everybody wants a box of chocolates, Duncan? And a long-stemmed rose?'

And everybody knows: Cohen. Duncan was sick of pretending. 'Yes, Boss. That's exactly right.'

Beale sat up abruptly, his elbows on the table. 'Trevor, Duncan. Enough. Not another word. Let's just enjoy this dinner tonight and sleep on things. Okay? It is a bad business for a small country town. No-one could disagree with that. Lots of unknowns. And yes, Duncan, it probably is quite complicated. We've had one casualty and hopefully he'll be alright in the morning. So, let's just let things rest for now. I'm hungry. I hope this chicken is as good hot as it was in those sandwiches!'

Unlike the flat that Ben had been staying in, Chloe's apartment was part of the pub's original structure. The walls and floors were the same tired, worn boards and exuded the same noises, independent of human passage. Chloe had painted one wall bright orange and the others an off-white. The high plaster ceilings were enamelled. The effect was pleasing, although felt to Ben more like an art gallery than a place to live. The furnishings were sparse. A graceful, aged leather couch occupied one wall of the living room with an over-stuffed armchair next to it, in the corner. There was no TV, but Ben noticed a Bang and Olufsen reel-to-reel player and speakers.

Chloe nodded towards it. 'My uncle's. He's got lots of tapes for it in the safe. Thinks the whole set-up will be a collector's piece one day and worth more than the pub. Took it as payment from a bloke for some carpentry work on his house. He never used it much, but I love it. Wait till you hear how this classical piano stuff sounds.'

Chloe picked up one of the large tapes that lay on a coffee table beside the player, and threaded it carefully. Chopin's 'Prelude Opus 28 No. 15'. The 'Raindrop Prelude'. A-flat, pattering delicately. Incongruous. Change of pitch. D-flat to C-sharp-minor. Miraculous. It saturated the apartment for five minutes or so, before a click. Then silence.

'God, that's beautiful.' Ben was stunned.

'Chopin, I think. I don't know much about classical music. I don't even know if my uncle would be happy for me to be playing his tapes.'

'Is the collection only classical?'

'No, there's a lot of stuff from the sixties and seventies. Crosby, Stills and Nash, that sort of thing. Have a look and see if there's anything you want to listen to.' She showed him to the safe, which wasn't locked.

Ben found a Donovan recording. 'Dad used to go on about this bloke. Do you mind?'

'Go for it.'

The finger-picking prelude to Yeats' 'Song of Wandering Aengus'. Simple. Promised something special. Then Donovan's voice. The soft Scottish lilt. The man goes out, fire in his head. While moth-like stars are flickering. Catches a fish with a berry, on a thread. It becomes a girl. Glimmering. Apple blossom in her hair. Calls him, and vanishes into brightening air. He looks for her. He grows old looking, through hollow lands and hilly lands. The fire in his head. But the glimmering girl is out of reach. Always.

Donovan keeps singing. Nothing compares. Nothing is really heard. She's standing too close. A skirt tonight. Cotton shirt tucked in. Low shoes. No stockings. His hand goes to the curve of her waist. Settles. They're almost dancing now. Down to her hip. Up to her chest. The side strap of her bra. To her breast. Small. Nipple hard through her shirt and bra. Her eyes closed. Arms by her side. Both unmoving.

He looks at her face. Knows it could happen now. And knows it would be worse than killing people. Harder to bear. She knows it, too. The music comes back. Simple music. The Scottish lilt.

They sit down on the couch. Hold hands, then let go. Her hand lies on his leg.

'It's okay, Chloe. I know.'

'I'm sorry, Ben. I shouldn't have let that happen.'

'Nothing really happened, Chloe. It's okay. Really.'

'I don't know what will come about with Duncan. Me and Duncan.'

'It's what you want though, isn't it?'

'It really is. But I can't get past him. He shows me enough of himself for me to fall in love with, then hides behind his big body. He hates that big body. You know that? Most blokes I've known seem to spend their lives trying to be bigger. Duncan's enormous. And tougher than anyone. But he doesn't want to be. I think he wants to be like you, Ben. Nice hair. Not tall. Polite.'

'You think Duncan wants to be a poof?'

Chloe laughed, relieved. 'No. Definitely not. But you know what I mean. Duncan just wants to be an ordinary bloke. He doesn't feel like he can be with me when he's such a bear.'

'But you like him how he is?'

'I really do. There are times when I think someone spunky would be nice. But I love how solid Duncan is. Bear is the best word for him. He's seriously like a huge bear. That's nice. Very secure. And he's smart as well. Not just the reading. He knows a lot of music, too. He can talk about anything. We both want to travel.'

'I think you're going to have to force him a bit. Corner him and throw yourself at him. Try to get him drunk first.'

She laughed again. It was a nice sound. 'I want to get out of here, and he knows it. He can't stay here forever. He's wasted in this job. I know he does it well, but he's too good for it. We're country people, but I wish we could go to Brisbane together.

I want to do nursing. I've been looking into it. Duncan could work in one of the Brisbane stations for a while. Maybe become a detective. Something that needs smarter people.'

'Do you think Duncan wants to leave?'

'Not urgently. He likes Warkon, and I think he likes our little routine. But it's been good having you here as it's somehow pushed all that as far as it can go. We need some change now.'

She stood up and stretched. 'I'm going to make a pot of tea. Would you like some?'

'That would be great.'

'Has Duncan told you anything about himself? His childhood?'

'No, not really. I know he comes from a property in Queensland, but that's about it.'

She was in the kitchen, her back to him. 'It's a big property and pretty well known. His stepfather owns and runs it. His father died when Duncan was very young. He was a drummer in a local band. His car was in one of those horror seventies drink-driving accidents, somewhere in the bush. Everyone was killed.' Chloe paused, rinsing the kettle. 'Duncan's stepfather was divorced at the time with custody of their young son. Apparently fought his wife for it and got there through some sort of local clout. He married Duncan's mum for mutual convenience. She got security, and went up a hundred social grades, and he got a pretty young wife. And Duncan, of course. But he never liked Duncan. He always rubbished him. His size made him look like a dumb lout. He told Duncan he'd never be any good at farm work and discouraged him from learning to work horses and cattle. All that stuff. I guess he hoped Duncan would leave the place when he was old enough, and not come back. Which is pretty much what happened.'

'Were there any more kids?

'Yes, a daughter. His mother was pregnant when she remarried. The daughter's a physio in Brisbane and still very close to Duncan. She's been here a few times. First time, word got around and the pub was packed. We reckon everyone wanted to see what a female version of Duncan looked like. But she's tiny. His mum is, too, and his stepfather's a little ferret. It was his real dad, the drummer, who was the giant—like Duncan.' She poured the tea. 'Anyway, it was a pretty hard childhood, I think. Duncan took himself off into the bush a lot and developed his knack for observing things. He was often asked to do little local security jobs—you know, doorman—and on the strength of that his stepfather encouraged him to join the police. My hope is that the force will recognise his smarts and put him into an unusual job. Trev does, and I think he'd really stick his neck out for Duncan.'

'You really should talk to him about this stuff, Chloe. He adores you. You can see it in the way he behaves around you. His face when he's opening those bloody sandwiches. Like Christmas for him, every day.'

'Does he really like them? The chicken parmigiana sandwiches?'

'I don't know. I don't think anyone could like them. As a main course, it's bad enough.'

Chloe looked appalled. 'Really? Isn't it good?'

'No, Chloe. It's foul. No pun intended.'

'I thought everyone liked it.'

'Everyone likes you. They don't care what they're eating. Duncan loves that wrapping. And the pink lunchbox.'

Chloe was laughing now. 'We'd better get to sleep. Another big day tomorrow. What did Trev want to say to you tonight?'

'I think Trev knows. Under that eccentric old man thing, I think he knows. He grilled me about the shooting. How hard it would be? Could I do it? Even asked me what would make me do it. Pretended it was hypothetical, but he was trying to catch me off-guard. I bet he knows I took the Norton out there on Monday, too.'

'Do you think he'll do anything?'

Ben was suddenly exhausted. 'I really don't know. He seems to be trying to work out why things have happened. If he suspects me, then he suspects Duncan, too. But he knows that Duncan wouldn't get involved with something like this unless he had no choice. And I think he's trying to understand why he had no choice. I reckon he'll get there. They know there was a woman. Hopefully I'll be in Western Australia by then.'

'Trev really likes Duncan. He treats him like a son. All his other policemen are dumbos, really. I've met a lot of them. He and Duncan are both smart and they like playing games with each other. It gets a bit annoying sometimes, actually. I don't think Trev would turn on Duncan, unless he also had no choice.'

'No. I get the same feeling. Anyway, let's get some sleep. I'm really sorry about before.'

Chloe kissed him lightly. 'It's okay. I brought it on. Sleep well. The bed's probably better than the one in the flat.'

CHAPTER 8

I was discharged from hospital two weeks later. The agitation had continued to increase until one night, nurses came into my room to calm me, and to stop me screaming. They gave me an injection of something and sat with me until I went to sleep. And as I slept, I went back to the cold of the snow and the forest, the injection shrouding me in warmth like a lambs-wool coat. I lay down among the bracken and watched again. I watched everything. I lay in the warmth of my cocoon and watched. And then I understood.

I woke with a nurse sitting by me and stroking my forehead. It was astonishing. I didn't really know where I was, or what was happening, but felt that I could drift off again and be completely safe. So I closed my eyes and this time disappeared into endless blue, letting the warmth seep through me until it took the form of the sun. Below me was the scorched earth and, rising from it, an ageless magic rock. Twisting tortured bloodwoods and parched turpentine. Little canyons with their bottomless green pools. I had wings. Enormous wings that let me ride endlessly on the warm air. I could see everything. And everything made sense.

I opened my eyes again and gradually the room came back into focus. The nurses were smiling now. One of them held my hand. I tried to squeeze it, but didn't have the strength. I couldn't find the words to thank them.

I didn't tell Dr Gidleigh or Anna or Dania anything about this. The feelings were suddenly raw, but I could use some of Anna's techniques to talk myself through them. Dr Gidleigh saw the improvement and lowered the dose of the drug, and with that I started to see the rest of the world more clearly. I also started to feel real emotions again. Not so much the waves of anxiety and euphoria, but happiness and sadness and perspective. The plan was to continue at that dose for a couple of months then see how I felt when the drug was slowly withdrawn.

Winter had given way to spring and Sydney was warming up again. The rains had started and had an urgent tropical feel to them. I was pleased to leave the hospital. I could probably have taken myself out for day trips here and there, but hadn't done that. I had felt a bit self-conscious about being a patient. I had also wanted to focus on getting the job done, so that I could leave—and hopefully never go back.

I had promised Dr Gidleigh, Anna and Dania that I would change a few things. I stopped the dope altogether and cut the drinking back to small amounts here and there. Anna had also been concerned about the music. I was surprised by that. I knew I had a bit of talent, and all the practice and performances had given me some skills, but she thought it was just another form of escape and was concerned about how powerful it had become for me. She hadn't come across that before and thought I should take a break from the highly-emotive performances. I had always wanted to play the oboe. I loved its sound. Anna thought it might be helpful to take that up—to concentrate on reading music and developing technical skill and leave the guitars alone for a while. She thought that if I went back to rock and folk music then it would hopefully be for pure enjoyment, and not escapism. Interestingly, she thought the same way about my little Zen technique with music on headphones. Her rule was that I should connect with what was real and all around me.

I embraced all this, with the exception of the quiet story-telling. Now that I was thinking more clearly again the voices were no longer garbled and I could once more control events. Make them right. Sometimes when sleep wouldn't come, I would lie until late at night with my eyes lightly closed and my hands on my chest, and just let it work its way into me. I knew that I wouldn't be able to put a lot of it down on paper. It wasn't just a question of remembering the dialogue, as sometimes there would be no talking at all and I would just be experiencing things—physical things, as well as feelings—things that were all around me.

Dania was all around me. When I came home from hospital, she stayed. She didn't return to her mum's place in Randwick. I made room for her clothes and she became a part of the household. It was fantastic. Dom seemed to have headed in the same direction as me, without going through hospitalisation and medical treatment. Aud had bought him an electric drum kit that he could play through headphones without driving us crazy. We went busking one afternoon down by the Quay. I just played the music. I didn't try to live it. People weren't as arrested by the whole thing as they had been previously, but they still stopped and clapped. We could play pretty well. I had my eyes open the whole time and I think I laughed a lot more.

Around that time, Dania went with me to see the dean of veterinary science and some of our lecturers. Dr Gidleigh had written the dean a letter. They had also spoken on the phone. The dean was a nice old bloke. He was very understanding. Very lenient. He told me that I could continue in my current year as long as I could pass the upcoming exams. He also told me not to overplay the negativity associated with repeating the year if need be. He said that lots of good vets had done that. That mine was a difficult age to be. Difficult to cope with life changes and maintain a high academic standard. He didn't want me to become too stressed by the exams. He thought that if I started feeling bad again, I should just pull out from everything and take it all up again next year. Dania asked him questions. His receptionist made us coffee. I felt like an adult.

I wanted to see Professor Greene, as well. Little Fat Man. He had been upset when I told him to fuck off, and had discussed it with the dean. We found Prof Greene in his office, scribbling out another crazy roll of overhead projection plastic. I knocked.

'Yes.'

The door was open. He looked a bit shocked, then recovered. 'Come in. Please.'

'Professor Greene, this is Dania. My girlfriend.'

'Hello, Dania. And hello, Devlin. You're looking much better.'

I blushed a bit. Dania squeezed my hand. I thought I should get on the front foot. 'We've been to see the dean. He's given me permission to try and continue with the year. I'm really grateful for that, but I also wanted to apologise to you for my rudeness that day. It was unacceptable. I'm really sorry.'

He looked very happy. 'That's okay. I was a bit upset at the time, but it was obvious that something was wrong. At first, I thought maybe you'd had a tragedy in the family. Something like that. I was happy to let it go. But I'm pleased that you've come to see me. Thank you.'

He offered his hand and again I felt like an adult.

He gestured vaguely at the mess of scrolls strewn across the floor of his office. 'You've missed quite a lot, obviously, but you seemed to have an interest in microbiology. Come along to the lectures and do your best. But please let me know if I can do anything to help you catch up.'

'Well, I've got some notes from one of the others but I was actually wondering whether I could borrow your overhead spools? I'll look after them and bring them back. But it would be useful to read the notes you were talking to. I can then pad that out from the textbook.'

Prof Greene seemed surprised, but thought that was a great idea. I fully expected the horrendous spools to be difficult to follow but it wouldn't hurt to have something to correlate with my photocopied notes.

We thanked him again and left with armfuls of plastic. I deposited them in the ute and we then continued to make our way around the other lecturers. It was great. Nobody was angry with me. Nobody seemed to think I was bludger. A few of them thought I might struggle with the exams, but reaffirmed what the dean had said about the fact that many good vets had not gone through in the minimum period of five years. The statistic was actually about twenty percent.

We went from the vet school to Ernie's cafe for afternoon tea. Ernie had been very happy to see me back and I had so far done enough hours for one-and-a-half free breakfasts. He wouldn't let me pay for the tea and cakes. I still felt bad for reminding him of his son's death. That must have been awful for him.

'He is getting fit again, I think. I see him running up and down the road when he should be working. Riding that bike. You are good for him, I think, no?'

Dania was pleased about this.

'I'll get that mower out tomorrow afternoon and we'll be back for breakfast on Sunday.'

'That will be good. My lawn, it is eating away the back of my shop, I think. I will cook you nice pancakes on Sunday. Your lady should be much fatter.'

Dania thought she was getting a little 'pot'. She had modelled it for me. I couldn't see anything at all. When she lay down, her hip bones jutted out. That would probably have horrified Ernie, but I liked it a lot.

I was working hard now, reading and writing notes every day and late into most nights. Dania was pleased to begin with, but then started to seem pre-occupied. She had told me that sometimes she felt alone in the house. Dom and Aud never deliberately excluded us, but really only had eyes for each other.

I was still surprised by the change in Dom. In truth, I think this was his natural environment. The lonely inner-city grunge thing had never sat well with him and had probably been wearing him down. He'd spread his books and notes out on the couch, tapping on the window ledge with a drumstick. Aud would be bustling around, feeding him bits and pieces. Sitting on his notes and chatting to him. The radio would be on with noise all around, but he seemed to be able to work like that. Happily scribble things out on a spiral pad and write all over his textbooks. He would stay there for hours on end while I beavered away upstairs. And his marks had gone right up. He told me quite seriously that he was going for a distinction average and thought he could probably do it. Aud knew he could.

But Dania was increasingly restless and distracted. Her old friends were mostly on the other side of the city. Randwick area. On weekends, she would usually take the ute over for the day. She had become used to driving it. She had a little cushion to bring the seat up a bit. Sometimes she would take some clothes and stay back at her mum's place. I just wanted to keep working. I thought there was a real chance that I could catch up most of the ground I'd lost in hospital and make it through the end-of-year exams. I really wanted to do that. But Dania seemed to be getting a bit tired of everything revolving around me. She wanted a bit of her life back. She went out with girlfriends. A bloke called her at our place one evening, but she laughed it off. Dom looked at me. I shrugged. I didn't know what to do.

And most of the times we had together were still beautiful. I went up and down a bit sometimes but we never fought about anything. We had our big breakfasts at Ernie's place and he always made a fuss of her. We went to the Botanic Gardens, and then on to the zoo. And sometimes I went with her to meet her friends. But I still felt self-conscious in public and didn't have much confidence. It was easy to get upset, and then we would generally just go back home. She kept lifting me back up and never complained about the bad days. I was always grateful for that but felt as though I could become a burden. It was sometimes a relief when she went off on her own and came back happy. I could also be happy then and we could share some nice time together.

'Devvo! Dania!' Dom was yelling up the stairs. It was late morning. I had got up some time before and made coffee, then brought it back to bed.

'Two secs, mate.'

We pulled on jeans and t-shirts and went down to the sitting room. Aud was pacing. That was a bad sign. Biting her lower lip. Dom caught her hand as she walked past. Dragged her down to the couch. She was holding a letter. I thought maybe her mum had died.

'They're coming.'

I resisted the urge to make an ET joke.

Aud was pale. 'Dad and Mum. They're coming to Sydney. They want to have dinner here. They wondered whether they could ask my godmother, Marjorie, and her husband as well.'

Dom was looking uncertain. I went in for the kill. 'He's probably going to shoot you, mate. Know that, don't you?'

Dom looked as though he did know that. But the reality was actually a bit worse. Aud adored her dad. If he didn't like Dom, then that would definitely put a strain on things. I asked her when they were coming.

'Next weekend. This letter got lost somewhere in Dom's notes.'

I chuckled. Dom went in for the whole deep-litter approach to filing his lecture notes. But I could sense that they really were quite worried. 'Do they want to stay here, Aud?'

'No, they'll stay in a hotel somewhere. Mum's got a medical appointment.'

'Okay, well, look, we have to take it seriously. Me and Dom will go berserk on the house and garden. I've got a bit of time this week. You two think about dinner. Do something amazing. We'll help. We'll overwhelm them a bit.'

Dom and Aud looked at each other. Dom was still holding Aud's hand.

Dania took over. 'Come on, Aud. We'll make an enormous lasagne. Maybe two of them. Start with barbequed prawns. You said your dad loves those. Then maybe sticky date pudding. That's easy to make big. There will be six of us.'

Aud looked brighter. Sticky date pudding always did that. Dom still looked a bit concerned. I thought I should help. 'It'll be right, Dombo. We'll get the yard done today. Then we can focus on the house during the week. You girls start making a list of the food you'll need. You'll have all Saturday to cook it and do the last-minute stuff. We'll get dressed up. Buy some nice wine. It'll be fine.'

Dania sat down on the other side of Aud. 'It'll be really fun, Aud. Honestly, we'll blow their socks off. Everyone loves Dom.'

'It's true, Aud. He doesn't smell as bad these days.' Dom threw a drumstick at me.

'I'll give him a haircut. Devlin, too.' Dania cut mine and Dom's hair. Dom's was perennially wild. And that beard needed a trim.

'And, Aud, I promise not to howl at all. Not even a little howl. And I won't dribble in the soup.'

The three of them laughed. Aud was looking better. 'Mum thinks you're lovely, Devlin. She was very worried about you.' Aud had told them everything. I wasn't completely happy about that, but with Aud you just had to putt along and not try to change anything.

'Okay?'

'Okay.'

'Right. Brekky. Then Dom, get ready for some gardening.'

Dom tickled Aud. Aud smiled a bit. I put the toast on.

It was late the following Saturday afternoon and preparations had gone well. The yard looked fantastic. We had done a lot of pruning and taken it all to the tip in the ute.

Dom was back to his usual bubbling self. 'Mate, you'll have to put a lid on the slurping tonight. No slurping. No groping. No foreplay. Just act like normal people.'

I punched him and he feigned pain. 'I'm serious, mate. You and Dania just maul each other wherever you go. No shame. Dad will have a heart attack.'

Aud's dad did have a name. John, apparently. But we found it hard to call him that. 'Boss' might have worked, but we settled for 'Dad'. Aud's mum was more difficult. She didn't seem to have a persona. We went with 'Aud's mum', so as to keep the point of reference.

'Word of advice, mate. That topic. Don't chase Dad's cuddly little defenceless daughter 'round the house in your undies. Get yourself shot.'

Dom laughed. It cracked me and Dania up to watch them. Aud loved being tickled, but got all panicky about it. So, Dom would stalk her. She'd squeal and run away. He'd follow her, slowly. Catch her in the end.

We were stringing some coloured lights up around the trees in the backyard. It was warm enough to eat outside now and the forecast was good. A clear night. Aud and Dania had prepared the lasagne during the week. One great big one. Lasagne always tasted better when it had sat for a bit. The house was spotless. We had cleaned the windows, architraves, everything. With the monster lasagne back in the oven the place smelled sensational.

Dom had had a severe haircut. Half a ton of black ringlets left all over the floor. Beard cut back. Had even shaved around it a bit. Looked arty. Strangely, Dom never looked particularly intelligent. Tobe did. Arty was the best Dom could do. We had been out and bought him some new clothes. Dom had a seemingly limitless collection of t-shirts advertising every band that had ever played in Sydney. And about ten pairs of identically ruined jeans. And virtually no socks. We found a shirt with a collar that he thought might be acceptable. I had had some quiet instructions from Aud. And a pair of black pants that he loved. And we had stocked right up on socks. I was sick of him flogging mine. We came back with ice creams for the girls.

Aud was definitely winding up now. She was still wearing her working scarf. We'd seen a docco ages ago now that showed impoverished women tilling the fields somewhere in eastern Europe. In the snow. One of them might even have been in harness. And they were wearing scarves. So Aud bought a scarf. She wore it while vacuuming. Cleaning out the coffee machine. Solidarity with working women the world over.

Dad/John and Mum/name-unknown would be arriving soon. Dania was upstairs in the bathroom doing her hair. I would go in after her. I loved the smell of perfume and hairspray. She didn't have as many bottles as Aud, but still a fair number. Dania usually did her makeup in undies, sitting at my desk with a little mirror propped up on a book. Sometimes stockings. Sometimes without the bra. It was always pretty much unbearable.

We finished the lights and straightened cushions, then lit some candles. Aud had lots of amazing candles. We put on some music. Quiet. No singing. Nothing that might make me shut my eyes and become transported, fork halfway to mouth. I had strict instructions about that. And no drumming on the table. Dom's innumerable sticks had been cleared away. We looked around. Aud was ready. Me and Dom needed five minutes each. The house looked great. Smelled great. We smiled at each other. I trotted upstairs towards the sound of the hair dryer.

'Devlin and Dom, this is Gordon and his wife, Marjorie. Gordon is my accountant. Marjorie is Audrey's godmother.'

'Bullshit.'

John looked at me. Dom closed his eyes. We were standing in the doorway. Aud, Dania and Aud's mum, Janice, were in the kitchen.

'Sorry?' John wasn't sure he had heard correctly. Gordon was looking at the ground.

'This bloke's not your accountant. He can't be.'

John looked at me. He clearly wondered what dark and lonely road this might be heading down. He spoke quietly. 'Well, actually, he is, Devlin. I've known Gordon for more than thirty years and I can very definitely say that he is my accountant.' Police voice. *Sir, I need you to put the child down. And step away from the ledge.*

Dom's eyes were still closed. Behind them, he seemed to be drumming that opening riff from Led Zep's 'Rock and Roll'.

Gordon looked at me, pleading.

But I wasn't going to give way. 'No way. He's a cop.'

Aud's dad peered hard at me. He was obviously beginning to question the efficacy of my treatment. Probably wishing he was armed. Dom was withdrawing still further.

I dropped the pretend outrage. Thought I should explain. 'This clown and a mate of his came around just after I moved in and put the heavy word on me. Told me they were cops. Did the whole Dennis Waterman thing. Told me that if Aud was unhappy then it would "go hard for me".'

I looked at Gordon. He seemed to be suffering some sort of acute visceral pain.

'Gordon, you didn't?' Marjorie managed to combine a question and an outraged accusation into a single statement. Wifely technique.

'*Go hard for him?* We don't say that. No-one says that.' John was struggling. I was smiling broadly. Dom was laughing. Untold relief.

But Gordon didn't think he was out of the woods. A bit frantic. 'John, look, I'm sorry, mate, but you told me to keep an eye on Aud and I was a bit worried when she said that a young bloke was moving into the house. I thought a little scare might work well. My brother Andy came with me.'

John was incredulous. 'You and Andy pretended to be police officers? And told Devlin that it would *go hard for him* if Aud was upset?'

Gordon couldn't immediately see a loophole in the English language that might get him out of it. 'Basically, yes.'

'But that's illegal, Gordon! And really stupid!' He turned to me. 'And you believed him? You really thought Gordon and Andy were from the police? Even saying stupid things like that?'

I didn't think John would necessarily enjoy an opinion on the commonly held view of police stupidity. 'I was really frightened, John.'

'Bullshit.'

Everyone laughed.

'Gordon, you really are an idiot. And if this bloke ever earns any money, then I think you should do his tax returns for free.'

The dinner was a huge success. Dom was a bit nervous at first and laughed too much. Aud was okay now that people had arrived, and busied herself with drinks and nibblies. Aud's dad had told them about Gordon and Andy's impersonation of police officers. Aud's mum was horrified. Gordon had stopped being ashamed and was now thinking it was all a great joke.

'So, how are you feeling now, dear? Are you able to keep going at university?' Aud's mum had taken me aside.

I wasn't very comfortable talking about it, but I couldn't be rude. 'Thanks, yes, I think it's all okay now. The exams will start in a few weeks. I guess I'll find out then. But I think it's okay.'

'Well done. We're very impressed with you. And we like your girlfriend. She's just delightful.'

I blushed a bit. Dania was charming everyone. She looked amazing in a simple fitted grey dress. Her hair pinned up. Slender as a reed. 'Dania's been fantastic. She's helped me so much. And it's nice that she gets on so well with Aud and Dom.'

'We can see you've got a lovely household. It really does make us so happy. John worries a lot about Audrey, but she's obviously over the moon with your friend, Dom.'

I sensed that this was what she really wanted to talk about. 'I think she liked him straight away. He's really settled down a lot now that he's with her. Dom's an amazing bloke. Has John told you about him?'

'He said Dom's going to be an astrophysicist. I'm not really sure what that is.'

I laughed. 'I don't really know, either, but I get the feeling it's about mathematical physics. Theoretical models for things we can't imagine. Dom's the only true genius I've ever met. That's not an exaggeration. Technically his IQ is at that level.'

'I think John's a bit scared of him. He thinks he'll say something silly. John often wishes that he'd studied something. He was a very successful policeman, but it was never really enough. He envies you and Dom.'

Aud came in carrying a big tray. Dania went to fetch the cream and Belgian ice cream. We all sat back down.

Dom was suddenly looking pained. I gave him a questioning look. He nodded towards Aud. Aud tapped a glass with a spoon. Dom got up and went and stood behind her. Hands on her shoulders. I looked at Dania. She didn't know, either.

Aud had everyone's attention. 'Mum and Dad, it's so nice to see you. You, too, Gordon and Marjorie, although Gordon, you shouldn't have been so mean to Devlin.' More laughter. Aud wasn't big on speeches, but she was on a roll. 'Me and Dom have something to tell you all. This will be news to Devlin and Dania, too. Sorry.'

Dom squeezed her shoulders.

'We're going to have a baby.'

Silence.

'Devlin, could you please serve everyone some pudding?'

Even Dania was astonished. Chicks are supposed to know these things. John looked completely lost. Janice looked at me, but could see that I was also speechless.

Dom coughed. He was clearly suffering. I wanted to be able to hand him a small, palliative drumstick. Everyone turned to him. 'We know it's a big shock. Aud only found out yesterday.'

She reached up and put a hand over his. She looked completely oblivious to the anguish all around her.

Dom rallied himself. 'But look, we reckon it's fantastic. We love each other, and we're really excited. I don't know what it will mean from a practical standpoint, but we'll make it work. Yesterday was the best day of my life.'

Aud was now crying a bit.

John looked at his wife. She also had tears in her eyes, but was smiling. He stood up with his glass. 'In theory, I think I'm supposed to shoot you . . .' Everyone laughed. He held up his hand and looked again at his wife. 'But I'm just overjoyed. Honestly. And so is Janice. We're so happy for you. It's wonderful news. A toast to Dom and Audrey!'

We drank. Dania got up and hugged the sniffling, giggly Aud. I served up the pudding. Completely speechless.

'Mate, that was the bombshell to end all bombshells.'

We were lying back on the couches. The guests had gone.

'Sorry to spring it on you both like that. We didn't want to tell you beforehand, because we thought you might then feel funny with Aud's parents.'

'That's okay. Probably true. Big night for them.'

Dom chuckled. 'I liked Aud's dad. It went really well. He wants to see the labs at uni. We'll do that on Monday while Janice is at the doctors.'

Dom was drinking happily now. Hugely relieved. I don't think I'd seen him nervous before that night.

Aud and Dania were making coffee. Having their own chat.

'Mate, do you think we might be growing up?'

Dom smiled. 'I was just wondering whether it was going to be a drummer. Little drum kit, mate. Little guitar. Can you fucken believe it?'

I chuckled, reassured.

Later, upstairs, and Dania seemed restless. She got up and sat in a chair. Still naked. The candle had burned down low.

'Come back to bed, hon.'

She padded back and sat on the bed. I knew what was bothering her. It was not something I could talk about directly.

'I think it's great. Aud is so different now. She'll be a really good mother. And Dom will be good, too.'

'I know. It is really good news. It's probably just because I'm a girl. I want one, too. But I don't really. I just feel that I do. I feel jealous.' She lay back down. 'In a way, they're a lot simpler than we are. Even though there's nothing simple about either of them. Especially Dom. But their love is simpler.'

I knew what she meant.

'We've got something fantastic, Danny. I love you so much. I never thought I could love anyone like this. I thought it was bullshit.' I put the cover over her and snuggled her in.

'Can you give me the next chapter of your story? I've missed reading about Warkon.'

'I'll write it down for you tomorrow. '

Dear Dania,

It's been a bit of a strange time lately.

Ups and downs, and then Aud's big news.

And we're getting towards the end of the story.

Love, Devlin xxx

Thursday

'Ben, mate.'

'G'day, Byron. Hoots.'

'A fresh new day in paradise.' . . .

. . . 'Ben, mate.'

'G'day, Byron. Hoots.'

'A fresh new day in paradise.'

'Possibly. Hard to tell. A long way from here.'

Byron chuckled. 'Don't be like that, mate. Beautiful place, this. What do you reckon, Hoots?'

Hoots was having a better morning. He'd slept well and received his medley of pharmaceuticals a little earlier than usual, and was at that point lying on a trampoline bed in the sun and happily chewing on a roo bone.

'You know, when he was a pup—probably six months—he dragged that tramp out from the shade and put it there in the sun. Then he moved it when the shade moved around. Ever known a dog do something like that?'

'Does sound unusual. They're supposed to be the smartest of all dogs.'

'All fucken true. Those little Jack Russell things are pretty cluey too, but nothing stacks up against a well-bred heeler. The reds are a bit out there. Dingo or something in them. Blues can be snappy too, but reds are definitely more feisty. None of them much use for running. Need a kelpie for that. Yard dogs, really. Built like fucken wombats.'

Hoots was not obviously well bred, but did resemble a wombat. An aging red-roan wombat that had been skittled by a car and left by the road for a week.

'Clean his teeth, that bone. Smell his breath after. Fresh as a daisy.'

'I won't be doing that, Byron.'

Byron could see Ben's point. 'No, well, anyway, your bike.'

They moved into the garage.

'Now, you'll be pleased to see that the little bits have become big bits again, and the big bits are getting put back in or on the frame. I know you were getting a bit nervy about the little bits. Necessary part of the strategy.'

The bike was definitely taking shape. It was supported on a stand and balanced by chains attached to the beams of the garage. The motor was in place and the twin carburettors fitted. It had been cleaned meticulously and looked almost new. The exhaust headers and mid-pipe shone. The forks were attached, as were the driveshaft and shock.

'The tank is almost done. Should come up well. The back wheel I've cleaned up. Some new spokes. Front wheel was fucked, so that's brand new. All trued.' Byron was on a roll. 'New tyres. Military. You'll like them. Better than the roady rubbish on there. Getting low, anyway. I'll balance 'em up for you. Seat I sent to a mate in Barker. Needed a bit of upholstering. Back later today. Got some new guards and plastics. Bars and controls all good.'

'That's fantastic, Byron. Really, it's looking brilliant. When do you think it'll be ready to ride?'

'Bit keen to leave town? Well, I reckon it'll be right tomorrow morning. Should get this lot organised today. Then you can piss off across the desert and hide under a rock for a year.'

'Reckon a year would do it?'

Byron chuckled again. 'Year should be right. Might even have a beard by then.'

Ben sat down on a drum. 'I'm pretty sure that Trev knows.'

'Well, be surprised if he didn't. I'd call you blokes Dumb and Dumber if I wasn't a little bit worried that Dumb might call round and pull me fucken head off.'

'We had no choice. Seriously, there was no other choice.'

'Want to tell me how it happened? Brief overview?'

Ben went through the events of the previous Saturday.

'Fuck me. That's a day-and-half. Geez I wish I'd been asked to go along. I'd have gone down there and gutted the pricks.' Byron sat down on a discarded part of a tractor's transmission.

'Byron, you've been to a war. How do people usually behave?'

'Open question, mate. Gather you're talking about the killing bit? Hard to predict. Some tough blokes tear up and fall apart. Some of the emotional ones go quiet. Some of the quiet ones go mental. Mostly it's short term. Mostly they revert back to being whatever fuck-ups they were beforehand. Some don't. Some are changed by it.'

'How did you feel?'

'Mate, I was an end-stage dickhead when I joined up. I reckon I would have driven a car into a tree or something if that war hadn't happened when it did. I was drinking pretty much all fucken day. Smoking a bit, too. Fighting any prick who looked at me. Couple of arrests for assault. No charges. Matter of time.'

Byron got up and moved over to the low window. Looked out at the yard strewn with the sand-browned carcasses of broken vehicles. 'Army saw something in me. Pricks harder than I was beat the shit out of me. Taught me discipline. Taught me mechanics. Taught me to survive. And to kill. Joined a small group in Nam as the mechanic. General purpose. More of an engineer, really. Fix anything. Didn't see a lot of fighting till the convoy we were travelling in got ambushed. Fought our way out. Had to hike into a river valley, then follow that back to the coast. Plenty of shooting along the way. Pretty much no food. Never dry. Fuck-all sleep. Six days all-up.'

He rested against a work bench. Idly scraped up some filings. 'Five blokes died along the way, but eleven of us made it home. Got medals. Sold mine.'

Ben was watching him.

'You know, mate, I reckon those six days were the high point of my life. The killing had nothing to do with it. It was the survival. The feeling that you might just live if you could be everything you could possibly be. Make sense? Plenty happened after that. More shooting as well. Then the war ended and we snuck home like whipped fucken dogs.'

'How did the others handle it?'

'The walk out? Well, the blokes who died didn't. Simple as that. Maybe they were the better blokes. Don't know. The others? Two went home. Pretty much fucked. Three got so sick they went home later. The rest? I don't know, mate. You didn't talk about it. We survived. One or two might have enjoyed it. One or two might have been nutters, too.'

'Do you still think about it?'

'Sometimes. Not that long ago, really. I don't stress about it, but sometimes the feeling of being hunted comes back. Terrifying, that. Knowing a mob of seriously hard bastards are after you. Vicious killers. Torturers. Not big blokes, but way worse than those biker pricks. You've got to fight to live, or die fighting. Can't get taken prisoner. Took an oath to kill each other if there was no way out.'

Byron put his face in his hands. Spoke through fingers like tyre leavers. 'Truth, mate, it's just an experience. No place in reality.

You experience it, then let it go. Get on with life.' He softened. Smiling now. 'Get a dog.'

'You and Hoots are a good pair. Got the whole district terrified.'

Byron smiled sadly. Kicked at chips in cement. 'Mate, the poor old bastard's dying. Hard to talk about but I know it's happening. Good day today, out in the sun there. But he's going downhill quick now.' In the background, they could hear Hoots chewing on his bone. 'Me and Hoots came out here twelve years ago now. Been great. Met some good blokes. Had some good fights. Made a bit of cash. When Hoots is gone, I'll fuck off, I reckon. Thought about it. Got a mate goes back to Nam doing jobs for villagers in one of the places we were based. Helping them out. Gets a bit of government money. I reckon I'll join him. Mechanical skills be appreciated, though they're all pretty smart like that. Probably live over there somewhere. Try and give something back to the place. Fucken beautiful country.'

He rose. 'But today we have to fix your bike. Mate, don't stress about the bikers. You've done what you can and if the cops come for you then don't fight it. The courts will like you and there's a good chance the cops will be able to put the avenging gang nutters on a leash.'

'Thanks, Byron. I'll go and give Chloe a hand in the pub. Duncan's gone back to the escarpment with Trev and the Homicide blokes. I reckon we'll probably know tonight how things are going to pan out.'

Hoots looked up from the bone held deftly between his forepaws. Stared at Ben. Ears pricked. Ben took the long way around the garage compound.

'Duncan.'

'Boss.'

It was late afternoon. Forensics had completed their investigation during the morning and had returned to Barker to organise transport back to Sydney. Beale and Mitchell had also returned to Barker, with a pair of constables assigned to help them to locate and interview suspected local drug dealers and pushers.

'Thank you for being charitable to the sergeant today. I appreciate your efforts.'

'Pleasure, Boss. Tell you the truth, a bit worried about Mitchell. Don't like him, but he's a tough bloke and probably has half a brain when he's not being a dickhead. Seems like someone's pulled the plug out at the wall.'

'Yes, I suspect some leave may be advised when they return to Sydney, but for now he will be needed to help Beale work through our local roughnecks.'

'They're not very rough, Boss. Most are just dropouts with bugger-all work or life prospects. One or two might like a bit of a brawl, but just frustration. No real shit in them. Beale will scare the bejesus out of them, I reckon.'

Trev laughed. 'Senior Sergeant Beale, yes. And I suspect you're right.'

'So, what's next for us, Boss?'

'For now, Duncan, you go back to Warkon. Talk to Chloe. That's important. And a direct request. I'll explain in a minute.'

'Do that, Boss. On my mind, anyway.'

'Good. Now this investigation. Beale and Mitchell will return to Sydney when they've ploughed through the locals. I suspect that will be early next week. Perhaps as soon as Monday.' Trevor paused. 'John won't be expecting to solve this one. I know that. And I also know that this will not be a concern for him. He has told me these things.' Trevor looked at Duncan. 'The aim will be to use the killings to highlight the movement of biker gangs out into rural communities, and the need for more resources and better police coordination. John will also be looking closely at the current structure of the Sydney gangs and the key personalities, and the extent of any rifts or cooperation among them. This will all be valuable to various units of the Sydney police. But it won't solve what happened out here last Saturday.'

'Why do you say that, Boss?'

'Because, Duncan, this was not done by biker gangs and it was not done by our local louts.'

Silence.

Then Trev went on. 'I have followed up a few small leads, with interesting results. The Visitors Centre in Barker tells me that a couple with some sort of European accent—possibly German—were asking questions about the escarpment just last week. They had a small white campervan. It was parked in the bay outside the centre. They set up a table outside the van and brewed some coffee. The staff recall this quite clearly.'

Duncan remained silent.

'One female member of said staff has a particularly clear memory of the man, who apparently was very tall and very blond and had very blue eyes. She talked to this man at length, as he was interested in the ghost stories about the escarpment. The couple planned to camp out there and do some hiking.' Trev paused, then added, 'I think this couple stumbled upon a gathering of bikers, or perhaps the other way around. I think they were attacked and that the woman was raped—or was going to be. I think that the man probably has an unusual blood type.'

Trev squinted into the afternoon sun. 'What happened then? Well, I think that two or more hunters discovered the scene. They considered the range of possible options. They decided that one of them would approach the group and order the bikers to stop, while the other would provide covering fire. This second person was, fortunately, a marksman.'

Trev returned his gaze to Duncan. 'But something happened and the bikers attempted to locate their weapons and fight back. They were all killed. One was shot with a rifle at close range, and presumably by the negotiator. The leader was killed outright while reaching for a shotgun. Another was killed when the tank of his bike exploded and the fourth was also killed outright.'

Trev wasn't finished. 'This is just a theory, Duncan, you understand that?'

'Perfectly, Boss.'

'The men then helped the couple to their van and they left. To where, who knows? Possibly they have resumed their travels. Possibly they returned home to Europe. The hunters obliterated their footprints and returned to their own vehicle. And presumably this was in the car park on the other side of the escarpment.'

Trev prodded Duncan's boot with his own. 'So, what do you think of my theory, Duncan?'

'I'm terrified by it, Boss.'

'Yes, then there's the lone biker filling up at Polka station. A not-tall, blond man. Not a biker, really. A bike rider.'

Trev smiled to himself. 'I suffered a telephone call with the outraged Mrs Folton and discovered that this man did not have a patch on his jacket and was not what she considered to be a biker. I also discovered that the man was quite young. Mrs Folton believes that she could pick him out from a line-up or identify him in a photograph.'

Duncan put his head in his hands.

'Yes, exactly, Duncan.'

'So, Boss, what's next?'

'Duncan, I'm not sure that you have been listening to me. Senior Sergeant Beale is leading this investigation and will take it first to Barker and then to Sydney. He will not solve it here or down there, but he will gain considerable leverage from it to undertake some tasks that will benefit us all.'

'What will you do, Boss?'

'I have done my bit, Duncan. John knows my theory and completely discredits it. That said, he and I agree on two things.'

'They are? Boss?'

'Your friend Ben should seek to have his bike repaired post-haste and should take himself to Western Australia. There he should enjoy the beaches and beautiful women, and should perhaps languish for some time.'

'The second point of agreement?'

'You should go to Brisbane in the company of Chloe. We had an interesting conversation this morning. She wants to hone and formalise her skills in dealing with the sick and the lame. John and myself have made some enquiries as to your eligibility for the position of Community Liaison Officer. John has gone so far to provide a recommendation for you, which can be taken as a *fait accompli*.'

'Community Liaison Officer?'

'The Brisbane police are suffering from a poor image. They need someone to help local communities to see that the police are on their side. Someone to get to know community leaders and stare down the troublemakers. I think you'd be ideally suited and do a great job.'

'Why do you think I could do this, Boss?'

'I have seen the way you handle people here, Duncan. You use your not inconsiderable size without violence or malice. You even appear to be able to make friends with people as you are taking their bottled refreshment away from them or ejecting them from the premises.'

Duncan chuckled. 'So, you've talked to Chloe about this, then? Boss?'

'Well, if I'm honest, Chloe came and talked to me. She wants to precipitate something, and you will prove yourself to be considerably less intelligent than I suspect should you overlook this extremely attractive gift horse.'

'Okay, Boss, I'll do it. And please thank Senior Sergeant Beale for me.'

'I will certainly do that. Now, I think we should both go and use the remaining hours of the day to best advantage.'

'Hot dog.'

'Don't push it, Duncan.'

'Mate, talked to Byron a little while ago. Bike will be ready by tomorrow morning.'

'Great news, Duncan, thanks. Why do I get the feeling that the sheriff is running me out of town?'

'Because he is, mate. Bike is fixed, you go. And keep going. Due west.'

'And your boss knows about this plan?'

'Close to his heart, mate. Fail to start this bike and we'll put it on a ute and personally drop you off in Eucla. Uncomfortable trip, cuffed to a bike on a ute. Recommend you do it unaided.'

'Do I get a full tank of fuel?'

'No, you get told to fuck off. Way pointed. Due west.'

'Okay, just checking. So, what will the happy couple be doing then?'

Chloe had been listening. Resting against the windowsill in the front room of Duncan's tiny police station. 'We're going to give it a go in Brisbane. Trev has found Duncan a good job with the police, and I'm going to register for nursing training. Think I might need to do some more schoolwork at TAFE. Duncan will keep me and provide for lots of shoes.'

Ben chuckled. 'And you, in return, will continue to cook parmigiana and brownies and make exotic lunches?'

'I'll do that. All of those things. Duncan's sister has agreed to put us up while we look for a house or a unit. It's a big step, but I reckon we'll be okay.'

'I think you'll be fine. Make him keep his boots outside somewhere. A shed maybe, or a dog kennel.'

Duncan thought he'd better start talking again. 'So, aside from heading due west as instructed, what are your plans?'

'I'm going to hit Perth for a while. If Chloe could give me a reference for bar work, I might do a bit of that and just get a feel for the place. I then want to head north to the Kimberley and across the Gibb River Road to the Territory. From there, it's further east to Queensland, then down the coast. I reckon I'll be in Brissie in about six or eight months. Might look you up.'

'That would be good, mate. Trev says no postcards or contact. Either way. Till things settle. Six or eight months should be okay, but just arrive and get in touch through the cops in Brisbane. They'll know where I am.'

'No worries. I think I'm getting the full picture now.'

'That's right. It's a big picture. Don't have to tell you not to talk about this thing. Not to anyone. Not even in vague ways. No idea how easy a rumour can spread to the biker community.'

'I won't say a word. This has panned out better than we expected and I won't rock the boat.'

They heard commotion from across the street. Old Cecil appeared on the veranda of the pub and put his hands to his mouth, yelled, 'What's a bloke have to do to get a drink? Fucken shoot someone?'

CHAPTER 9

It was a new year. A completely new year. I made it through the exams. Passed everything. I even managed a sprinkling of credits. The dean's office had called me at home. I made an appointment to see them. I thought I must have failed something and they wanted to break it to me gently. Didn't want me taking a swanny off the Harbour Bridge. But the dean just wanted to congratulate me himself. Shook my hand again. It was a really nice gesture.

I was coming down off the Prothiaden now. Dr Gidleigh thought I should keep it going during the exam period, and until the results came through. Then slowly reduce it. See how I felt. All okay so far. I hadn't seen Anna, the psychologist, for some time. She thought I might need to come back to her within a year or so. She said that it was often a case of three steps forward and two steps back. I should expect that.

I had Christmas with Dania and her mum. It was quiet, but really nice. The cat still hated me. I had to stay around Sydney for most of the holidays as Ernie had left me in charge of the cafe. He wanted to see some of his rellos back in Turkey. Gave me some emergency phone numbers and called in every few days. Heidi, who had been doing some of the cooking on a casual basis, stayed on to cook full time. A cousin with another cafe in Surrey Hills would supply the pastries. Ernie was famous for his pastries and hoped the business wouldn't suffer too much. I told him I'd let everyone know that this was only a temporary arrangement. Boss had gone off somewhere with an eighteen-year-old waitress. Left the monkey in charge.

'I know you like to make silly jokes, but I think you will take this thing seriously, no? You did well to pass all your exams. You work hard. You're a good boy.'

He patted me like a dog. I told him I'd definitely take it all seriously. And I did. I got up ridiculously early each morning to have the place firing for the commuter traffic that staggered down to the wharf each morning. Ernie had shown me how to make good coffee, and how to keep the queue as short as possible by slotting in the small orders. I already knew about cleaning tables and taking money. Heidi also got there early. She was cute and a bit younger than me. Studying acting at NIDA. Her mother was a chef and had taught her the ropes so that she could work her way through.

I hadn't been working at the Jungle Bar for some time, so this was my only income. Ernie told me to pay myself a small wage. He would then look at the profits when he got back and give me a share. I had no idea how much money a cafe would make. I had never been very interested in money. But it felt fantastic to be running something. Taking responsibility for it.

And I could take a lot of the expiring stuff and unsold pastries back to the flat. Aud loved the pastries. Perhaps too much. Heidi took some, too. She lived with some friends in a house in Pyrmont and rode an old Lambretta scooter to work each day. Open face helmet, scarf and sunnies. Knees together. I told Dania how cute she'd look on a scooter. A red one. But Dania was scared of the Sydney traffic. And a bit uneasy about Heidi.

'Mate, this is such a great little place.' Tobe was happily eating a piece of baklava that would have had to have been turfed overnight. Ernie had strict rules about freshness. I privately thought that baklava got better with age. It sort of disintegrated into a delicious, sticky mess. But Ernie's rules had to be observed to the letter. Tobe had a little box of the stuff to take home with him.

I was closing the place up for the day. Heidi had helped with the cleaning. Tobe had then enjoyed watching her ride her little scooter back up the hill. And I think Heidi had enjoyed Tobe enjoying it. I realised that this could get complicated. Tobe had also passed everything. He had done a bit better than me and had even started thinking that he might be able to get through with honours. I had no doubt that he would. Wazza had had a couple of near misses and needed to do two second exams in early February. Posts. They let you do this if you were borderline. Wazza was at home working hard.

I did one last check of the power and cookers, then pulled down the steel shutters. We headed off to the Townie. Wednesday. Book Club.

'Girls!'

'Fuck off, Tobe.'

I always thought Tobe's traditional greeting for the Wild Boys was a bit dangerous. They sometimes got to the pub pretty early. With a skinful, Will was quick to ignite. Not a big bloke but very tough. And old Bill always seemed like he'd be right at home in a jungle war.

'Refreshment for you.'

We added two jugs to the carnage on the table. Hector took one and refilled everyone's glasses.

'Your missus coming?' I think Bill had a gentlemanly crush on Dania.

'Yeah, mate. Dom and Aud are in town. They'll pick her up and come over. Probably another hour or so.'

The gathering had changed a bit. Dania was usually there, and Dom and Aud as well. Dom and Hector liked to argue about Jethro Tull. They could maintain it for hours. Dom and I loved Tull's music. Tried to adapt the flute to tin whistles. Dom had modified an old tape player so that it played at half speed. He had pulled it to pieces and put lacquer on one of the cogs to make it bigger. Only Dom would think of doing that.

We used the slowed-down player to try and analyse songs, including some of Ian Anderson's amazing acoustic guitar stuff. We had 'Thick as a Brick' pretty much nailed now. Individual notes with a hard plectrum. A pick. Moved the D-shape up three frets with a capo, then used the little finger to change the D-shape through the riff. It was one of those songs that is completely original—like 'Bohemian Rhapsody' and 'American Pie'. Difficult to imagine how Anderson could have dreamed it up. Very clever bloke.

We occasionally took the guitars to the Townie and played quietly out on the balcony. A little crowd would gather. But you couldn't talk then and that was really the point of the get-together.

Book Club itself had fallen apart a bit when I had started going downhill. I had been the one to keep people reading, especially when it was left-field things like Hector's *Clan of the Cave Bear* or Tobe's earlier impractical fascination with Tolstoy. It wasn't completely dead, but now we just talked about any book. And sometimes music. And sometimes just told filthy jokes.

I was still drinking tiny amounts. Aside from the drug, I had to get up before five now to get the cafe organised. The others knew about the trip to hospital. And the rest. Bill seemed to have a genuine respect for the fact that I'd gone completely crazy. He thought that was a major achievement and was fascinated by the hospital stories. The early morning commotion in the corridor. I suspected he might give it a go one day. Terrify Angela and Alan.

I took another sip from my special glass. The glass had caused turmoil when I had first produced it, a month or more ago. I'd found it in an antique shop. Will had been appalled.

'What the fuck is that?'

'A pony.'

'Fuck off.'

I held it up to the light. 'Seriously, mate, in country New South Wales everyone used to drink beer out of these. Before there was good refrigeration. Meant that the beer stayed cold and bubbly.'

'Stayed cold and bubbly because it was still in the cellar in the fucken barrel.'

It was like a miniature schooner glass. I think it held about half a middy. Maybe a small rum-and-Coke. But the shape meant you could get a nice head. Just like a normal beer. But tiny. I liked it. I brought it along with me each week. `

'You're a fucken idiot.' Will still hadn't got over it.

We drank and chatted for about an hour. Dom and the others hadn't turned up yet. Tobe was still eating the soggy baklava. No-one else was keen. Will rose to get some chips and dip.

'Thanks, Will, mate. Th'art a good cunt.' Tobe had been reading *Lady Chatterly's Lover*. It was always just a matter of time. Will looked at him. No idea of the context. Tobe really had no fear.

Hector saved the day. 'Devvo, how are you going with *Catcher*?' He'd had lent me *Catcher in the Rye*. It was my idea. He wasn't taking the piss. I had read it at school and wanted to read it again.

'I think it's terrific. I like it. I really do.'

Hector and Tobe chuckled. Everyone loved Salinger's syntax. I was also a bit intrigued by the central idea. The catcher in the rye. The spin on Robert Burns's old poem, which had then become a children's song. Salinger's Holden Caulfield misheard the song and thought that a catcher was someone who protected little kids. Stopped them blundering off a cliff, hidden in a field of tall rye. Holden himself wanted to be a catcher. Protect kids everywhere. Protect their innocence. I liked that idea. Dr Gidleigh was a catcher. So was Anna. And Dania. I think I had made Dania into a catcher, when she just wanted to be a pretty girl. Adored. But together they'd caught me. Stopped me from falling off the cliff. I sometimes wondered whether there might be other catchers out there. In hills and cold forests. In the bush. High up in the silent open skies. Writing the script. Telling the story. Watching, and making magic. Catching.

I looked up. Dom was carefully piloting a now visibly pregnant Aud to a seat. Aud looked great. She was wearing all the primary colours at once. And eating an ice cream. And smiling at everyone.

'Dombo! Aud! Where's Dania?'

Dom sat next to me. 'Mate, Dania wanted to go to the cricket. Day-night game. Australia versus . . . I don't know, some flogs who don't mind losing. Friends from work. Free seats.'

'Okay.'

'Fill up your little glass, mate.'

'Okay.'

Dania had moved back in with her mum. She had done it just before Christmas. That was fair enough. Her mum was getting sad on her own. But after Christmas, she stayed there. She told me that I would also have to move soon. Aud hadn't said anything yet, but they'd need the room for the baby. I knew that was true. I was dreading trying to find another place. I loved living in Balmain, but there was bugger-all cheap rent there.

Things with Dania had started to slip a bit again. I was pretty much okay now, except some times when I was with her. Mostly it was good. Just like it always had been. But every now and then I found it hard not to lose confidence and get panicky. I guess I could sense her pulling away a bit and that terrified me. And Dania definitely had been pulling away. When I felt like punishing myself, I imagined there was someone else. Someone a bit more normal. I had to be careful because the pain of that was almost unbearable.

But increasingly, she was doing things with her own friends. I didn't seem to be invited. Or I was, but it had already been agreed that I wouldn't like whatever it was.

One Sunday afternoon in early February, we agreed to meet at a coffee shop in the Rocks. It was a place that we liked and one that had lots of nice memories for us.

It was really just a Sunday like any other. I had been working at the cafe till two o'clock or so. The locals always enjoyed a leisurely Sunday breakfast. Brunch. We didn't roll out the lunch menu on Sundays. Had to have some time off.

When the last of them had left we cleaned the place and packed up. Heidi putted off up the hill on her scooter. I counted takings. We had had a couple of groups and long sittings. Big breakfasts with many coffees. Overall, it was almost a Sunday record. I locked the steel shutters and made my way down to the wharf.

It was a beautiful summer day. Not too hot. Clear skies. And pretty sails all over the harbour. I caught the ferry over to the Quay and walked across to the Rocks.

I thought I was early, but she was already seated. Big sunglasses. That scrunchy. She looked beautiful.

We kissed briefly and sat down. Ordered coffees and small things. Talked about Aud. How good she looked. Talked about Ernie's cafe. So much fun. I thought I might have a vet practice that served coffee and cakes. Breakfast. Brunch. Sick animals would be discouraged. Maybe just vaccinations. It was hard to kill anything when you were only vaccinating it. Free muffin with every kitten immunised.

Dania smiled, but the big sunnies stayed on. I looked across at the Quay.

'Devlin, honey.'

And everything snapped inside me. 'I can't see you with those fucking glasses on.'

She took them off. Her eyes were red and she was blinking back tears.

I stared at her. She nodded and began to cry.

'How long have you known?'

She reached out for my hands. I let her take them. I was shaking inside. It seemed surreal.

'I started thinking about it while you were in hospital. At first it felt like a silly idea, then bits and pieces began to make sense.'

'I didn't know it myself until the end. Not really.'

'I know. And do you remember when you were back home and I took your car to the Hunter Valley for a concert?'

I nodded.

'Well, while I was there, I drove into Singleton to look at the microfiche in the town library. It took me most of the day, but I found a local newspaper article about the incident. And then several others.'

She stopped to take a mouthful of coffee and looked out at the harbour. 'Then I went to the police in Singleton.'

She looked across at me and flinched at the horrified expression. Gripped my hand hard. I let her continue. 'I gave them a made-up name and told them I was a friend of the girl— the woman—who was killed. I said that I wanted to know if they had found out anything more than was reported in the papers. A detective sergeant talked to me for a long time. He told me that the case was still open, but that they didn't expect to make any more progress unless a reliable witness could be found.'

We were both quiet. I was breathing heavily.

'What happened, honey? What happened that you couldn't let yourself remember? What is your Warkon story really about?'

Now that it had been said, it seemed that the worst was over. I let go of her hand and massaged my eyes. 'I really didn't know, Danny. I swear to you that I really didn't know. If deep down the story meant something else, then it was a message to myself and not you.'

She nodded. 'When did you start to remember?'

'I had a nightmare. I was having lots of nightmares in hospital, but this was worse. It was more like pain than fear. I must have been screaming because they came into the room and sedated me. Then sat with me while I slept. I think the writing and stories had kept it at bay, and when that started getting more difficult the agitation began. I felt that something was trying to get out. I guess the sedative they gave me just opened the gate.'

'Why didn't you tell me this? I thought we were honest with each other.'

'I was going to, honey, one day when everything was okay again.'

'Tell me now. Tell me what happened. Please, just tell me everything.'

So I told her. It was the trip along the Barnard two years ago. I had been thinking about setting up a campsite, and trying some fishing, when I heard the screams and shouting. I was surprised by how close they were as I had thought that I was alone in the forest. I crept forward around the boulders and looked down to the clearing through the rifle's scope. There were four bikers, but there was also a girl. She was screaming. I crept back behind the boulders, and just sat there. The screaming was intermittent and every now and then I could hear laughter. I didn't know what to do. I knew I couldn't leave them and walk out to get help, as the bikers would be long gone by then. I thought about going down there with the rifle, but there were four of them and I'd seen a shotgun leaning against a stump. The blokes had looked as though they'd been drinking and would definitely fight back.

I sat still for ages, and was still sitting, clutching the rifle and listening and trying to think of something when the screaming suddenly increased and was then followed by a lot of shouting. I scrambled around the boulders to the shelter of the bracken and looked back down to the clearing. One of the bikers was crying and two others seemed to be consoling him. The fourth was raging and trying to reach the crying biker through the other two. Eventually the angry one moved off to start a small fire with a rag he'd soaked in fuel from the tank of his bike. The others found logs to sit on and they all seemed to settle down a bit.

But the girl was on the ground, alone and at some distance from the group. Through the scope I could see her clearly. She was a little bit chubby. She had blonde hair, and blood down one side of her face. And her head was turned back on an awful angle. A crow was perched nearby on the stump against which the shotgun was resting. It seemed to sense me, or perhaps had seen a glint of evening light reflected from the rifle scope. It held its head on one side and regarded me coldly, unmoving.

I knew then that I had had the chance to save her. Or at least try. It was only a few minutes, but if I had acted immediately, she might still be alive. I was choking back tears as I turned the rifle across to the bikers and loaded the first round into the chamber. I had five bullets. One spare. I still don't recall how it happened. I really don't. But when the echoes around the deep forest valley had fallen away, I knew that they were all dead. And that the crow had gone.

I lay back in the bracken and closed my eyes. When I awoke it was completely dark. I was very cold and felt only an urgency to leave the place. I looked at the clearing once more through the rifle scope and saw the shapes of four bodies that seemed to have fallen asleep around the coals of their fire. I crept back up the river, set up my tent and slept for a couple of hours before packing it away again and heading back to the property where I was working.

I didn't think of anything much during that long hard walk, but by the time I got back the only truth I knew was that I'd seen a group of bikers and had left them sleeping around their fire. And after I had left the mountains and hitchhiked west to the edge of the desert, then north through to the huge stations in the Queensland gulf country above Charters Towers, even that memory was blurred and indistinct.

Dania had been staring down at our clasped hands as I told her this. I wanted desperately to hear her say something, so asked, 'How much do the police know?'

She looked up. 'The sergeant told me that he suspected that something had gone wrong with a local drug deal, but he didn't have any leads. All the immediate suspects had alibis. And that was what the local papers reported. It was in the Sydney papers too, but only a small article.' She looked up at me. 'He said that they had seen a place where they thought someone had been lying, about seventy-five meters away, but they never found the shells. And because those horrible hunting bullets break apart on impact, they could never hope to identify the gun.'

I nodded. 'The gun is probably still sitting where I left it in the corner of the old bloke's cabin. I almost threw it away. It felt evil. And since this has come back, I've been wondering what sort of forensic information they might have.'

Dania's eyes were tightly shut. 'It's over now, Devlin. Not just you and me, but this terrible thing. It's all over, honey'

I became aware that she was half-speaking to someone behind me and turned to see a tall man standing respectfully about a metre back, his hands in the pockets of his jacket.

'John? Dania, what's going on?'

Dania was frantic now, almost panicking.

'I called John and asked him to fly down and meet us here. He's come straight from the airport. Devlin, I haven't told him anything. You have to do that. You can't hide from this thing anymore. You'll have to tell the police what happened and trust them to look after you.'

For a split second, I had the irrational urge to run. And just keep running. But Dania had already beckoned Aud's dad over to the table and asked him to join us, and I could only stand up and shake his hand, then collapse back again in my chair.

'So, son, what it is that you need to say to me?'

Dania looked at me and reached out again for my hands.

'I'm sorry, honey. I didn't think you would take this step yourself, and I couldn't bear to see you carrying around this awful secret any longer.'

John was sitting quietly, looking out towards the harbour. I stood up again, then Dania did the same and I held both her hands self-consciously. I went over to the counter and shakily counted out the money, then walked back to her and hugged her for a long time. Drank in the smell of her hair. The feel of her body. The scrunchy.

I took a large envelope out of my backpack and passed it to her. 'I knew something would happen this morning, Danny. It's the last chapter.'

She took it and smiled. Kissed me. Tears on her face. Put a wet hand to my cheek, then turned towards George Street. People milled around her like sticks in a flooded stream, then someone took an arm and she was gone.

Dear Dania,

The last chapter.

Friday, Ben's last day in Warkon.

And now you've got the whole little book.

I've been back there several times since writing this out, but it's very quiet. Summer has set in and the heat of the bush is all but intolerable. Except for the evenings and early mornings, when the colours change before your eyes and life seeps out of the rock, pooling in small holes and gullies and trickling lightly over the burnt scree, looking for a story.

Love always, Devlin xxx

Friday

'Mate, I reckon we're ready to go.'

'Byron. Hoots.'

Ben had a surprise for Hooty. He reached into a paper bag and brought out a cooked sausage . . .

. . . 'Mate, I reckon we're ready to go.'

'Byron. Hoots.'

Ben had a surprise for Hooty. He reached into a paper bag and brought out a cooked sausage. One of Chloe's breakfast sausages. Beef, bacon, tomato and herbs. And lots of sausage in between. He lowered the sausage gingerly, with one end pointed towards Hooty.

As a result of being vaguely homicidal, Hooty had never been shown kindness by anyone other than Byron. Ever. Not once in his fourteen angry years. He regarded the sausage with astonishment, then looked up at Ben, lifted his lips on principle and gently took hold of the other end. Ben let his end go and straightened up. Hooty remained in a state of disbelief just long enough for the smell of cooking to reach deep into his bear-like nose. Then swallowed the sausage in two loud bites.

There was silence for a few seconds while Hooty regarded Ben with some seriousness, before stabbing the air with his snout and emitting his squeaky heeler bark. Ben had seen the game with the plastic hammer. He knew what that bark meant. He bent down without hesitation and ruffled Hooty's ears. Hooty smiled.

'Well, fuck me. You're the first bloke to have done that and kept his fingers.'

'He likes me. He knows that I kill people.'

'Yeah, I reckon that's probably it, mate. Smell the blood on you. Brother in arms.'

'He's a great dog, Byron.'

'He is that. And fuck he's had a great life.'

Ben crouched down and Hoots licked his hand.

Byron shook his head. 'Mate, I'm completely fucken amazed. All it took was a sausage. Should have been handing the fucken things out to customers all these years. Feed the dog. Your mate for fucken life.'

'No, Byron, it's the blood. Cordite. Powder burn. He knows I'm another nutter, like his dad.'

'You're not like me, mate. If you were, I'd have known it, and stuck your bike back out on the fucken road where I found it.'

'Well, let's have a look at this bike.'

They pushed open the big doors. The garage had been cleaned out and the floor swept. Loose tools had found their hangers or boxes, and equipment was stowed. The bike was on its centre-stand. Ben stood back, astonished.

'That's bloody amazing! It looks like a new bike.'

The tank had been resprayed after the dents were beaten out and it gleamed in the slanting light from the small, high windows. The tyres, as promised, were new and had a more rugged, off-road tread pattern. The new bars had been painted and controls attached. The modified engine protection was in place.

'Seriously, mate, this looks better than new. I like the seat. It's a bit more orange than the old one. Looks great.'

'Yeah, well, it's been good to work on one of these things. Constantly finding these stupid fucken ideas, then looking closer and seeing why they work. Not like any other bike. Nothing like the Norton. Which I've washed, then carted up and down the dusty road on the ute, just to prove that it's been sitting here gathering red dirt the last year.'

'Sorry about that. It was stupid to take it back to the escarpment. Duncan was right to get the shits with me. Now you've had to lie to the cops.'

'Mate, Trev knew exactly what I was saying. He's okay. He'll look after the big fella.'

'I think you're right. I think it's going to turn out okay. But I do need to fuck off to Western Australia. In Duncan's own words.'

'You do, mate, you do. And to help there, you've got a full tank of fuel. Courtesy of the big fella. And you've even got some sandwiches. And there's this.' Byron handed Ben a worn envelope.

Ben looked inside. 'There's heaps in here.'

'I've taken out three-fifty to cover parts. Called in a few favours. Don't worry about the labour. Been a joy and an entertainment, and you've tamed my dog. Should be sixteen-fifty left over. Get you to the other side no worries.'

'I don't know what to say, Byron.'

'No need to talk, mate. Let's start the fucken thing and see how it sounds.'

The bike turned over easily and fired up on the third go.

'New battery. Lighter. Last longer. Carbies a bit out and a bit grubby. Should run much better. Less fuel. Valves are okay. Small adjustment there. Fair bit of shit in the fuel lines and filters. Fuel from old drums will do that. Serviced the forks. New oil there. Shock was okay.'

Ben twisted the throttle slowly. 'That's heaps better. Much crisper. Mate, this is just fantastic.'

'Well, Ben, get your gear organised on it and me and Hoots will see you off.'

In the rear-view mirror, a tall bloke and a stumpy dog. Fading. Obscured by red dust. There were fewer houses out here on the edge of the town. Empty lots. A cattle truck parked, its driver checking tyres.

The road was hard beneath him but the corrugations were absorbed by the bike's suspension. The balanced wheels tracked perfectly. Behind him on the seat was his waterproof roll with tent, sleeping bag and thin foam mattress. Panniers on each side held food, cooking gear, clothes and some other bits and pieces. A small bag on the tank carried his wallet and maps. And the brownies.

Ben opened it up a little, listening to the big motor. It was breathing properly now, the flat twin running in sync. Smooth power so different to the Norton.

Completely free. Everything changed. A new life.

Beside the road ahead stood a wedge-tailed eagle. Huge. The leg of a road-killed kangaroo in her claws. Ben watched closely and slowed the bike, but the bird didn't flinch. Stared straight at him. Into him. Through him.

He rode past it and accelerated away, due west. At least a hundred kilometres before the next corner. Right over the horizon. The end of the world.

But the hard stare followed him through the dust. Through the thick leather of his jacket. Across the aching, empty, arid plain.

And he began to realise that it would be there forever.

9 781922 792563